Ex-fashion designer, ex-model, ex-roadie and inveterate gym-rat, Jack Dickson has been writing since 1994. Previous books include *Oddfellows* (Millivres 1997); the Jas Anderson mysteries *Freeform* (GMP 1997) and *Banged Up* (GMP 1999); and *Crossing Jordan* (Millivres 1999). *Some Kind of Love* is the third Jas Anderson novel. Jack's collected erotica, *Out of this World*, will be published by Zipper Books later this year, and his short screenplay *The Sucker Punch* goes into production in May 2002. Jack lives in Glasgow with his man and his dog.

Also by Jack Dickson

Thrillers:
Oddfellows
Freeform
Crossing Jordan
Banged Up

Erotic fiction:
Still Waters
Out of this World

First published 2002 by GMP (Gay Men's Press),
PO Box 3220, Brighton BN2 5AU

GMP is an imprint of Millivres Limited,
part of the Millivres Prowler Group,
Worldwide House, 116-134 Bayham Street, London NW1 0BA

www.gaymenspress.co.uk

A CIP catalogue record for this book is available from the British Library

ISBN 1-902852-31-1

Distributed in the UK and Europe by Airlift Book Company,
8 The Arena, Mollison Avenue,
Enfield, Middlesex EN3 7NJ
Telephone: 020 8804 0400
Distributed in North America by Consortium,
1045 Westgate Drive, St Paul, MN 55114-1065
Telephone: 1 800 283 3572
Distributed in Australia by Bulldog Books,
PO Box 300, Beaconsfield, NSW 2014

Printed and bound in Finland by WS Bookwell

Some Kind of Love

JACK DICKSON

For Raymond and Jackie.
For Bishops Loch at sunset.
For everyone who finds *some kind of love*
and makes it work for them.

Prologue

'Ah got him.'

Three monosyllables chilled on the side of his face. He could smell the adrenaline, feel the tremors from the body against his. Breath on his neck:

'That bastard'll never hurt onywan again, Jas-man.' The bear-hug tightened.

He buried his face in a tangle of brown hair and inhaled the familiar scent of one of two men who had haunted his mind for the past three months. What remained of the other now lay in some hospital mortuary, awaiting post-mortem.

Mongrel emotions coursed through his body. He wanted to know Stevie'd had the sense to wear gloves – and didn't.

He wanted to know where he'd abandoned the vehicle – and didn't...

Jas closed his eyes, instinctively stroking the tee-shirted back.

... wanted to know Dalgleish had seen the face of his killer before the front of the car had hit him, wanted to know there had been pain and crumpling bone and a sudden, heightened sense of utter helplessness.

Breath quickened on his neck. Other, still-trembling hands gripped his shoulders and a groin began to grind against his.

Veins pulsed on the insides of his eyelids, mirroring the pulse in his swelling cock.

Then the face beside his was turning and his open mouth found another. The force of the kiss drove him back. Spine jangled against cold metal. The handle of the fridge dug into his kidneys.

Stevie's lips were hard and dry. Desperate.

Jas returned the motion, pushing with his hips and thrusting his tongue deeper into the warm mouth.

Stevie's fingers moved over his bristling scalp. Broad hands were cradling his crew-cut head and the mouth had moved back to his neck.

Jas moaned, tasting the other man's saliva. Air rushed into his lungs.

The lips were on his shoulder, now. A tongue was licking fresh sweat from his shivering skin. Vibrations in the chest against his told him there were syllables amidst the kisses.

He wanted to feel this was wrong.

He wanted to feel guilt.

He wanted to push this man away and walk to the telephone, report what he knew about the death of ex–Hadrian Security Solutions prison officer Ian Dalgleish.

Jas opened his eyes.

Stevie's fully dressed body still pressed against his own half-naked form.

He stared beyond to the front door. His thumbs lingered on the waistband of Stevie's jeans. As four fingers splayed down over two hard buttocks, his right palm cupped an unmistakable, rectangular bump. Moving his left hand between them, Jas eased Stevie away. 'How much?' His palm was solid against an equally rigid chest, elbow locked.

From the prison-pallid face, brown eyes met blue.

Even at arm's length, his stomach flipped over.

'Two grand...' Brown glowed to amber. Stevie stuck a hand into his pocket and hauled out a folded brown envelope.

An empty folded brown envelope. And an eight-times creased sheet of A4: release-papers.

'... never seen that much money in wan place before!' Laugh. Forearm rubbed. Envelope shoved back in pocket. Like nothing had happened.

Jas removed his palm and walked away.

'Carole can find a use fur it. Family Allowance disney go far, these days.' Stevie followed him into the bedroom, still talking. 'When ah git a job an' that, ah'll be able tae gie her mair – oan a regular basis.'

Jas stopped at the window, hands resting on sill.

'Man, ye dinny ken how guid it is tae see ye!' Uncertain for the first time.

He tried to close his ears.

'Jist tae be oot – tae be walkin' the streets again!' Voice less uncertain... He knew Marie McGhee and whichever of the Johnstone brothers had arranged the hit would cover everyone's tracks well. But it didn't make him feel any better.

... for a different reason.

'Sam an' Hayley ur sproutin' like weeds. Ah canny believe how much they've grown.' Voice yards away.

He didn't want to know.

'When ah git masel' sorted oot, ah'm gonny get a wee flat. Mibby huv the kids round, at weekend, an' that.' Footsteps.

He didn't care.

'Ah'm no' the same guy that went intae the Bar-L. An' ah'm never fuckin' goin' back.' Footsteps stopping.

The unadulterated optimism in Stevie's voice hurt his chest. Eyes narrowed, Jas stared out over sodium-lit streets and fell back on small-talk. 'Where dis yer sister live?'

'Cranhill – Starpoint Street. Ye ken it?' The voice was close. Too close.

Jas continued to stare.

A sigh. 'Ah gave her address tae the Probation Officer, but Carole's man's no' that keen oan huvin' me aroon' the place.' Another sigh. 'Canny blame him: he's awready hud ma kids fur two years.' Pause.

'Ony idea when the GE or the Jimmy Duncan lock the doors?'

He continued to gaze over sleeping roof-tops.

Less than a mile to the south, The Great Eastern Hotel and James Duncan House: fine names disguising two of Glasgow's main, all-male hostels. Some kind of home to myriad homeless. In his mind's eye, he could still see the stubby fingers of HMP Barlinnie's grey chimneys. Steven McStay had been released less than twelve hours ago. Straight from one violent institution to another?

Minutes passed...

He could hear breathing, rapid and uncertain. Jas let it stay that way. Fingers gripped the windowsill. Around his lips, his ex–cell-mate's saliva was drying to a tight web. Jas thought about spiders and flies.

... two, three...

Floors below, Cumbernauld Road was quiet, apart from the odd car. Further afield, throughout Glasgow, those who spurned the hospitality of hostels or were too late to get a bed, slept where they could.

... four, five...

No address, no dole-money. Forget even applying for jobs, never mind getting a flat.

... six...

'Widda bin madness no' tae take the money, since they wur offerin' it, eh Jas?' Apologetic. Unnerved by the silence.

A smile twitched his lips and broke the web: two grand was the least of it. The whole thing was madness. But madness with method. Unlike what he was at present considering.

'Whit ye lookin' at?'

The voice was closer. The heat from Stevie's body narrowed the gap between them. Jas released the windowsill and turned. He frowned at the 6'1" man, inches away. 'You tell me.' Blue eyes bored into brown.

Confusion creased the pallid, angular face.

The frown hardened to a scowl. Loose declarations slipped easily from the lips of every ex-offender in his first 24 hours of freedom. Jas stared – at a man who had just finished an eighteen-month sentence for the aggravated assault of two gay men.

A man with whom he had shared a prison cell for two brief weeks of that eighteen-month sentence.

A man with a wife, somewhere, and two children in Starpoint Street.

A man who had bathed his body, after four faceless others had abused that body against his will.

A man who had killed in cold blood, a mere five hours ago, the prison-officer responsible for that abuse.

The pale face reddened. 'Ah... dunno whit ye mean.' Head lowered. A tangle of brown hair fell across angular features.

Jas wondered if it was the truth. Then wondered why he was even wondering.

'Jist thought ah'd hand-in yer jacket.' Moving away. 'Ah'll mibby seeya aroon'...' Head still lowered.

Jas stretched out a hand and gently gripped Stevie's chin. Tilting the prison-paled face up to his, he looked into the eyes of a gay-basher and murderer. 'Jist till ye git yersel' sorted oot, okay?'

Black pupils ringed with hazel. Stevie nodded.

'This flat's too small fur two...'

Another nod.

'... an' it's ma work-address, as well as ma home. '

'Mibby ah could... help-oot wi' yer business...' Eager-to-please. '... typin' an' that. Ah wis forty words a minute, in The Shotts, and ah ken ma way aroon' maist applications if...'

Jas frowned. 'This is a wan-man business.'

Obedient nod.

'Coupla days – a week at maist.' The drumbeat in his chest was moving into his head. 'Ye dae yer ain dishes, an' ah want the place kept tidy. There's a laundrette up the road. Service-washes ur two quid extra, but she eyeways loses at least wan sock.' The drumbeat changed to a slow, tolling bell.

A further nod.

'Ah'll git ye some covers.' His voice was hoarse. 'The couch isney too bad.' Stevie's chin was damp and bristly. With each nod, the skin moved between Jas's fingers. The hardness in his jeans became a little harder...

He released the chin and walked towards a wardrobe.

... and the alarm-bells in his head rang a little louder. Jas ignored both, hauling open the door and fumbling in the dark depths. He grabbed what felt like the spare duvet, turned.

Orange sodium streaked the angular face. Black pupils almost eclipsed the hazel. 'Thanks, Jas-ma...'

He dropped the duvet and silenced the final syllable of a nickname he needed to forget. 'It's jist Jas, okay?' One knuckle brushed Stevie's lips. 'An' this is jist temporary.'

Huge pupils stared at him. Shaking fingers stroked the side of his face. 'Can ah...' Words barely audible. '... sleep wi' you? Jist fur the night?'

His mind was a thumping black 'no'. He seized a white-scarred wrist.

Then he was kissing Stevie's clenched fist and easing him backwards onto the bed.

One

His left index-finger hovered above the 'l'.

The phone rang.

Jas glanced from notes to keyboard to monitor, then lowered his hand. In the background, the answering-machine version of his own voice launched into the preamble:

'Anderson Investigations. Leave a name and number, and I'll get back to you.' Beeps.

He looked back at the notes, then at the keyboard and let the answerphone pickup. The first screening: these days, he checked-out clients thoroughly before returning the call. Jas frowned at the monitor, lowered his left index-finger towards 'g'.

The voice which followed the beeps was female and unused to answering-machines. 'Mr Anderson? This is Margaret Monaghan. Could ye phone me... er, back on 875 – 6632. Er... thank you, Mr Anderson.' Pause. 'Oh, er... Marie gave me yer number – Marie McGhee? She said maybe you could help me. Er...' Another pause. '... bye-bye.'

He sat back in the chair, rubbed his face. The frown remained in place. When he removed his hands, the letter was still only half-finished. Jas peered at the monitor. Voice-activated software: he'd read about that. Quicker, easier and...

The bedroom door opened. 'Wis that the phone?' Hoarse voice.

Jas turned his head. The frown removed itself. 'Aye, but it wis fur me.' He watched his previous expression settle on Stevie's sleep-relaxed face. 'Ah telt ye ah'd wake ye, if it wis yer solicitor.' He glanced at his watch. 'Go back tae bed – ye've still goat a coupla hours.'

'Ah'm up noo...' The bulky figure rubbed red eyes, then hauled open the fridge door. Sounds of knees cracking.

Jas focused on the long sweep of Stevie's back, then returned his attention to the keyboard.

Voice-activated software: was it as straightforward as it sounded? He stared at his notes, then the monitor. Lubricated tones reading over his shoulder:

'That the wuman whose man's cheatin' oan her?' Stevie took another slug from the carton of orange-juice. Eyes on the half-letter.

'He wisney cheatin'...' Jas depressed 'i' and looked back at his notes. '... just goat a job he disney want her tae ken aboot.' Sceptical voice in his ear. Warm hand on his shoulder:

'Whit sorta job?' The warm fingers began to knead. 'Christ, yer muscles are like fuckin' cables! Ye're no' sittin' right again.'

'Ah'm sittin' fine.' The hand moved round to his collarbones, then slipped beneath the neck of his polo-shirt.

'No ye're no'...' Sleepy reprimand. Two hands pulling at his shoulders. 'Ye're aw' hunched-up.'

Jas fought a frown and aimed for the 'h'.

'See?' Fingers on his right deltoid. 'It's aw' that typin'-wi-'wan-hand stuff.' Less-sleepy reprimand.

The frown won. 'Willya go back tae bed an' let me finish this?' Jas rotated shoulders, shrugging off the hands.

They lingered. 'Canny sleep.'

'Well, go an' huv a shower, then.' Jas peered at the notes. He searched for his place and tried to ignore the hands.

Which moved lower. 'Wash ma back?' Fingertips brushed through the hair on his chest and began to circle his pecs.

A shiver erected his nipples.

The response registered against two rough palms. 'C'mon…' The voice was closer, hoarse again. Not sleep-hoarse. '… ah'll dae yer letter fur ye, later.'

Jas stretched out long legs beneath the small table. Rubbing the crown of his head against the pale skin of Stevie's stomach, he looked up. And gave up.

Amber eyes glinted down. Stevie smiled. 'Eh?'

The hands were now stroking his sides, fingers moving over his ribs. He groaned, raising his own arms to grasp two handfuls of tangled brown hair. 'You go oan an' let the water heat up – ah'll be through in a minute.'

A grin. 'Don't be long.' Strong fingers gripped his wrist, moving the hand down behind the chair.

Prick twitched against the fly of his jeans. His guided hand felt the outline of Stevie's morning glory. Out of sync, like all night-shift workers, at half-five in the afternoon. 'Jist a couple more lines…' A veil of tangled hair descended towards his face. Stevie's lips brushed the tip of his nose:

'Whit's that guy doin' onyway, that he canny tell his wife aboot?'

'He's a life-model – up at the Art School.' Jas grinned, fingers closing around Stevie's length.

'A whit?' Half-quizzical, half-pleasure.

Jas explained.

Amber eyes widening.

Jas grinned. 'Fifteen quid an hour – pays better than ony job the dole ur offerin' him.' He winked. 'How much you oan, doon at Hovis?'

'Five quid an oor…' The shadow of frowning disbelief. Then the hands wrenched themselves from beneath his shirt and Stevie was slowly peeling off underpants. '… ah believe in miracles / Since ye came along – ya sexy thing!'

Jas laughed. 'It's no' strippin' – jist posin'.'

One heel snagged in underpants waistband. Stevie staggered,

kicked the knickers into the air and continued to sing.

Jas whistled through his teeth, caught the underwear and waved it.

Stevie bowed, then winked. 'Ah'll run the water, eh?'

Smiling, Jas nodded. He watched a pair of tight, white buttocks sway rhythmically past the fridge towards the bedroom to the accompaniment of an out-of-tune Hot Chocolate, then looked back at his notes.

Sometime later, he sealed an envelope. A shard of blinding orange hit him in the face. Jas switch the PC off and shifted position.

This side of the building never got any direct sunlight, but each July late afternoon-reflected rays from a window opposite filled the normally dark living room with light.

Rotating shoulders, he moved out of range, walked to the answerphone and played back the day's three messages.

The first was the woman whose PO box address adorned the envelope. The second thanked him again for work done two months ago, and promised a cheque in the post.

Jas mentally moved the name to the top of the Bad Debt file and rubbed his right biceps. Stevie was right: he wasn't sitting properly. He'd find out about voice-activated software.

The third message finished. The tape rewound itself.

Jas sat down on the sofa and continued to rub.

Margaret Monaghan. The name meant nothing.

Marie McGhee. That name did.

A lot of business was repeat, or referrals. But the check still went through: Private Investigators had an obligation to stay on the right side of the law. He replayed the message again, then got up from the sofa and walked into the other room.

On the bed. Stevie. Sprawled and naked. The tv was on. Loud. Jas moved to the four-drawer filing-cabinet and opened the middle drawer.

'Ach, away – it wis aff-side!' A growl from the bed, directed at the screen. Volume increased.

Jas flicked through suspended files. Maybe he'd go to disc-storage, when he got the voice-activated software.

'You fuckin' blind?' Astonished laugh.

The tv commentator denied the accusation. Jas paused at 'McGhee', lifted a foldered bundle of papers and began to sift. Marie moved around a lot, but her mobile number should be the same.

'Get yer fuckin' eyes tested, pal!' Stevie continued to shout at the tv.

He spread the file on top of the metal cabinet and continued to search. In the background, the tv sports commentator talked very fast over an increasingly deafening roar. After a while, he found her number. After less of a while, his head was throbbing. Jas looked up. 'Turn that doon, eh?'

Scowl to the screen. Remote aimed. Volume increased.

Jas sighed. At least he was getting better at reading the signals. Rotating his right shoulder, he slipped Marie's card into his pocket, closed the file and sat down at the foot of the bed. 'Whit's wrang?'

No response.

Jas racked his brain, then remembered the reason Stevie was up and around so early, in the first place. 'Did yer solicitor definitely say he'd phone the day?'

A muscle pulsed in Stevie's newly shaven neck.

'Mibby it's a guid sign – nae news is guid news.' He began the lies. 'Ye said yersel' Maureen canny just waltz back intae Sam and Hayley's lives efter four years an' take over.' The name of the woman with whom Stevie had spent eight years of his life felt strange on his lips. 'Mibby yer solicitor's still… negotiating wi' hur solicitor.' Jas wondered if James Firestone, Llb, had got around to telling his client that, estranged or not, a mother was a mother and, as such, had rights. 'That'll be why he's no' phoned ye.' Jas studied Stevie's profile for a reaction.

The angular features were set hard.

A decibel-loaded blast of music signalled the end of Scotsport. Stevie continued to stare at the screen, remote in fist.

Jas moved up the bed, reached towards it. 'Whit did Firestone say, last time ye talked tae him?'

Stevie turned onto his side. The remote disappeared from view.

Jas stared at a pink ear. 'Turn it doon, eh?' His voice filled the room, barely competing with the massed voices of the Gap generation.

'Ah'm watchin' it.' The tone cut through the roar.

'The adverts?'

'Ah like the adverts.'

He focused on the loop of Stevie's hair, now secured in one of Hayley's scrunchies: the eleven-year-old always left behind at least three, each visit. 'Yer solicitor's no' said onythin' aboot suspendin' yer access, hus he?'

The only response was a deepening of the frown.

'So we're aw' still oan, fur the weekend, as usual?'

Remote aimed. *Coronation Street*'s theme-tune cut off in its prime. 'Ah've goat tae take ma holidays soon – afore the end o' the month.'

Realisation dawned with a vague recollection of an even vaguer discussion of a joint, two-week break. 'That's good, eh?' His voice was too loud. He lowered it. 'Gies ye mair time tae...'

'Ah better get ready fur work.' Stevie rolled off the bed and stood up.

'Whit aboot that shower?' He leaned across and grabbed one hairy knee.

Stevie pulled away.

'If ye still want me tae dae yer back, we can...' He glanced towards the en suite shower-room. The floor was draped with wet towels.

The sound of Stevie dressing filled the bedroom.

Jas watched. Regret tightened the muscles in his right arm. 'Ah'm...'

'Disney matter.' His apology cut short.

Jas rotated his shoulder: it didn't help. 'Ye ken ah eyeways dae the paperwork, afore ye get up. Ah lost tracka time an'...'

'Ah said it disney matter.' Stevie struggled into jeans, pushed past him and strode into the hall.

Jas followed. 'Talk tae me.'

'Nothin' tae talk aboot.' In the living room, Stevie was pulling on boots, eyes floorwards.

Regret slipped into irritation. 'Ye kent ma oors wur weird when ye moved in.' Frustration hardened his voice.

Stevie looked up. 'Ah took the bakery work so's we could... see mair o' each other.'

The hurt in the amber eyes hit home. Jas scowled. 'You took the bakery job cos it gies ye mair time wi' yer kids!' He regretted the words as soon as they were out.

Then Stevie was on his feet, fists clenched. 'Ah took it cos night-shift wis the ainly thing they offered me, an' gettin' a job wis wanna yer precious ground-rules!' Hazel irises glared.

Jas narrowed his eyes and lowered his voice. 'Ah ken – ah'm sorry.' He stretched out a hand.

'Fuck sorry!' The pale face flushed up. 'Ah'm oota here!' Jacket grabbed from sofa. Stevie pushed past him into the hall.

'Ye don't start till nine – we've goat ages yet.' Jas followed. 'That's the typin' finished – we can...' The draught from the slammed door was warm and smelled of exhaust-fumes. He stood there, listening to Stevie's receding bootsteps.

Still frowning, he waited until the sound faded, then withdrew the card from his pocket and walked back into the living room.

'Ah wisney sure if she'd gie ye a ring – ye dinny mind, dae ye?'

Work was work. Jas balanced the receiver between chin and shoulder. He lit a cigarette. 'How come Margaret Monaghan kens you – she sounds like a nice wuman.'

Marie McGhee's laugh cackled down the telephone-line. 'She's in ma Victim Support Group – an' Maggie is a nice wuman.'

His shoulder was less stiff. Her voice or the nicotine? Jas smiled: neither seemed likely. 'This nice wuman a rich wan tae? Ah hope ye made sure she kens how much hirin' me costs.'

No laugh. 'Since Joseph's insurance paid oot, Maggie's goat money tae burn – an' that's whit she'd dae wi' it, if it wid gie her peace o' mind.'

Reflected sunshine vanished, like the touch of a light switch. The living room darkened. Jas watched the end of his cigarette glow. 'Okay, ah'll gie her a ring.'

'Thanks, Big Man. Dunno if ye'll be able tae dae much, but jist tryin' might help.'

'That's whit ah'm here fur. Thanks fur confirmin' she's kosher.'

A laugh. 'Business must be boomin', if ye can afford tae pick an' choose yer clients.'

'Ah git by.' He inhaled. The glow crept up the cigarette's length.

Pause, then: 'An' how's yer lodger?' The word loaded.

Jas exhaled. The tightening returned to his shoulder. 'He's fine.'

'Tell him ah said hello, eh? Ah've goat a lotta time fur Stevie...'

The tightening spread into his right biceps.

'... canny be easy fur him, whit wi' that bitch o' a wife o' his, turning up oota the blue, like that.'

He was surprised more by her interest than the fact she knew so much. And not surprised.

'But he's doin' okay?'

'Aye...' Something was being talked around, here.

'An' you an him ur okay?'

Something which was never mentioned. One thing amongst many. Jas inhaled, then exhaled.

Another pause. 'You two been thegether – how long, noo?'

'Fourteen months.' His biceps throbbed.

Low whistle. 'That's a while, fur you, Jas.'

He frowned. Smalltalk wasn't like Marie. She was working up to something. He wondered if it was the same something.

'It'll be two years in September, since wee Paul died. Weird the way things work oot, eh Big Man?'

It was...

'Neil lost somethin' special, in the Bar-L, an' you an' Stevie found somethin'.'

... and it wasn't. Jas leant back on the sofa, flexing his arm. Through the window, the evening sky was clouding over.

Neil. Neil Johnstone.

Serving life for the murder of another prisoner. Briefly the lover of Marie McGhee's brother Paul, serving eighteen months for possession of Ecstasy. And responsible by proxy for the scar on Marie's face.

Their thoughts moved along parallel lines. 'Ah visit, when ah can.'

Not so much losing an enemy as gaining a... brother-in-law? 'Neil still in the Bar-L?'

'Aye.'

'Wi' Jimmy?'

'Jimmy wis moved tae Carstairs, last November.'

He tapped the end of his cigarette against the edge of a smoked-glass ashtray. 'Here endeth the history-lesson.' A smile twitched his lips.

'Whit?'

'Nothin'...' Jas drew the last millimetres of cigarette deep into his lungs, then stubbed the remnants into the ashtray. Maybe the something was better not talked about. Like abracadabra, maybe saying the words would give someone, somewhere, power. 'Well, cheers fur shovin' some business ma way.' He hauled himself upright. His right arm refused to move, so he used his left. 'Ah'll gie Mrs Monaghan a ring, the night.'

'Make it efter nine. Maggie's holding the meetin' at hur hoose, this week. Eyeways lays oan a guid spread, tae – ah think she likes the bakin' as much as the company.'

'Okay.' Jas removed the receiver from the crook of his neck, holding it in his left hand while trying to flex the fingers of his right. He waited for her closure.

It came after another pause. 'Luck efter yersel, Big Man. Say hello to Stevie, fur me?'

'Aye...' He severed the connection.

Victim Support. Insurance. Joseph. The voice on the answerphone had sounded mid-fifties. Husband? Brother?

Jas played back the tape, wrote down the number and returned the phone-call.

Son.

Just after nine-thirty pm, the large living room of the second-floor flat in Rutherglen still bore traces of Marie's recently departed Support Group...

'Thanks for comin', Mr Anderson. Sorry aboot the mess.' Wearing the sort of pinny his grandmother had rarely taken off, Margaret Monaghan deftly placed a variety of cups and plates on an already laden tray.

... and testament to another, less-accepted departure. Jas pulled his eyes from the illuminated, framed photograph which sat on top of a well-polished sideboard. 'Lemme give ye a hand.'

'You sit doon, Mr Anderson – ah'll just be a minute. Ye'll take a cuppa tea, won't ye?'

He knew better than to refuse. 'That'll be great.' Jas sat on a worn but solid armchair. He didn't usually do home visits – for obvious reasons – but Margaret Monaghan suffered from arthritis and seldom left her flat. As her ample, shuffling form disappeared through a doorway, Jas craned his neck to take in more of the makeshift altar.

A photograph. A large photograph in an ornate frame. Looked like a detail blown-up from a holiday snap. A football scarf curled around the base of the frame, a green-and-white guardian snake.

Draped across one corner, a small gold cross on a chain. On the wall above the photograph, a larger, gilt crucifix. Above that, a bleeding Sacred Heart.

The whole scene was lit by two, obviously new, desk-spots. And a small votive candle which flickered in front of a bevy of Mass cards.

Jas stared at the face in the photograph. Head-and-shouders shot.

Mid-teens. Sandy hair cut into a bowl-shape, skimming pink ears. Green eyes. Which were smiling at someone just out of sight.

'That was taken at his cousin Fiona's wedding. Last spring.'

Jas turned his head towards the voice. For a big, arthritic woman, Margaret Monaghan moved silently.

She placed cup, saucer, milk and sugar containers on a small table to his right. 'Joseph said it made him look like a wee boy, but ah eyeways liked him in it.'

He knew better than to comment: listening was part of his job.

'Would have been eighteen, next week, Mr Anderson.' She sat down in the armchair opposite him. And the shrine. The pinny was gone, exposing blouse, cardigan and pleated skirt. Broad fingers smoothed the fabric, picking at invisible threads. 'His whole life ahead o' him.' Eyes fixed on the spotlit scene.

'You mind?' Jas removed the small device from his pocket. He sat the voice-activated tape-recorder beside the cup and saucer, nodded to it.

She barely heard. For the next thirty minutes, tiny wheels turned and he watched her talking to Joseph Monaghan. He turned the tape when she paused:

'Marie said you could maybe… find oot how the police ur gettin' oan wi' things.'

Jas kept his face impassive. 'It's an ongoing enquiry, Mrs Monaghan. The police will be doin' everything they can.'

She nodded. 'Aye, ongoin' – that's whit ah keep gettin' told.' She was picking at the imaginary threads again. 'Ongoin' fur nearly a year, noo.' No resentment in the voice. Just a little disappointment.

Jas didn't tell her the official stats on detection-rates.

He didn't tell her that, after a year, unsolved cases were put on the unofficial back-burner, and left there to dry out. She probably knew. Private Investigators were often straws to be clutched at.

'Marie said ye wurney cheap.' With some effort, she got out of her chair and walked to the altar.

Jas smiled at the bluntness and didn't offer to help.

Margaret Monaghan pulled open a drawer in the highly polished sideboard. 'Ma sister keeps tellin' me ah should use this tae get a new hip.' She turned.

Jas stared at the thick sheaf of notes.

'But ah'd sleep easier, if ah kent everything that could be done wis bein' done tae catch the animals who murdered ma Joseph.' She shuffled towards him, dumping at least ten thousand in crisp pink notes into his lap.

He was intending to tell her the police were unlikely to co-operate with the private sector, full stop, if an investigation was ongoing.

Instead, he counted the money, gave her a receipt for his five hundred pound retainer and advised her to keep the rest somewhere more secure. Then he switched off the tape recorder, put it back in his pocket and told her he'd be in touch.

Two

Back at the Cumbernauld Road flat, he made notes from the tape, then showered. In the cramped, plastic cubicle, Margaret Monaghan's calm words replayed themselves in his head. Jas washed the day from his body, while another, less-calm voice replaced that of his new client.

Drying himself off, he picked up Stevie's towels from earlier and shoved them into the laundry-basket. The flat was silent. Jas straightened the duvet and pillows, easing himself between the sheets. He drifted off to memories of hard, angry words and a pair of mahogany eyes...

'Ah'm sorry.'

... woke up to soft words and cool hands on his body. Jas blinked in seven am sunshine.

Arms tightening around his waist. Lips near his ear. 'Ah'm...'

''S okay...' He relaxed back against the warm body. '... it wis ma fault too.' Knees dug into the back of his knees. Thighs shadowed thighs. Two erect nipples ground into the skin on either side of his spine:

'Ah thought aboot ye aw' shift. Wis gonny phone, but ah didney want tae wake ye.'

Voice-vibrations trembled into his chest. Jas pulled up his legs.

Stevie mirrored the movement.

He inhaled deeply, filling lungs. Over the smell of his own sleepy body, the scent of yeast and antibacterial soap made his cock twitch. Jas reached round, stroked the curve of Stevie's arse-cheek and smiled at the windowsill.

This made it all worthwhile.

He luxuriated in silence and the languid motion of their bodies. No kids. No phone-calls. No clients. No worries.

The best part of the day. Listening to another man fall asleep beside him.

Stevie's balls nestled beneath Jas's arse-cheeks. One yeasty hand travelled down his stomach and settled in his groin. He grinned. He grabbed a wrist, returning the hand to his stomach. 'Listen, we'll...'

Less languid movement cut the sentence short. Stevie's arm slid under his body and a well-muscled leg pressed down on his. Seconds later, he lay on his back.

Sunlight filled the room. Stevie filled his eyes.

Freed from the scrunchie, brown hair scorched chestnut by the rising day. Pale chest stained with a rosy blush, which was spreading down over stomach to brush the pink head of Stevie's prick. Above one nipple, a triad of white lines refused tainting.

Jas focused on the scar-tissue. Similar skin circled Stevie's wrists like chains to the past. Broad palms flattened themselves over his pecs, pulling him back to the present. Hair tickled his face.

One palm on the small of Stevie's back, the knuckles of his other hand stroked the side of a starting-to-bristle cheek. The smile hurt Jas's face. He stared into glowing brown eyes.

Stevie's expression was tight against his fingers, pupils swollen with another purpose.

The knowledge stretched his prick a little more. Then a hand slipped between them, yeasty fingers curling around his length.

Jas arched up off the bed, thrusting into Stevie's fist and searching for a mouth...

… and finding it. Stevie's body was rigid.

Something in Jas melted. He thrust his tongue in between open lips. Two groans synched as one. His hands roved down over the hard cheeks of Stevie's arse, cupping and kneading.

Another need tightened Stevie's fist.

Jas increased the force of the kiss, pulling Stevie down onto him. Index fingers stroked the moist furrow, searching for the heart of the man.

Stevie broke the kiss, straddling Jas's thighs.

The fist was moving now. Brown eyes fixed on the movement.

Jas groaned. Blood and desire pulsed against Stevie's fingers. Sleep was a million lust-soaked miles away. He replaced Stevie's hand with his own, gripping the root of his prick.

A lunge towards the bedside table. Cigarettes and lube scattering to the floor. 'Fuck!' Stevie dangled over the side of the bed.

Jas ignored the cursing. The pad of one finger pressed against the opening to the man's body, he began to massage.

Stevie moaned, a veil of hair whipping across his face.

Then his finger was inside and his cock was pulsing in his own fist.

Stevie lurched upright, sinking down onto the intrusion.

Jas released his prick, gripped Stevie's hair and dragged him into another kiss.

Then they were rolling and his finger was moving and Stevie's hands were under his shoulders and…

… ringing. Muscle clenched around him. Stevie tried to move.

'Let the machine get it.'

'It might be…'

'It's hauf-seven in the mornin'!' Desire made him scowl. 'Whit solicitor phones at…?'

Stevie wrenched himself off Jas's finger. Hard-on slapping stomach, he bounded from the bed and ran through to the other room.

The scowl deepened. Jas slumped forward onto rumpled warmth. He could still smell where Stevie had been. Eager voice from the other room:

'Aye?'

Jas rolled over, pawing the floor at the side of the bed. From the other room, eager into irritation:

'Naw, this isney Jas Anderson. Who's this?'

He found, opened the cigarette packet. More irritation:

'Haud oan...'

Jas stuck a cigarette between his lips and rolled out of bed.

Disappointed face in the doorway.

He snatched the lighter from behind a pile of books. 'Telt ye tae let the machine take it.'

Stevie padded over to the bed, threw himself wordlessly onto it.

He sighed, lit the cigarette. In the living room, the receiver lay on the couch. He picked it up. 'Jas Anderson.' His voice was thick.

'Tom Galbraith. Sorry for the dawn call.'

The voice was deep. Accented. English, but not London. 'Whit can ah do fur ye, Mr Galbraith?'

'You don't remember me, do you?'

Jas stuck the cigarette between his lips and sat down. Galbraith... Galbraith. 'Should ah?'

Brief pause. '1989. Workshop on interviewing techniques. Divisional Headquarters. Pitt Street?'

A cop? Jas looked around for an ashtray. The occasion vaguely placed itself. The name remained stubbornly unfamiliar. 'Naw – sorry.'

'1991? Edinburgh?'

He found an ashtray, used it. 'Still rings nae bells. Whit can ah do fur you, Mr Galbraith?'

Uncertain. 'Like to talk to you, about a private matter, Jas.'

'Ye want to hire me?' A naked shape wandered into the room, heading for the kitchen. Jas tried to catch an eye. Stevie's gaze dropped to the floor.

'Not exactly, but I would appreciate a word.'

The accent wasn't local, but a potential job was a potential job. He gave the address and suggested a time.

Relief. 'That'll be great. Thanks, Jas. Look forward to seeing you again.' The connection severed.

Jas slowly lowered the receiver. 1991. Almost ten years ago... Galbraith?

From the kitchen: 'Who wis it?' A tangly head poked round the side of the door.

Jas inhaled on the cigarette. He continued to stare at the phone. 'Nae idea.'

Head back into kitchen. Sounds of a kettle switching off. 'Whit did he want?'

Jas walked towards pouring noises. 'No' sure.'

'Seemed tae ken you...' Mirthless laugh.

He watched Stevie heap his own coffee with sugar, then lift both cups. His mind was back with a career long over and done with. 'Tom Galbraith...'

Stevie looked at him. 'Aye, he said that.' Quizzical. 'An' ye really don't ken him?'

Jas caught a tone in the question. He didn't want another argument...

The smell of the coffee sharpened his brain.

... another, much-anticipated telephone call pushed itself into his mind. 'Dae ah no' owe ye a shower?' He slung an arm around Stevie's shoulder, nuzzling the neck beneath the hair.

'Whit aboot...?' Eyes to the coffee-mugs.

Jas guided Stevie back through to the bedroom.

An hour later, Stevie lay in his arms:

'Ah ken Mo's got rights – Firestone telt me that. Ah don't mind hur seeing Sam an' Hayley...'

Jas smoothed slowly drying hair from the concerned face.

'... an' she's fine aboot them stayin' wi' Carole. But she's gonny make trouble...'

He could feel the tension. Jas continued to smooth.

'… aboot…'

Jas sighed. He'd been waiting for this.

'… this place.'

Jas stopped stroking. 'Whit ye mean – this place?'

Stevie leant his head against Jas's shoulder. 'Firestone sez…' Brain searching for exact words. '… ma present accommodation isney ideal, fur the weekend stay-overs.'

Jas frowned. 'Whit else did he say?'

Sigh. 'The sleepin' bags an' the couch urney guid enough…'

'We'll git wanna they fold-doon sofabed things.' He mentally added it to the voice-activated software.

'That wid be great, but it's mair the… layoot.'

Jas resumed stroking, gathering Stevie's hair into a thick length behind a bristly neck. 'The bog an' the bathroom bein' in different places?' He knew it was an anachronism: most tenement flats were being upgraded to meet more accepted standards. But the convenience of an ensuite shower-room had always seemed worth hanging onto. 'Mibby the couple that owns this place'll be amenable tae some… alterations.'

The tension was back. 'It's mair where the… bathroom is.' Sigh. 'The fact Sam an' Hayley huv goat tae come into the bedroom, tae wash their hauns an' stuff.'

His fingers tightened in the thick loop of hair. No our. Merely the. He turned Stevie around to face him. 'Maureen does ken, doesn't she?'

The pale face reddened. 'Ah'm no' sure.' Stevie stared at his lap.

'Whit dae ye mean, ye're no sure?' Something was starting to explain the sullenness which had tinged the atmosphere for the past two weeks. 'Yer wife's been back three months an' ye've no' telt her who ye're livin' wi'?'

'None o' her fuckin' business…' Deeper blush. '… but ah think the kids mighta said somethin'.'

Irritation tingled in his stomach. Jas pushed it away. He draped his arms around hunched shoulders and leant his head against another.

'Ye shoulda put her straight, at the start. Now it looks like ye're tryin' tae hide somethin'.'

'Ah ken, ah ken... ah wis gonny tell her, but...'

He tilted Stevie's chin upwards. 'So whit's the state o' play, at the moment?' The reasons didn't matter. The damage was done.

Dull brown eyes refused to meet his. 'She's no' happy wi' unsupervised access.' An explosion of movement. Stevie pulled away, eyes blazing. 'She fuckin' walked oot on us! She's been fuck kens where doin' fuck kens whit an' noo...' Stevie leapt off the bed. '... she's goat the cheek tae say ah'm no' fit tae be alone wi' ma ain kids?'

Jas watched the pale body pace. Part of him had avoided involvement, from the word go. Another part of him had known involvement was inevitable. 'It's no' you.'

Stevie's fists were clenched. 'She's the wan who's no' fit tae be wi' them! Whit if she decides tae dae a runner again? Whit ur me an' Carole meant tae tell 'em this time?'

Jas raised his voice. 'It's no' you she thinks isney fit tae be alone wi' them.'

Stevie thundered on. 'Ah'm no' goin' through aw' that again! We wur aw' fine, till she turned up. Carole hus them durin' the week, when ah'm workin'. We huv them at weekends. Ah...'

'It's no' you, ya stupid fucker.' Jas gripped a rigid arm. 'It's me – us!'

The thunderous face stared at him.

Jas stood up, blue eyes never leaving brown. There was so much he didn't know...

Like, why Maureen McStay had left her husband with two young children, four years ago.

... so much Stevie probably didn't know either. He wanted to ask...

... and he didn't.

Maybe the one person who did know was the only person he'd never met. Someone who had packed her bags and walked away from an eight-year marriage.

Stevie's pupils remained tiny black dots. 'Whit we dae is none o' her business.'

Jas massaged the rigid arm.

Microdot black telescoped a little.

'If her kids ur stayin' here…' Jas pushed a hank of still-damp hair away from a storm-cloud face. '… it is her business. An' her solicitor's business.' He knew it wasn't what Stevie wanted to hear.

Ex-offender counted against him enough. Ex-offender, living with a man – in a flat where the bathroom was ensuite to the only bedroom?

He relaxed his grip on a less-rigid forearm. 'Ye gotta co-operate.'

Stevie looked away. 'That's whit ah'm doin'.' Eyes narrowed in morning sunshine. Voice belying the words.

'Ye gotta trust Firestone: he's lookin' after yer interests…' Jas moved behind the tensed, naked man. '… an' ye gotta stop bottlin' this aw' up.' The irony of the instruction made him smile. Wrapping arms around Stevie's waist, he followed the gaze through the window, over rooftops to Christ knew where.

Stevie leant back against him. 'Ah'm goin' oota ma fuckin' mind here, man.' Voice barely a whisper.

Jas inhaled the smell of freshly washed hair. 'Gie it till this efternoon, an' if Firestone husney phoned, phone him, eh?'

'Aye. Okay.' The voice was unconvinced.

Jas began to move. Steering Stevie towards the bed, he lowered him onto it and sat beside him. 'It'll work oot – you've goat rights tae.' He watched long, pale legs slip under the duvet.

True – and not true.

Stevie's record was for a crime of violence: Maureen McStay had reason enough to object to her estranged husband's influence on their children, with or without the knowledge of who he shared his bed with.

'Ah ken…' Stevie pulled the quilt up. '… ah suppose.'

Jas stared at the fan of tangle-dried brown hair, eyes moving to the now-relaxed face. Tiny lines furrowed out from the corners of each brown eye. Leaning over, he kissed the right. 'So git some sleep, Snow White.'

The first laugh in a while. 'Dis that make you Prince Charmin' or the wicked queen?'

Jas forced a smile: it made him part of all this, whether he wanted to be or not. 'Well, ah'm no' yer fairy godfather!'

A lower, sleepier sound.

Jas sat there, stroking Stevie's face until the man fell asleep. Then he grabbed a jock from the floor, walked through to the living room and began to exercise.

An hour later, he was dressed and leaving.

An hour after that, he was sitting in a familiar seat in the Mitchell Reference Library, scanning microfilmed newspapers for October, last year.

The game had been Celtic vs Dundee United, the score: 3-2.

Seventeen year-old Joseph Monaghan was attacked by person or persons unknown on Saturday 5th, less than a quarter of a mile from Celtic's recently refurbished stands at Parkhead.

D Division territory. London Road: his old patch. His five-year-old, old patch. Cops made elephants look absent-minded.

Jas scanned on. The following day's *Scotland on Sunday* carried pictures of a heavy police-presence within Queen Street Station, a good two miles away. Several arrests had been made, mainly on minor disturbance of the peace- related incidents.

He stared at the photographs. In microfilmed reproduction, football- colours didn't come up. One fan looked very much like another.

From Monday 7th to Wednesday 9th, both tabloid and broadsheets carried details of the attack. True to Margaret Monaghan's version of events, Joseph had been found in a gutter, near The Forge Shopping Complex, with massive head injuries. He was pronounced dead on arrival at hospital.

Monday's *Record* showed the same detail from the same photograph which sat in Margaret Monaghan's living room, amidst the usual police appeals for witnesses.

The *Herald* had an editorial, on the Tuesday, bemoaning a resurgence of organised football violence. Plus another appeal for anyone who had witnessed the attack to come forward.

The same day, in the *Record*, a feature headline screamed: 'Someone who didn't walk on by.' Jas paused. Read. Amidst the tabloid rhetoric, a passing, unnamed motorist had stopped that Saturday afternoon...

His eyes moved from screen to notepad. Jas clicked his pen, scribbled.

... called 999 from his mobile phone, then personally driven the dying teenager to Glasgow's Royal Infirmary, when ambulance and police had been slow to arrive.

Jas frowned, winding forward to Thursday. A small paragraph on page eighteen of the *Herald* told him police were pursuing a number of lines of inquiry, in the murder of Joseph Monaghan...

'Mr Anderson?'

Jas looked up.

A slender boy in a CK One tee-shirt held out three stapled pages. 'That's your fax here.'

'Thanks.' Jas smiled, accepting the requested document. He took in the cropped-and-bleached hair. And the returned smile.

The blond lingered a few seconds, then walked back to the reference counter.

Jas watched him go, then stood up and made his way to the door.

It made a change to be sheltering from the sun. Sequestered in a stone alcove with two freckled students and an emphysemic old man, he smoked and read.

Post mortem reports were a matter of public record: anyone could get a copy. It didn't make pleasant reading. Despite the head injuries, technically, cause of death was asphyxiation: Joseph Monaghan had drowned in his own blood, following extensive trauma to the breastbone which had perforated one lung.

Jas frowned: it took a lot of force to shatter a breastbone...

The pathologist's report pointed to repeated stampings. The imprint of a boot had been visible on the skin of Joseph's chest.

... a lot of anger.

Jas read on, exhaling grey smoke through his nose. Football violence was touch-paper ignited, burning brightly for a few frenzied seconds then fizzling out.

He thought about the *Record*'s tribute to the motorist who had found and driven Joseph to hospital. Grinding out the dog-end under the sole of a Doc Marten, he levered himself off the alcove wall and made his way back inside.

Another two hours and he knew everything in the public domain it was possible to know.

In the weeks following Joseph's death, there had been two further mentions of the crime: Tayside Police were working with their colleagues in D Division, on the organised football violence angle, and Joseph's body was finally released to his family, almost two months after the attack. The discovery of a bathtub full of Semtex in a Sighthill flat had elbowed the case from journalists' minds, early November.

Jas leant against the bus-stop and narrowed his eyes.

Technically, the investigation was still open. Technically, the police could refuse to talk to him...

A number 51A rumbled into sight. Jas fumbled for the exact change.

... technically, Tayside Police were involved. The crime wasn't their patch. Their detection-record wasn't on the line.

The bus stopped. Doors wheezed open. Jas dropped ninety-five pence into the slot, took his ticket and walked upstairs.

But they still had no reason to co-operate with the private sector...

... and no reason not to. Sometimes being ex-polis was an advantage. DC Frank McKenna, of B Division, in Dundee, couldn't be more helpful – or as young as he sounded on the phone.

Jas leant back on the sofa. 'So there wis nae joy, your end?'

'We ran the description details past a couple of beat-patrols, hauled in a handful o' casuals. Nothin'. There wis talk o' your guys bringing a witness over – fur an ID parade, ken. But it didney pan-oot.'

Description-details...

Description-details...

Jas rubbed his forehead. 'Ah don't suppose ye...?'

'Never goat the witness's name. Like ah telt ye, ah wis jist the liaison. Aw' phone an' fax-work. Cross-referencin' an' the like.'

The east-coast accent was barely noticeable. Frankie McKenna was good on the phone. 'Thanks anyway.' The name of a contact at D Division would have been useful too. Jas didn't push it: information had a way of tracking itself backwards, and McKennna had told him more than he'd expected.

'Glad ah could help, Mr Anderson.'

Jas returned the pleasantry and severed the connection. He glanced at his watch. Nearly four: he'd put off the phone-call to D Division long enough. Punching in a number he knew by heart, he reached for a cigarette.

Maybe he'd get someone as helpful as Frankie McKenna had been.

Three minutes later, he knew better.

'We cannot comment on an ongoing case. Thank you.'

Jas lit a cigarette. He'd uttered the same words countless times, over twelve years.

Policy. Procedure. Par for the course.

He thought about Margaret Monaghan's hip-replacement money. He thought about returning the five hundred pound retainer he'd taken last night...

... then thought about that large, pink bundle steadily eroding away as she hired PI after PI, none of whom would get even as far as he had. He was still thinking as he punched in another, memorised number.

He was asked his name by three people, then eventually put through to the correct extension.

'DI McLeod.' Crisp precise diction. Clear, cool voice.

Jas smiled. 'Hi, Ann.'

Three

'Who's this?' Automatically suspicious.

His smile broadened. 'An' they spend thoosands sendin' ye all oan Public Relations courses!'

A sigh of recognition. 'What do you want, Jas?'

He laughed. 'Can ah no' phone up an auld colleague just fur a chat?' She could read him like a book.

'Cut the flannel. It's been a very long time.' Voice cold.

The laugh died. About a year since they'd last spoken. Hardly aeons, in the grand scheme of things. She sounded stressed and tired. The knowledge made him glad he'd resigned when he had – not that he'd ever have made the rank of DI. 'No' that long...' Jas pulled his work-diary from beneath the transcribed Monaghan notes. Eyes fell on a name and a time, for later that afternoon. '... an' ah'm no' flannellin'. You wur at a seminar on interviewing techniques, in eighty-nine, were ye no'? Pitt Street?'

Surprise. 'That's going back a bit.' Tone warming.

'That's whit ah thought...' Maybe this wasn't the time to ask about the Monaghan Case. '... ye don't remember a Tom Galbraith, dae ye?'

'I remember three days listening to some bigwig bluster on about game strategies and psychological interview tactics...' Thawing further by the minute. A soft laugh. '... and setting off the fire alarm. Divisional Headquarters had just introduced the blanket No

Smoking rule, remember? You braced the elements and went outside for a cigarette – it was freezing. Me and Allan McVey found an empty room...' A louder laugh. '... the whole building was evacuated, and I ended up outside anyway!'

He listen while she reminisced, adding a word or two in the right places. DI Ann McLeod sounded like she didn't get many normal conversations, these days.

'Galbraith... Galbraith...' Eventually, she got back on track. '... what was the first name?'

Jas supplied it and explained the circumstances. 'He's no' local, goin' by the accent, but he seems tae ken me, an' ah've nae idea who he is.'

'Sounds vaguely familiar...' Thoughtful pause. '... and he wants your services?'

'Presumably, but ah'll find oot fur sure soon enough...' Jas lit another cigarette. '... so how's life, onyway?'

The sigh was back, but less icy. 'Don't ask.'

He took her at her word and plunged into the thaw. 'You workin' on the Monaghan murder?'

Pause. 'Was this... Galbraith involved in...?'

'Naw, naw...' He filled her in.

The sigh dropped in temperature. 'Jas, I...'

'The kid's mother's just lookin' fur reassurance everythin' that can be done is being done.' He talked on, not giving her the chance to intervene. 'Goin'- through-the-motions work, really...' Summarising what he already knew, Jas continued firmly towards the climax. 'Just the witness's name an' a phone number, eh? If whoever it is disney wanna talk tae me, ah'll no' push it. Ah just want somethin' tae justi-fy whit the family's payin' me.'

Silence.

He shuffled transcribed details and waited.

'If the case is ongoing, Jas, I...'

'We both ken it's ongoin' nowhere – no' after nine months.'

Crimes were solved in the first three or not at all. 'An' it's no' even your division. Monaghan, Joseph: type in the name fur me, see whit comes up.'

More silence.

'Come oan – whit harm can ah dae? Ah might even come across somethin' your lot missed.' The implication out before he could stop it.

And registering. 'Give his mother her money back and tell her to get in touch with us, if she wants to know how things are progressing.'

D Division's phone number was top of Margaret Monaghan's redial list. Jas frowned. 'The wuman's been fobbed off fur months as it is. Whit'll wan name hurt?'

Icy words. 'Sorry, I can't help you.' Connection severed.

He lowered the receiver and cursed his heavy-handedness. Jas walked to the window, stared out into the back-court. He should never have taken Margaret Monaghan's money.

In the communal triangle between three adjoining tenement-blocks, lines of washing hung motionless in a no-wind.

Another of Strathclyde's unsolved crime statistics rose from the recesses of his mind, dirtier laundry unaired for almost two years. Jas stubbed out the cigarette, pushing the death back down where it belonged and turned away. Opening the bedroom door quietly, he poked his head in.

Beneath a crumpled duvet, the judge, jury and summary executioner of ex–Prison Officer Ian Dalgleish scowled in restless sleep. James Firestone had obviously yet to phone.

Stevie had other things to worry about...

Jas looked at his watch.

... and so had he. An unrecognised voice on a telephone was due in less than half an hour.

Closing the door softly, he returned to the living-room-cum-office and pondered Tom Galbraith's identity while attempting to make the room more presentable.

*

'Again, apologies for the wake-up call...' Five-ten of trim early fifties sat easily in the armchair, barely registering his surroundings.

Jas had taken the couch. The phone had rung twice, in the past fifteen minutes. He'd turned the volume down and let the machine pick up. 'Nae problem ...' Despite the exposure and a distinctive, neatly clippered moustache, the heavily lined face still meant nothing. But at least he recognised the type. A smile played around his lips: Stevie would appreciate the ex-army posture. You could drop a weight from the back of Tom Galbraith's head and watch it fall straight to his tailbone.

'... debated phoning you for a week now...' Hands held loosely in lap. 'Wasn't sure it was the same James Anderson from way back. Heard you'd set up in the private sector.'

No unnecessary use of pronouns. Sentences clipped as neatly as facial hair and fingernails. An efficient man, in everything. Jas nodded. 'Aye, ah'm thinkin' o' addin' an extra A tae the Anderson – get first in the phone-book's business-section.'

The joke acknowledged briefly. 'Finally got round to it at half-seven this morning.' One end of a neatly trimmed moustache scratched with an equally well-manicured thumbnail.

Recognition dawning. 'Ah'm glad ye did.' Jas smiled at the man who filled the chair opposite. Where the face and bearing remained oblique, the mannerism placed Tom Galbraith firmly in his mind.

The years fell away and he was standing outside Divisional Headquarters in Pitt Street with a pipe-smoker from West Yorkshire Police whose right hand was unable to leave a neat brown 'tache alone. 'You still in the Force?' The hair on the upper lip was now tinged with grey.

A nod. 'CIB now – been there for the past decade. You resigned on... health reasons?' Beneath thick matching eyebrows, insightful grey eyes studied him.

'Five years ago.' Jas lit a cigarette. If Tom Galbraith knew that, did he also know the circumstances of the resignation? Official, or unofficial?

He inhaled. They'd hit it off, more than ten years ago, but he was a different man, now. 'So whit brings ye back tae Glasgow?'

'Work, as ever.' Dismissive smile. 'Hope to get the chance to see more of your architecture, though, while I'm here.' Speech-pattern relaxing.

Another conference? Jas blew a smoke ring. Bits and pieces were coming back.

A couple of lunch-breaks spent strolling around the area. Stopping in front of what was left of the Alexander 'Greek' Thompson church to shelter from February sleet. Talk of a wife. The production of snapshots showing a chubby kid in school uniform. Outlines of a life he'd been unable to reciprocate. Falling back on impromptu details of the building behind them. And landing on common ground. 'Ye'll huv tae hurry before whit's left either crumbles away or gets torn doon.'

A less dismissive smile. 'You should see what they've done to Manchester.'

'You still based there?'

'London, these days. Nicholas has just finished a year at a sixth form college.'

Jas tapped the cigarette end in the ashtray. The chubby kid in the private school uniform. 'Yer boay'll be...' He searched his memory. '... late teens, noo?'

The moustache tugged. 'Seventeen. Off to Oxford to study law, in the autumn.' Pride in the voice, tinged with... something else. 'Eileen and I brought him up with us. We've rented a flat in the city – a sort of last family holiday, before he moves away.' Moustache tugged again. Throat clearing. 'In fact, that's ... mainly why I rang you.'

Jas cocked his head.

Tom Galbraith got up from the armchair. Pipe withdrawn from the pocket of a well-cut barathea blazer. 'You mind?' Pipe waved.

'Go ahead...' He stared at square shoulders, wondering as he had ten years ago if it was good tailoring or the army background. Jas watched the pipe-lighting process. The Tom Galbraith he'd known had talked easily about everything and anything. Now the space between them filled with the fumbled rasp of match after match on sandpaper. A neatly manicured hand shook uncharacteristically. Finally:

'Christ, why is this so difficult?'

'Get yerself a pipe-lighter.' Jas disregarded the obvious bush-beating. He grabbed the matchbox, struck and cupped his hand around the flare.

Tom Galbraith lowered his pipe to the flame.

Their eyes met. Jas smiled. Grey looked away. Jas watched the man suck deeply on the stem. 'Ye wur sayin'?' The room filled with a rich, warm smell.

'Need a favour.' Square shoulders sloped slightly.

'Whit kinda... favour?' He opened the notebook and picked up a pen.

The military bearing faded further. 'It's Nick.' Tom Galbraith sat down. Legs crossed, arms folded, he seemed smaller in the chair.

Jas looked from the slumped, worried form to the notebook and closed the latter. And waited.

The smell of smouldering tobacco eased off as the pipe went out. 'Eileen and I brought him up here with us because we didn't want to leave him alone in London.' Folded arms folding more tightly. 'Sixth form college wasn't choice: his last school expelled him for repeated breach of curfew.' Insightful grey eyes everywhere but his. 'How he managed to get four A-levels is a miracle. He doesn't know anyone up here, but he's still out every night, never says where he's going and even when Eileen can persuade him to stay in, he barricades himself in his room with the telephone and his computer and refuses to talk to me.'

Jas smiled. 'Sounds like at least seventy percent o' teenagers.'

Head raised. 'His mother and he still communicate, to a certain extent...' Regretful eyes. '... seems I'm the problem.'

Jas extinguished what was left of the cigarette. 'And where exactly dae ah fit intae this?'

'Would you... talk to him?'

Jas laughed. 'Me?' He leant back on the sofa. 'Ah wis wanna the... thirty percent, at your Nick's age.' Good exam-results, waiting patiently to join Strathclyde's finest: the perfect son. 'If he's goin' through a rebellious phase, ah don't see talkin' tae an ex-cop's gonny...'

'Think Nick's gay.' Moustache tugged vigorously.

Jas blinked.

'Think he's gay and he's... afraid to tell me.' Arms unfolded. Broad palms rubbed a confused face. 'Obviously, with all the associated risks, it's not a lifestyle I'd... choose for him, if it was up to me...'

Jas stiffened. He'd seen his own father... three times in the last decade? And then by accident.

'... but he's still my son, and I love him...'

Jas picked up the pen and turned it over between his fingers. They'd exchanged a similar number of sentences in that time.

'... and I want him to know if... that's the way he is, I'm...' Arms tightly refolded. Discomfort increasing. '... cool with it.'

The slang was at odds with what was left of the military bearing. Despite other memories, Jas found himself grinning. 'So tell him that.'

Tom Galbraith was on his feet again, pacing. 'We barely exchange a civil word, these days. Thought maybe...' Pause. '... you could...' Head raised. Prompting.

Jas met uncertain grey eyes.

'... have a talk with him – man-to-man, as it were. Find out if he's being...' Term sought for. '... safe, does he have a... boyfriend, or whatever they're calling it these days.' Uncomfortable grey eyes. 'It would put my mind at rest, a little.'

The role of counsellor was completely alien. Jas sighed.

Seventeen.

Maybe gay. Maybe not.

Oxford-bound and evidently enjoying life.

The common ground between himself and Nick Galbraith would be limited, to say the least. He gripped the pen. 'Whit did ye have in

39

mind: you march him round here an' ah dae some palsy-walsy act?'

'No, no...' Tom Galbraith sat down again. He lifted the pipe and the matches. '... thought perhaps you would like to come for a meal. Eileen'll make sure Nick's there – and we'll see how things go.'

Jas stared at the concerned man before him. Another man, and a lack of social life shimmered in his mind. 'When wur ye thinkin'?'

Relief poured off the face. 'Whenever suits you – the weekend? Eileen and I will make ourselves scarce, after dinner, and the two of you can...'

'Okay if ah bring someone?'

Eyebrow raised. 'You have a...?' Another term-search.

Why was it a surprise? Jas suppressed a frown. 'Ye spoke tae him this mornin' – he works night-shift at the bakery doon the road, so the dinner'll have tae be early-ish.'

Nod. 'That's fine.'

'Oh, an' we huv Stevie's kids at weekends, so that's oot.' Jas mentally scanned a very uncrowded social calendar. 'How's Monday or Tuesday, next week?' He watched Tom Galbraith quiver under the weight of a lot more information than he'd been prepared for.

A momentary fluster hidden quickly behind yet anther tug at the moustache. 'Tuesday's fine. When does your... er Stevie start work?'

It made a change to be the comfortable one. Jas smiled. 'Ten till six. Eatin' at seven-ish'll suit us fine.' It made a change to say *us*.

'Good, good...' Pipe bowl tipped into ashtray. More than singed tobacco spilling out. '... even if Nick refuses to talk to me, just having you two there will show him I'm not the... monster he thinks I am.'

His hand seized abruptly, gripped tightly:

'You have my eternal gratitude, Jas.'

He managed a laugh, returned the squeeze. 'Aye, well keep it till we see how this goes.' His hand released:

'Of course, of course...' Tom Galbraith was refastening the buttons of the barathea blazer. He looked taller than when he'd entered the flat, half an hour ago. 'Oh…' Pipe and matches replaced in pocket. '… either you or… Steve vegetarian?'

'Naw…' Jas grinned. '… wan deviation fae the norm's enough fur us.'

No laugh.

Jas stood up. 'A joke, Tom…' He lifted the business diary. '… ye're allowed tae laugh, ye know.'

Still uncertain. 'Ah…'

Jas grabbed the pen. 'An' yer address wid be helpful.' He regarded the confused face and wondered if Nick Galbraith knew how lucky he was.

'Albion Buildings – flat three. Ingram Street, just along from…'

'Ah ken it…' Jas wrote. '… nice. Didney ken they did short-term lets, though.' Eyes from the diary. 'How long's this conference oan fur?'

'Oh, the flat's rented for a month…' Tom Galbraith was already striding towards the hall. '… and I'm not up for a conference.'

Jas followed, waiting for more…

'Tuesday, at seven, then?'

… which did not come. Jas nodded. 'We'll seeya then.' He steered the figure in the barathea away from lethal artexing and opened the outside door.

Tom Galbraith paused. 'Looking forward to…' The first genuine smile, over a blazered shoulder. '… meeting Stevie. And great to see you again, Jas.'

He grinned. 'You tae, Tam.' The old name came automatically.

The smile broadening. 'Bye.'

Jas stood at the top of the stairs, listening to descending feet and remembering more of ten years ago.

The smile.

The complete physical unselfconsciousness.

A decade had done nothing to diminish Tom Galbraith's appeal…

Jas closed the door.

… but now it was merely one detail amongst many. In the living room, the warm smell of pipe-tobacco lingered. He rewound and turned up the volume on the answerphone, still thinking about a square-shouldered outline and an easy manner.

The first voice was female, and talked for a while. Jas emptied the ashtray as Margaret Monaghan's halting inquiry on his progress eventually ended.

So was the second. Much more brief. 'Give me a ring back when you can. I might be able to help.'

He picked up the receiver, pressed Recall and wondered what had happened to change DI McLeod's mind.

Stevie was up and morosely around by the time A Division's switchboard tracked Ann down to her mobile.

Jas shook his head at a non-verbal enquiry from a pale, anxious face, writing as Ann provided a name and a phone-number. Then the proviso:

'Should this Guy Walker have remembered anything else since his statement was taken nine months ago, you phone D Division straight away, okay? No following up on your own.'

'Nae problem...' He underlined the name twice. '... like ah said, Joseph Monaghan's mother mainly wants reassurance. Ah'm plannin' tae give her jist that.'

'I've heard that before.' Sceptical.

'This time ah mean it...' Jas tapped the pen against the notepad. Margaret Monaghan's eager voice from the answerphone echoed in his head. '... ah don't wanna tread oan onywan's toes.' And he didn't intend to take any more of an arthritic widow's money than he had to.

'Make sure you don't...' More scepticism. '... and if anyone should ask, you didn't get the name from me.'

'Ma lips ur sealed.' He circled the name and what looked like a West-End code. 'An' thanks.'

Resigned sigh. 'I suppose I should be grateful you didn't want more.'

He laughed. 'Wid ah push a friendship, Ann?'

The sound almost returned. 'Bye, Jas.'

He replaced the handset.

Steve lifted it almost immediately. Large bitten fingers punching in a number committed to memory.

'That's gone half-five...' Jas lit a cigarette. '... Firestone's office'll be...'

'Fuckin' answering-machine.' Receiver strangled by a huge fist.

'Leave a message...' He watched a heavy jaw clench.

Brow furrowed in concentration. Then receiver banged back down. 'Ah canny talk tae they things...' Stevie lumbered through to the bedroom. '... ah'll go round there, first thing the morra morning.'

Jas stared at the name and number of the only witness to Joseph Monaghan's death. Guy Walker could have one of myriad attitudes to what he'd stumbled across near The Forge Shopping Centre, Parkhead, late on a Saturday afternoon in October of last year.

Sounds of discontented dressing in the background dogged his thoughts.

Some people put what they'd seen out of their minds, tried to get on with their lives...

Jas leaned over, closed the living-room door and pressed the first three digits of the telephone number.

... a few seized on the importance-by-proxy as a way of brightening up otherwise drab lives, pestering the police more diligently than even Margaret Monaghan...

He let the code register, then continued.

... others refused to admit it had happened, giving reluctant, sketchy statements if they even lingered at the crime scene at all...

At the other end of the line, a phone began to ring.

... it all depended on a number of factors, stretching from the severity of the crime to where it had happened. Guy Walker lived in the West End: opposite side of the city from where Joseph Monaghan had been kicked to death...

The phone rang on.

... being non-resident in the area where the crime had occurred sometimes gave a useful detachment. A double-edged detachment. Jas frowned. Guy Walker may have given his statement then happily put what happened that afternoon in October to the back of his mind and thanked his maker he didn't have to live in Parkhead. Part of Jas wouldn't blame him if he had. Part of him hoped he had. Part of him wanted to...

'Hello?' Breathless-sounding. 'Sorry, I just got in.'

'Mr Guy Walker?' Jas gripped the pen.

'Speaking.' Cheerful-sounding.

He took a deep breath and went into the introductory spiel.

Ten minutes later, Guy Walker's tone had changed. But he agreed to a meeting and gave unnecessarily detailed directions to his first floor flat in Athol Gardens.

'Thanks, Mr Walker. Ah'll see ye... 'bout eight?'

A pause. Then: 'Yes, eight.'

Progress achieved in one area. Jas severed the connection, made his way through to the bedroom to try for progress in another.

Four

The first floor flat had an open aspect. As did its occupant. Just before eight, a pleasant-faced middle aged professional with thinning brown hair ushered him into an airy lounge. The room blazed in setting sunshine.

Going through the motions...

Jas sat down on a beige-coloured sofa and took out the tape recorder.

... half an hour, at most...

He refused the drink offered, began the preamble.

... home by nine. He pushed another fractious exchange with Steve from his mind, activated the tape recorder and looked encouragingly from rosy-tinged walls to an eager, open face.

Forty-five minutes later, both were haunted by shadow. 'I'll never forget it...' Guy Walker padded to the window, paused briefly then flicked vertical blinds. '... every time I get into the Honda, I see him lying in the back seat. He probably died there.'

'You did aw' ye could...' The first surprise: D Division's witness and the *Daily Record*'s Good Samaritan were one and the same. '... more than a lotta people would have.' Jas turned the tape-recorder's cassette then returned his attention to the tensed shoulders.

'I've taken two First Aid courses, since – did I mention that?'

Three times. The second surprise: after nearly a year, the recall of a forty-six-year-old financial adviser was sharper than dodgy pension practices.

'Maybe I could have saved his life – maybe if I'd known what to do, maybe if I hadn't panicked, if I'd waited for the emergency services instead of...'

'Better dyin' in the backa your car than alone oan a pavement, Mr Walker.' You could wait all day for an ambulance in the East End, and the police would be stretched to the limit, with a match on. 'Ye did aw' ye could.'

The PM details swam in his mind. There was the shattered breast-bone, the punctured lung... Jesus himself could not have saved Joseph Monaghan.

'Now, if we could just go back a bit tae...'

'Sure I can't get you a drink?' The hunch-shouldered figure pulled itself from the window and headed for a stack of bottles.

'No thanks...' Jas watched the third G&T poured. More G and a lot less T than the last. '... so ye wur picking up a new car, that after-noon?'

Nod. 'The company has a deal with Shettleston Motors. I was still getting used to it – driving slowly, you know? That's the only reason I... saw the fight at all, I suppose.'

'How many were involved?'

'At first I thought three...' Guy Walker wandered back to the win-dow, sipping the G&T. '... it was only when they bolted across the road in front of me that I noticed... Joe.'

Some bright spark at D Division had obviously told Guy Walker the victim's name.

'Seventeen – Christ, he was only seventeen.'

Jas watched the glass sipped from. A name personalised things. Made it real. 'You got a good look at the three who ran aff?'

'One practically fell onto my bonnet. If the brakes hadn't been so new I might have...' Pause. The glass drained.

Jas waited, watching Guy Walker gather himself:

'Yes, I got a good look at one. The other two were blurs.'

'Football colours?'

Guy Walker turned. 'What do you...?'

'Were they wearin' Dundee United football colours – scarves? Shirts? Hats?'

Uncomprehending blink. Then understanding. 'No – I don't think so. Nothing that registered, at least.'

The real thugs never did.

'Joe was, though – green and white scarf, baseball cap.' A slight tremor in the voice.

'Tell me mair aboot the wan who fell onto your bonnet...' Jas steered the conversation back on track. '... you said you got a good look at him?'

Another nod. 'I'll never forget that face...' The shadow of a frown. '... I picked it out of a book of photographs, on the Monday afternoon.' Guy Walker made his way back to the bottles. 'Maybe if I'd gone after the three of them – maybe if the ambulance and the police had got there a bit faster.' Words speeding up. 'Maybe if traffic hadn't been so damn heavy I...'

'The man you ID-ed, Mr Walker?' Jas applied the breaks. It was one thing letting them talk. Letting them wallow in self-recrimination did no-one any good.

A sigh. 'Yes. Sorry...' Veering away from the bottles and perching on the arm of the three-seater sofa. '... it's just, on top of everything else, picking out the wrong man is...' Small laugh. '... nearly as difficult to live with.'

'Whit dae ye mean?'

A hand through sparse, brown hair. 'Christ, it looked so like him.' Frown. 'I was seeing that face everywhere – in the street, on tv... but when it came to the ID parade, the body-type was all wrong.' Guy Walker raised his eyes from the empty glass. 'He was brought in for questioning, though – on the basis of my... photobook ID.' Regret. 'Turned out he had an alibi, anyway. The police were very nice about it, all the same. But I felt I'd let everyone down...'

Jas nodded sympathetically. The brain could play tricks – as could the memory.

'... especially Joe. I couldn't get him out of my mind. I kept remembering the way he cried in the back of the Honda as I drove him to hospital.' Self- deprecating smile. 'I think I wanted to identify someone so much I...' Words tailing off.

'It happens.' Jas returned the smile. Regardless of the crime-stats, most people's lives were never touched by violence. But when they were...

'He wouldn't let go of his hat – even at the hospital. God, there was so much blood. On his face, his hands – the cap was soaking...' Guy Walker was off again, reliving the event.

'Thanks for yer time, Mr...' When Jas reached to switch off the tape-recorder, he was still talking:

'It was white – at least, it had been white... with three letters embroidered on the front. You know the type?'

Jas raised an eyebrow.

'His cap.' Anguished face.

'Ah...' Jas nodded, wondering if Marie's Victim Support Group would be of any use to Guy Walker. The man obviously still had a need to talk it out of his system.

'Strange what sticks with you – I can remember his knuckles shining through all that blood. But his face faded months ago.' Guilty-sounding, like it was a betrayal.

Jas nodded again. His mind was back with Margaret Monaghan's shrine. A scarf, a small cross on a gold chain, a photograph...

... he paused on his way up from the comfortable sofa. 'You sure it was a cap – no' a woolly football hat?' Margaret Monaghan's shrine had featured no headgear.

'A baseball cap – you know? With a skip. A large skip. And three letters on the front...' Impatient. '... all the kids wear them.'

Jas switched the tape-recorder back on. 'Can we go back a bit?'

Eager open face. 'Of course. What do you...?'

'The cap, Mr Walker...' Maybe it was nothing. 'Tell me when ye first noticed it...'

Fifteen minutes later the sun was a red streak beyond the roofs of Dowanhill. In a phone-box on Byres Road, Jas cradled the receiver between face and shoulder. 'Aye, Mrs Monaghan. A baseball cap. White, wi' three letters on the front – mibby 'J-o-e'?'

Soft laugh. 'He was always Joseph, Mr Anderson – even wi' his pals. But he did wear baseball caps – no' tae a match, mind ye.' Pause. 'Why dae ye ask?' A tinge of hope.

'Jist checkin' ma facts, Mrs Monaghan...' He made himself downplay the significance. '... did ye get aw' Joseph's personal effects back fae the hospital okay?'

Surprise. 'Aye...' Sudden sadness. '... right doon tae his loose change an' his Celtic season-ticket.'

He had to ask. 'And there wis nae baseball cap – ony kinda hat?'

More hope. 'Ah saw Joseph aff masel', that afternoon. He wis bareheided.'

It was probably nothing. 'Did the police ask about a cap?'

Hope mixed with confusion. 'No' that ah remember, Mr Anderson. Want me tae go an' look through Joseph's stuff? He hud quite a collection – Air Jordan, Nike. A white cap, ye say? Wi'... letters on the front?'

'No, don't bother...' She'd kept his clothes. Jas sighed. As it was probably nothing, it wasn't worth stirring up further memories. '... ah'll be in touch soon.'

'Right ye are, Mr Anderson...' Hope vanishing with the last shreds of sunlight.

Jas terminated the conversation. His index finger hovered over the 'next call' button.

A cap.

A baseball cap...

White, with a three-letter word on the front.

A three-letter word. A name?

... which apparently didn't belong to Joseph Monaghan, but which he had resolutely refused to release, even in death.

Jas moved his finger to the return coins button and listened to the clatter of metal on metal. Beyond the phone-booth's glass walls, a row of figures waited impatiently. His watch told him it was nine fifteen: common sense told him the police already knew about the baseball cap. Jas scooped the coins from the phone, pushed open the door and walked down to a bus-stop.

An accident at St. George's Cross. Traffic tailing back for a mile. Jas focused on Stevie...

... and a dinner-engagement, in four days' time. Maybe that would put a smile on his face.

There was no face to put anything on. Signs of a hastily eaten meal lay in the kitchen. Jas shoved Steve's plate into the sink and turned on the tap.

Guy Walker's information drained back into his mind.

The cap...

The cap...

... sometimes it was strands of hair. Often blood or skin, either beneath the fingernails or mixed with the deceased's own.

Rarely, an item of clothing was snatched and held onto. Such mute witnesses to an attacker's identity were more useful than a hundred Guy Walkers. In scientific terms. Eyes could play tricks, time distorted memories but forensic evidence rarely lied.

Going through the motions slipped into real work. In the lounge, Jas switched on a corner lamp, lifted the business-diary and flicked.

The answerphone's display read '1'. He didn't play it back.

Nowhere in the extensive newspaper coverage of Joseph Monaghan's murder had any such cap been mentioned.

He located the number for The Royal's pathology department, punched it in.

*

'You surfin' that Information Superhighway again?' It was after eleven by the time he located head mortuary porter Jimmy McQueen.

'Jist widenin' ma horizons.' Chuckle. 'Whit can ah dae ye fur, Mr Anderson?' The youthful voice was cheery.

'Can ye check a name, and a list o' personal effects fur me, Jim? It's goin' back a bit...' Jimmy had worked at the Royal since he'd left school, longer ago than anyone in admin liked to dwell on. Retirement age was strictly sixty-five. Jimmy had to be pushing that. Maybe inhaling formaldehyde kept him young.

'Nae sweat, Mr Anderson – since ah goat tae grips wi' they CD Roms, there's nothin' ah canny git ma hauns oan.'

Jas laughed. 'October 5th, last year...'

'Ach, that's probably still oan disk. Haud oan...'

Jas held. Where a lot of his colleagues – and not a few doctors – moaned about the recent transfer of patient information to computer, Jimmy had taken to technology like a fish to water. These days, he spent more time hunched over a glowing terminal than pushing cadavers from the wards to the mortuary. Most of the Royal's pathology department came to Jimmy, rather than risk a toe in the fathomless depths of the hospital's computerised record-system.

Jimmy seemed to like it that way. Jas had a feeling Jimmy McQueen arranged it that way: even when he went over retirement age, could admin sack the only employee in pathology who could find anything?

'That wis a Setterday, right?'

Jimmy was back. 'Right...'

'Name?'

Jas supplied it. 'DOA. Brought by car tae A&E, late afternoon an'...'

'Here we go: Joseph Monaghan. DOB 2/8/85?'

The date brought the age home. Jas frowned. 'Aye, that's him. You got a list o' his personal effects there, Jim?'

'Nae sweat...' Pause. '... did somethin' git lost again?' Irritated. 'Ah've telt them a thoosand times: first thing a boady comes in, get a bin-liner an' tuck it under yer gurney. Keeps everythin' in the wan place...' Sigh. '... whit happens is, ye see, jaickets come aff in A&E, if there's ony attempt tae resuscitate. Falsers come oot. Or wanna their shoes falls aff in the lift...'

'The effects, Jim?' Jas interrupted the impromptu lecture. Despite his addiction to the digital world, Jimmy McQueen was as chatty as ever.

'Callin' them up, Mr Anderson...' Pause. '... is it the jewellery that's missin'?

'Jist tell me whit's listed.' Jas picked up a pen: Jimmy was too quick for his own good.

'Okay-dokay... wan Nevis Sports jacket, wan paira Adidas trackies, wan paira black Caterpillar boots, wan Celtic Away shirt, wan Celtic scarf...'

Jas listened. Waited for the one effect which interested him...

... at the end of a meticulously recorded list, he was still waiting. 'Nae cap?'

'Cap?'

'Baseball cap. White, big peak, three letters oan the front?'

'Nothin' here aboot ony cap, Mr Anderson. Ye sure he wis wearin' wan?'

Holding, not wearing. 'Dis it say who collected his stuff?' Jas tapped the end of the pen against the side of his hand. Maybe the police went through them before...

'A... Mrs Margaret Monaghan signed fur them, Tuesday the ninth. The Away shirt went tae the lab, oan the Setterday night – fur the blood-typin'. But it wis back within the oor.'

Jas increased the speed of the tap, remembering Guy Walker's photo-freeze memory of knuckles squeezed shiny. 'Stuff gets... lost often, Jim?'

Regretful sigh. 'Like ah said, aw' the time. Ah dae ma best, Mr Anderson, but summa the young porters ur affy haphazard. Think jist cos somewan's deid, the claes dinny matter...' Pause. 'You an' me – we ken different, eh?' Another sigh.

Jas stopped tapping. DI Ann McLeod's proviso circled in his mind. It wasn't his problem. Maybe it wasn't anyone's problem. Maybe the cap had been spotted by some eagle-eyed uniform, passed straight to CID.

'It's a guid few months ago, Mr Anderson, but ye could try A&E's Loast Property department.'

Not his problem...

'They haud on tae jewellery an' the like, usually. But ah dunno about... caps.' Pause. 'Mean somethin' special tae somewan, dis it?'

'It might, Jimmy...' He put down the pen and stretched. '... thanks fur yer help, pal.'

'Ach, ony time, Mr Anderson. Drap me an email if ah can dae onythin' else.'

Jas replaced the receiver, eyes back on the diary. From twelve years with Strathclyde Police, he knew all evidence and information concerning the Joseph Monaghan inquiry would be subjudice. Whoever was – or had been – in charge of the case at London Road didn't have to tell him anything. What was left of Margaret Monaghan's five hundred pound retainer pressed down on him...

Jas rubbed his face. Today was – Friday? He'd leave it till Monday. Jas leant back on the sofa.

The weekend...

The weekend...

... Stevie's nights off. The only part of the week when their jobs came anywhere near sync.

Jas got up from the sofa, walked through to the bedroom and began to undress.

Most weekends he made a point of working. In the Mitchell Library's reading-room. Or working-out. With two, the flat was cramped enough. Four was impossible, even if two of those four were under twelve.

He shoved shirt, socks and underpants into the laundry basket, folded his work-trousers and replaced them in the wardrobe.

Weekends. Family time.

Jas moved into the shower-room, turned on the faucet. A dinner-date on Tuesday seeped back into his mind.

That was something. Something they'd never done, in fourteen months... together. Jas had no idea what Steve's work-colleagues at the bakery knew of his home-life, but his own job gave little scope for social contact.

He leant against the small plastic cubicle, removed his watch and stuck a hand beneath still-cool water.

Maybe Stevie could take Tuesday off. Make a night of it. Maybe...

... the phone rang. Jas sighed, switched off the shower and padded through to the living room. 'Hello?'

Silence.

Jas sighed. 'Hello?'

More silence.

Jas scowled, replaced the receiver. Happened all the time, but never failed to irritate.

From the darkness beneath the table, a red '1' shone up at him. A long-awaited call from a solicitor pushed itself into his mind. Jas pressed 'play'.

The machine rewound. Then a voice. Not Firestone's voice:

'Steve, it's me. Sam's got a bit of a cold. Nothing serious, but ah think it wid be better if Hayley an' him both stayed here, this week-end, if he's no' shaken it aff by the mornin'...'

Jas stared at a flashing red line.

'... ah don't want either of them sleepin' on a draughty couch. Hope you haven't arranged anythin' special. Give me a ring tomor-row, okay? Ah'll see how he is then.'

Maureen McStay's message ended. Jas stood there, lips pulled between two responses.

Three weekends ago, it had been Hayley. With a sore throat.

Two weeks before that, something else.

He listened to the machine reset itself.

Never any notice – always last minute, usually the Saturday morning. Jas frowned: Stevie's responding mood lasted all weekend. He pushed the feeling aside.

This time would be different.

Two days.

Two whole days. Dinner on Tuesday. Stevie was due a fortnight's holiday, before the end of July. Jas smiled, mentally thanking a woman he'd never met or spoken to directly. Her own deviousness would backfire.

Two days.

Two whole days to work on Stevie...

... about the Firestone stuff. About the Maureen-and-kids stuff. About calming down. Accepting the situation.

Maybe buy the fold-down bed. Maybe think about rearranging the rooms, so that Sam and Hayley didn't have to walk through the bedroom to wash their hands.

Maybe...

... Jas reset the answerphone, scribbled a note and sat it on top of the machine: the one place Stevie would check in these days of long-awaited calls from solicitors who never phoned back. Then he walked through to the shower-room and washed under cold water.

Not his problem?

He tilted his face up to meet icy jets.

Stevie's problem – his by proxy.

Jas turned off the water-control and grabbed a towel. Ten minutes of brisk drying got his prick half hard. He debated a wank, then thought about the first Saturday's long lie-in for months.

The bedroom was in darkness as he slipped naked between the sheets. A series of Stevie-centred thoughts got him fully hard. Jas savoured the tease and drifted off with a hand curled around eight inches of anticipation.

Five

Traffic woke him. And sunshine. Plus the scent of yeast.

Jas peered at the bedside clock: 9.30am. Turning onto his back, he looked left to the broad, rigid shape inches away.

Stevie was fully dressed and staring at the ceiling.

He propped himself up on one elbow.

Narrowed brown eyes continued to stare upwards. Shards of sunlight streaked the angular face.

Jas sighed. 'Come oan, it's no' the enda the...'

'Ah wis gonny take 'em tae the zoo, efter we'd bin tae see Firestone.' Words aimed ceilingwards. 'Wanna the lions huz had a baby. Ah read aboot it in the *Times*, thought they'd like tae see it, then mibby go fur a burger an'...'

'It'll aw' still be there, next weekend.'

Eyes from ceiling. 'An' Firestone's fuckin' closed, oan a Saturday.' Amber irises glinted. Arms rigid at sides.

'So do it Monday...' Jas stared into a furious, hurt face. '... that gies ye two days tae work oot whit yer gonny say an'...'

Stevie leapt from the bed. 'Ah saw Sam, yesterday efternoon up at Carole's an' he wis okay then.' Pacing.

Jas hauled himself upright, leant against the metal headboard. 'Ye ken kids: wan minute they're fine, the next they're...'

'She jist disney want them seein' me. She wants tae keep 'em wi' hur!' Pacing faster. Arms still rigid at sides. Fists clenched into tight balls.

And the phone-call was designed to provoke exactly this response. 'Well, she'll no' get whit she wants, will she?' He spoke slowly, quietly. 'You're their dad, Stevie. You've got...'

'Ah should go roon' there, check fur masel', eh?' Pause in the pacing. Amber irises glowing with fury. 'Ah'm their dad – if Sam'll no' well, ah wanna...'

'Sure that's a guid idea?' Jas swung his legs over the side of the bed and got up. He moved slowly, quietly towards where Stevie stood. He tried not to dwell on the consequences of the suggestion.

A thin thread of blue pulsed in a pale neck.

Jas dragged his eyes from the vein and stopped inches away. 'Eh, Stevie?'

Angry eyes focused somewhere to his left.

Jas cocked his head, meeting an impotent gaze. It tore at his heart. 'Whit good wid it dae?' He grabbed two iron shoulders. Bunched muscle quivered in his grip. 'If ye wanna check how Sam is, phone... Maureen.' The name felt strange on his lips.

'Ah did...' A tangled brown head lolled forward. '... there's nae-wan in. If ma boay's no' well enough tae spend the weekend wi' me, how come he's well enough tae be oot wi' her?' Words mumbled bootwards.

Jas frowned at the wall beyond the lowered skull. Part of the plan – part of Maureen McStay's little game. A game Stevie couldn't win. He moved a hand to the back of a bristly neck and pulled Stevie closer. A tangly head leant against his chest:

'Whit did she huv tae come back fur? We were aw' gettin' along fine, withoot her.'

That much was true. He cupped a palm over bristly skin, rubbing. Stevie's sister Carole had the kids during the week. Stevie had them at weekends, and when his job would allow, longer. The reappearance of Maureen McStay – also with a job, a house in Coatbridge and a car – plus the school holidays, had thrown a spanner into an arrangement which, though far from ideal, suited everyone...

He frowned.

… almost everyone.

'Whit dis she want?' Irritated confusion.

Not for the first time, Jas wondered the same thing. Custody? Both she and Stevie were dependant on Carole, during times such as these: Sam and Hayley were under twelve. Maureen McStay knew Carole's good graces were only obtained as long as her brother remained in the picture.

A reconciliation?

Jas pushed the possibility away. His other hand moved between them. Fingers slowly unbuttoned Stevie's shirt.

Fists uncurled, loosely settling on his waist.

He felt himself start to respond. Fingers brushed the muscle on Stevie's chest. Jas eased back a little and slipped the shirt over sloping shoulders.

The garment hung from broad wrists. Stevie's head moved from Jas's chest, resettled in the crook of his neck.

The weekends…

He ran his hands up and over the smooth curve of Stevie's back.

… she wanted the weekends.

Jas scowled. Like he did.

Tensed sinew flinched beneath his palms. A leg moved between his. He ground his half-hard prick against a denimed thigh, hating the selfishness.

And wanting the man. 'It'll be okay… we'll talk aboot it later, eh?' The platitudes came easily. Hands moved between them, searching for the buckle of Stevie's belt and further justifications. 'Git yer mind aff it, there's nothing ye can do till Monday…' Fingers found the buckle. Then other hands were helping and he was walking backwards towards the bed.

Somewhere in the distance, traffic roared down Cumbernauld Road.

Jas covered Stevie's body with his own, holding him against the bed and burying his face in the depths of an armpit. Damp, musky hair filled his mouth. Laboured breath filled his ears. He slipped his hands beneath the hollow of an arching back. Palms gripped two hard mound of tensed muscle.

Somewhere in the distance, car horns honked and engines revved.

Legs curled around his back. Stevie's crotch rasped against his stomach. A hard length of need pressed between his nipples.

Jas opened his eyes, spat hair from his mouth and licked the distance between the pit and the head of that need. Between his own thighs, balls tight and sore with postponement.

Stevie groaned, bucking up from the bed.

Jas ran his tongue down a flexing length, nuzzling the root.

Somewhere in the distance, the outside world of estranged wives and much-loved children faded away.

He inhaled the sweat of Stevie's balls, rubbing the soft hairy flesh with his chin. The body beneath his tensed. Then he was under the quilt, lifting heavy thighs over his shoulders and spreading the cheeks of Stevie's arse. Dark warmth filled his eyes. Jas elbowed the duvet aside and folded heavy legs up onto a hairless chest.

Hands grabbed for his shoulders, gripping and kneading.

Another need pulsed between his legs. Jas moaned, holding the man open with his thumbs. Heart pounded in his chest. He plunged between twin mounds, exploring well-charted territory which still never failed to take his breath away. Suffocating in the smell of the man, Jas felt the orifice spasm against his lips.

Stevie ground down onto his face. Knees slipped from nipples, splaying each side of his face.

Jas continued to delve, licking around dark crinkled skin.

Feet planted on the bed, Stevie pushed back.

Somewhere in the distance, two sharp honks of a car horn. Somewhere closer to home, one hand left his shoulder and pawed the bedside table. Seconds later, a squashed metal tube hit the side of his face. A condom landed on the bed beside his elbow.

Jas grinned through parted lips. He grabbed what was left of the lube and reluctantly pulled his face from Stevie's arse. Unscrewing the top one handed, he looked up the bed.

The pale angular face creased with urgency.

He locked eyes with rich, mahogany irises and lubed Stevie by touch alone. Each time a greased index-finger pushed into the hard, sweating body, black pupils enlarged a little.

Stevie's mouth was open, half scowl, half smile.

Jas watched the expression stretch beyond both as he continued to widen. His other hand covered Stevie's prick. Tacky skin flexed against his palm.

Somewhere in the distance, noise in the hall.

Jas moved onto knees: the post was late, today. His shaft bounced off stomach. He coated it quickly, tossed the tube in the direction of the bedside table and...

'Dad?'

Stevie lunged for the duvet, pulling it over two naked bodies. 'Sam? Ah though you hud a cold?'

Jas fought his way free of the quilt and made a grab for dressing-gown. Head swivelled.

'Jist sniffles...' In the doorway, a smaller chubbier version of Stevie beamed at them both. 'Hi Uncle Jas!' Bright, unbroken voice.

He tried to smile, managed a nod. At his side, Stevie was searching the floor for underpants:

'Ah, that's guid, son. Where's yer...?'

'Mum sez you've tae make sure he disney get a chill, but.' On command, a less-friendly, bob-framed face appeared behind Sam's. Overnight bag gripped in front of Tommy Hilfiger-ed chest.

Jas found the dressing-gown, shoved arms into sleeves and avoided Hayley McStay's suspicious brown eyes.

'There's juice in the fridge, hen. You an' Sam go get a can and ah'll be through in a minute.'

Jas searched the bedside table for cigarettes. Found them and waited for the sound of departing feet.

It didn't come. 'Mum sez smoky atmospheres urney guid for us.' Disapproving voice.

'Well we'll open the windaes, eh? Noo go an' get yer juice.'

Silence.

Jas turned slowly back round, marvelling at how guilty they could make you feel.

Two small figures regarded the scene with varying degrees of curiosity.

'Go oan, eh? Ah'll be through in a minute.' Stevie's voice radiating forced normality.

Jas risked a smile. 'Ye can pit the computer oan, if ye want.'

Sam's grin split the chubby, eight-year-old face. Five fat fingers tugging at the sleeve of a Tommy Hilfiger jacket. 'C'mon...'

His sister remained sober-faced, but allowed herself to be dragged back into the hall. Over sounds of a fridge opened then closed, the side of Stevie's head briefly met his:

'Sorry, man...'

'Disney matter.' He cupped the back of a bristly neck, then slapped a shoulder. 'Go oan before they wipe ma hard-drive!' An attempt at levity.

Stevie smiled, levered himself out of bed and began to dress.

Jas watched the way his body moved. Maureen McStay won every time...

His receding hard-on flexed against the inside of his thigh.

... one way or another.

'You workin' the day?' Said without turning.

Jas remembered plans and cases put on hold. 'Aye.' He lit a cigarette.

'We'll keep oota ye way.' Stevie had opened the wardrobe and was rummaging in its depths.

Jas gripped the filter between thumb and forefinger, watching a clean sweatshirt hauled over a tangled brown head.

When he turned, Stevie's eyes lit-up the sallow face.

He couldn't compete. Jas met hazel sparks, smiled. 'Have a guid time, eh?' If Stevie was happy...

'Bring ye back a lion-cub.'

A hand ruffled dirty blond spikes. Then Stevie grabbed cigarettes from the bedside table and strode into the hall. 'Okay, who wants tae go see the baby lions?'

Sam's yell of matching enthusiasm made up for eleven-year-old Hayley McStay's silence. Jas leant back against the metal headboard and continued to smoke over the sounds of imminent departure and complaints about having to take a bus.

Ten minutes later, the flat was quiet. Jas lit another cigarette. If Stevie was happy...

... ten minutes after that he walked through to the living room, unplugged the computer and pushed it back into its weekend quarters.

He showered.

He aimed for eighty sit-ups but gave up at fifty.

He made himself eat toast and let the answerphone pick up three potential clients.

In the laundrette, he watched his socks twine with Stevie's and tried not the think about the zoo. In the supermarket, he bought spaghetti hoops in tins, four packets of biscuits and wondered what Maureen McStay was doing.

Back in the flat, he replayed three messages and took notes. The sun had moved. Shadow draped both rooms.

Jas rubbed his face and switched on a light. The laundry had been put away. He'd hoovered. Two reports lay untyped beside the computer. A couple of final reminder letters still to be printed out. He had a full caseload, three new jobs to consider.

He stood up, walked through to the bedroom. He'd never been busier...

More money in the bank than he knew what to do with.

... or lonelier. Jas stared at the bed. Their bed. At one time, sharing a bed would have been enough. At one time, he wouldn't have cared what whoever he shared it with did the rest of the time. Now?

He walked to the window, stared down onto Cumbernauld Road. Below, ordinary people doing ordinary things. Men pushed prams. Women talked in small groups. Teenagers lounged at both bus-stops, flirting with and ignoring each other by turns.

Jas gripped the sills, raised his eyes over the roofs opposite in the direction of Calderpark.

The zoo. A cliché. Like Burger Kings and cinemas all over the city, on Saturday afternoons. Over-anxious fathers over-anxiously over-compensating. Stuffing a week or a month's worth of attention into eight short hours.

Jas frowned, then pushed the expression away.

Tuesday.

Dinner with the Galbraiths...

He found himself smiling.

... it almost sounded normal. He pulled himself from the window and made a mental note to tell Stevie tonight. Bending to plug-in the computer, the smile stayed in place. Jas switched on, reached for a blue file and began to flick. As he located the paperwork, he hoped the lion-cubs made their intended impression.

Six-thirty, he slipped two A4 manila envelopes into the post-box.

Seven-thirty, burger-fed and gorged on fresh air, a threesome trouped back to the flat. They left again ten minutes later for the eight-o'clock showing at The Forge multiplex of the Pokémon film.

In the bedroom, Jas made a start on the report for Margaret Monaghan. A brief phone-call to A&E's Lost Property Department failed to turn up any baseball caps.

He'd written the first paragraph when the front door opened and reclosed to the accompaniment of exaggerated shushing sounds from Stevie. Jas stayed in the bedroom, only leaving when two tired-looking figures trotted through to wash hands and faces.

In the living room, Stevie was unrolling sleeping-bags.

Jas smiled. 'Wis the film ony guid?'

A laugh. 'Loast me in the first ten minutes, but they seemed tae like it.' Stevie darted into the hall. 'We okay fur milk?' Yawn over the sound of the fridge door opening.

Jas sighed. Enough spaghetti hoops to feed an army, though. 'Ah'll nip up tae Rehamndi's while you put them tae bed.' He grabbed his jacket.

Abstracted nod.

Jas shoved arms into Levi sleeves, lifted keys and left the flat.

He returned to darkness. Thrusting the milk into the fridge, he eased open the living-room door.

Hayley and Sam lay at opposite ends of the sofa. The spare duvet over the sleeping bags.

In the other room, Stevie was dead to the world. Jas stood at the side of the bed and listened to the sound of shallow breathing.

A faint smile stained parted lips.

Jas leant down, pushed a brown curl from the peaceful face. Twenty-four hours without sleep had caught up with Stevie.

He returned to the computer, re-angled the small spotlight and made another start on another client-report. The dinner-engagement with the Galbraiths could wait...

'How come ma dad lives here?'

Late Sunday afternoon, it was still waiting. Stevie and Sam were playing football in the back court. Hayley was washing her hair.

He raised eyes from notepad and stared at the thin figure with the towel-draped head. Jas tried a smile. 'It's close tae where he works.' He returned his attention to the details of one of yesterday's phone-calls, wondering what Stevie had told them.

'Ah mean, how come he lives wi' you?'

Jas blinked. Her brother took the situation at face value: eight-year-old Sam accepted anyone who could kick a ball about. Hayley was a different matter. 'Ye wanna plug yer hair-drier in, in here?' He nodded to a spare socket beside the wardrobe.

'An' how come the two o' yous sleep in the same bed?' Narrowed eyes refused to be side-stepped.

Jas sat the pen on top of the notebook, placed both on the work-station and stood up. The eleven-year old was usually silent to the point of rudeness. Part of him wanted to seize on the interaction, for Stevie's sake. Another part balked at having to explain or justify. He fought the resentment, opened his mouth.

'Ma mum says you're queer.' She was in there first.

'Okay...' He found himself smiling. 'Whit does she say aboot yer dad?'

Frown. 'She says he disney ken whit he is.' Hayley looked away for the first time.

The unintended insight made him grin. 'Mibby it's who ye ur, no' whit ye ur that matters, eh?' He walked to the bed and sat down.

She continued to stand in the doorway of the shower-room. 'Whit?' Brown eyes from the carpet to his. Antagonism replaced by confusion.

He repeated the sentence more slowly.

She seemed to consider it. For a long time.

Wetness between his fingers told him his hands were sweating. Jas wiped palms on thighs and tried to think what to say next.

'You an' ma dad met in prison, didn't yous?'

Jas returned a gaze now more curious than confrontational. Queer, ex-jailbird and antisocial workaholic: no wonder Hayley was suspicious. He decided to spare her the 'I was only on remand' spiel and nodded. Jas had a feeling the interrogation wasn't really about him anyway. 'Ye like comin' here, at the weekend?'

'It's okay.' Sulky, preteen play down.

Progress of a sort. 'Better than the weekends wi' yer mum?' He seized the opportunity.

'She's gotta car. And MTV.'

Jas suppressed a laugh. The sum of one's possessions, nothing more. He suddenly felt sorry for Maureen McStay. 'Whit aboot yer Auntie Carole's? Ye like livin' there?'

'Mum says Auntie Carole canny keep her legs shut.'

Jas blinked. Stevie's sister was evidently pregnant again. Mum seemed to say a lot, to an eleven-year-old who was having trouble processing it all.

'Mum says when the baby comes, me an' Sam'll go and live with her, in Coatbridge.' Eyes again on the carpet. The towel had slipped from the wet head and now hung around slender shoulders.

Jas wondered if Stevie knew any of this. 'You want to go an' live with yer mum?'

Wet head shake. 'None o' ma pals live in Coatbridge. It's horrible.' Droplets of water dribbled down a now-worried face.

Even with the car and MTV. Jas got up from the bed, took the towel from around unhappy shoulders and began to rub long blond hair.

She didn't pull away.

'No-one can make ye dae onythin' ye dinny wanna dae, Hayley...' Jas rubbed on, teasing tangles apart. '... yer Auntie Carole'll git a bigger hoose...' Stevie's kids had lived with his sister for more than four years, now. That was home – not some cramped flat in Dennistoun or the splendours of a Barratt house in Coatbridge.

Her head dipped lower. The top came to rest against his chest.

Jas smiled. 'Where's yer hair-drier?'

'In ma bag...' Mumble floorwards.

He patted her shoulder. 'C'mon through and we'll dry it. Don't want ye gettin' a chill, like Sam.'

Head slowly raised. 'Mum made that up. He disney huv a cold.'

The shared confidence was more progress than he'd expected. Jas returned the compliment. 'Ah thought that.' He nodded towards the living room. 'But we'll dry yer hair, onyway.'

Small, sceptical smile. 'Ye ken how tae use a diffuser?'

Jas winked. 'Me an' diffusers ur like that.' He held up two crossed fingers.

A disbelieving laugh. 'Aye, right...'

He raised both eyebrows, waggled them. 'Wanna put money oan it?'

A giggle.

Jas grinned. The eyebrows did it every time. 'C'mon. A pounds says ah kin make ye look like...' He searched his memory. '... Baby Spice in ten minutes flat.'

'She's no' called that ony mair!' Scornful giggle. 'Make it a fiver.'

'Okay, ye're on.' He tossed the wet towel into the laundry basket and ushered her through to the living room.

A small victory. But a victory, nonetheless.

Half past six on the dot, two honks of a horn summoned Hayley and her brother from the flat.

Jas let her off with the bet, promised a rematch. He stood beside Stevie at the bedroom window waving as two small shapes got into the back of a red Ford Fiesta. An arm slipped around his waist:

'Christ, they take it outta ye.' Weary laugh.

The car pulled away. Jas peered, trying to see the driver past two still-waving hands in the back seat. Maureen McStay was a blurred outline. He wondered what the kids were telling her. He wondered how it made her feel.

Stevie's eyes remained on the vehicle until it disappeared round the curve in Cumbernauld Road. 'Ye shoulda come wi' us, yesterday.'

'Next time, eh?' Jas pulled his gaze from the quiet, Sunday evening street and slung an arm around broad shoulders.

Tangled head turning. 'Ye mean it?' Brown eyes widening.

'Sure...' Jas grinned. '... we're gonny dae mair things... thegether...'

Stevie whooped.

'... startin' wi'...' Jas laughed, leading the sparkling-eyed figure through to the living room and detailing the plans for Tuesday night.

Six

Monday and Tuesday passed the way they usually did. Two reports required in-depth searches. His eyes stung from hours in the Mitchell's Internet Suite. Jas wondered how Jimmy McQueen could stand it.

Tuesday evening. 'Whit aboot this wan?'

Critical eyes peered back at him from the mirror. 'Fine – it looks fine.' Stevie had tried three ties already. Jas slapped a suit-clad arse and went to check his wallet.

'Ah hate fuckin' ties.'

'Don't wear wan, then.' He grabbed wallet and keys from the desk and walked back through to the bedroom.

'This suit disney look right withoot a tie.'

Jas laughed. 'Wears yer jeans and yer Wrangler jaicket, then.' He stared at the broad figure.

The suit had been bought for Carole McStay's fortieth birthday celebrations, last year. It... did something for Stevie. He looked older. More like a thirty-eight-year-old father of two.

A phone-call and an appointment with a solicitor pushed itself to the front of his mind. Jas sobered. 'What did Firestone huv tae say fur himself, by the way?'

'Nothin' much.' Fourth tie torn from neck and thrown into the wardrobe.

Something in the voice. Jas touched a shoulder.

'Lea' it man, eh?' Warning tone.

Jas removed his hand.

'Mibby it's this shirt...' Stevie fell to a crouch, hauling garments from the floor of the wardrobe. '... think ah should change it?'

A change of attitude would be more useful. 'Ah think ye look fine the way ye are.' Jas bit back irritation and concentrated on another father...

Stevie sighed heavily, plucking at a fifth tie. A long sliver of muted blue thrown around shirt collar.

... and another son. Expectations of Nicholas Galbraith formed in his mind: sullen, obstreperous, uncommunicative. Jas pushed them away. Preconceptions never did anyone any good. He patted his pockets, checking for the thousandth time. On the periphery of his vision, white-shirted elbows came and went:

'Ah Christ...'

Jas returned his attention to where Steve was still struggling. The effort and the nervousness made him smile. 'Whit are you like?' He seized both ends of the tie, pulling them free from hands all thumbs. 'Haud still.'

A sigh. Then Stevie did as he was told.

Jas deftly whipped thick end over thin, lessened the knot then slid it slowly up towards a bobbing Adam's Apple.

Worried brown eyes pinned his. Collar folded down. Brown eyes back into mirror. 'Are ye sure ah...?'

He turned the anxious face back to his. 'Ye'll be the bella the ball, okay?' The smell of newly washed hair drifted into his nostrils.

The joke fell flat. 'Ah wish ye'd asked me, afore ye invited us both tae this ... thing.' More apprehensive than ever.

'It's no' a... thing. It's jist dinner. Wi' a guy an' his wife an' their son.'

Unconvinced scowl. 'Folk like me don't... dae dinner.' Another sigh. 'Whit the fuck am ah gonny huv in common wi'... a polis, his missus an' some wee nyaff that's daein' law at university?' Worry reclaiming ground from annoyance. 'Whit am ah gonny say tae 'em? Whit we gonny talk aboot?' Stevie sat down on the bed, grabbed a boot and shoved his foot into it.

'Football, cookin', yer work, Sam an' Hayley – onythin' ye like.' Jas watched the process. 'It's no' a big deal.'

Stevie's hands shook slightly as he tried to feed laces through eyelets.

The extent of the apprehension sank in. Jas crouched beside the bed. 'If it's really botherin' ye that much, ye can...'

'Naw, ah'm comin' – nae fear...' Head lowered, the last of the eyelets skipped. Stevie wrapped a length of lace around the top of his boot. '... canny let ye go oan yer ain, can ah?' Head raised. The first smile of the day.

Jas returned it, laid his palms on suited knees. 'The food'll be first class, if nothin' else. An' ye'll like Tom. He's a guid guy.'

A flicker of suspicion in gold-flecked irises. 'You an' him...?'

Jas laughed. 'Oh aye – roon' the backa Pitt Street polis headquarters, in the conference coffee-breaks.' He pushed himself to his feet.

Another joke flat on its face. Suspicious eyes narrowing. 'Ye're no'... still interested, ur ye?' Pale skin paling further.

The laugh died. 'Ah never wis.' He gripped a shirted wrist, pulling Stevie upright. 'The guy's an auld friend – ah'm doin' him a favour. Tom Galbraith's son gets tae see how...' He paused. '... cool his faither is wi' poofs, an' we get a free meal. Aye?'

'Ah suppose so.' Hands thrust into pockets.

Jas took a step back. Stevie looked decidedly uncool with the whole thing. 'Relax...' He found a smile. 'Jist be yersel' an' everythin'll be fine.'

'It will?' Amber eyes searched his.

He nodded. 'An' if it dis start tae drag a bit, we can eyeways lea' early, causa yer shift.'

Almost convinced. 'Aye, that's true...' A last uncertainty. 'This... Tom – whit dis he ken aboot me?'

Stevie's record was his own business: no preconceptions – on either side. 'He kens you an' me ur... thegether, but that's it. Onythin' else is up tae you.' He ruffled tangle-free hair.

'Don't dae that!' Anguished howl. 'Took me ages tae get it aw' flat...' One hand smoothing imperceptible waves.

Jas glanced at his watch: 6.45 pm. He walked into the hall, lifted a pink-paper wrapped bottle of wine from the top of the fridge.

Behind, the sounds of final readjustments executed in the mirror. Then Stevie was opening the door and they were going to do what normal people did.

Albion Buildings had a security entrance.

Stevie shuffled his feet and lit a cigarette from the stub of another.

'Pit that oot, eh?' He grabbed the packet, shoved them into pocket then pressed bell 3.1 and waited.

Crackles then: 'Jas?'

He lowered his face to the grill. 'Aye, Tam.'

'Come in, come in...' A buzz.

Jas nudged Steve and pushed the smoked glass door.

Three flights of steep stairs later, another door. Open. Tom...

'Hope ye've goat the oxygen masks standin' by...' At his side, Stevie was panting. Jas smiled at the moustached face and held out the wine.

... and a woman. Smaller. Blonde. As nervous-looking as Stevie.

Tom laughed and took the bottle, moving back into the spacious room. 'Eileen? This is Jas Anderson and...?'

He stuck out a hand towards the blonde. 'Good to meet you.' Behind:

'Er, Stevie – Steven McStay.'

'Ah, yes – we spoke briefly on the phone, Steven... er, Stevie.' Tom moved to close the door. 'Eileen? See what the lads are drinking.'

Jas squeezed Mrs Galbraith's warm hand and smiled at the lads. 'Mineral water wid be great.' He looked to where Stevie was awkwardly surveying his surroundings. As did Eileen Galbraith:

'Stevie?'

Uncertain eyes dragged from marble-effect walls.

Jas smiled reassuringly, releasing Eileen's hand. He raised a prompting eyebrow.

'Oh, er – onythin'. Water's fine fur me tae. Ah gotta work, later oan...' Stevie moved forward, following Jas who followed the small blonde woman into another room.

'What about a lager, Stevie?' Tom brought up the rear. 'Just one, before we eat.' Dressed in open-necked shirt and jeans, one hand tugged at the end of a newly trimmed moustache.

The mannerism was the only indication the man was anything other than completely at ease with the situation.

'Stevie and me'll have McEwans, pet – that okay for you, Stevie?'

He walked over to a pair of generously upholstered sofas and sat down.

'Er, aye – yes, cheers. That'll be – '

'Good, good – and leave the glasses...' A last order-cum-request, thrown in the direction of the departing Eileen. 'Just bring the cans.'

He caught Stevie's eye, nodded to the sofa.

Bemused expression settling into edginess again. Stevie stood in the middle of the high-ceilinged lounge, gaze flicking between where Tom was lighting his pipe and the door through which Eileen had recently disappeared.

'Nice flat – the Force ur doin' ye proud.' Jas stuck a hand into pocket, produced cigarettes and held out the packet.

The gesture provoked a response. Stevie strode across the room, snatched his property back and immediately lit up.

'Not bad, is it?' Pipe stem sucked. 'Private parking, too – round the back.'

Stevie hovered around the arm of the sofa. Jas tried to draw him into a conversation about room-sizes and placement-amenities.

Eileen returned with the drinks and two ashtrays.

Talk moved on to Tom's hire-car, the weather and the building-work across the road.

They were given a tour of every room except one.

Stevie drained his can, was handed another while Eileen asked Jas about his job and Tom inquired about Stevie's. She received the usual spiel. The response from the ponytailed, suited figure was monosyllabic.

Conversation moved on to more general generalities. Jas's eyes strayed to the clock on an immaculately restored mantelpiece.

Hands ticked towards seven-fifteen, then seven-thirty.

He accepted another bottle of Volvic, watched Stevie pop a third can. Appetising smells drifted through from the well-equipped kitchen. A ping sent Eileen back in that direction.

No-one mentioned that dinner-for-five had now become dinner-for-four.

Jas looked to where Tom was now pointing out something beyond the large bay window to a less-stiff-looking Stevie. Despite the strain of the evening so far, he smiled as a grin split the pale face:

'You a United fan, pal?' Stevie's laugh was lager-loud.

'That shower? Followed City since my dad took me to my first match, at eleven, along with West Yorkshire...'

'They're doin' no' bad this season, eh? Ah catch the odd high-lights, when ah'm waitin' tae see how ma ain team fared...'

'You follow...? Let me guess.'

Jas lit a cigarette, listening to the interaction animate. He'd never known Tom was a football fan. Cricket, yes...

Stevie laughed. 'Ainly two choices, really – if ye're fae Glasgow.'

Tom chuckled. 'Let's see...'

'Ah'll gie ye a clue. ' Stevie nodded left towards the bay window. 'If the wind's in the right direction, ye can probably hear 'em score fae this windae, Setturdays!'

Another chuckle. 'You're a Celtic man, right?' Hard 'C' pronunciation.

Jas frowned. Parkhead. Joseph Monaghan. A missing baseball cap...

Stevie's laugh was explosive and genuine.

Tom's turn to look bemused.

Then Stevie was loosening his tie, detailing recent disappointments and less recent victories. Tom was nodding. The room filled with genuine conversation.

... he didn't want to think about work. Not now. Jas wandered through to the kitchen.

Eileen Galbraith's carefully made-up face was near to tears. On what looked like an Aga, pans of vegetables edged closer to overcooked. Brimming eyes to small expensive watch. 'Seven o'clock, he promised!'

It was now almost eight.

Jas sighed sympathetically. 'Smells great. Want a hand?' From the lounge, he could still hear the sound of loud, laughing voices.

Red eyes raised from examination of oven-contents. 'We should wait until...'

'Dunno about Tam and Stevie, but ah'm starvin'.' He smiled, wondering if he'd ever caused his own mother this sort of anguish and knowing he had. 'Let's eat before it's ruined, eh?'

'You're right.' Weak smile. Hands wiped on apron. 'Why should our evening be spoiled just because my son is too rude and inconsiderate to...?'

A door banged.

Silence, then: 'Mum?'

Footsteps. Running footsteps. Then a head around the kitchen door. A bleached blond, French-cropped head. The most flawless skin Jas had ever seen on a teenager...

'Nick, where have you...?' Relief mixed with annoyance.

... and a sense of timing designed for maximum impact. 'Sorry, got held up.' Nicholas Galbraith moved casually into the kitchen. Apology to his mother. Wide, far-from-sorry eyes on Jas. 'Not missed dinner, have I?'

He flinched under the blatant stare, refocusing to register the rest of the figure while Eileen Galbraith reprimanded in unconvincing tones.

Tall – almost six-foot. None of the gawky, physical awkwardness Jas remembered in himself at that age. Shoulders at present encased in green-and-white rain-proofed O'Neill jacket. Narrow waist. Long denimed legs ending in fluorescent green trainers...

Jas moved back, spine impacting with the edge of a worktop.

... which were now elegantly hoisting the rest of Nick Galbraith onto the worktop at the side of the Aga. 'Smells great...' One hand raising the lid of a saucepan, the long fingers of another deftly removing a spear of what looked like asparagus. The vegetable nibbled '... thanks for waiting for me.' Gratitude added at just the right moment.

Relief and tolerance eclipsing irritation. Mrs Galbraith's voice admonishment-free. 'Go through and tell your father and... Stevie we'll be eating in...' Apron removed, folded and draped over a rail. Oven-glove lifted. '... five minutes.'

'Okay!' Jaunty-sounding. 'Just let me wash my hands and...'

'Ah'll tell 'em.' He made the offer to get away from a stare he could still feel on his body. And to convince himself he was still here.

'Thanks, Jas – oh, Nick, this is...'

'I know who this is.' Leisurely slipping from the worktop. Licking the taste of asparagus from full, bee-stung lips. 'You're one of dad's tame benders, aren't you?' Unflinching, vaguely amused eyes.

'Nick, please...' A tone of complete helplessness entered Eileen Galbraith's tired voice.

He'd been baited by better than this – much better. This time, he held the stare, stuck out a hand. 'Jas Anderson...'

His open palm regarded. Then eyes back to his face. 'Jazzz...' Nick lengthened the final consonant. 'They call you that in the army?'

He smiled. 'Wisney in the army.' Jas lowered his arm and turned away.

'You're not a cop, are you?'

Nick Galbraith's vaguely surprised question followed him back into the lounge, where Stevie was still grinning loosely and popping the ring-pull of his fourth McEwans.

Other, stiffer fingers tugged at a recently trimmed moustache. Tom Galbraith's irritation was palpable.

Jas kept his face relaxed, delivered the message and followed a ramrod-straight form through to the dining-room.

'Glasgow has some good clubs, but nothing like London. Trade, Fist...'

Now free of the O'Neill jacket and clad in a tight-fitting white top, Nick Galbraith ate with relish...

'More wine, anyone?' His mother raised a bottle.

... and dominated the conversation. ' No thanks – this is fabulous by the way, mum. Do you do the clubs, Stevie?' Wide-eyed openness to the man opposite.

'Er... no' really.' The ponytailed head remained resolutely lowered.

He'd been the object of the same studiedly interested attention over the starter. Jas speared a broccoli floret, eyes moving from brown tangles to Tom Galbraith's thunderous features and back again...

'You don't?' Exaggerated surprise. 'I'm sure I've seen you around. What about Archaos, Saturday nights?'

Jas frowned: he could handle it. Give as good as he got. But what he could see of the lowered face was reddening:

'Wisney me, pal.' Stevie ate slowly, as if searching the food for an excuse not to look up.

'You've got a double, then.' Nick carefully laid his knife and fork on top of his place, leaning back casually in his seat. Long legs stretched out.

Beneath the table, a trainered foot brushed his.

Jas looked at Nick.

Wide grey eyes directed opposite. 'Same hair, same eyes, same...'

'Give it a rest, Nicholas.' Tom's voice was icy.

Exaggerated hurt look. 'I was only making conversation – isn't that what you want me to do? Talk to your friends? Make them feel welcome?'

'Nick, I think we need more...' Eileen Galbraith's placating tones cut through mock-injury.

'You don't mind, do you Stevie?' A wide, winning smile across the table.

Beneath, Jas edged a reassuring boot Stevie-wards. And encountered the same, alien trainer. He stiffened, wondering how long Nick had been attempting to play footsie with Stevie.

Clutched cutlery gripped more tightly.

'Stevie... Stevie...' Blond, French-cropped head cocked thoughtfully. '... no, sorry – my mistake. The guy I met wasn't a Stevie. He said his name was...'

'Can ah use yer bog?' Chair-legs scraping on polished wood. Stevie lurched to his feet. Eyes to clock then door.

'Yes, of course...' Eileen Galbraith matched the movement. '... second on the left, down the hall to your...' She started to clear away plates.

'I'll show you.' Long, demin-clad legs fluidly manoeuvred out from beneath the table.

'You'll stay where you are.' The words almost trembled.

'What is your problem?' More exaggerated injury. 'I was only...'

'Go and help your mother.' Nod to where Eileen was carrying plates kitchenwards.

Nick Galbraith moved round towards the head of the table and Stevie.

Tom was on his feet, now. 'Do it!'

Father and son eyed each other.

A furious fist gripped a bare, muscular arm.

Nick shook off the gesture. Tom regripped, hauling the protesting figure to the other side of the large room and out of earshot.

Jas looked to where Stevie was now hauling his jacket from the back of the chair and thrusting arms into sleeves:

'Listen, er... thanks for the meal, an' everythin', Mrs... er, Eileen. Ah gotta get tae work.' Pale face still pinkish.

In the background, Tom was talking in low rumbles.

Jas tried to catch Stevie's eye. Failed.

'I'm sorry you couldn't stay longer, Stevie...' Eileen was back, half-embarrassed half-relieved at least one guest would not witness what was evidently about to erupt at the far side of the dining-room. '... it was nice to meet you.'

'Aye, you tae...' Stevie backed towards the door. '... thanks fur... everythin'.'

Before either Jas or Mrs Galbraith could move forward, Stevie was out of the room. Seconds later a door banged. Jas sighed.

This had been a mistake. He cursed himself for putting Stevie through it. Then remembered his hostess. As the only member of the party still seated, he managed a smile at Eileen's distraught face. 'Ah'm lookin' forward tae the pudding, even if nae-wan else is hungry.'

She managed a smile back. 'Jas, I'm sorry about...' Embarrassed eyes to the adjacent room and increasingly raised voices.

'Nae problem.' He reached over, topping up his wineglass and groping for platitudes. 'It canny be easy for...'

'Well, fuck you!'

They both turned in time to see a white tee-shirted form stalk past the arch which separated the two rooms.

Eileen Galbraith rushed into its wake. 'Nick! Wait! Don't...'

The sound of another door banged theatrically.

Jas lifted a saltcellar, fiddled with it. At least Stevie had missed this part. He waited for Eileen to return. When she didn't, he stood up and walked through to the lounge.

At the bay window, Tom Galbraith looked smaller. Shoulders slumped. Rigid fingers again trying to light the pipe.

Jas watched three attempts, then pulled matches from his pocket and strode across thick carpeting.

*

Migraine forced a tearful Eileen to a darkened room with a cold compress. He never got the pudding.

'See what I mean?'

Twenty minutes later, Jas declined whisky for the third time and watched Tom refill his own glass. He nodded, sitting across from the still-standing man.

'Know it didn't help matters, but I couldn't sit there while... he interrogated the two of you like that.'

A smile shadowed Jas's lips. Interrogation to one set of eyes. Blatant, unabashed flirting to others. 'Ah'll tell ye wan thing...' He stood up, inhaling a fragrant cloud of pipe-tobacco. 'Your Nick's ten times mair thegether than ah wis, at his age.'

Surprise in the tense face.

He leant against the mantelpiece, remembering how long it had taken him to acquire skills Nick Galbraith already used with practised ease. 'He kens... who he is, an' whit he is, Tam.'

Surprise growing to irritation. 'He's an ignorant, ill-mannered little...'

'He wis playin' wi' us aw' ...' Jas laughed. '... can ye no' see that?'

Irritation giving way to confusion.

Jas pulled a cigarette from the packet, ignited the end. 'When ah wis that age, the biggest thing wis knowin' ye wurney the same as everywan else...' He drew heavily on the filter, aware he'd rarely talked as openly before – to either Leigh Nicols or Stevie. '... they're the norm, ken? An' you're some kinda freak – the wan that disney fit in?' He searched the face for any shred of understanding.

Tom ventured a slow nod.

'Whit happened through there, the night, wis...' He smiled. '... that turned oan its heid, if ye see whit ah mean. You an' Eileen, as far as Nick's concerned, ur the...' He grinned. '... deviants. You're no' like him, an' he's his ain norm.' Part of him still smarted from the flirting – the part that felt Stevie's discomfort at the open attentions of a younger, more confident man. But another part admired Nicholas Galbraith. And envied him.

'So he is... gay?'

Jas tapped the end of his cigarette into an overflowing ashtray. 'Gay as a goose, as the yanks put it. Everythin' else – the sulkin', the tantrums – is jist teenage rebellion stuff. Fae whit ah saw the night, he's a bright, articulate boay, Tam.' A shadow floated in front of his eyes. Jas recalled wasted years hiding and trying to fit in. 'Nick's no' ashamed o' whit he is. Be grateful fur that.'

A slow, almost embarrassed nod. 'So where's he liable to go? I mean, what's he... up to, when he's not here? He doesn't know anyone in Glasgow.'

Jas frowned. The implication was obvious. 'It's no' aw' aboot sex...' He knew a great deal of it was. '... Archaos's straight, as far as ah ken – a dance club. He's probably made masses o' wee clubby pals.' A sudden intrigue, as to what Tom Galbraith thought of himself and Stevie pushed its way into his mind. Jas elbowed it aside.

Unconvinced frown. 'What if he's not? What if he gets...' Throat clearing. '... I mean, what if some... er, older... er, man gets...?' Tactfulness overcoming the ability to finish the sentence.

His frown deepened. The other stereotype. The predatory homosexual stereotype.

Then he found himself smiling: the kid would eat most older men for breakfast – if he was even interested.

Confused frown.

'Tam, he's young, he's bright, he's gorgeous...' Jas stubbed out his cigarette. '... he's no' gonny settle fur onythin' less in a...' The word came uneasily. '... boyfriend.' He watched Tom Galbraith bite the stem of the unit pipe and consider the information.

Jas took in the implication of his own words. Like attracted like – whether looks, education or income. Occasionally, an anomaly occurred...

An articulate, blond discrepancy floated in his memory. Jas pushed it away.

... but rarely lasted.

Leigh Nicols and Stevie had ponytails in common. Nothing more. Before he had time to dwell further on the past, Tom Galbraith recovered his voice:

'You're saying I shouldn't worry?'

Jas looked at the concerned face. 'Ah'm sayin' teenagers ur teenagers, across the board. Nick'll tell ye onythin' he thinks you should ken – when he's ready.'

A half-hearted tug on the recently trimmed moustache. Tom Galbraith walked over to the fireplace, tapped out singed tobacco remnants into the ashtray.

Jas inhaled charred shag and the faint smell of lemon soap. 'Aw' ye can really dae noo is gie him space.' He smiled wryly: when had he become such an authority? Other offspring and their constant effect on another father edged into his mind. The thought was picked up:

'Shame Stevie had to leave so early – he works night-shift, you said?'

Jas nodded, glancing at the clock and remembering the look on the angular face under the onslaught of Nick's flirting: just before nine. If he got a taxi straight away, he could be home in time for another row.

'Nice bloke, Stevie – didn't know you followed the football, Jas.'

'Ah don't...' He lifted cigarettes, crammed them into his pocket. 'Listen, ah'll git aff noo, if ye're...' He smiled. '... a bit happier aboot your Nick.'

Wry laugh. 'Not been... my Nick for a good two years now.'

The knowledge tugged at his heart. Jas laid a warm palm on a shirted, well-muscled shoulder. 'You an' him'll be fine, pal – jist gie it time.' He patted lightly, then removed his hand and made his way towards the door.

'Short of falling back on handcuffs, don't see what else I can do.' Tom followed.

A glimmer of lightness in the tone. He was glad. Jas turned. 'Thank Eileen for me, eh?'

A nod. Tom reached past, fiddling with the snib.

Jas inhaled the lemon smell again. He regarded the moustached face. 'It wis guid tae see ye again, Tam.' It had been. 'Aw' the best, eh?'

The expression returned. 'You too…' The door opened.

He moved out onto the landing. Jas shoved hands into trouser pockets, lingering for reasons he didn't want to think about.

A shadow across the moustached face. The mouth opened, then closed again. Tom Galbraith had obviously decided not to say whatever he had been about to.

Jas filled the space with a smile, then jogged down three flights of steep stairs and out onto Ingram Street.

A taxi had him home by 9.15, well before the start of the bakery's night-shift.

On the bed, a dozen ties remained. The wardrobe door was open, the way they'd left it.

But no Stevie.

Seven

He showered and changed into shorts.

From beneath Stevie-concerns, work-related matters edged upwards. Jas opened all the windows, switched on the PC and hauled out the Monaghan file.

Balmy evening sounds drifted in from a dark back court. Kids laughing. Dogs barking. A distant radio. The arrhythmic thud of football on wall.

Jas stared from notes to screen and listened to the thump. A bleached-blond, French-cropped head superimposed itself over Joseph Monaghan's smiling face.

Two seventeen-year-olds.

One dead. One very much alive and kicking back at everything his parents tried to do. One with the life stamped out of him. The other living life to the full. One straight. One gay. And determined to live that way.

Jas frowned at the screen then switched the PC off. In the dark lounge, he walked to the open window and stared out.

Stevie...

He gripped the sill.

... eight years of marriage. A two-year prison sentence for violence against gay men, perpetrated during those eight years. The white scars of self-abuse still ringing broad wrists...

He stared across the back court, past telephone poles and wires to a bank of illuminated and other, darker rooms.

... visible ties to the past. Kids. A sister. A wife. A life lived in bits, here and there...

His own family, seldom heard from. More rarely seen. Fragments of a biological link. Nothing more. Jas inhaled warm night smells then turned and walked through to the other room. He sat on the edge of the hastily made bed and stared at two pillows.

The flat was huge and too small at the same time.

Too big when Stevie wasn't here. Tiny, with the two of them and the kids...

He thought about a three-bedroom Barratt house in Coatbridge with MTV and a proper garden – not a concrete back court.

... ammunition for an estranged wife whose clip was already near to full. And he thought about two weeks' holiday which had to be taken before September. His own workload demanded no breaks. He usually liked it that way...

Joseph Monaghan's smiling features lingered.

... such a waste.

He lay down, burying his face in Stevie's pillow.

Maybe it was time to move on.

Jas slipped his hands beneath softness and inhaled the smell of Stevie's hair. Three feet below, a twitch inside his shorts. He smiled wryly. This wasn't about sex...

Hips moved by themselves, grinding languidly into the mattress. Another, animated seventeen-year-old face edged in.

... and it was. But not just sex. About living. About a life worth living. A life outside work, a life worthy of the name.

He lay there, listening to the sound of cars on Cumbernauld Road and grinding his hardening prick against a rumpled duvet. Just before the point of no return, a white baseball cap sprang to the front of his mind. Jas rolled onto his back and sat up.

The image vanished, immediately replaced by a promise made to

Ann McLeod. He rubbed his face, snatched the transcription of Guy Walker's statement from the top of the filing cabinet and walked back into the living room.

All other cases could be held for a week or so.

He switched on a light, lifted the receiver and punched in the number for D Division.

It was just before ten pm.

Fifteen minutes later, he was put through to the night sergeant.

Jas identified himself for the third time.

Bemused irritation. 'Can this no' wait till the morning, sir?'

Rarely had the epithet delivered less respect. Jas frowned. 'Ah need tae either speak tae the officer in charge o' the investigation, yer collator or lea' a message fur both.' It could have waited, but why should it?

'Hold on, please...' Long pause.

Jas sighed and held. He wanted to get this wrapped up fast. After an eternity:

'Neither o' them ur available...' Different-sounding. 'Whit did ye say this wis in connection wi'?' Less bemused. And no sir, this time.

'The Monaghan investigation.' Jas gripped the receiver more tightly: no wonder the public were reluctant to co-operate with the police. It was hard to know who was doing who the favour, here.

'Why don't ye tell me, sir? Ah'll pass ony information oan tae the officers concerned.' More alert. And the sir was back.

Jas scowled. He made a mental note to inform Ann that he had at least tried. 'Okay – write this down...' Two could play the patronising game. He didn't have the case number, nor the names of any officers involved, but how many Monaghan investigations could there be, ongoing?

Ten minutes later, he made an increasingly irritated night sergeant repeat the words back to him. 'A white baseball cap, right? Three letters oan the front. It might be nothin', or your boays might already huv it. But better safe than sorry, eh?'

Breathing sounds over vague writing-sounds.

The irritation contagious. 'An' ah want two copies o' that intae Internal Mail. Wan tae yer collator, the other tae whoever's in charge o' the case.'

'Yes, sir. Ah'll see tae that, Mr Anderson.' Somewhat more respectful. 'It'll be oan their desks, first thing.'

The courtesy gave him little satisfaction: he'd rather have talked to whoever was in charge of evidence-collation personally. Strathclyde's collators were now potentially drawn from the civilian population and were, as such, potentially more human. Communication with one not tied to the ranks was always easier. And more productive.

But at least it was done. Now it was up to those to whom Margaret Monaghan paid her taxes. 'Thanks...' He made to sever the connection. 'Guid...'

'Can ah ask how you came by this information, Mr Anderson?'

The sudden curiosity was unexpected. Jas hesitated. Annoyance at previous phone-calls to discover the state of play, re a dead seventeen-year-old, tightened his shoulders. And the stock phrase he'd been palmed off with, each time. 'Ah canny comment oan that, pal.' He put the phone down and lit a cigarette.

Couple of hours, typing up the report and his conscience would be clear...

Jas smiled.

... as would be the next two weeks. Rotating his shoulders, he got up and switched the PC back on.

From six-thirty onwards, he drank coffee and looked out the bedroom window down towards the bakery. Sunshine bathed his face. Inside shorts, he'd been hard for the past twenty minutes.

Two weeks...

His balls tingled. Jas stuck a hand beneath white meshed cotton and readjusted his cock. The touch of his own fingers made him shiver.

... two weeks to sort out a life. Put down roots...

Three floors below, the odd car drove up Cumbernauld Road. Jas moved, leaning against the panelling at the left window. He craned his neck to catch a glimpse of the red Hovis bakery flour-silos.

... he could afford it...

He narrowed his eyes.

... his accountant was always banging-on about the madness of paying three hundred a month to rent. Two hours ago, at four in the morning, he'd surveyed the windows of three Parade estate agents. An hour after that, he was waiting outside Rehamndi's to buy every local newspaper with a Property section...

The first ripple of night-shift workers washed onto Cumbernauld Road.

... property. Bricks and mortar. Solidity. Permanence...

Jas scanned heads for ponytailed brown.

... buying furniture. Furnishing a flat. Nesting? The thought made his prick twitch. Jas frowned. The more you had, the more there was to get rid of. When it was over.

Four years ago, he'd sold the flat he'd shared with Leigh Nicols 'contents included in the price'. Eastercraigs was less than two hundred yards from Cumbernauld Road. He'd never been back.

The ripple became a wave. Cars too, now. Jas followed groups of men and women with his eyes. He watched some halt at the bus-stop while others headed for Rehamndi's and remembered his own occasional night-shift with Strathclyde police.

Coming home from the blue to the blond.

The boot was on the other foot, these days. Jas pushed the frown away and rescanned the street below...

The tide of bakery workers was ebbing, now. A few stragglers drifted up from the direction of Duke Street.

... the expression refused to leave. His stomach tightened. The sound of keys in the door made it flip over. He moved from the window and walked swiftly across the room.

Stevie was struggling out of the suit jacket when Jas grabbed shoulders and pushed him back against pink artexing. 'Whit you daein' up so...?'

He cut the question short, sealing lips over startled lips and shoving a knee between Stevie's legs. The smell of antibacterial handwash and yeast filled his head. Pink spikes scraped knuckles. Jas thrust with his tongue.

The body beneath his stiffened for a second. Then warm hands were on his waist and a startled mouth was returning the pressure.

Jas moaned into the kiss. Hands moved down between the wall and a still-suited back. Knuckles grazing raw.

Stevie's spine arched off artexing.

Jas cupped two hard arse cheeks, grinding his cock against the top of Stevie's thigh. He broke the kiss to push his face into the side of a yeasty neck. Part of him wanted to apologise for the fiasco that had been dinner with the Galbraiths...

Harsh breathing in his ears.

... part of him wanted to share the news that they were going house-hunting later...

Against his own thigh, Stevie's balls were hard and tight. Hands left his waist. Fingers trying to grip less than an inch of dirty fair hair. Open mouth fumbling for another.

... noble, extravagant gestures of selflessness faded. He raised his head from a bristly neck, kissed Stevie again and began to steer him backwards into the bedroom.

The responding shove was stronger.

Somehow they ended up in the living room. Still half-in, half-out of the suit jacket, Stevie pulled away, hauling down matching trousers. And underwear.

His cock throbbed against meshed cotton. Jas stared at the whiteness of the man's arse, fingers fumbling inside shorts.

Fabric bagging somewhere around knees, Stevie threw himself over the back of the sofa. Shaking hands wrenched arse cheeks apart.

Blood pounded in his ears. He stared at the darker furrow and the dusky rosette at the heart.

He wanted this slow.

He wanted the bed.

With the sun streaking white walls and Stevie gazing up at him.

In the gloomy living room, with a man still wearing jacket and shirt, Jas wrenched down the waistband of his shorts and gripped his prick. His could smell himself over the stink of antibacterial soap. Staggering over to splayed legs, he pulled Stevie's suit trousers down further and rubbed his leaking cock up and down the moist crack.

Pale flesh shuddered. The soft hair on Stevie's arse stood on end. Somewhere over the back of the sofa, a husky voice cursed harshly.

Jas leant forward, covering the still-clothed body with his own. He nudged a ponytail aside, mouth open on the back of Stevie's neck. Three feet below, velvet continued to trace crinkled skin.

Movement beneath him. Other fingers on his wrist, pushing his hand forward.

He frowned. Needing a condom. Needing lube. Wanting neither. Wanting…

… Jas leant back, re-angling his prick. Positioning the head. Contact.

Knees into the back of knees.

Shaft flexing against fingers.

His balls clenched. Hips moved by themselves, left hand on Stevie's waist.

Warm skin quivered. Surface tension tested, but held.

Balls tightened. A muscle thrummed in his left thigh. Hips jutting forward again. Delicate skin chafing around the head of his prick. Sandpaper on silk.

A grunt, lengthening into a moan.

Then Stevie's hands were back on spread arse cheeks. Jas covered whitening knuckles with his own, staring down between their bodies. Bracing his arms, he watched his glans edge into the man.

A low groan from the other side of the sofa.

Jas closed his eyes and continued to push. Jaw clenched against sensation.

The moan lower in pitch. More urgent.

He barely heard it, sinking into the warm tight embrace. Fists curled around other fists, dragging pale hands from paler arse-cheeks. Two sets of arms braced, twenty fingers clenched against the pleasure.

Then his balls brushed Stevie's balls. Jas shook fists free, hands slipping beneath the groaning body. He gripped hipbones, pulling Stevie back against himself.

Wanting more.

Wanting deeper.

Wanting...

... the body beneath his lunged up from the sofa. Shivering arse cheeks curving into his stomach. A hand behind his neck, pulling a crew-cut head down into tangles of brown.

He mouthed sweaty hair, one arm curling around a scarred chest. Knees shook.

They stood there, trousers around knees, shorts at ankles. Thigh to thigh. Nipples to spine. Pubes rasping against pale curved mounds.

Like some anonymous, hurried, half-dressed fuck...

Jas smiled wryly.

... with a married man. Then he was pulling out and thrusting back in again. Fucking the way they used to fuck.

Before solicitors entered the scene.

Before Maureen McStay began to make trouble...

... he opened his eyes. Stevie braced one arm against the back of the sofa. The other hand curled around his own cock, dragging in sync with the thrusts.

He gripped hipbones and increased the speed of the fuck, grinding into tight moistness and loving the drag of it. Stevie's grunts and the sound of his own breathing filled the dark, dank living room.

Calves cramping. Cock burning. Neither registered...

... then Stevie was rearing up from the sofa, knees bent. Arse thrusting back.

Fingers slipped on sweat-sheened hipbones. Jas bit the back of a shirt-collar and ground his prick into the heart of the man. The tightness around his length tightened abruptly. Lips parted. He scowled, feeling the first tremble shake Stevie's body. Jas released the shirt collar. Forehead impacted with the top of a suit-covered spine as he thrust with short jabs.

Then his mouth was open and he was falling forward, arms wrapped around a white-scarred chest, cock flexing violently.

'Ah'm sorry ah left like that – Tam an' Eileen wurney annoyed, wur they?'

Jacket and shirt lay in a crumpled heap. 'Naw – they both said tae apologise tae you, fur Nick's performance.' Jas kissed the top of a tangled head and tried to kick off Stevie's trousers with a bare foot.

Relaxed for the first time in weeks, the body in his arms stiffened.

He gave up and twined his legs with what was available of Stevie's. 'Onyway, forget aboot aw' that – ah've gotta a... proposition fur ye.' Sprawled on the living-room floor, he turned from back onto side.

Apprehensive brown eyes raised from his chest hair.

Jas reached round, peeling the front page of the *Record* from a damp shoulder-blade. 'When can ye take these holidays o' yours?' He hauled them both upwards, propped himself against the edge of the sofa.

Apprehensive to curious. 'Onytime, really – they're owed me, so...' Stevie settled in the crook of his arm.

Jas flicked through pages, pausing near the back. 'The morra?' He folded, then refolded, placing the section in Stevie's lap.

'Probably...' Curious eyes to the Property section, then his face. Panic. 'Jas-man, ah...'

He laughed. Stevie's insecurity was ten times his own. 'Ya stupid bastard – ah mean fur both o' us...' He remembered the excuse. '... so the kids can huv a room o' their ain, eh?'

Panic to incomprehension. Then brown glowed amber.

'An' a bog wi' a wash-hand basin!' Jas looked away, not wanting the gratitude. He disentangled himself and stood up. 'You huv a look – you ken whit we need.' He stretched muscles still tight from the fuck, tugging crystals of spunk from foreskin.

'Jas...' The voice was husky. '... man, ah...'

'Make a list, eh?' He strode towards the door. 'Ah've got a coupla loose ends tae tie up, but ah'll be back by the efternoon.' He moved into the hall, heading for the shower.

Everything else could be done by phone.

Margaret Monaghan needed face-to-face.

He was pulling a towel from the cupboard when a hand grabbed his arm. Jas turned.

Amber eyes glinted with tiny chestnut flakes. Stevie's hair was a tangled mess. Pale skin flushed pink. From the sex?

A large hand seized his.

Jas grinned. 'Ur you gonny look at they listings or...?'

Stevie raised the hand. Dry lips brushed grazed knuckles. Glinting eyes never left his.

Jas's stomach flipped over. He tried another laugh. It caught at the back of his throat. He smiled, swallowed the lot. 'Somewhere wi'... grass in the garden, eh?' He ruffled messy hair, eased his hand away. 'Noo, lemme huv a shower in peace.'

Amber eyes smiled.

Jas pulled himself away before their draw became too strong.

By ten-thirty, he was catching a bus to Rutherglen.

By eleven, Margaret Monaghan had made him three cups of tea and was about to press scones in his direction. She'd not even opened his report. 'Like ah said, it's an ongoing enquiry, so ah couldney get much.' He knew delaying tactics when he saw them.

In the chair opposite, ancient hands were smoothing invisible ruffles from a pleated skirt. Eyes again stared past him to the spot-lit shrine.

Jas sighed: he was getting soft. 'However...' Raising hopes was pointless. But the baseball cap still tugged at his instincts. '... the police may huv received a new piece o' information on Joseph's death, so don't be surprised if ye get a call in the next coupla weeks.' He tried to keep any undue optimism from his voice.

It didn't work. She beamed at him. 'Marie McGhee said ye wur the best, Mr Anderson. Ah knew ye widney let Joseph doon.' Hands from skirts. Arms braced against chair sides. 'Noo, how much dae ah owe ye fur...'

'The retainer covered it.' He stood up, watching her ignore his words and limp slowly to the sideboard.

'Not at all, Mr Anderson...'

He frowned at the back of her carefully set hair, noting she had failed to take his advice about banks.

'... your time is money, and ah ken ye spent a fair bitta both oan this.' Margaret Monaghan closed the drawer, turned. Two wads held out, broad elastic band around each. 'This enough tae cover yer expenses?'

Jas walked towards her: he knew better than to argue. 'Another five hundred's fine.' He clocked the ten fifties in each, took one of the bundles and nodded to the other. 'Put the rest towards that new hip, eh?'

Small smile. 'You're a good man, Mr Anderson.'

All-round saint, that was him: widows, single parents...

... Jas returned the expression. He moved towards the door, wanting to escape the compliments and the scones. 'You look efter yersel', eh?' He skipped the line about getting in touch, if she ever needed any more work done: repeat business of this nature he could do without.

'You too, Mr Anderson...'

'Ah'll see myself oot...'

Uneven footsteps followed in his wake, ignoring his words.

Another generation's mores and manners. At the front door, she reached past him to unlock the double dead bolt. 'They'll get them, won't they? The animals who murdered ma Joseph?'

Jas stepped out into the close, eyes straight ahead. 'Aye, they'll get them, Mrs Monaghan.' He couldn't look at and lie to her. 'Take care...' Jogging down two flights of stairs, he was at the bottom before the door closed.

She'd at least get a phone-call: if nothing else, he'd shoved Joseph Monaghan's murder back into the minds of those employed to deal with it.

Not his problem.

Not any more.

Crossing Caledonia Road, he inhaled traffic smells and tried to push the odour of ever-burning votives from his mind.

Eight

Stevie's two-week holiday commenced on the Thursday.

''Scuse me a minute, boays...' In the spacious lounge of a ground floor in Onslow Drive, fifty-year-old Mrs Gilhooley smiled and moved towards the sound of barking.

Jas looked from the printed schedule to where Stevie was peering out through vertical fabric blinds. 'Whit dae ye think?' By Friday afternoon they'd viewed seven flats, price-range twenty-three thousand to forty-eight, in an area spanning Bridgeton to the south and north as far as Springburn. And almost everything in between.

'The school's jist across the road...' A Wranglered back turning. '... but it's affy near the... ground.'

'Ground flairs tend tae be...' He walked over to the window. Whitehill Secondary sat in summer-holiday silence. '... an' ye're right – come August, it's gonny be chaos oot there.'

'Nice garden, but...' Stevie nodded behind them. '... an' ah like the way she's partitioned off that wee room.' Eyes to where an ancient bed-recess now had its own frosted glass door. 'You could keep yer... business-stuff in there – it's goat a power-point.' Enthusiastic. 'An' the kitchen's great – no' like that poky wee wan of oors.'

And the flat had two bedrooms. Plus a back-court with a well-kept square of grass and a flowerbed. Jas frowned. You could tell a lot about a tenement from its garden...

Stevie was gazing up at a high ceiling. 'Big, eh?' Impressed.

... but twelve years with Strathclyde police told him more: ground floors were the biggest security risk. Somewhere in the back of the flat, the large, as yet unseen dog, barked for emphasis.

'How much she want fur it, again?' Steve was tightening the scrunchie around ponytailed hair, leaning on his shoulder. Eyes to the schedule.

'Fixed price – forty-seven five.' He walked back to the window, noting recently applied putty around one of the panes.

Beyond vertical fabric blinds, a tree, in the small square of ground which set the red sandstone row back from the street. But no fence.

Controlled-entry...

'Guid value, eh? Better than that place in Garthland Drive – it wis forty-eight.' Stevie followed him to the window. In the distance, the invisible dog continued to bark.

... which said exclusive and desirable, in the Merchant City or West End...

'The swimmin'-pool's just along a bit, tae. That's guid fur the kids...' Hands rubbed together.

... break-in or vandalism problem, elsewhere.

'Ah like this place...' More enthusiastic than ever. '... whit aboot you?'

A hand lightly on his shoulder. Jas smiled. If it had two bedrooms and a bathroom with wash-hand basin, Stevie liked it. He'd raved about every flat they'd viewed over the past two days.

'Sorry aboot that, lads...' The owner was back.

Instinctively, Stevie put distance between them.

'... noo, onythin' else yous wanna huv another look at?'

Jas turned towards Mrs Gilhooley's well-preserved, smiling face. It almost equalled Stevie's in the enthusiasm-stakes. 'Ye get much trouble fae the kids?' He nodded towards the recently replaced window and the school beyond.

Smile fixed. 'A wee bitta noise sometimes...'

Noise rarely broke windows.

'... but it's a nice area, lads. Guid neighbours – maist ur auld folk. Nae...' Small laugh. '... aw' night parties, or onythin'...'

He wondered how they'd react to Sam's football in those neat flowerbeds.

'An' baith bedrooms ur good-sized, eh? Yous work locally, lads?' Now eager to change the subject.

'Doon at Hovis...' Stevie's first contribution to the dialogue seized on:

'Ach, well ye'll be really handy fur yer work, eh son?' Beam. 'Two single boays like yersels couldney find onythin' better, aroon here...'

Jas almost smiled.

Mrs Gilhooley talked on. 'Since the council blocked-aff the end o' the street, it's been really quiet – residents' parkin' only.'

He frowned. Cul-de-sacs were up there with ground floor flats, security-wise.

'Freshly decorated, coupla months ago – an' that bathroom suite's brand new...' Concentrating on the inside. Which meant there was a problem with the outside.

'... ah'm movin' in wi' ma sister, in Condorrat – that's why it's fixed price, son.' Words now aimed at Jas: Stevie didn't need convincing.

He smiled politely. 'Thanks fur showin' us round. The estate agent'll be in touch...' Better to pay twenty-nine-five in Bridgeton and know what you were getting. He folded the schedule, shoved it in back pocket and moved towards the door.

'There's a young married couple interested, son...' Desperation setting in. '... if ye're gonny put in an offer, better get yer survey done fast.' Mrs Gilhooley scurried ahead, into the showpiece of a hall.

Jas nodded noncommittally, then paused looking to where Stevie was still scrutinising the ceiling. A faint, heavily painted-over bump around the light-fitting caught his eye. 'Ony recent subsidence?'

Eyes immediately upwards. 'Ach, that's nothin', son...' Eager face flushing. 'Aw' the tenements aroon' here huv cracks.' Too-quick answer.

True, but some subsidence was more recent than others. It explained the too-fresh paint and plasterwork. And maybe the council's closing of the road to heavy traffic. 'Aye, ah ken…' He reached for the door handle, noting three double locks he'd not noticed on the way in. '… we'll be in touch.' He opened the door, standing back while Stevie nodded wordlessly to a disappointed owner.

Somewhere in the distance, her dog barked on.

'Well, ah liked the first flair flat in Firpark Terrace.' An hour later, Stevie sprawled on the bed, surrounded by schedules and property-details. 'It's no' gotta garden, but there's that big bitta green opposite.'

He was losing track of what they'd viewed and what they hadn't.

'Whit aboot… organisin' a survey oan that wan, then?' More eager than ever.

Jas sat down on the edge of the bed. 'We should look at a coupla mair…'

'How come?' Turning onto back. Enthusiastic face creased by disillusionment.

He sighed, explained.

Stevie sat up. Embarrassed. 'So… you gotta pay fur the survey?'

Jas nodded. Plus there was organising the mortgage: despite the estate-agent's reassurances and his accountant's enthusiasm, self-employed status did change things.

Blunt-nailed fingers self-consciously scooped schedules into a semblance of order. 'So… this is gonny take a while?'

He stared at the lowered, ponytailed head. More than two days, anyway. 'Whit's the hurry?'

'Nae hurry…' Suddenly sullen-sounding.

Jas sighed: everything had to be instant. Now. 'Whit aboot… viewing a bit further afield, eh?' He took the schedules from a clenched fist, smoothed crumpled paper and scanned. Eyes stopped at Charing Cross. 'You widney mind a bitta travellin' tae work, eh?' Detached property. Two-bedroom. Modern. More expensive than the East End, but a house would have a garden, and a…'

'Timbuctoo... Easterhoose – onywhere! Ah'm past carin'!'

Stevie's lunge knocked the schedules from his hand. He fell backwards, laughing.

Hands gripped wrists, forcing his arms onto the bed behind him and holding them there.

He gazed up at the pale grinning face. 'This isney gonny get flats viewed, is it?'

Stevie straddled his crotch, arms braced.

The pressure and the closeness had his prick stretching in seconds.

A pale face loomed closer, tangled ponytail wisping his collarbones. Jas bucked up, trying to kiss grinning lips.

Elbows bending. Arms paralleled his. Weight used to prevent the movement.

Jas laughed, parting legs and wrapping them around other legs.

Grin wavering. Groin met groin.

Not now. Jas ignored a tingle in his balls. He bucked again, using Stevie's legs for leverage. 'C'mon – we've goat stuff tae dae...'

'Fuck... stuff.' No grin. The full mouth was a tight line of desire.

Two hundred pounds of bulk and muscle held him there. The thick outline of Stevie's hardness ground against his hipbone. A moment suspended in time and bright sunshine...

Helpless.

... the first shiver of panic came from nowhere...

Powerless.

... growing in seconds to a full, bone-jarring shudder. The beginnings of arousal swept away by spurting adrenaline. Prick shrinking. Balls clenching tight against his body. A roar trembled in the back of his throat. Jas wrenched one wrist free from the grip and grabbed a ponytail.

'Ow, ya...' Both hands flying to head.

He tugged back and hard, wriggling awkwardly from beneath Stevie. Fingers curling into fists, Jas leapt from the bed.

Wanting to hit.

Wanting to run more.

Get out of there.

Get as far away as he could from the sudden, unwanted memory of one night in Barlinnie's gymnasium two years ago.

'Man, whit's wrang?' Fear and concern in the voice. 'Jas, whit...?'

He got as far as the hall when the phone purred into life. 'Ah'll get it...' His voice sounded miles away, weak and distant.

Belonged to someone else...

Blood pounded in his ears. He ducked into the living room.

... someone who couldn't fight back. Not against four. Not with wrists and ankles tied to a vaulting horse, splayed open and vulnerable and...

The receiver was in his hand by the third ring. 'Yes?' The roar escaped.

'Jas?' Shock on the other end. 'You okay?'

His legs gave way. He sank onto the sofa, fingers tightening around the handset. He clutched at normality. 'Aye, ah'm fine, Tam. Fine, fine...' If he said it often enough, maybe it would be true. 'Whit can ah dae fur ye?' Rapid breaths echoed back into his own ear, obliterating the caller's response.

Then Stevie was crouching beside the couch. One tentative hand reaching for his knee. Face all eyes. Eyes all confusion.

He managed a weak smile, turned away. From the other end of the phone, words burbled into his ear, bypassing his brain. Jas shook his head to clear it. 'Sorry, whit wis that?' On the periphery of his vision, denimed legs straightened up and carried Stevie back through to the bedroom.

'I said, your answerphone isn't working. Tried to leave a message earlier, but the phone just rang and rang.'

Switched off for two weeks' duration. Officially, he was on holiday. Jas closed his eyes and tried to breathe more slowly. 'Aye, ah ken. Sorry.' Automatic words.

Two years ago...

He inhaled deliberately, held the breath then let it go. Then repeated the action.

... no nightmares. He couldn't even remember their faces. No need for counselling, even if it had been offered: nothing to counsel.

So why now?

And why with the man who had bathed his body afterwards, held him in scarred arms and stroked his hair?

Prickling anger behind his eyes. Jas sniffed, wiping his nose on the back of a still trembling hand. On the other end of the phone:

'Look, is this a bad time?'

'Naw, naw – go on...' He opened his eyes. The surface of the sofa blurring. 'This aboot your Nick?'

'Business. Bit of work. Interested?'

'Aye, why not?' Anything to take his mind off what had just happened. Jas fumbled for the notepad. 'Gimme the details an' ah'll...'

'Rather do this face-to-face.'

Fingers refused to obey. Elbow knocked the notepad onto the floor. 'Nae problem...' Any excuse to get out of the flat. '... want me tae drop round tae Albion Buildings?'

The excuse went the same way as the notepad. 'At work, at the moment.' Voice lowered. 'But I can... call in, on my way home, fill you in then. Say... six-ish?'

Jas looked at his watch: just after five. 'Fine...' Figures swam before his eyes. A tremble shot up his arm. He tried to replace the receiver. After three goes, he managed it.

Ten minutes later, the strength returned to his legs. He pushed himself from the sofa and walked through to the bedroom.

Stevie was watching tv. Volume barely audible. Confused brown eyes from the screen to his.

Jas walked to the window and searched for something to focus on.

'Er...' Uncertainty from the bed. '... ye're right. We should view mair flats. Ah've... er... marked a coupla, up the West End, fur the morra?'

Same bright, sunny day. Same cloudless sky. The newly tiled roofs of Haghill glinted scarlet in late afternoon glow.

'Will ah... er, phone yon estate-agent-wuman noo?'

'Aye, aye...' It was fading. The last dregs of terror receding back into the depths of memory. Sights. Sounds...

He opened the window, inhaling the stench of passing buses.

... the smell was the last to go. Old plimsolls. Worn leather. Sour arousal. And the stink of his own fear.

'Er... okay... ah'll go do that then, eh?'

'Aye.' He drew warm dusty air into his lungs. The smell of outside. Of summer. Of now.

Not then.

Behind, footsteps retreated from the room.

Jas waited until he heard the sound of Stevie's voice addressing someone else. He turned and walked towards the shower.

Tom Galbraith was in a grey suit. And holding a leather document-case.

Jas closed the bedroom door against the sound of the tv and ushered him into the living room.

Clear grey eyes met his, smiled. 'Your time's money, so I won't beat about the bush...' Pipe produced from pocket.

Jas pushed the ashtray between them.

'... know about the circumstances of your resignation from The Force.' Admiration in the voice. 'Took a lot of guts to expose a senior officer. Cost you your job, Jas.'

'Ah woulda resigned onyway – nae wan wid work wi' me.' All in the past. He lit a cigarette.

The crew-cut head nodded. 'Up against that sort of attitude all the time, in CIB. On the few occasions we can find an officer willing to co-operate, he usually hasn't got a job to go back to afterwards.'

Gay or grass? Which had endeared him less to former colleagues? Jas inhaled on the cigarette.

'And I read about the Hadrian fiasco. Ian Dalgleish was ex-Force, wasn't he?' Cheeks hollowed. Pipe stem sucked.

'That wis different – ah wis jist workin' fur a client.' He waited for the name of the man who had orchestrated his rape to bring back the panic...

... and waited.

Smile. 'Always did have a problem with authority, didn't you? Even way back, when we first met.'

The forwardness made him grin. 'Bent authority's no' authority at aw'...' The grin slipped. '... an' Ian Dalgleish wis ten times worse than ony of the prisoners he wis put in charge of in Barlinnie.' The strength of the declamation took him by surprise.

The smile fading. 'Sorry – corrupt authority, more accurately.'

Exposure of Hadrian Security Inc's cash for contracts scam was an aberration, in his day-to-day business life. Jas gripped the cigarette between thumb and forefinger, tapped the end against the ashtray. 'Maist o' ma work these days is followin' cheatin' husbands, chasin' up bail-dodgers an' servin' summonses.'

'Aware of that...' Tom Galbraith leant back easily in the chair. '... but you have the kind of attitude I'm looking for.'

The tip of his tongue burned with what he'd told every other potential client.

Two weeks' holiday.

Two weeks' flat-hunting and relaxation...

Jas frowned.

... with a man to whom he'd barely uttered a word, since earlier that afternoon. He watched the cigarette's smouldering tip. 'So tell me aboot the work – then ah'll tell ye if ah'm interested.' The curiosity which had been pricked by last week's visit was genuine enough.

No policing-conference, this time.

What else could second an inspector from CIB north of the border?

Ten minutes later, he was finding out.

'As separate incidents, they're all just par for the course...'

Jas digested the information: a Muslim officer turned down for promotion. Several applications for transfer to E Division refused.

'… but taken together – and with this alleged campaign of harassment towards Allistair Gibson getting as far as the papers, it's got to be dealt with.'

Jas nodded. He'd had little time for the Fast Stream Graduate Promotion Scheme himself: university overachievers went to pieces on the streets…

… pieces ordinary officers like himself had to pick up, or cover for.

'Your Chief Commissioner has the press breathing down his neck. He needs impartiality – which is why I was drafted. And he needs the rumours about E Division quashed, once and for all.' Controlled bass tones a little hoarse.

Jas stood up. 'Want a drink?' It was working. Information as distraction was working just fine.

Laugh. 'Technically, I'm off-duty now so…'

'Ah meant water – or we've goat tea.' He opened the living-room door, just in time to catch the bedroom door closing. Jas sighed, reached into the fridge and grabbed a two-litre bottle of Strathmore Spring. As he returned to Tom, the tv was turned up.

'Water's fine.'

He plucked glasses from the draining board in the kitchen, carried the lot back and poured. 'Ye've talked tae this Fast Stream graduate guy – the wan who says he wis being harassed?'

The glass lifted, drained. 'First thing I did, when I arrived, last month. Gibson's subsequently applied to the Civil Service. His resignation from Strathclyde Police is on hold, pending the outcome of his final interview, but it seems a foregone conclusion. He now says his would-be harassers did him a favour – off the record, naturally.'

Civil Service pay was streets ahead of cops'. Jas grinned. 'Typical graduate!'

The grin unreturned. 'Jim Afzal – the Asian officer passed over for promotion – is being moved sideways. Collator…'

Jas sipped from the glass. A civilianised post – a desk-bound post. A cushy number or general dumping-ground, depending on your viewpoint.

'... and two of those initially refused transfers have received them. The third officer's taking early retirement.'

Jas cupped his glass. 'So what's yer problem? Bringin' you up's had the desired effect. Easterhoose Division's cleaned up its act. Everywan's happy.' He looked at a far-from-happy face.

'It's all a bit... too neat.'

Tom was sounding like bad crime-fiction. Jas smiled. 'Don't look fur problems when there's none there, pal.'

A frown. 'Rot sets in from the top down. E Division stinks so much I'm surprised they can't smell it down south.' Tom stood up. 'We're not talking the usual racial slurs and comments from beat-cops.' Grey eyes sparking with irritation. 'They don't make policy-decisions.' Fingers clenched around pipe-bowl. 'Top brass does.'

Jas refilled Tom's glass, held it out. 'Who's in charge, oot in Easterhoose, these days?'

Glass regarded, then taken. 'Fraser – Chief Superintendent Eric Fraser.

He spun the name around in his mind, then shook his head. 'Did a stint with their Juvi-crime fifteen years ago. But things huv probably changed a lot, since then.'

In Easterhouse?

He considered the inaccuracy of his own words.

The sprawling scheme lay on the eastern fringes of Glasgow. Lauded in the fifties, a town-planner's brave new world built to house occupants of demolished inner city slums. Ignored in the sixties, when brave new world turned bad and even a visit from Frankie Vaughan failed to halt razor gang-violence. Held up in the seventies and eighties as one of the most socially deprived parts of Europe. The nineties had brought millions from the European Union Social Fund and a visit from Jean-Marie Le Pen.

Houses refurbished.

Money pumped into amenities...

Jas smiled wryly.

... and a proposed name-change. Back to Provan. 'How ye findin' them?'

'Couldn't be more helpful. Been allocated an office, access to everything and more civilian assistants than I know what to do with – including Jim Afzal.'

Jas's mind was still on a part of the city he'd not seen for years. He had memories of eighteen months in Easterhouse – hard memories...

Kids written-off by everyone. Out of their heads on glue. Then H.

... good memories. Of a division united by local antagonism. Guys who stuck by you when thirteen-year-olds produced machetes bigger than their own arms. 'Much sign of this... rot ye're so convinced of?' His own defensiveness took him by surprise.

'I'm still elbow-deep in station records...' Eyes to the bulging document-folder. 'The snout-fund's abnormally high, and their detection-rate leaves something to be desired, but that's the only discrepancy, so far.'

The words synched with his own thoughts. 'Ye're talking about the Greater Easterhoose Area, remember? Even the victims o' crime oot there dinny trust the polis.'

Blank look. 'Know it's a little rundown, but...'

'Ye've heard aboot the CS Gas trials, ah take it?'

One eyebrow raised.

Jas lit another cigarette, filled in the blank.

Sceptical. 'Those trials were random – you know that.'

'Random madness – oota aw' the areas in Scotland tae test officers carrying gas canisters, top brass in Edinburgh pick the wan where the polis ur awready aboot as safe – an' aboot as welcome – as a Celtic supporter oan the Glorious Twelfth!'

Scepticism blurring into confusion. 'Run that past me again?'

Jas inhaled deeply. 'Takes the polis aw' their time tae protect themselves in Easterhoose. They trials didney dae a lot fur... awready strained community relations.'

In the background, a door opened. Then another. The tv blasted through.

Jas stopped talking.

A toilet flushed noisily.

He waited for the door to close again. Instead, the hum of the fridge became audible.

'Oh, I know E Division have had their problems, but...'

'Ye seen whit they huv tae patrol? Ye seen the size of it alone?'

'A lot of greenbelt out there, I know...' Wry smile. '... down south we'd have built over that, decades ago.'

Most of it was marshland. Froze almost to tundra in the winter, attracted flies and midges by the swarm in summer. Undevelopable. A concrete overcoat for the whole area was the only step left.

'And it's well-served by the motorway. Ten minutes max, city centre to the station along your M8.'

Fridge door closing. The tv blared louder than ever.

How many Easterhouse residents saw the M8 from anything other than the seat of a bus? And how much could Tom Galbraith gauge about the region, skirting the edge from the safety of his car every day?

'Could do with some help – impartial help, Jas. Someone outside the Force. There's a budget for this, so money's not a problem.'

He glanced towards the door and the racket, wondering if Stevie was listening. They should talk...

... but not now. Not yet. 'You in any hurry tae get hame?' Jas stood up.

Curious. 'Got about an hour – why?'

'Lemme show ye the scenic route.' He grabbed jacket from the back of a chair and opened the living-room door. Jas glanced once in the direction of the bedroom, then lifted his keys and ushered Tom Galbraith down onto early evening Cumbernauld Road.

Nine

The hire-car was a metallic turquoise Proton, parked in Birkenshaw Street. As he followed Tom across Cumbernauld Road towards glinting paint work, two familiar honks behind.

Jas turned, watching the red Fiesta disgorge its enthusiastic contents. Sam and Hayley McStay bounded into the close of 247.

He sighed. Friday evening – he'd forgotten.

The idling Fiesta moved off smartly, leaving him staring at the back of a Maureen McStay's head.

Jas turned away, jogging down into Birkenshaw Street. At least they'd talk to their dad. He slipped into the passenger seat, slammed the door:

'You're the navigator...' Good-natured, crew-cut nod towards the M8 feeder-road. The car reversed over the uneven surface. '... which way?'

'Right, then straight oan through the lights.' Jas buckled up, eyes fixed on the bedroom window of the top-floor flat.

He should have stayed. Maybe the kids would have taken his mind off things as effectively as a drive through the East End's less salubrious fringes...

Engine vibrations hummed against the back of his thighs.

... Jas looked away from the window and focused ahead.

Traffic was light. Mainly buses. And taxis. Women dragged dogs and pushchairs along dusty pavements. Pensioners chatted in easy groups. The odd drunk reeled from a pub. Teenagers strutted in expensive sportswear, rubbing shoulders with older men in shiny, thrift-shop suits.

Jas rolled down his window. Laughter drifted in.

'Nice little community, here.' Tom curved right, cruising past Rehamndi's, two off-licences and a small supermarket.

'Aye, Dennistoun's okay.' A bank, a bookies', another Asian newsagents –cum-grocers and a third off-licence hid the newly refurbished Haghill. The council kept trying. Kept failing.

The car slowed behind a bus. 'Small enough to still keep its sense of itself.' Tom stared left, to Kennyhill Secondary School and Alexander Park beyond.

His own eyes darted to the foot of Aberfoyle Street and the back of two Umbro-ed shoulders hunched in a tenement doorway.

'Swans, boating-pond. And a sports-centre.'

The badly bitten fingers of a thin hand snatched a cling-filmed square from another and palmed back what looked like a tenner.

The bus moved off. So did Tom. 'You don't know how lucky you are up here. All this green space and trees.'

Newly painted park railings flitted past in evening sunshine. Jas pulled his eyes from the doorway transaction and allowed Tom his rose-tinted glasses. 'Straight ahead.' He pointed away from another M8 feeder lane and down Edinburgh Road.

Tom flicked the indicator on. 'This is D Division's province?'

His old patch. 'We're jist leavin' it.' Jas nodded, eyes scanning the wide dual-carriageway which skimmed the top of Carntyne and the bottom of Riddrie. The road was almost deserted. As were the pavements: most bus-routes twisted up or down, at this point.

'Great view...' Tom was glancing right over Shettleston to the tower blocks of the South Side.

Opposite, steep green banks hid most of Cranhill.

'... didn't realise this part of the city was as high up.'

It was about to get higher. 'Turn left at Kwik-Save…' Jas leant forward in his seat. He stared up Ruchazie Road. '… then fourth right.'

Tom obliged, wound down his own window. 'The air's so fresh, out here.'

Jas wound his up and waited for the Bellrock to put air-quality into perspective.

Tom drove through Cranhill in silence, just managing to avoid a pack of mongrels. Both car windows were now tightly closed.

The area mirrored its dog population. Jas looked out at Bellrock Street's boarded up, graffitied three-storeys. In a parallel curve to the south, Starpoint Street had been bought over by a housing co-operative. Carole McStay's home was refurbished. A showpiece, featured in recent Millennium Regeneration publicity.

It was a start…

Jas frowned.

… a start long overdue. It had taken the OD of a thirteen-year-old, his body found semi-gnawed by the family Rottweiler in a damp back bedroom, to force the council's hand.

Tom cleared his throat, slowing behind a number 51 bus.

Jas felt the man's discomfort. There was hope here. Needle in a haystack stuff, though. And this drive wasn't about drawing raw edges together and sewing hopelessness unseen inside.

The car paused at the intersection with Stepps Road. Jas looked right at a familiar landmark. 'They used tae illuminate that thing.'

Tom's exhalation of relief at leaving the Bellrock was audible.

Jas nodded to the Cranhill water-tower. 'Well, wance – cost… so many hundred thousand tae light it up fur wan night. Ye could see it fur miles, but.'

Disbelieving tones. 'With… all that back there, someone saw fit to spend money lighting up eyesores?'

'It's called… creatin' a sense o' local pride.' Looking at a giant, twinkling metal structure from the window of a crumbling second-floor flat created something in the looker. Jas wondered if pride was the best word for it.

On the other side of Stepps Road, the number 51 disgorged women with kids, buggies and trolley bags. Between the back of the bus and Tom's Proton, vans and lorries streamed up towards Queenslie Industrial Estate.

Tom shifted into first and edged across the road.

'SoapWorks is a big local employer...' Jas nodded to the Body Shop logo on the side of a green transit van and wound down his window. '... an' a good wan...'

Gardenias filled the car.

'... coupla IT companies ur up there, too...'

The car sped along Blairtummock Street, climbing higher.

'... wi' work comin' intae the area, an' the Housing Co-ops, things ur changin'...'

Craggy peaks of semi-demolition ranged the roadside. Behind, new roofs and neat gardens struggled to make their presence felt. Quieter here too: the packs of dogs had been rounded up, packs of kids redirected to either of two huge new sports-centres.

Jas smiled. 'Ah used tae live...' He craned his head towards what was left of Horndean Crescent. '... jist up there.'

Tom slowed.

Jas continued to crane. The block of three polis flats had been subject to vandalism for years. Now, more authorised vandals with bulldozers and a wrecking ball were finishing the job.

Blowing up from the distant city, wind buffeted the car. Jas wound down his window, inhaling faint gardenias. And dust. As the road curved, he looked right. 'Stop here a minute...' Jas nodded past boarded-up Blairtummock Primary School.

Tom pulled into the grass verge at the side of Lonmay Road.

Jas got out. The wind stung his face. He walked to the edge of the steep slope. Behind, the slam of a door told him Tom was following.

Hundreds of feet below, Glasgow spread herself for them.

Jas shoved hands into pockets, bracing himself against gusts. He watched tiny cars make their way along Edinburgh Road. Behind, hidden by banks of green belt, the M8 was unseen.

The process worked both ways.

'It's so desolate.' The comment shouted over howls of wind.

Jas smiled. 'At night, ye can stand here and watch the lights go oan aw' ower the city.' The sheer scale of the view still took his breath away...

A sudden blast of air battered them both. Jas grinned.

... with a little help from the elements.

'What's that?' A shout by his side. A grey-suited arm pointing left.

Jas narrowed his eyes. 'Recycling plant – goes day an' night...' He turned. '... ye huvney seen it from the motorway?'

Slow head shake. 'Seen... nothing of all this.'

Jas watched the wind erect Tom Galbraith's severe crew cut into iron grey spikes. A sudden urge to run his palm over that head made him frown. He slapped a grey-suited arm. 'C'mon, there's mair.'

Together they jogged back to the car.

Westerhouse Road was busier. Late-night shoppers. Kids and families streaming to and from the swimming pools in early evening sunshine.

Jas thought briefly of Stevie, wondered about this weekend's outings.

As they passed the seventies-built stone fortress that was Easterhouse police station, Jas pointed across the street. 'You up fur a walk?'

Tom edged the car into a side road, slowed further then switched off the engine. 'Walk?'

Jas unbuckled his seat-belt. 'Ye've been away fae the streets too long, pal. If ye really wanna see whit E Division huv tae police, ye need tae dae it oan yer feet.' He opened the car door, got out and tried to get his bearings.

On the far side of the road, beyond John Wheatly College and the police station and the sports centres, the M8 continued its oblique path east.

Jas looked back to where Tom was removing his jacket and thrusting the garment into the car. He smiled. 'When ah said… streets, ah didney mean Tarmac. You goat onythin' else ye can put oan?' Eyes to dress shoes with an army shine.

Frown. 'There's… a pair of Nick's trainers, in the boot. We're about the same size.'

Jas grinned: the father stepping into the son's shoes. He watched Tom walk to the rear of the car; then hauled arms out of his Levi jacket, tossed it into the Proton's interior and glanced towards a bank of trees.

Stevie, the kids and four faceless men in Barlinnie's gymnasium were receding by the minute.

'There really wis an Easter Hoose, wance…' Beneath his boots, marsh grass crackled dry. '… a castle – well, no' quite a castle. An estate, wi' a hall an' grounds. There's a bitta auld wall aroun' here somewhere.' Eyes scanned a distant group of kids on Quad bikes and the remnants of a closer, recently burnt out car. 'The local landowner or laird or whitever ye wanna call him…' Jas nodded left. '… planted they trees an' Lochwood plantation, ower there…' He pointed further afield, beyond a wooded area to where two redbrick towers poked up from behind the trees. '… an' he introduced the deer. Ye dinny see 'em often, but they're there.'

At his side, Tom kept pace in fluorescent green Nikes. 'That's the nurses' home, isn't it?' A bare forearm waved to an out-of-place looking concrete outline.

He nodded. 'Gartloch Hospital closed in the eighties – a near ruin noo, an' a fuckin' fire-hazard. Still looks good, though…' He pre-empted a question. '… an' naw, ah've nae idea who the architect wis, but we'll see it soon enough.' Jas paused at a fence, turning to gaze back over marshland towards Conisburgh Road.

From the upper windows of three houses, Union Jacks fluttered in the evening breeze.

Marching season. He frowned.

'Was there ever a loch?'

Jas looked back to where Tom was watching him, elbowed the frown away and raised an eyebrow.

'Gartloch, Lochwood, Garthamloch – it's in so many place names.'

'It's Garthamlock, no' Garthamloch – probably cos o' the auld canal.' He grinned at the slip. 'But aye, Bishops Loch's still there.'

'You had a bishop around here?'

Jas laughed. 'The Catholic Church owned aw' o' this, at some point, so ah widney be surprised.' He watched Tom push shirtsleeves further up over well-muscled forearms. 'Wanna take a look?' He turned away before his eyes lingered too long.

'Why not.'

The laugh died in Jas's throat. He wondered when this impromptu tour-cum-history-lesson had moved from instruction to pleasure. Then he stopped wondering, levered himself from the fence and broke into a sprint. 'C'mon – while there's still enough light.'

They circled the derelict, Victorian-built hospital then ducked through a rusting iron fence beside a large, odd-looking tree.

'Juniper grows here?' Surprise.

A lot could grow in Easterhouse. Given the chance, the right conditions. And the nurturing. 'Probably just likes its roots kept wet.' Jas plunged into dense undergrowth.

Tall reed beds housed unseen squawking water-birds and shielded the loch from sight. The ground was damper here, even after two weeks of a sun now low in the sky...

Behind, the sound of slapping and swearing.

... and the midgies were out in force. Jas padded on, heading for the patch of drier, higher ground he remembered from years ago. The wet green smell of vegetation seeped into his nostrils. 'You okay, back there?'

A snort. 'Didn't know this would turn into a safari – ow!' Another slap.

Jas hid a smile. 'Midgies seem tae like Yorkshire blood.'

Crunching beneath his feet. And a clearing ahead. 'No' much further.' He veered right, stepping over a rotting tree trunk and up a slight incline.

Swans had nested here, when he'd been with Juvi-crime.

Swans mated for life, returned to the same nesting spot each year...

... Jas pushed undergrowth out of his way. And stepped into daylight. Evening light.

Surrounded by dense foliage, the small patch of dry ground was oblique to all but knowing eyes. Jas stared down the length of pink, sky-reflecting water. Behind:

'Christ, I'm getting eaten alive here. Are we...?' The question cut short.

He sat down on a large rock and fumbled for cigarettes. Tom stopped slapping his neck, grey eyes over the mirror-smooth loch. Jas sparked a lighter, watching the figure in shirtsleeves take in the view. He drew on the cigarette. Vague squawking in the reed-beds quietened.

Less than half a mile from rotting council-stock. Less than quarter of a mile from the burnt-out car. Another world. Here before they built Easterhouse.

And would outlast it.

'Got a match?' The voice was close, low.

Jas raised the lighter.

They smoked in a silence broken only by lightly rustling reeds. As dusk deepened and the water turned vivid red:

'Beautiful...'

Jas stood up, dropped the remnants of his cigarette and ground out the smouldering end with the heel of his boot. Inches away, his eyes brushed a discarded condom. He smiled. Local kids had obviously discovered the secluded spot.

'... and terrible, at the same time.'

'Nae area's aw' good or aw' bad, up here – or onywhere, fur that matter.' He looked to where Tom was a dark outline beyond the pipe's glowing bowl.

As a CIB officer, the man's work was unavoidably internal: rooting around in the viscera of divisions, investigating irregularities and complaints against police officers themselves. But external influenced internal to create a working environment of sorts.

An environment which had to be worked in.

Okay, E Division weren't saints.

Jas thought about Allistair Gibson, the accelerated graduate promotion scheme cop. He'd have been as welcome in E Division as pork at a bar mitzvah.

But Gibson was now up for the Civil Service. Two thirds of the refused transferees had eventually got their transfer. From what he'd seen, on his first visit to the area in years, Easterhouse was no better or no worse than it had ever been. E Division, under the command of Superintendent Fraser, were doing as good a job as anyone.

He listened to the silence, caught one grey eye in the gloom. It crinkled around the edges. Jas returned the smile, enjoying the quiet. And a comfortable ease which needed no words.

Silences with Stevie soon filled with unasked questions and unspoken thoughts, cranking up tension levels. Uncomfortable. Uneasy. A silence crackling with discontent...

... on both sides?

A frown twitched his lips. And did not go unnoticed:

'Does this mean you're not interested in the work?' Matter-of-fact. No disappointment in the voice. Just an understanding of how things were.

Somewhere in the reed beds, a coot hooted. Jas thought about twelve more days, looking at flats...

A concerned, angular face superimposed itself over the memory of four, unidentified others.

... and trying to accommodate the unaccommodatable.

It would be light work. More money would be useful, if the hundred percent mortgage didn't pan out. Stevie could have the kids round, during the week. They could both have a bit of breathing space.

'Ye can fill me in oan exactly whit ye want, over a drink.' Cooling night air erected the hair on his arms. Jas shivered and moved back towards dense undergrowth.

One drink became two.

The barman in the Caledonian Vaults on Lochdorat Road didn't blink an eye at one mineral water and an orange juice.

Jas carried glasses across the quiet lounge and smiled wryly. Maybe things were really changing, in Easterhouse...

... or maybe they took whatever business they could get.

Ninety minutes wandering around marshland gave them both an appetite. Two drinks became jumbo sausages, beans and chips, twice – all-day bar lunches meant exactly that, at the Cally Vaults.

They talked. He told stories of his days with Juvi-crime. Tom's grey eyes smiled. His laugh was genuine.

Half an hour later, Jas smoked while the conversation turned to business:

'Routine surveillance, basically. What Fraser gets up to, when he's not behind his desk. Where he goes, who his friends are – and a photographic record of those friends.' The voice was low. Tom Galbraith's iron-grey crew cut was inches from his.

Jas nodded. 'It'll cost ye...' And keep himself away from home more than he normally liked. '... if ye want mair than a week o' it.'

'Start with the weekend. Don't want to waste your time and CIB's money, if we can wrap this up quickly.'

Jas exhaled over a white-shirted shoulder. 'Fine with me.' Maybe two days would be long enough for him to be able to face Stevie, explain why he'd nearly wrenched the man's head off in his need to be away from under that strong, restraining body.

'The file's in the car...' Tom drained the orange-juice. '... talking of which, you okay for a vehicle?'

Jas nodded: Donald up at Alexandra Parade Motors had an endless supply of nondescript-bordering-on-unroadworthy transport.

'Now, what's your usual retainer?' Hand to the back of the chair for a jacket still in the car.

'Lea' that fur noo...' Jas tipped the last of the mineral water bottle into his mouth: after this afternoon, he'd almost pay for the excuse to work. He stood up. '... but ye can get the meal.'

Hands now patting trousers. Sigh.

Jas laughed, pulled a tenner from the pocket of his jeans. 'It's goin' oan yer invoice, mind.' He nodded in the direction of the door, then walked towards the waiting barman.

Tom guided the Proton onto the M8 for the return journey.

Jas looked at the shadowed profile inches away. 'How's things wi' your Nick, by the way?'

'Progress of a sort – I think...' Small smile to the windscreen. '... been badgering Eileen about you and Stevie all week.'

Jas remembered the footsie and grinned. He wondered vaguely what Eileen Galbraith had told her son. And what Nick had asked.

Small smile shrinking. 'Still practically ignores me, though.' A sigh. 'Is that better or worse than the two of us screaming at each other?' Forehead wrinkling.

He thought about rows and awkward silences closer to home. Outside the close of 247 Cumbernauld Road, Jas unbuckled his seat belt. 'Ah'll gie ye a ring?'

'Monday – at home.' Tom turned. The smile was back. 'Glad you decided to take the work, Jas. Knew you were the man for the job.' One hand extended.

He didn't want to think about his motives for taking either. Jas laughed, gripped strong knuckles. A wedding band dug into the side of his ring finger. 'Ah'll be in touch.' He withdrew his hand and opened the door.

As the car sped on towards the feeder-road, he could still feel another man's warmth on his palm.

Ten

The flat was in darkness.

Jas stuck the Fraser file under one arm, walked into the living room...

On the sofa, two small heads protruded from two sleeping-bags.

... and walked out again, closing the door quietly. In the hall, he opened the fridge and grabbed a bottle of mineral water. Eyes to wrist, in the triangle of light.

Just after eleven.

Maybe Stevie would be asleep...

He closed the fridge, glanced towards the bedroom. Listened.

Voices just audible.

... maybe not. Fingers tightening around the plastic bottle, Jas walked towards the sound of a low tv.

Reflected light bathed the angular face blue. 'Ah wondered whit had happened tae ye.' Propped up against the metal headboard, Stevie looked from the screen to Jas. Words somewhere between concern and annoyance. Expression somewhere beyond both.

Jas looked away from awkward eyes and pulled off his jacket.

'Sam an' Hayley wur askin' where ye wur...'

Jas placed the Fraser file beside the PC, pulled out a chair.

Behind: '... Carole an' her lot ur aw' goin' doon tae Glasgow Green, the morra, fur face-paintin' or somethin'. Ah thought we could...'

'Ah've goat a job oan.' He opened the file, pulled a sheaf of papers from blue cardboard and stared at words he couldn't read.

Movement. 'Whit happened tae the fortnight's holiday?' Voice at his shoulder. Annoyance creeping ahead of concern.

Jas sat down. 'Somethin'... came up.'

'Must be an affy important somethin'...' Voice closer. Annoyance cut short. An attempt at lightness. '... well, ah kin live withoot huvin' ma face painted. Whit ye say tae me helpin' a bit wi'...'

'Naw, you go wi' Carole and the kids.' He slipped the sheaf back into the cardboard folder and stood up.

'Ah don't mind – tae tell the truth, ah don't think ah'd really be missed. Carole's...'

'There's nothin' ye can help wi', Stevie.' The edge was in his voice before he could stop it. The wider implication of the sentence echoed in his ears. Jas stared at the wall above the PC.

He wanted to explain. He wanted to give two-year-old terror a name, hear his own voice say the words. He wanted to hurl the Fraser file out of the window and throw himself into Stevie's arms. He wanted to be held and reassured and told everything would be all right. He wanted – needed – Stevie to understand...

The wall shimmered with colours from the tv.

... and he wanted to pretend nothing had happened...

The edge parried, returned. 'Huz this goat somethin' tae dae wi'... Tom Galbraith?'

Jas spun round. 'Whit?'

'Don't gimme whit, man!' Light from the tv screen splashed across the pale, confrontational face. 'Ye nearly tear ma fuckin' heid aff, ye'll no' talk tae me then ye walk oota here wi' some guy ye say ye hardly ken an' ye're gone fur fuckin' four hours!' Dark, angry eyes sparkled in coloured light...

He wanted to laugh. Jas stared at 6'1" of heavily built maleness. Dressed only in underpants, Stevie was kneeling on the bed. Glowering:

'Well?'

He scrutinised the half-naked man, searching for the Stevie who had understood enough to drive the car which had killed Ian Dalgleish, the instigator of the rape.

'Ur you an'... Galbraith...?' The words low. The sentence unfinished.

Fists tightened. Revenge was easy – instinctive. No thought, just action...

Eye for eye.

Death for rape?

... and did little to make anyone feel better. Least of all, the victim. Jas scowled. 'Aw', grow up, pal!' He strode to the filing cabinet, thrust the Fraser file inside then stalked towards the shower.

Icy needles battered knots of tension into submission.

He stood there, tilting face up towards the shower-head and waited for the water to do the same to his brain...

Stevie.

Four faceless men.

Tom Galbraith's easy silences.

The memory of a fear, as real today as it had been two years ago.

... ten minutes later, cheeks scarlet and stinging, he was still waiting. Jas switched off the shower. He continued to stand there. Water dripped from his body, impacting on the plastic cubicle in tiny, slowing explosions.

He breathed in time with the sounds, drawing air into his lungs and holding it there. When the last droplet fell, his heartbeat was almost normal. And beyond the shower's sliding door, the tv volume had been lowered completely.

Grabbing a towel, he dried his numb body and enjoyed near-normality. In his head, at least. Beyond the closed door, he had no idea what Stevie had made of the past nine hours...

Ur you an' Galbraith...?

… or maybe he did. Jas rubbed his face.

He needed to say something. He needed to at least say what wasn't responsible for his behaviour. Wrapping the towel around his waist, he slid the door open.

The bedroom was lit only by orange sodium from below. A humped shape lay, facing the window.

Jas stared at Stevie's outline, then untied the towel and sat down on the side of the bed. His hand moved towards a tangled brown head, pausing an inch away. 'You awake?'

No response.

A shiver, half-relief, half-disappointment tingled down his spine. Fingertips brushed hair. Jas pulled back the duvet with his other hand, slipped legs into Stevie-scented warmth. Lips replaced fingers. He eased arms around the lightly snoring bulk, inhaling shampoo and cigarettes.

The curve of Stevie's arse moved into his groin.

Jas tightened the embrace. He kissed the back of the tangled head then pressed his cheek into the hollow between chin and shoulder. 'Aboot earlier…' His voice was a whisper.

In sleep, Stevie shifted onto his stomach.

Jas draped a leg over hairy thighs and continued.

Sometime later, he stopped whispering.

Just saying the words aloud had brought back shadows of the fear. But the dark had helped…

… the dark and the warmth and the slow, solid beat in the chest beneath his. Jas kissed a shoulder one last time then eased his face from pale, sleeping skin. He had to face the fear himself, before he could share it with another.

And that would take time.

Rolling onto his back, he glimpsed the moon through the top floor window.

Maybe tomorrow night.

Maybe a day spent focused outwards would allow the space inside to gather itself.

Eventually, one arm trapped beneath Stevie, he fell asleep.

Seven hours later he was up, dressed and scribbling a note of apology. Jas removed the Fraser file from the filing-cabinet, stroked the side of a still-snoring face and left the flat quietly.

He bought a take-away coffee from Mrs Rehamndi, sipped from the polystyrene cup in a public phone-box and listened to Donald Gaetano's home number ring five times. Then listened to Donald's sleepy voice.

Just before eight, he was watching a grumpy, out-of-condition Scottish Italian in dirty overalls fill the tank of an equally out-of-condition-looking Vauxhall Astra. He doubted it would take him to the end of the road, let alone the stars.

But looks deceived – as always.

Donald flicked at a patch of rust with a rag, then got into the driver's seat and turned the ignition. Accelerator pumped.

A roar filled the small, dark space which was Alexandra Parade Motors. Over the revs:

'Keep her topped up, Mr Anderson – she gits a wee bit sluggish if her tank's less than hauf-full.'

Jas nodded.

Donald left the engine running, eased his bulk from behind the steering-wheel. 'Two days, ye said?' Registration, tax and MOT papers held out.

'Aye...' Jas took the documents, shoved them into the pocket of his jeans. '... gie ye a ring, the morra night, if ah need her longer.' He walked to the car, threw the Fraser file onto the passenger seat and got in.

'Nae sweat, Mr Anderson.' Donald's voice was louder as he cranked open the garage's metal shutter. 'Happy motorin'!'

Jas buckled up and reversed out onto the Parade.

Half an hour later, he was sitting outside eighteen Broomhill Drive and waiting for the Frasers to stir.

He followed Eric Fraser and a well-preserved blonde who fitted the description of Lila Fraser to Comet in the Hillington Industrial estate, where they purchased a fridge freezer.

Next stop, the Anniesland B&Q Garden Centre. Two trays of geraniums and a quantity of strawberry netting joined the fridge freezer in the back of the year-old Isuzu.

Lunch in the garden centre's cafeteria. Then back to Broomhill. A tall, mid-twenties man with Eric Fraser's hairline helped his father manoeuvre the fridge freezer into number eighteen. Mrs Fraser carried the shrubs and the netting.

On the other side of the road, Jas flicked his cigarette into an overflowing ashtray and read the file again.

Ten years with Larkhall.

Thirteen with Maryhill.

Fraser accepted the promoted, mainly administrative post of Chief Superintendent with E Division two years ago.

Jas drew the last millimetres of cigarette smoke into his lungs. He opened the Astra's window, stubbed the filter out on top of a pile of others. His eyes remained trained on details of Eric Fraser's professional life.

A couple of commendations, here and there, over the years. Nothing spectacular, but nothing damning either. Eric Fraser had never left uniform, evidently earning his present position by sheer years of service.

Twenty-five years...

Jas turned his face towards the neatly kept front garden of number eighteen.

... retirement due any time. Mortgage paid off with the golden handshake. Kids all grown up and settled elsewhere...

He replaced the service record and withdrew a copy of the

comprehensive personnel file Strathclyde Police kept on every officer in their employ.

... two girls and a boy. The former both married – one still living in Glasgow, the other down south, in Yeovil – the latter still single, serving the last few months of his legal probationary period with a firm of solicitors in Byres Road.

No scandal in the family – not as much as a divorce or a visit to AA.

Jas smiled: none of the Fraser offspring had followed their father into the Force.

Nothing unusual in that. Nothing unusual in any of it.

He glanced again at the door of number eighteen. The quiet, prosperous suburb of Broomhill was a long way from the desolation of Easterhouse.

Whatever Tom Galbraith's instincts were telling him, Eric Fraser would be mad to risk anything which might nudge that approaching golden handshake out of reach.

But instincts were instincts.

And a job was a job.

Jas glanced at his watch, lit another cigarette and settled back down.

Two hours later, the son left.

An hour after that, just before seven, a taxi drew up. Eric Fraser and wife – now more smartly dressed – emerged and got in.

Jas followed at a discreet distance, back onto the Clyde Expressway then the M8. Just before half-seven, he parked Donald's Astra in the non-members' car park of the new Tollcross Leisure Centre and watched other dinner-suited couples appear from taxis and private cars.

Tollcross: still relatively affluent, for the East End, but closer to E Division's patch than Jas expected, for Broomhill residents' Saturday-night socialising. He knew the leisure centre had a function suite. He also knew it was popular with the local Masonic lodges...

In the car's darkening interior, he peered again at the personnel file.

... no mention of Masonic membership, but Fraser's ownership of a Rangers Football Club season-ticket spoke volumes.

Jas frowned, unbuckled and got out of the car. Might as well do what Tom would be paying him for. Wishing he'd worn slightly smarter clothes, he locked the Astra's door and headed for the entrance to the recently refurbished Tollcross House.

The bar was full of glowing men with squash-rackets and less fit-looking locals.

Jas ordered a mineral water and grinned at the barmaid. 'Whit's oan in The Ballieston Room, the night?' Straight questions sometimes got straight answers.

Overly made-up eyes rolled. 'Civil service retirement do – the karaoke's cancelled fur this week.'

Jas feigned disappointment and paid for his drink.

The barmaid lingered over his change. 'No' seen you before – here fur the big prize?'

He masked ignorance.

She nodded to a garish poster on the wall behind the bar. 'Five hundred quid fur warblin' "Ah Will Survive" in tune.' More rolling of thickly mascara-ed eyes.

Jas grinned. 'They'd pay me five hundred no' tae sing.'

She laughed. 'Aye, ye dinny look like the usual heid-cases karaoke night dredges up.'

His first mistake: standing out. Never a plus point. A shout from one of the squash-racket crew took her attention before he had to conjure some justification for his interest. Jas seized the chance to move from the bar to a table with a view of the leisure centre's foyer. And the continual trickle of evening-dress into the Ballieston Room.

It was just before eight pm.

*

Just before eleven he phoned Stevie from the public phone in the foyer.

Jas stuck a finger in one ear and listened to his own voice on the answering machine. He wondered when it had been turned back on. Clearing his throat, he shouted over informal karaoke from the bar. 'It's me. Gonny be late the night. Ah'll try an' catch ye the morra, sometime...' He made to sever the connection, then remembered Glasgow Green. '... hope they painted ye a new face.' Jas regretted the attempt at intimacy as soon as the words were out.

Lingering in the reception area, he glanced towards the now-ajar door of the Ballieston Room. Laughter and the smell of cigars drifted out.

Hunger and loneliness tugged at his guts. He went back to his car and waited for Eric and Lila Fraser to leave.

They did so just after midnight.

He was back at the Cumbernauld Road flat by half-one, limbs cramped and sore from fourteen hours' surveillance.

Part of the job.

It went with the territory.

Jas undressed in darkness and began a workout. In the narrow space between bed and window he pumped his body, floor then ceilingwards.

Gradually, blood began to circulate more quickly. Gradually, muscle tightened then loosened. By the time he'd completed eighty press-ups, a damp sheen cloaked his naked body.

Jas flipped onto his back and raised his knees. Pushing the base of his spine onto the worn carpet, he concentrated on vertebrae. And the spaces between them.

In his mind's eye, his spine began to loosen and stretch.

Jas stared at the ceiling. He listened to his breathing and the shallow, more even sleep breath of the man in the bed above him.

In his mind's eyes, spaces grew between the vertebrae. The distance between his shoulders widened. Knots of tension in his neck began to release.

A sudden crack made him flinch. Jas stiffened...

... then visualised his body, heavy and limp, sinking slowly into the carpet.

The relaxation workout took three times as long as the press-ups. He didn't do it as often as he should...

Jas blinked at the ceiling.

... but it usually worked, if he made the effort. When he finally rolled onto his right side and stood up, taut, cramped sinew was a distant memory...

Jas smiled.

... as was Friday afternoon. He showered quickly, then slipped into bed behind a sleeping Stevie.

The bedside clock read 2 am. He nuzzled beneath a ponytail, surprised how awake he felt.

Between tingling thighs, his cock twitched. As he gripped bedwarm shoulders and turned the lightly snoring shape towards him, the resistance was less of a surprise...

A mumble. A frown. Stevie gripped his pillow and pulled away.

... and more of a disappointment.

Jas stared at the hunched shape: he'd been like a bear with a sore head for the past thirty hours. None of this was Stevie's fault. He reached over the near-foetal hump and set the alarm for six-thirty.

Less than four fours away.

Hardly worth sleeping...

Jas moved to the far side of the bed and onto his back.

... but at least worth a try.

Seven am. He was back at Broomhill Drive. With the camera. And a notebook.

Three and a half hours later, Eric and Lila left.

Jas sat outside a Presbyterian church in Victoria Park Gardens and thought about Stevie.

The afternoon saw the Frasers tee-off on Scoutstoun golf course, in the company of another couple.

Jas used the camera for the first time. He thought about Stevie and stared past four appropriately dressed figures. Twenty-four-hole course – at least three hours' worth, from what he'd seen of Lila's drive.

He reversed out of the non-members' car-park and headed for the Clyde Expressway.

Sunday traffic was heavy. It was just before four when he pulled Donald's Astra into a space in front of 247 Cumbernauld Road. Jas stared through the windscreen.

Three cars down, a red Fiesta glinted in afternoon sunshine...

His hand found the door handle.

... a driverless red Fiesta.

Fingers tightened. The top floor flat was crowded enough, with two adults and two kids. A third thrown into the mix?

His flat. His home.

A frown creased his lips. More time spent sitting outside flats while other people's families got on with family life?

Jas released the handle, lit a cigarette. And waited.

Fifteen minutes later, Maureen McStay ushered Sam and Hayley into the back of her car.

Jas watched them drive off, wondering vaguely about the early pickup.

Only vaguely.

The flat was empty. Apart from the one man he needed to talk to.

He ground out his cigarette in the full-to-brimming ashtray, got out and jogged towards the close of Number 247. Jas followed a faintly floral scent up four flights of stairs.

In the bedroom.

Stevie.

Standing at the window.

A tangled brown head lowered. Reading something…

Jas walked towards the engrossed form. Arms slipped around a tee-shirted waist. He rested his chin on one broad shoulder. 'Man, ah'm sorry. Ah want tae…'

'Christ, where did you spring fae?' A folder slipped from suddenly rigid fingers.

The smile froze. Jas stared, watching highly sensitive details flutter to the floor.

'Ah, fuck… sorry, ah…' Stevie fell to a crouch.

'How much o' that did you read?' Jas beat him to it, snatching Eric Fraser's personnel file from apologetic fingers.

Surprise. 'None o' it – ah just lifted it tae…'

'Ma business stuff is confidential – you ken that.' On hands and knees, Jas scooped papers and photographs back between blue card-board.

Surly snort. 'Since when did ah huv tae sign the Official Secrets Act tae git a clue aboot whit's keepin' you oot hauf the night?'

'Ah telt ye – it's work. Polis work…' He stood up. '… so keep yer nose oot, eh?' The words more harsh than he'd intended.

Sceptical snort from the floor. 'An' when did the polis start usin' private investigators?' Stevie sat back on his heels, scowling.

Jas returned the expression. A retort formed on his lips. He turned away and walked through to the dark living room before he said something he'd regret.

Sleeping bags and the spare duvet still draped the sofa. The Fraser file gripped in one fist, he swallowed down further irritation, stalked past the mess and leant against the window sill.

From outside, the rhythmic thump of football on sandstone echoed the thud of his heart.

Jas stared into the back-court and willed himself to calm down. Eyes searched for something to concentrate on. A focal point other than the tightening in his stomach.

In the shady triangle between three tenements, a red-haired woman in ski-pants was trying to stuff a bag of rubbish into a bin. Three wee girls sat on concrete, chalking on slabs. At the foot of a telegraph pole, a Portacabin had been erected. Yards away, a small boy in a green and white striped jersey continued to kick the ball.

Jas stared until his eyes hurt.

Then breathing. Behind.

'How come the kids left early?' Eyes still focused on back-court activity. He struggled to maintain a neutral tone.

A sigh. 'Maureen's ma's in hospital. She wanted tae take 'em oot tae the Southern General wi' her, tae visit.'

'Nothin' serious, ah take it?' Beneath the inquiry, thoughts spun off at tangents. He'd never thought of Stevie's ex-wife as having parents. He wondered how long she'd been in the flat, whether it was her first visit, what she thought of the mess, what she and Stevie...

'Jist tests, ah think.'

Jas nodded. Below, a figure in workman's overalls lumbered from the Portacabin with a bag of tools and guided the tangents back to base. Distant memories of an offer to provide tv and telephone services filtered back into his mind. He seized at it. 'That CableTel finally gettin' round tae daein' the work?' Cheaper than BT's line rental. Plus dozens of free channels. He found himself wondering about MTV.

'No' sure...' Stevie moved to his side. '... they wur buildin' their wee hut when we goat back fae the Green yesterday. No' bin much activity since.'

They were getting good at this. Jas sighed. Four hours' sleep and at least another six hours' surveillance made him weak. He smiled, looked away from the back court. 'Ah see ye kept yer auld wan.' He stroked the outline of Stevie's jaw.

A flinch. Then a quizzical eyebrow raised.

His smile broadened. 'The face-paintin'.'

A laugh. 'Oh, aye – lived wi' this wan that long ah've kinda got used to it.'

You could get used to a lot of things. Jas slipped his other arm around a solid waist. A hand on his shoulder, palm sliding up to his neck:

'Ah'm sorry ah looked at yer... private stuff.'

'Disney matter.' It did, but other things mattered more. He traced the outline of dry lips with his index finger. Another hand on his shoulder. Then the lips were on his neck and Stevie was grinding his crotch against Jas's thigh.

Eric Fraser.

A case taken.

A job had to be done. Jas ran fingers through brown tangles. Lila Fraser's handicap was high, but not that high. Gently, he seized well-muscled shoulders and moved away. 'Ah gotta get back.'

Muscle stiffening. 'Jist ten minutes.' Voice low.

Lips nuzzled his ear. Jas frowned. 'Ah can't.' Face from his neck:

'Five, then.' Amber eyes huge and glowing.

Fingers on his belt-buckle. He swatted the hand. For the second time in forty-eight hours, Jas pushed Stevie away. For a different reason. 'Ah said ah canny!'

Huge eyes confused. Confusion into hurt. Then sulk. Stevie spun round and stalked into the bedroom.

Jas stared into his wake, sighed, then lifted his jacket and left.

Eleven

Lila Fraser's drive had obviously improved over the course.

Jas tracked the foursome down to the clubhouse bar, then followed the Isuzu and an olive-green Range Rover to a smart bungalow in Bearsden. From the other side of the road, he noted house number and reg. Eyes remained on the two parked cars. Mind wandered off down one-way streets and Stevie-centred cul-de-sacs.

A No Entry sign in front of one night in an old gymnasium brought him back to Ralston Road's evening peace. And twilight.

It was dark when the Isuzu pulled out of the gravel driveway and headed back to Broomhill. Three miles south, Jas watched two smiling figures carry golf bags into number twenty-seven then glanced at his watch: half-eleven.

A very unsmiling face shimmered in his mind. And a pair of dark, sulky eyes.

He waited fifteen minutes in case Eric Fraser re-emerged. When he didn't, Jas switched on the ignition and drove towards the twinkling Expressway.

Five past twelve.

No note.

No light.

No Stevie.

Jas frowned, walked into the living room. One hand hovered over the telephone. Carole McStay's number was committed to memory. He wondered if Stevie talked to his sister.

Jas removed his hand and sat down in darkness. He lit a cigarette and wondered if Carole was a good listener. Then he stopped wondering. Jas stood up, walked through to the bedroom and switched on the PC.

Ten minutes later he was transferring the meagre results of forty-eight hours' surveillance from notebook to screen. Even meagre took close on an hour. By the time he'd finished, shoulders ached and the flat was still in darkness.

Jas looked towards the other room, wondered if talking to Stevie via telephone would be easier. He pushed the thought away, switched off the PC and began to undress. By the time he'd showered and smoked another two cigarettes, sleep had edged to the top of his priorities.

He woke to the familiar presence of another body inches away.

Jas smiled and eased himself out of bed. First things first. He grabbed the printed surveillance summary from last night and padded naked through to the living room.

Tom answered on the third ring.

Jas dispensed with pleasantries and gave him the gist. 'Nae secret assignations, nae dodgy characters. Why make work fur yersel', Tam? Instincts can be wrang.'

Silence. A sigh, then: 'Let me check the address and registration.' More silence.

His turn to sigh. Surveillance work was worth it for the money, usually...

Jas looked towards the hall, and the bedroom beyond.

... but money wasn't everything. Tapping on the other end of the phone took his attention.

Keyboard tapping.

'Ah thought you wur at hame?'

'Am – if I connect the mobile to the laptop, I can access the PNC direct.'

Jas laughed and thought of Jimmy McQueen in the Royal's mortuary. 'Very high-tech.'

'Yes, but there's only so much I can do remotely: E Division's records are still mainly paperbound – especially the recent stuff.'

Jas scratched his balls and wished he'd lifted his cigarettes. 'Well? Any joy? Fraser's golfin'-pals aw' goat records as lang as yer arm?'

'Hold on...'

Jas frowned and held. He tried not to think about Tom Galbraith, in shirtsleeves and pipe, on the other end of the phone. Eventually:

'You up for some more work?'

Refusal formed on his lips. Too slow.

Tom read his mind. 'More specific, this time. Some... gaps here, in Fraser's schedule for the next five days I'd like confirmed.'

Jas fiddled with the telephone cord.

His silence interpreted. 'Mainly evenings, and the odd afternoon. Nothing marathon.'

He let the information circle, then provided some of his own. 'Ah kin recommend of a coupla other PIs, Tam. Guid guys – they...'

'Want you, Jas.'

A scowl and a smile fought on his lips.

'Someone I can trust – someone I don't have to spend hours explaining the sensitive nature of this all to.'

Mainly evenings.

The odd afternoon.

Still time for flat-viewing.

Still time for quality time. The smile won. Jas grabbed a pencil. 'Dates an' times?' He wrote while Tom detailed. He didn't want to think about his motivation.

'Phone me with an update... say, Wednesday?'

'This time okay again?' He looked at the clock just before eight am.

'Yes, fine.' Happier-sounding. 'Oh, and give me your bank details. I'll get that retainer authorised and deposited this afternoon.'

One last chance. He recited sorting code and account number, then an outrageously large amount.

'It'll be there by the end of business today...' Not a blink. '... talk to you Wednesday, then. Bye.'

Jas listened to the disconnection tone. CIB – on Tom Galbraith's recommendation and instincts – were willing to put a very large sum on the line. He replaced the receiver, switched the answerphone to Home and wandered over to the window.

In the back court the figure in workman's overalls approached the small Portacabin, unlocked it and entered.

Jas glanced down at the notebook. Six time periods, spanning the next five days. Two during Eric Fraser's working hours. Four evenings.

Plenty of opportunity to view flats...

He walked back to the telephone, lifted the receiver and rang Donald Gaetano.

... by car. Quicker. More efficient.

With the Astra's rental increased until Friday, Jas moved to the kitchen and filled the kettle. Property details were scattered around the flat. He gathered most of them up while the kettle came to the boil, noting an appointment had been made to view the Charing Cross semi at eleven that morning. Still naked, he carefully made two cups of coffee and carried them through to the bedroom.

Just before eight-thirty, he sat two mugs on the bedside table and knelt at Stevie's side of the bed.

The angular face was frowning in sleep.

Jas pushed the last two days aside and gently shook a hunched shoulder.

'The rooms ur a bit wee.'

'Easier tae heat.'

'The wallpaper's fuckin' horrible.'

'We kin redecorate – dae onythin' ye want.'

'Ah don't like the looka him next door.'

'The guy wis jist bein' friendly...' Jas struggled to keep his tone light.

A brooding storm-cloud stalked past the nervous owner and back into the hall of the semi-detached. 'An' it's miles fae ma job.' Stevie continued to voice objections from beyond the lounge door.

Jas and the thin, dark-haired woman exchanged glances. He shrugged.

The house was immaculate. Move-in condition.

Nice garden. Three bedrooms. Double glazing. Central heating. Even an alarm.

A bargain at Fixed Price fifty-five grand.

'Where does your friend work?' Whispered enquiry from the thin brunette.

'East End – the Hovis bakery?'

A nod. 'It is a bit far for travelling.'

Jas conceded the point. Especially with the shifts. But there would be a bus – there were always buses. 'Ye had much interest?' Maybe he should buy a car.

'Two couples are having surveys done – and it's only been on the market four days.' Nervous optimism.

Jas folded his schedule in half. The semi would go fast. And it was too far from Stevie's work.

'Naw, it feels... poky...' The storm-cloud was back. '... it's these wee rooms.' Stevie glowered ceilingwards then to the startled brunette.

Jas didn't point out the modernness of the house.

The fact it was south facing with open aspect and would get the sun all day. The fact that there was no shared back court. The fact that it would be theirs. And more than a match for any Barratt house in Coatbridge.

He smiled noncommittally at the owner. 'Thanks fur showin' us round. We'll be in touch.' Before Stevie could find anything else to criticise, Jas steered him to the front door and out into Donald's Astra.

In the car, Stevie lit up. 'That wis a waste o' time.'

Jas flicked through the schedule, pausing at each asterisked property.

Last week.

Lying on the bed with a red pen.

Laughing.

Asterisking.

Less than... five days ago.

He stopped flicking, looked at his watch. 'That big wan in Craigpark's next. Hauf-eleven the appointment's for – nae poky rooms there, an' it's handy fur Hovis.'

'Aye, whitever.' Amber eyes focused left.

Jas followed the gaze to the guy in the house next door, who was cutting grass.

Stevie's sulk extended to everyone they encountered. Part of his punishment. Jas looked away, switched on the ignition.

A half-hearted rev. Then nothing.

Jas turned the key again.

Not even a half-hearted rev. The engine wheezed once, then died.

Harsh laugh from the passenger seat. 'Ye shoulda made sure yer pal Tam got ye a hauf-decent car.'

Jas remembered Donald's caveat. He switched off the ignition and scowled at the fuel-tank gauge. The small needle hovered between half and empty. 'Did we pass a petrol station, oan the way here?' He presumed there was a can in the boot.

'Didney notice.'

Jas turned the ignition a last, futile time. Not even a wheeze.

Stevie wound down his window and flicked a cigarette end into the gutter. Studiously disinterested eyes to the gauge. 'Yer tank's hauf full, so it's no' that.'

Jas debated explaining then decided against it. 'Can ye no' remember if we passed a garage? Wis there no' wan jist…?'

'Ye've plentya petrol…' One blunt-nailed finger stabbing at the small gauge. '… but wi' this wreck o' a cor, it could be ony o' a hundred other things.' Scowl.

He didn't want another argument. Not now. He unbuckled and got out.

'Where ye…?'

Jas walked swiftly to the guy with the lawnmower.

There was a petrol station two streets away. Lawnmower man had a spare can. Jas thanked him, refused the offer and almost apologised for Stevie's sullen stare. He unlocked the boot, grabbed a red plastic container and jogged down the street.

Half an hour later he'd phoned the flat in Craigpark and told the owner they'd be a little late. As he poured petrol into the Astra's sludgy fuel tank, Jas stared at the back of a sulky, ponytailed head.

By two pm he should be watching E Division's car park, eyes trained on Eric Fraser's Isuzu. Jas wondered what Stevie had planned for the rest of the day, thought about asking…

The sound of a window wound down, then: 'Christ, we'd be quicker walkin'!'

… petrol-fumes filled his head and killed the thought. Stevie's mood at the moment, maybe a morning together was enough.

He replaced the fuel-cap, slung the can into the boot and got back in.

'Dunno why ye bothered – yer tank wis hauf-full an'…'

Jas turned the ignition. A roar trembled beneath them, cut Stevie's comment short.

They drove in silence towards the M8.

The large ground floor flat in Craigpark was too big, too draughty and had no central heating. The ceilings were too high and the garden would require too much upkeep. Blunt fingers tightened the scrunchie around a loop of tangled hair, pointed to the polished beech flooring throughout. Tight lips grumbled about the lack of carpets.

The floor brought back memories of Eastercraigs and another, less difficult-to-please ponytailed man. Jas bit his tongue when Stevie told the owner he'd never get forty-nine thousand for it and left first.

They stood at opposite ends of Donald's Astra.

Jas glanced at his watch.

Stevie glanced away. 'Ah'll walk hame.' Turned towards Onslow Drive.

'Ah'll drap ye – goin' as far as the feeder...'

'Ah'll walk.'

'Okay, see ya later. Ah'll no' be ony later than...'

Hands thrust into pockets, Stevie was already slouching out of sight...

'Haud oan!'

... and earshot. Jas leant against the Astra's bonnet and rubbed his face.

He didn't need another flat. He didn't need any of this. He was quite happy where he was. All this was for...

... Jas pushed irritation away, unlocked the Astra and drove down Craigpark towards Duke Street.

With a bit of luck, he'd get pictures of Eric Fraser doing deals with the cream of Glasgow's criminal fraternity and all this would be over.

A talk on the evils of drugs to students at the Shettleston campus of John Wheatly College. In full uniform.

Drinks at the MOD headquarters in Anderston. In full uniform. With suits and other uniforms.

Jas got photographs, phoned Stevie at six-thirty when it looked liked turning into an all-evening reception. The phone rang and rang. He cursed himself for switching off the answerphone.

He bought a late-edition *Times* from a vendor on the corner of

Argyle and Waterloo Street, read it cover-to-cover then followed Eric Fraser back to Broomhill.

The Cumbernauld Road flat was empty when he got home.

Hayley McStay's Hilfiger body-warmer lay on the sofa. Jas debated returning it. Starpoint Street was less than fifteen minutes away, in the car. His legs rebelled.

Another twelve-hour surveillance shift had taken its toll on his body. Pulling on Nikes, he left the flat and jogged round ten pm Dennistoun Streets. The pubs were coming out by the time the smell of cigarettes and Donald's Astra finally left his nostrils.

The flat was still in darkness when he returned.

A humped shape in his bed snored gently. It smelled of soap and shampoo.

Jas sighed, showered and crawled in beside it.

Tuesday morning brought grey skies and solicitous brown eyes.

Jas swam from a dream in which Eric Fraser was playing golf with Michael Johnstone and Reggie Kray while a telephone rang somewhere in the distance. He blinked into an angular face.

Bottom lip chewed. 'Ah'm sorry ah wis such a prick, yesterday.'

'Ah'm sorry ah ever took this fuckin' surveillance job.' He pushed himself up from under the duvet and slipped one hand beneath a tangled ponytail.

Stevie flinched. 'So pack it in.'

He felt the resentment erect the hair on the back of a tensing neck. 'It's ainly till the end of the week...' Jas began to stroke bristly skin. '... an' maistly in the evenings.' He looked into suspicious amber irises.

Which flickered. Stevie cocked his head.

Jas circled tee-shirted shoulders with his free arm. He wanted to explain – wanted to share the tedium of sitting in a car for hours on end, with only thoughts for company...

The tangled head remained cocked. Eyes expectant.

... but knew he couldn't. 'It'll no' affect... oor plans.'

Glinting scepticism.

Jas met the stare head on. 'It'll no' – ah promise. Okay?' He felt the hesitation in the body beneath his arm.

Amber disbelief changing...

Jas drew Stevie closer.

... into another warning-sign. 'Kin ye be here, Friday mornin', at least?'

His turn for curiosity. 'Probably – whit's happening Friday?'

Angular face folding. 'We're gettin' a visit. Fae Welfare. Tae see if this place is... suitable fur Sam an' Hayley's... sleep-overs.' Stevie buried his head in Jas's neck.

The man seemed to shrink in his arms. Jas stroked the tee-shirted back, listening to mumbled explanations and fears from a source further from home.

Maureen McStay. Via her solicitor and John Firestone, who recommended compliance and co-operation.

Ostensibly, it was a reasonable request.

Ostensibly, it was only natural for a mother to be concerned about where her children spent weekends.

And with whom.

They'd both known Friday morning would come sooner or later. Part of him warmed with the knowledge Stevie wanted him there. Another part...?

Jas draped one thigh over a denimed arse, holding the tense body closer. 'It'll be okay.' He kissed a bristly neck. 'We kin tell the social-worker we're lookin' fur somewhere bigger – wi' a wash-hand basin in the bog.' Wry laugh against his chest:

'Christ, that's gonny be the least o' it, Jas-man.'

He continued to stroke, staring beyond the lowered head to grey clouds beyond the window.

Speeches from Glasgow City Council's Social Work department and a non-discriminatory policy on gay and lesbian parents burbled at the back of his throat. Publicity photographs shimmered in his memory: shots of two smiling men holding each other's and the hands of a similarly smiling teenage girl, one of whom – it was hard to tell which – was her biological father.

Intent was one thing. Action was something else.

Stevie's arms tightened. 'Fuck her!' Anger in the voice. 'Why did she have tae fuckin' come back?' Pain in the voice. 'Why kin she no' jist… lea' things alain!'

Jas closed his eyes. Hate for a woman he'd never met tightened his stomach. But hate never helped anything. Slowly, he eased Stevie's head up from his chest.

The angular face was blotchy. Amber eyes dulled to lifeless brown.

'It'll be okay. There's nothin' wrang wi' this flat, an' there's nothin' wrang wi' you. Ye're a guid dad…' He spoke slowly, wanting the words to sink in. '… an' nothin' can change that.' Holding Stevie's face between his palms, Jas smiled.

Half-smile back.

He brushed still-uncertain lips with his then swung legs over the side of the bed. 'Wanna… move some furniture'?' Jas stretched and regarded Stevie.

Confusion.

He laughed. 'Make room fur the sofabed, eh?' It was long overdue, anyway. 'Ah'll phone the property managers o' this place, see if they'll find a new hame fur that hellish couch through there.' Maybe even rearrange the accommodation: no reason why living room and bedroom couldn't be reversed.

The first genuine smile in nearly a week. 'Ma wages'll be through, so ah kin go haufers.'

Jas nodded, heading for the shower. 'Gimme fifteen minutes, okay?'

'Want yer… back washed?' Uncertain again.

Jas smiled. He couldn't remember the last time he'd felt as comfortable with Stevie…

He shook his head. 'You go cancel the viewings fur the day – we can dae they the morra.'

... or as unaroused. He grabbed a towel and stepped into the shower room.

The sofabed was flat-pack and cheaper than he'd imagined. They bought two, crushing boxes and futon mattresses into the back of Donald's Astra.

In the afternoon, Sam and Hayley came down to help build them. The old moulded sofa stood on its side against pink artexing.

Jas left overcrowded chaos just after four, picked up Eric Fraser's Isuzu and followed E Division's head to The Copthorne Hotel.

No uniform, this time.

Dinner with a guy about the same age.

Jas photographed from a stone lion in George Square, then thought about Stevie. He smiled and smoked for two hours until Fraser and his dining companion emerged.

They shook hands before departing for separate cars.

Jas noted the Toyota's reg then tailed Fraser back to Broomhill. Just after ten, seated on a surprisingly solid-feeling sofabed, he punched in the number for Flat Three Albion Buildings while Stevie swore at the new sofa's half-completed companion.

The phone was answered on the second ring.

'Tam, it's Jas.' He covered his other ear against increasingly frustrated cursing.

'Jazzzzz...' Giggle.

He sighed. 'Hi Nick – yer dad there?'

Pouting down the line. 'Won't I do?'

'Is yer dad there?' He bit back irritation.

'Oh, he's here...' Another giggle. '... how's Stevie?'

'He's fine.' Jas looked from notebook to where the object of the enquiry was watching him. He rolled his eyes.

Stevie looked away.

'And you, Jazzzz...' The low, teasing voice purred on. '... how are you?'

Vaguely amused irritation solidified into annoyance.

'Tell yer dad ah'll phone back in...'

'Jas?'

'Tam?'

'Yes, Tam and Jazzz...' Overdone Cilla Black impersonation. '... you have successfully selected each other to win a...'

'Get off the line, Nick!'

Pouting. 'Say please... Tam.' Name stressed.

'I'll ring you back, Jas.' Weary sounding. Then disconnection.

He put the receiver down.

Stevie was engrossed in plans and diagrams.

The phone rang almost immediately. Jas picked it up.

A sigh. 'Sorry about that – wasn't expecting you till...'

'Ah ken. Thought ah'd catch ye the night.' Rustling, then hammering in the background. 'Haud oan.' He placed palm over mouthpiece. 'Gonny gie it a rest, fur a minute?'

Stevie raised a sweaty face.

Jas nodded to the kitchen. 'Ye've earned a tea-break.'

Sweaty smile. A hand through damp tangles, Stevie bounded to his feet and padded from the room.

Jas removed his palm. 'Right...' He flicked through notebook and parroted activities, times and car registration numbers.

By the time he'd finished, Stevie was sitting at his feet, head on Jas's knee. One large hand held a mug of tea.

'Business lunches, business dinners – jist the usual toap-brass socialisin'.' He stroked sweaty hair. 'Ah'll dae the morra, use up the rest o' the film but ah think ye're oan a hidin' tae nothing, Tam.'

Sigh. 'Getting nowhere at the station either – despite half the division falling over themselves to help me.'

Jas fanned his fingers beneath Stevie's ponytail.

'If they devoted a fraction that energy to tackling crime...' Another sigh. 'The detection rate's appalling.'

Jas laughed. 'At last ye canny accuse 'em o' fittin' up.'

'Suppose not...' Wry chuckle. 'Par for the course, from all accounts.'

'Aye...' Jas remembered Joseph Monaghan. He kissed the top of Stevie's head and sobered. '... they can arrest 'em by the hundred, but if the evidence isney cast-iron the PF's office'll no' take ony case tae court.' Between his legs, Stevie's face was warm against a tensed thigh. A broad hand roved up and down his calf.

A twitch in his groin.

Jas flinched. 'Onyway, Tam, whit aboot a meet – the enda the week?'

'Sounds good...'

Stevie was moving now, tangled head lowered. Jas shifted his hands to beneath a damp tee-shirt.

'... what about...?'

'Ah'll ring ye an' we'll arrange something.' Stevie's back was warm and damp. Full lips nuzzled the outline of his hardening prick. 'Bye.'

Surprise. 'Ah... bye...'

Then the receiver was knocked from his hand and he was on his knees, on the floor amongst empty futon boxes and grinding his mouth against those full lips.

Twelve

Groin tingled.

He moaned. Hands resting lightly on a tee-shirted waist, Jas let the kiss deepen and drew Stevie closer.

He needed this…

… after days of sniping and sulking and long hours alone in Donald Gaetano's old Astra, he needed warmth and affection and…

A strong chest ground against his.

Jas moved his hands up a tee-shirted back.

A web of muscle expanded beneath his palms.

Fingers hooked over solid shoulders. His right hand brushed the ponytail.

A twitch in his groin. Jas broke the kiss and buried his face in a bristly neck.

Stevie's arms tightened around him. Lips nuzzled his ear.

Belly to belly. Thigh to thigh. A vein throbbed against his cheek. Beneath his knees, empty futon boxes groaned and crumpled. Jas followed their lead, relaxing into the powerful embrace. Inches from his mouth, an Adam's Apple bobbed convulsively. He kissed Stevie's throat, then leant his head on the broad shoulder.

Holding.

Being held.

Feeling safe.

Protecting.

Feeling wanted...

... wanting?

Stevie's crotch pushed against his.

Jas closed his eyes. Breath quickened in his ear. He could feel the hard outline. He could smell arousal. He could...

... hands between them, blunt fingers tugging at the belt of his jeans.

Eyelids flew open. Jas lurched away, staggering to his feet. Calves cramped.

The fingers held firm, unbuckling then unzipping.

Sharp spasms in his right leg. He gasped. Then blunt fingers hauling down jeans and underwear. The gasp hardened into a frown. From a yard above the lowered, ponytailed head, Jas winced as Stevie curled a fist around his half-hard shaft.

Breath on his balls.

Arms hung limp at his sides.

Another's arm curled around bare thighs...

Jas inhaled sharply.

... and a warm tongue licking the lolling head of his prick.

Jas scowled. The cramp increased. He barely felt it. Abs tightened, sinew twisting and knotting. At the end of stiffening arms, hands curled into fists. Shoulders squared. Knees locked. Jas stared straight ahead.

The tongue moved down his shaft, dragging lips in its wake.

A tremble erected the hair on his chest.

Then Stevie's lips were a tight 'o' and the hand was cupping his balls and every muscle in his body was rigid...

... except one.

Heart hammered against ribs.

Jas stared down.

An alien, half-hard length of flesh appeared then disappeared into the 'o'.

He tried to relax.

Somewhere beyond the pit of his stomach, clenching. A film of sweat clung to his skin. Mouth was a desert.

Another mouth was wetter. Warmer. Stevie sucked desperately, speeding up the blow job.

The hand left his balls for his arse. The fist around his shaft tightened.

His head filled with the wet slap of lips on prick...

... and the thunder of blood which refused to leave his brain. Eventually, he managed to move one arm. He stroked tangled, lust-dampened hair.

Lips paused just below the head of his prick. Face tilted upwards.

Jas met confused, amber eyes. He looked away from the man on his knees, pulling his shrinking prick from between wet lips and hauling up underwear.

'Whit's wrang?' The voice was hoarse.

Jas zipped up and groped for levity. 'Sittin' in a cor aw' day's mair strenuous than ye'd think.' And came away empty handed.

'Huv ah done somethin'?'

His skin flushed icy. 'Naw, it's nothin' tae dae wi' you.' He wanted to hold. Be held. Stroke. Be stroked. Reassure and feel Stevie's body warm and powerful beside his. Jas walked to the window and searched for distractions. Right foot impacted on an empty futon box. 'Ye made a great job o' the sofa-beds...'

No reply.

He stared down into the back-court, watching everything. Seeing nothing. '... this place'll be like a wee palace, by Friday.'

Still no reply...

Behind, he sound of packaging kicked aside. Then footsteps.

... verbal, at least.

Solid, pacing footsteps.

Jas gripped the sill. 'When the social worker comes, ah don't see ony reason why...'

'Fuck the social worker!'

'Come oan – ye've gotta be reasonable aboot...'

'Fuck hur an' aw' hur fuckin' spies!' More pacing.

He wanted to turn. Wanted to soothe. Jas continued to stare out the window. 'The social worker's no' a spy, Stevie. They're...'

'That's no' CableTel!'

Rigid fury at his shoulder. A hand shot past his face. Jas flinched, following Stevie's arm to the small Portacabin. 'Whit ye oan aboot?'

On command, the same figure in workman's overalls emerged, turned towards the back door.

'Ah rang 'em yesterday – there's nae work scheduled here till October!' Stevie was wrenching the window. 'Oi! Ya... peepin' Tom, ya!' Belligerent tones echoed around the triangular back court.

Jas grabbed Stevie's arm. 'Whit ye...?'

'Aye, you pal!' The arm hauled free. 'Seen enough, the day?'

The workman paused, gazing at dozens of windows for the source of the voice. Three women and a boy looked over from beside drying lines.

'Up here, ya fuckin' snoop!' The voice dropped an octave. 'She payin' ye enough?' The question growled.

Jas gripped both arms, moving behind Stevie.

'Aye, well there's nothin' goin' oan in oor bed these days ye couldney invite hauf o' Glasgow in tae watch!' Fury provided extra strength. Tee-shirted bulk elbowed itself free. Then Stevie was hauling down his sweat-pants and gripping his thick, stubby cock. 'Want some, pal? It's goin' spare onyway...' He waggled the length.

The workman was walking quickly out of sight. Three women and the boy continued to stare. The boy was laughing.

'For fuck's sake!' Jas moved between the raging figure and the window. He shoved Stevie back into the living room. 'Ye wanna git yersel' arrested?' Jas closed the window, flicked down a venetian blind and frowned.

Stevie sprawled on one of the newly built sofabeds. Fury gave way to worry. 'Dae ye ken him, Jas-man?'

He raised an eyebrow in half-light.

'Ah mean, dae ye recognise whoever she's hired tae snoop oan us?' The angular face creased with impotent fury.

Jas made his way to the sofabed and sat down. 'Jist cos it's no CableTel, disney mean it's...'

'Kin ye... find oot?' His logic ignored. 'Ask aroon', like. You ken other PIs.' Stevie flattened himself against the wall, knees drawn up, hugged. Eyes past Jas to the screened window.

He stretched out a hand and clasped a knee. 'Calm doon.'

It trembled. ''Sno' your kids they're tryin' tae take away!' Amber eyes alight with panic.

Jas kept his hand there.

Stevie continued to stare at the lowered venetians. 'He'll huv cameras, high-powered mikes... he'll be reportin' back tae hur oan oor every move...'

Jas blinked. 'Okay, okay – take it easy.' Helplessness tingled in his veins.

'Will ye ask aroon' fur me, eh?' Pleading eyes from the blinds to his.

His guts clenched.

'Please?' Amber eyes rimmed red.

His heart thumped. The lie came easily. 'Gie it a coupla days, eh?' He pushed a damp strand of tangled hair back from the ashen face. 'If he's still there, ah'll go huv a word...' The strength of Stevie's panic was beyond subduing. '... but you dae nothin', right?'

A stare. Then a slow nod. And a sigh. Broad hands rubbing face.

Jas edged further onto the sofabed. Slowly, the rigid muscle beneath his palm relaxed. He stared at the backs of trembling hands. Irritation mixed with helplessness and churned into an unbearable brew. 'Ah've gotta go oot.' His hand moved from the knee to the thigh. 'Ye wanna make a start oan tidyin' this lot away?'

Face appearing from behind hands. 'Will ye be long?'

Jas shook his head. More lies. 'Ah need tae fill the tank and get the oil checked oan that wreck o' a cor.'

Shadow of a smile. 'Want a hand?'

'Naw, ah…' His reply too quick. 'Ah'll no' be long.' He withdrew his hand, stood up. 'You make a start here. Ah'll dae the rest when ah git back.'

'Nae sweat…' The lie swallowed whole. 'Fancy chips?'

Jas grinned. 'Aye, okay.' He grabbed jacket from amid the chaos and watched Stevie crawl off the sofabed. A bounce on the edge:

'No bad, this thing – no' bad at aw'…'

A loud creak.

Stevie leapt for safety.

Jas laughed. 'Mibby tighten yer screws a bit, eh?'

Broad smile. 'Aye… an' don't forget they chips.'

Jas mock-punched a now-relaxed face and moved into the hall.

As he left the flat, Mrs Gihooley's carefully plaster-coated ceiling cracks shimmered in his mind.

Thursday morning he ran Stevie up to Starpoint Street.

Thursday noon he used up the last of the film outside Civil Service headquarters in West George Street. And half-recognised the man who slapped Eric Fraser on the back as he left the building.

Thursday afternoon he handed the film to Donald Gaetano. 'Coupla hours?'

A nod. 'Pick it up at four, Mr Anderson.'

At five, he collected Stevie from his sister's showpiece semi. Hayley sneered at the Astra. Sam tried to drag him into a game of football. On the way home:

'Carole says play it cool, the morra…'

Jas frowned into rush-hour traffic: so had he.

'… says it's stability the social-workers look fur…'

He moved the car into first and edged forward.

'… we've both goat jobs, an' noo wi' the rooms rearranged an' that…'

He stopped listening, glanced at a slightly happier-looking face.

What did it matter where Stevie got the reassurance, as long as he got it?

Back at the flat, the answerphone read '1'. Jas plucked the Fraser file from beneath the PC and shoved the photographs inside. Stevie hit play, walked to the window. 'That bastard in the Portacabin's still there. He's...'

Beeps, then: 'Meeting the Greek tomorrow at 8. Sorry we can't get together.'

Laugh. 'Whit?'

Jas raised eyes from the Fraser file. He recognised the voice straight away. 'Play it through again...' He sat down on the edge of their bed, listened to Tom Galbraith's words a second time.

'Whit's aw' that aboot?' Suspicion directed from outside the flat to within.

Jas looked up. 'Nae idea.' At least the oblique message had distracted Stevie from the CableTel guy.

Sceptical eyes.

He met, held them then shrugged and switched the machine to Home. Senseless words circled in his head.

'Ah didney ken you knew ony Greeks.'

'Ah don't.' Jas replayed the message a third time, scribbled two sentences on the edge of the Fraser file.

'So whit's he oan aboot?' Reflected glare from the window opposite backlit the scowling shape.

Jas narrowed his eyes. 'Telt ye – ah've nae idea.' He walked through to the kitchen. 'If it's important, he'll phone back.'

Sceptical snort from the ex–living room.

Jas sighed. 'Bring somethin' through fae the freezer, eh? Ah'm starvin'.' He filled the kettle and let Tom Galbraith's message percolate at the back of his brain.

They showered. Separately.

They ate in silence.

Stevie switched on the tv. Jas dragged the PC through from the ex-bedroom. He flicked through a sheaf of twenty-five black-and-white glossies, waited for the machine to power up.

The Greek...

The Greek...

... an hour later, from the other room: 'Why don't ye jist phone him back an' ask whit he means?'

Jas rubbed his eyes. He'd wondered the same thing. Lighting another cigarette, he returned to the typing...

... an hour after that: 'Dis whit you're doin' fur him huv onythin' tae dae wi' Greece?'

Jas smiled. 'No' as far as ah'm aware.'

'Whit ur ye doin' fur him, by the way?' Studiously casual.

The smile faded. 'Ah telt ye – it's... confidential.' The word was theatrical. Something out of bad noir.

The tv volume increased.

Jas got up and closed the ex–living-room door.

Another two hours' typing cleared his mind. And allowed his brain to filter sense from Tom Galbraith's words. Jas saved the file, hit print and sauntered through to the ex-bedroom.

Now tee-shirtless, Stevie sprawled on one of the sofabeds. Soft snores over the sound of Scotsport Extra Time.

He perched on the edge, stroking the relaxed face. Which flinched awake.

Jas smiled. 'Ah gotta go out early the morra...'

Suddenly worried.

'... the social worker's comin'... when?'

'Eleven – can ye still...?'

'Ah'll be back in plenty o' time.' Jas watched the smooth chest. White scar tissue gleamed blue in tv glare.

Remote grabbed from floor. Aimed. Sound and picture vanished. 'Ye worked out whit he meant?'

In the dark room, Jas nodded. Tom Galbraith's memory was as

good as ever. He just hoped eight was am, not pm.

Expectant eyes.

Jas met them, shook his head. 'Efter ah hand in the report, ah'll tell ye everythin'.'

Stevie shrugged, looked away. 'Makes nae difference tae me.' He stood up.

Jas frowned through the darkness. 'It's cos it's polis business that ah...' He stretched out a hand to stroke the scarred chest...

'Ah'm beat.'

... which moved out of reach. 'Gimme a minute tae move the PC an'...'

Stevie was fiddling with the back of one of the sofabeds.

He blinked. A loud creak, then more bed than sofa.

Stevie breezed past, returning seconds later with the spare duvet.

His throat was dry. 'Aye, mibby it's a guid idea tae test it oot – case it collapses under wanna the kids...'

No response.

'... an' it'll save me wakin' ye when ah get up.' He tried to mirror studied nonchalance, watching Stevie silently undress. In the crotch of his jeans, an unexpected twitch.

One glimpse of firm, white arse cheek. Then Stevie was easing the rest of his naked body under the duvet. 'Don't forget aboot the social worker.' Quilted fabric hauled over a tangled head.

The twitch refused to go away. But the rest of him still had that option. Jas turned, walked slowly back into the new bedroom.

And an empty bed.

Half seven in the morning, he left Stevie hoovering. The Fraser file plus photographs nestled in a Farmfoods' bag beneath his arm. Jas walked past the Astra and caught a 51 into town.

Twenty minutes later he stood on Habitat's seventies' breeze-block roof, in the shadow of the Alexander 'Greek' Thompson Pharos-esque church. On the other side of the road, cars drew up and away from the

Albany Hotel. To his right, the sun glinted in a hundred mirrored, futuristic panes from BP's headquarters.

Jas smiled and lit a cigarette. Architectural influences straddled millennia. But the 'Greek' had the same significance it always had. Over the roar of the nearby Kingston Bridge traffic, his mind reeled back to nearly a decade ago.

Standing here in February sleet. A car-coated pipe smoker pointing and talking with the enthusiasm of an expert. Jas listening, nodding. Wondering how he could have lived all his life in Glasgow and noticed none of it.

He leant against a wall.

Anderston was all high-rise, multi-storey car parks and office buildings...

Jas walked to the edge of Habitat's roof, stared down onto Cadogan Street.

... at street level.

Sometimes it took an outsider to really see things. Sometimes all it took was raising the eyes...

He turned, leant against the roof-railing and stared up at a hundred feet of blackened stone.

... or stepping back. Distance. Objectivity. Really seeing what you looked at every day...

Stevie.

... with an outsider's eye. Jas turned away from the church tower. He scanned the street for a metallic green Proton and tried not to think about what a specific outsider would make of their everydayness, in a couple of hours' time.

At quarter to nine he was still scanning.

Cadogan Street busied up with shop-assistants and office workers. Jas now scanned for a phone-box. By nine he'd found one.

By half nine he'd phoned the Albion Buildings flat three times and got only an answering-machine.

By ten he was getting worried. And low on cigarettes.

Just after quarter past, footsteps on breeze-block. He walked to the top of the stairs.

'Sorry...' Slightly out of breath. '... should get yourself a mobile, Jas.' Two take-away coffees filled the hands. One extended.

He took the polystyrene container. 'An' fry ma brain? No thanks.' His eyes flicked to the street below. 'Where did ye park?'

'George's Cross.' Dressed in slacks and sportsjacket, Tom Galbraith walked quickly to the far side of the roof.

Almost a mile away. He thought of Stevie and the war with the CableTel guy then the oblique phone-message. Jas laughed. 'Paranoia must be catchin'.' Jogging across to a spot invisible from either above or below, he caught a serious eye:

'Just a precaution.'

CIB were disliked and viewed with suspicion across the board: did Tom's presence in Easterhouse render him potentially unpopular enough to merit this amount of cloak and dagger? He sobered, placed his coffee on a stone bench and whipped the Farmfoods' bag from beneath his arm. 'Here ye go...'

Folder taken, opened. The sheaf of photographs flicked.

Jas lit up. 'The wan at the end's...'

'Jim Taylor, head of Civil Service Recruitment in Scotland.' The sentence finished for him.

Jas smiled wryly, remembered Allistair Gibson and read Tom's mind. 'Nae law against helpin' wanna yer officers – ex-officers – git a foot in the door, is there?'

'Not at all.' A pair of half-rims produced from pocket, perched on nose. 'Fraser's very obliging all round.' More flicking.

'The rest o' the stuff's jist cor-regs an' addresses.' The glasses gave the already-commanding face a further edge of distinction.

'Mmm... good...' Magnified eyes remained trained on black-and-white glossies.

Jas de-lidded his coffee and sipped: white, no sugar. Like ten years ago. He watched Tom read the information. Then watched the other cup of coffee grow cold. Eventually:

'This is everything?'

Jas nodded. 'Like ah telt ye, Fraser's so normal ye widney believe it.'

Over the top of half-rims, intense grey eyes fixed his.

Jas met and held the stare. 'Mibby if ah knew mair whit ye think he's up tae, ah could...'

'Can't put my finger on it...' Glasses removed. Grey eyes rubbed. '... but there's something there.'

Something big enough to merit coded phone-messages and early morning meetings on roofs? A flip comment formed on his lips.

'... no-one's that normal, Jas.'

He let it pass. 'Tell me aboot it!'

Weary smile.

Jas stared. Strain stained the usually clear grey eyes. Work? Or home. 'How's Nick, by the way?'

Dismissive headshake. 'Don't ask.' Folder opened, photos slipped back inside. 'How are you for the weekend?'

He frowned. 'Tam, ah've goat... stuff ah need tae sort oot, maself. Whit aboot...?'

'Two more days – what do you say?' Glasses back into pocket. Pipe produced. Plus tobacco pouch.

Jas watch Tom's fingers deftly pinch a wad and press it into the pipe's bowl.

'That retainer go into your bank all right?'

Dead on time. No complaint there. He nodded, watching the way Tom's shoulders moved beneath well-cut tweed.

Pipe stem stuck between lips, clamped there by teeth. Hands patting pockets.

Jas flicked a lighter, moth to the flame. He held it to the bowl and felt ignited gas singe skin.

Sucking sounds.

The fragrant odour of smouldering shag filled his nostrils.

Grey eyes from the pipe bowl.

Fist tightened around the lighter. He could smell faint soap and the tang of unscented aftershave. Jas dropped his arm and moved back. 'Okay – just the weekend.'

Tom smiled. 'Thanks – you know I wouldn't ask if there was anyone else I could depend on.'

He returned a more wry version of the expression. 'That's me – Mr Dependable!'

A laugh.

A sudden warmth in his chest.

Then grey eyes to wrist. 'Put all this on your bill – I've kept you much longer than I...'

'Christ!' He glanced at his own watch: quarter to eleven. 'Ah gotta find a taxi.' Jas moved towards the concrete steps.

'Hold on – I'll give you a lift.'

Then they were both jogging down stairs and heading up Pitt Street's steep incline.

Thirteen

Mid-morning traffic was a nightmare. At quarter past eleven Jas took the stairs to the top flat three at a time and fumbled for keys.

In the bedroom, Stevie was standing at the window. Alone.

The apology formed on his lips... He glanced around the pristine room. 'She no' here yet?'

'Came early – hauf ten.' Said without turning. 'Ainly stayed twenny minutes.'

Relief fought guilt. And won. 'How did it go?' He walked towards the shirted figure.

'Hard tae tell.'

He paused six inches behind, then side-stepped left to lean against the window fame. 'Did she seem happy wi' things?' Jas looked at the side of a newly shaven face and tried to read it.

'Her an' hur... partner huv goat wanna oor futons. She says they're really comfortable.'

One hand moved to hover above Stevie's shoulder. 'Did she say onythin' else?'

'Telt me tae relax – said nae-wan wis oan trial, here.' Wry smile. 'She wis sorry tae huv missed you – an' apologised fur havin' tae come early. Ah telt her you'd be disappointed tae huv missed hur.'

He was... and he wasn't. But the voice was different. Calmer. Jas risked the hand. Stevie's shoulder flinched. Jas frowned. He was about to remove the palm when another hand covered his:

'Man, ah need a big favour.' Stevie turned.

Jas hid the frown. The guilt resurfaced. 'Onythin' – ye ken that.'

Fingers curling between his. 'Ye workin', the morra?'

He kept his face impassive. 'Why?'

Sigh. 'Firestone phoned, jist efter ye left. We've goat a meetin' wi' Maureen an' her solicitor the morra, at ten.'

He followed the brown eyes to some invisible spot on the floor. 'That's guid – that's...'

'Carole's got a scan, in the mornin'. Her eldest's goin' with Hayley tae queue fur tickets fur some... band...'

Jas cocked his head.

Brown eyes from the floor to his face. 'Kin you pick Sam up fae hur place at nine an' entertain him till somewan gits back?'

Jas blinked.

'Ach, it disney matter...' Brown eyes narrowing. 'Ah could lea' the boay wi' Carole's man, ah suppose.' Fingers disentwining.

'Naw, it's fine...' He gripped warm knuckles. '... nae problem.'

'You sure?' Gratitude tinged with suspicion.

Jas found a laugh. 'Sure ah'm sure.'

'Oh, cheers...' Relief. 'So ye've finished that job ye wur workin' oan?'

His nod was a silent lie, but a lie nonetheless. 'Nine, ye said? Want me tae bring him back here? Get videos or let 'im play oan the computer?'

Smile. 'If ye've still goat the cor, he'd love that. Likes cors best, next tae fitba' an' the computers.' The smile into a grin.

He tried to return it. 'Nae sweat – we'll drive aroon' a bit, eh?'

Stevie tugged at the tie around his neck. 'That's wan problem taken care of...' Tie wrenched off, tossed onto the bed. 'Noo ah need tae go tae the bank, get money out fur these fuckin' tickets.' Sigh. 'Twenty two quid, plus bookin' fee – can ye believe it?'

Jas let the hand slip from his and smiled.

'Who the fuck are S Shed Seven, onyway?' Stevie was rifling through the pockets of the Wrangler jacket.

Jas laughed. 'Fucked if ah know.'

Cashline card produced. 'Comin' wi' me? We could... celebrate that job o' yours finishin'.'

The lie was lengthening. But the truth would bring irritation and sulks and arguments. 'Ye're on – an' you can pay.'

Stevie grinned, shrugged on jacket and strode into the hall.

The job was finished. Or close enough to. Trying to convince himself it was the truth, Jas followed the jaunty figure out of the flat.

They ended up in Fat Cats. It was close to the bank and did all day breakfasts. Jas bought an *Evening Times* from a boy Sam's age, flicked through it.

Stevie ordered and joked with the barmaid.

The Property for Sale section was tiny, on a Friday. He glanced at the tv listings then closed the paper and folded it. A headline caught his eye:

'Second Man attacked at Gartloch.'

'Here ye go...'

He moved the paper.

Stevie placed a pint of heavy beside it, a clear glass before Jas.

He drank two mouthfuls of the mineral water, wondered why they didn't do this more often. Then remembered. Jas looked at the pony-tailed figure now flicking through the *Times*. ''Sno' bin much o' a holiday fur ye so far, hus it?'

Newspaper lowered. Questioning brown eyes met his.

'Wi' the social worker an'...' He short-circuited his own lack of presence. '... everythin'.' Jas sipped the cool liquid.

Stevie produced cigarettes, offered the packet. 'Better ah wis aroon' tae deal wi' it aw.'

Jas took one. Stevie lit it for him:

'This plus night-shift an' ah widda really bin wrecked.' Half-laugh.

Beneath the table, a denimed calf slipped between his. Jas closed his legs around it.

Brown eyes glowed. They continued to glow until the all-day breakfasts arrived.

They ate and talked... about flats viewed, tomorrow's meeting with Maureen's solicitor, Carole's pregnancy, the football. By the time the barmaid cleared the table, Stevie was laughing.

Jas enjoyed the sound more than the food.

'It's like...' Broad fingers stubbed out a cigarette. '... everythin' that can happen hus happened, know whit ah mean?' Cigarette packet grabbed, fiddled with. 'Christ, waitin' fur that fuckin' social worker wis worse than bein' up before the parole board.'

Jas lit another, listened to outpoured worries and fears now apparently in the past. He nodded periodically, his calf nestling between two denimed legs. His brain was moving on.

After the weekend.

Four days left of the holiday.

They'd view more flats.

Make a decision...

A brief, two-hour nightmare in a prison gymnasium was back in the pits of his mind.

... and talk. Really talk.

'Fancy the pictures?'

The question reclaimed his attention. Stevie's holiday. Stevie's time. Jas grinned. 'Aye, okay – whit wan?' He got up, shoved hand into pocket.

A hand on his arm. 'Ah'm gettin' this – you've done enough.'

He didn't want to think of what he'd done... or had failed to do. But he let Stevie pay.

And choose the film.

And stop off for a drink on the way home. Then another. Then he lost count. City centre pubs teemed with TFI Friday wage-slaves celebrating the start of the weekend.

Pints of heavy became vodkas.

Jas's belly sloshed with countless overpriced mineral waters. Someone was smoking a pipe nearby. The smell reminded him of metal-rimmed half- glasses and clear grey eyes. Out of the blue:

'Ah dinny ken whit ah'd dae withoot ye, Jas-man.' Slurred over music and chatter.

Crammed into a corner between the cigarette machine and the Gents, he laughed.

Drunken irritation. 'Ye don't believe me, dae ye?' Voice louder. A leaden arm around his shoulder. 'Ye're ma best mate... ma pal... an' ah love ye!'

Beyond the flushed face, a group of smiling girls. Jas caught the eye of one of their number. She grinned sympathetically at par-for-the-course Glasweigan sentimentality.

Jas managed to return the expression. 'C'mon, you – let's git ye hame.'

'Don' wanna go hame – ye love me, don' ye Jas-man? Don' ye?' The arm tightened, hugging him closer. Flushed face moving towards his. 'Cos ah fuckin' love you...'

Jas dodged parting lips. He knew it was time to leave when Stevie tried to kiss him in public. Just before ten, a tangled brown head lolling on his shoulder, he hailed a taxi and got them both back to Cumbernauld Road. He half-carried two hundred and fifty pounds of now-giggling bulk into the shower and undressed him there:

'Ah don' deserve ye... ah'm nothin' but trouble fur ye, Jas-man...'

'Aye, that's right...' He propped the swaying, semi-naked form against the cubicle wall and dragged down underpants. '... noo shut up an' git in there.' He heaved Stevie towards the shower-head. A hand grabbed his arm:

'Wash ma back, eh? C'moan...'

Jas placed his palm between pale pecs, pushed Stevie against the cubicle wall and fumbled for the temperature control.

'Ah love ye, Jas-man – ah've never felt this way aboot onywan in ma...'

He turned the faucet on full.

A shriek ended the sentence. Flailing arms fought the deluge of ice-cold water. Then legs folded. Stevie sank to the floor of the shower cubicle, gasping. Arms hung limply by sides.

Jas let the water do what he couldn't. When the gasping stopped, he gently eased the man to his feet, dried him then his hair and steered Stevie through to the ex–living room.

Silence replaced wild protestations of undying passion. It was easier to deal with. As he set the alarm and began to unzip:

'Ye don't, dae ye?'

Jas freed legs from jeans and hauled off shirt. 'Go tae sleep.'

'Don't blame ye, but ah can still love you, eh?'

A sudden shiver erected every hair on his body. Jas looked to where Stevie was now on his back. He couldn't see the face. The eyes he felt. He slipped into bed, pushing Stevie onto his side and curling his body around the icy one.

'Ah dae love ye... ye gotta believe me, Jas-man.'

'Ah believe ye – noo shut the fuck up and go tae sleep.'

Half laugh. In minutes the sound of soft snoring filled the room.

Jas rolled onto his back. He listened to the sound and put Stevie's declaration down to the vodka. The last thing he remembered before he fell asleep was the fragrant odour of Tom Galbraith's tobacco.

'Where we goin' now, Uncle Jas?'

He stared at the rear bumper of Eric Fraser's Isuzu. 'Wait an' see, eh?

In the passenger seat beside him, a ball clutched against a blue stripped chest.

He moved his eyes to the chubby face. 'Want mair juice?' Jas shoved one hand into the doorless glove-compartment and rummaged amidst bags of crisps. Fist tightened around a third can of Irn Bru.

'Naw...' A pair of clear, eight-year-old eyes remained fixed on the windscreen.

He replaced the can and followed suit.

Leaving his Broomhill home at nine fifteen, Eric Fraser took the city centre turn off at Anderston, driving down onto the Broomilaw. Saturday morning traffic was still light. Fifteen minutes later:

'Uncle Jas?'

They stopped at the Glassford Street intersection. He checked the rear of the Isuzu, two cars in front, then looked left.

'Can we huv a game later?' Open, enthusiastic face.

'Aye, Sam...' The lights changed. Jas winked, returned his attention to the road. '... in a wee while.'

'Cool!'

The word reminded him of Tom Galbraith. Jas grinned and moved off.

Fraser's Isuzu continued on into the Saltmarket and up towards London Road. Sam made a start on the crisps just before the Barras. By the time Donald's Astra turned down Templeton Street, he had finished two packets and was hitting the Irn Bru.

'You okay ower there?' Jas slowed, increasing the distance between his own front and the rear wheels of the Isuzu.

Sam beamed. 'Look!' One arm past him to the right-hand side of the road.

Jas turned slowly, following Fraser onto the grass verge.

Less than a hundred yards away, eleven-odd teenagers in a variety of non-matching sportswear dribbled eleven-odd balls around traffic cones. On the sidelines, a shortish, middle aged man in a washed-out Umbro warm-up suit blew a whistle and shouted by turns.

'Can we go an' watch, Uncle Jas? Mibby we can git a game.' Sam lunged dashboardwards, eyes moving past Jas's head then over his shoulder.

He parked a little away, watched Eric Fraser central lock and alarm the Isuzu then walk swiftly towards the shortish man with the whistle.

Stubby hands unfastening seat-belt. 'Can we? Can we?'

'Slow doon...' Jas unbuckled, glanced at the camera in the back seat and decided against it. '... we'll... oi!'

The passenger door pushed open.

He made a grab for the collar of Sam's tee-shirt. Too slow. Jas levered himself from the car and jogged after the small figure dribbling the football towards the training-session.

He caught up with Sam fifteen yards from the traffic cones. 'Haud oan...'

A yelp. A last, frustrated snap-kick.

The ball sailed through the air, landed at the feet of a tall, bleach-haired boy.

Jas hauled Stevie's son away from the demarked area. 'Calm doon, eh? They're practicin'. Ye canny interrupt 'em when they're...'

Sam wriggled free and ran backwards.

Seconds later, one chubby knee caught the returned ball, bounced it twice then steadied it underfoot.

Jas's head swivelled to where the bleach-haired kid was raising one thumb to an ecstatic Sam. For a second Nick Galbraith flashed into his mind, followed quickly by his father...

He glanced around.

... and his reason for being here at all. Over by a heap of sports bags and training-gear, Eric Fraser was chatting to the shortish man. Two pairs of eyes focused on the still-dribbling eleven. Then a warm fist on his wrist, tugging:

'Can we go watch 'em, Uncle Jas? Please...'

His returned his attention to the smaller, fatter version of Stevie. Jas grinned, plucked the ball from under one crooked arm and began to run. 'Ever considered rugby?'

Dismissive snort from behind. 'Rugby's an English game. C'mon, Uncle Jas... pass it tae me...'

He continued to run, circling the training area and only pausing when Sam's weight overcame his enthusiasm. Pausing by a tree, Jas let the eight year-old catch up. The vantage point was good...

He glanced to the Fraser/trainer huddle.

... and they could be back at the car quickly, should Fraser leave unexpectedly. 'Okay, fitba' it is...' He dropped the ball, controlled it with the side of his foot then gently nudged it Samwards.

'Where's the goals?' Panting enquiry.

'Nae goals, fur the moment...' Jas took off his jacket, sat it beside the tree. '... gonny practice yer ball-control skills...' He nodded to the traffic cones. '... like the big boays dae, eh?' Moving out from the shade, he nodded towards the football. 'Ah'll tackle you, then you tackle me, okay?'

Sam was on the ball in seconds.

Jas grinned, one eye on the approaching figure, the other over the top of the small head to the real object of this morning's exercise.

As they played, he took in more. A blue van sat beside Fraser's Isuzu. The legend Bridgeton Boys' Club painted in white, on the side.

Blue.

And white.

Jas knew, from the file, that Eric Fraser was the proud owner of a Rangers' life season ticket. He also knew both Glasgow Rangers and Celtic sponsored under-eighteens teams, the players scouted from local amateur and school clubs to be groomed for the adult league.

Fifteen minutes later, Sam was starting to flag.

They swapped over.

The eleven-odd teenagers were now gathered around the shortish man in the Umbro warm-up suit, who was handing out orange-quarters. The sight made him smile.

Amidst the corporate sponsorship and multi-million pound transfer fees, some things never changed.

'Can ah go get juice from the car, Uncle Jas?'

He pulled his eyes from where Eric Fraser was now talking to the tall boy with the bleached hair who had returned Sam's errant ball.

The eight-year-old face was pink with effort. He grinned. 'Aye – an' bring me wan tae, eh?'

Sweaty, enthusiastic nod.

Resting hands on knees, he watched the small figure half-run, half-stumble in the direction of Donald's Astra. Jas straightened up and strolled back to his jacket. He was just lighting up when:

'They things'll kill yer lungs.'

Jas raised his head.

The shortish man in the washed-out warm-up suit stood a few feet away, holding orange quarters in the palm of his hand. 'Not tae mention the example ye're settin' the boay.'

The reprimand was friendly, semi-joking. But the words hit the mark. Jas stuck the cigarette back into the packet. 'Ye're right, pal...' He remembered why he was here, stuck out a hand. 'Jas Anderson.'

The hand taken, gripped firmly. 'Malcolm Orr – Malkie.' Fingers released.

He stored the identification away for later. 'Makin' ye work, ur they?' He nodded to where ten-odd teenagers were now doing burpees. Eric Fraser was still talking to the eleventh, bleach-haired boy.

The nod followed. 'They're guid lads, but. Says a loat fur 'em that they'll show up, this hour oan a Setturday mornin' ' Eyes back to his.

Jas took in the open, hearty face. Veins broken through weather exposure rather than drink criss-crossed pink, healthy cheeks. 'Aye, it's no' ma first choice either.'

A laugh. An orange quarter held out. 'Bin watchin' the two o' yous.'

Jas took it.

A smile. 'A lotta faithers widney take the time tae...'

'Got 'em, Uncle Jas!' A small, chubby bullet shot between them, cans of Irn Bru clutched against chest.

The trainer laughed. 'An' here's the boay himself.' He sank to a crouch. 'That wis some fine tacklin' ye wur doin' there, pal. Whit's yer name – Jon Johansson?'

Giggle. 'Naw – Sam McStay!'

Orr eyed the cans of Irn Bru. 'See ma bag over there, Sam?' Stubby fingers past the small shoulder to the sideline.

'Aye…'

'Well, go look in' at ye'll find somethin' better tae drink.' Smile.

'Cool!' Then eyes to Jas. Enthusiasm tempered. 'Is it okay?'

He grinned. 'Aye, oan ye go…' He watched Sam tear off towards a large hold-all.

Malcolm Orr stood up, turned.

Jas pre-empted another lecture. 'Ah've… no' bin at this kid-thing long…' He picked up the discarded Irn Bru cans, sat them beside his jacket.

'Yer partner's boay?'

The easy use of the term surprised him. And the change of tone. Jas straightened up. His surprise noted.

Orr nodded to where the team were now running on the spot. 'Hardly a kid there that's no' goat an uncle or a new mum.' No judgement in the voice. 'Far as ah'm concerned, parentin's doon tae carin', no' genes.' Encouraging grin. 'An' you're doin' fine, pal.'

The presumption made him smile. The compliment tugged a guilt-string. Jas pushed it away. 'Aye, well… ah dae whit ah can.' He sucked on his orange-quarter.

Nod. 'The boay could dae a lot worse than git intae trainin' seriously.' Malcolm Orr moved to the tree, leant again it. 'See Gary there?'

Jas followed an Umbro-ed arm to the tall, bleach-haired boy who was now grinning at the head of E Division.

'That's Mr Fraser talkin' tae him. Dis a bitta scoutin' fur the Club. We're hopin' he can git Gary a try-oot fur Rangers' youth team, next January. A year wi' them – if he keeps playin' like he did last season – an' there's a guid chance he could git picked fur the squad.' Pride in the voice.

On the end of two stares, bleach-haired Gary was now executing a series of trick-kicks. Sam stood a yard away, spellbound.

Orr talked on. 'But whether he gits it or no', trainin's bin the makin' o' Gary. Gies him a goal – somethin' tae work towards... somethin' other than the drugs or the booze.'

The Glasgow obsession with football left him cold but he knew the truth in the words. 'Wi' Sam it's the computer – canny drag him away fae it.'

Orr turned. 'Listen: ah run a session fur under-elevens, Setturday afternoons up at Bridgeton Community Centre. Sam's...?'

'Eight.'

Orr levered himself off the tree and began to walk back towards where Eric Fraser was now chatting to other boys.

Jas flinched, grabbed his jacket and fumbled with the Irn Bru cans.

'... two o'clock, the community centre. Git him away fae his computer games, eh?'

Before he could find an excuse to leave, a small chubby figure was racing towards them.

Malcolm Orr repeated the offer to Sam.

Eyes lit up. 'Can ah, Uncle Jas? Can ah?'

Jas hesitated.

Orr spoke for him. 'Better ask yer mum first, eh son?'

Vigorous nodding. 'Can we dae that, Uncle Jas? Can we ask mum?'

On the edge of his vision, Eric Fraser was walking with the bleach-haired boy back towards the Isuzu. Two pairs of eyes in their direction.

Jas lowered his face to Sam's. 'We'll see...'

Two shouts resounded across the Green. 'Ah'll run him home, eh Malkie?'

'Seeya, Mr Orr...'

'Aye, Tuesday night, Gaz – an' watch that knee.'

'Ah wull, Mr Orr.'

Sam was tugging at his arm again. 'Can we go ask mum noo, Uncle Jas? Please?'

He took the opportunity. 'Aye, okay Sam.' Jas looked back to where Malkie Orr was watching the bleach-haired boy swing his sports bag into the back of Fraser's Isuzu. 'Bridgeton Community Centre, ye said?'

A hand into the pocket of the Umbro pants. Wad of cards produced. Orr flicked one from beneath the elastic band. 'This is ma number – the boy's mother can gimme a ring, if she wants to check me oot.' Good-natured grin. Card extended.

Jas took it. 'Thanks.' Name, address and phone number. He hadn't needed the camera anyway.

'Okay, okay...' Voice raised. 'Jim an' Kev – pick up the cones. Ashley and Gordon? Get the keys from ma bag an' open up the van.' Orr's attention was back on his charges...

Jas ushered Sam and the ball back towards the Astra.

... partly. 'Ah hope yer partner says aye, Mr Anderson. The boay could be good. Bye, Sam!' One hand raised in salute, Orr strolled towards the ten-odd teenagers.

Jas watched him as they walked back to the car. Regardless of his own reservations on the merits of football, Orr seemed to be doing a good job with the motley selection of teenagers. That fact said more about the man himself than a game with sectarian allegiances which split Glasgow right down the middle.

'Mr Orr said ah could be guid – ye hear that, Uncle Jas?'

Back in Donald's Astra, Jas nodded and buckled the seat belt around a now-effusive figure:

'Can we go home an' ask mum? Can we?'

He stuck the key into the ignition, watching the tail of Fraser's Isuzu disappear round into Landresssy Street. The morning's work had been quite productive: Tom Galbraith wouldn't grudge him the break. 'Aye, we'll go straight hame.'

'Cool!'

Jas grinned, continuing to do so over an enthusiastic babble all the way back to Cumbernauld Road. The grin only slipped when he saw the red Fiesta parked outside 247.

The empty red Fiesta.

Fourteen

She was blonde...

'Mum, mum – we played football!'

... younger than he'd expected...

'Mr Orr said ah was guid – said ah could come and practise with his team!'

... had her daughter's hair, her son's nose...

'Can ah go, mum? it's a... Saturday afternoon.'

... and stood in the living room of his flat, looking at him with a stranger's eyes while her son continued to hold his hand.

'Two o'clock, eh Uncle Jas?'

He eased his fingers from a smaller grip and met Maureen McStay's stare.

His territory.

His domain.

'Can ah, mum? Can ah – aw' go on...'

Sam continued to babble on about their morning, where they'd been and what they'd done. Beyond his estranged wife's slender form, Stevie's face was a mask of discomfort and confusion:

'Er... Mo, this is Jas – Jas Anderson. Jas, this is...' The attempt at introductions tailed off into awkwardness.

He stood there and let her scrutinise him, wondering why she'd chosen today to engineer an encounter.

Maureen McStay had been back in Glasgow six months. Six months of opportunities to inspect the man with whom her husband was now living. Why now? Why, full stop?

'Mr Orr said ye can phone him, if ye want, mum…'

'We'll see, son.'

'Oh cool…' A whoop of enthusiasm. '… can ah play on the computer, Uncle Jas?'

'Aye, on ye go.' He held her gaze. In the background, the sound of small trainered feet bounding from the room. He wondered how she felt about the 'uncle' title. He wondered how she felt about any of it.

Maureen McStay broke the stare and turned to Stevie. 'If ye couldn't look after him, ye only had to say.'

The twist behind the remark stopped him wondering. Stevie's blunt face reddened. 'The boay wis fine wi' Jas.'

'Ah don't want him with… strangers.'

'Jas isney a stranger! He's guid wi' them an'…'

'Ah need to know my son's safe. Ah need to know where he is, who he's with. Ah need to…'

She needed to score points where and however she could. He could understand that all too well. Jas took a step towards the door. But he didn't have to watch her manipulate an already guilt-ridden Stevie. As husband and wife continued the ritual torment, he walked through to the bedroom and closed the door.

Sam beat him twice at Worm before Hayley arrived and took over. Jas watched them do battle, waited for the front door to open and close again before returning to the scene of a less amicable encounter.

'It's still there.' Stevie stood in front of the window, gazing down into the communal back-court.

Jas leant against the sill, following a pair of narrowed amber eyes to the Portacabin. 'An' it's probably jist whit it looks like: work oan the telephone lines.' Maureen McStay's bitter, resentful voice circled in his head.

'It's an affy coincidence.' Unconvinced growl.

Jas frowned. 'Ye've had Welfare here – yer...' He could hardly say the word aloud. '... wife's bin in tae check me oot in person. Why keep a dog an' bark yerself?'

The ponytailed head swivelled round. Eyes amber slits.

'Why would she pay good money tae some private investigator when she can walk in here any time she likes and see fur herself whit the set-up is?' He tried to keep his voice even...

Confused amber slits.

... and failed. Jas slipped one hand beneath the ponytail and rubbed the back of Stevie's neck. 'Sometimes a Portacabin is jist a Portacabin...' Over a broad shoulder, he watched a small, nondescript man in an acid yellow hazard-jacket emerge from the structure and walk briskly towards the side of the tenement. '... eh?' He refocused on the amber slits.

Gradually, they widened out. The deep furrows on Stevie's fore-head followed suit. Then: 'It wis guid ye took Sam tae play fitba'...' The shadow of a smile. '... ye'll never git rid o' him noo.'

It was a relief to laugh. Jas slid his hand upwards, cradling Stevie's head then ruffling it playfully. He didn't ask how the meeting with Firestone had gone. There would be other times. Other opportunities when Stevie's frame of mind was not as finely balanced. 'You eaten?'

Headshake.

'Me neither. Wanna bung somethin' in the micro while ah type up some stuff?'

An obliging nod.

Jas stared at the side of the blunt, semi-relaxed face and wanted to kiss it. But this wasn't about sex. This was about keeping Stevie on an even keel. A large palm settled on his right shoulder. Fingers squeezed:

'Ah still think that Portacabin guy's up tae somethin', but ah take yer point.' The hand removed itself. 'Okay, you pair – nosh time!' Then Stevie was moving towards the freezer and Jas headed for the PC.

*

An hour later he'd committed that day's observations to hard copy and consumed something bland but filling. The kids were back on the PC. The man himself was snoring lightly in front of the tv. It was half past four.

Jas lifted the telephone receiver, left a message with Tom's answering service for the Greek at eight. He watched Stevie sleep until it was time to leave.

The sun hovered above the Kingston Bridge when he arrived at Habitat. Four cigarettes later it was sinking behind the Albany Hotel. Jas scanned the streets below for the green Proton and lit a fifth.

An hour later, a black cab disgorged the familiar figure in sports jacket plus pipe on the other side of a dusky Wellington Street. The expression on Tom's face was less familiar. Jas moved back into shadow and listened for the sound of footfall on concrete steps.

'The radio, my briefcase with all your notes and photographs – plus one of Nick's precious jackets…' Tom's teeth clamped around the pipe stem as he re-lit. '… all from E Division's car park. It would be funny if it wasn't so irritating.' One hand waved the lighter's flame above the pipe bowl. 'Still, the car's with SOCO so there's always the chance they'll catch the buggers.'

Car-crime was rife all over the city. Jas didn't hold out much hope but he nodded anyway. 'Ah can dae ye copies of everythin' that got nicked – an' the negatives are around somewhere.'

Tom inhaled deeply. 'I'll never hear the end of that damn jacket.'

The fragrant smell filled Jas's head. He laughed. 'Claim it back on expenses.'

A sigh. 'Apparently, it was something special – designer, sentimental value, something like that.'

'Nick'll get over it.' Jas watched the glow of smouldering tobacco in the near darkness.

'Hmmm...' Doubtful. '... anyway, sorry I'm late – it's going to be taxis for the next couple of days, I think.' Back in business mode. 'What have you got for me on Fraser?'

Jas pulled himself from the smell of the man and held out a folder. He briefly summarised that day's activities.

Tom listened and nodded. 'Orr... Orr...'

'Mean somethin'?'

Light from a window in the Albany Hotel illuminated the side of the tired face. 'Vaguely familiar – he runs a football club for kids?'

'Feeder club for Rangers – Fraser's a season-ticket holder an' obviously a fan.'

More nodding.

Jas leant against a breeze-block wall. 'Seemed okay.' He smiled, remembering Orr's easy manner with eight-year-old Sam.

'I'll run him through the PNC, see what comes up. Anything else?'

Jas detailed Eric Fraser's brief conversation with the platinum-haired boy. 'Gary somethin'. Orr's Great White Hope. He looked about fifteen. If Fraser's keen enough to have a season-ticket, he's keen enough to take a special interest in a potential home-grown striker.'

Tom smiled. 'It would make a change to have someone in the team with a name the fans can pronounce.'

Jas laughed. 'That's aboot it, then – want me tae keep tailin' Fraser?'

'Ease off for the next couple of days – he's station-bound till the end of the week. Meet me back here...' Tom turned, tapped the bowl of his pipe against the top of the breeze-block wall.

He watched the movement, eyes drawn to the strong profile in the dying light.

'... Friday morning, seven?' Tom tapped the pipe bowl a final time and turned back to face him.

Faint smokiness wrapped itself around the words.

'That okay for you? We can make it later if...'

'Naw naw – seven's fine.' Jas blinked in the dusk. 'Still think yer phone's tapped?' He tried a laugh to distract himself from the pull of the man.

'Let's just say I don't want to take any unnecessary chances.' The words were sober, serious. 'The less E Division and Eric Fraser know at this stage, the better.' Tom slipped the pipe back into the pocket of his sports jacket. Eyes focused beyond the edge of Habitat's roof to the city below. 'He's not twigged to you?'

'No' as far as ah'm aware.' Jas followed the eyes.

Brief nod. 'Good...' Tucking the folder under one arm, Tom Galbraith refocused on Jas. '... let me leave first – just in case.'

Coded telephone messages. Secret meetings at their special place. Nocturnal assignations. For the first time he could imagine the appeal of affairs. Jas smiled in spite of himself. 'On ye go, Sexton Blake!' His hand was on the man's arm before he knew what he was doing.

Just a pat.

A fraternal slap.

One friend to another.

He exerted the briefest of pressures.

Tom laughed at the reference. 'See you, then.'

And his palm was pressing air, his eyes watching an outline move through the darkness and disappear down concrete steps to the street below.

He never got around to asking how the meeting with Firestone had gone. Stevie was spending more and more time at Carole's. And when he did deign to return to the Cumbernauld Road flat, the amber eyes glowed with warning lights. Only a couple of days of the two-week holiday remained, and viewing more flats wasn't mentioned.

Jas took the opportunity to catch up on paperwork and obtain duplicates of the photographs and documents stolen from Tom's car. He still bought the *Times* on Thursday afternoon out of habit. The headline stopped him flicking straight to the property section:

'Third Serious Assault at Gartloch – Police Fear Homophobic Motive'.

He read the article twice, noting the warning issued to the gay community – by Superintendent Eric Fraser – to be on their guard. Since when had the area around the loch been a cruising ground? He was getting out of touch.

Thursday night, he was printing out invoices when Stevie got in. Late. 'You eaten?' Jas craned his neck into the hall. The bulk of their communications had been about food, recently.

No response.

He got up from the screen, rotating his shoulders and walking through to the other room.

Stevie stood in darkness, staring down at the vague outline of the Portacabin.

Jas paused in the doorway. 'Did ye eat up at Carole's?' He noted the man's rigid shoulders and knew food was the least of Stevie's concerns. Jas frowned. 'Ye wanna go... oot an' get somethin'? Ah think the café's still open if...'

'Ah'm no' hungry.'

'Ye gotta eat, man.' He seized on the reaction, moving into the room. And he had to talk – at some point. To someone. Jas paused a foot behind the motionless figure. Tension radiated off the solid body in huge waves. 'C'mon, wance ye smell they chips ye'll...'

'Ah said ah'm no' hungry!' Stevie spun round and marched past him.

Jas remained at the window, listening to the sound of the shower.

Space.

Time.

He'd give both, if that was the way Stevie wanted it.

Half an hour later, Jas made up the sofabed. He had to be away early anyway. It would save disturbing someone who seemed to spend most of their time in his company asleep anyway.

But as he pulled the duvet up around his ears, his arms wrapped themselves around the pillow and he finally knew there were lonelier states than being on your own.

He was on Habitat's roof by 6.45 am.

Tom was already there, drinking from one polystyrene cup and holding another. A briefcase lay on the top of the breeze-block wall.

Jas smiled for the first time since their last meeting. 'Ah hope that's got ma name oan it.' He nodded to the cup.

Tom extended the coffee.

Jas took, de-lidded it and sipped. 'Our friend bin behavin' himself?'

A sigh. 'Bring you up to date on that later – let me tell you what I've got on Orr.'

He watched Tom drain his cup, then pick up the briefcase and open it:

'Detective Constable Malcolm Orr. Forty three. Single. Address 16 Green Street, Bridgeton.' Tom read from a sheaf of paper.

DC. A cop.

'Fifteen years in uniform, with D Division. This is his first in CID – transferred over to E Division, under the auspices of Eric Fraser, after a very long wait. Malcolm Orr was one of the many who was initially turned down for transfer.'

A cop. Using a friendship with another cop to obtain favours? Nothing new in that.

Tom continued. 'At present, he's on two weeks' leave. The main reason he wanted into CID, apparently, is for the better hours – gives him more consistency with the...' Eyes from the papers. '... Bridgeton Boys' Club in which, from your report, we already know Fraser has an interest.'

Jas nodded. 'Nothin' wrang in that either.' As with Allistair Gibson and his smooth passage from the Force to the Civil Service, Fraser was using his influence to provide rather than deny. 'Fitba' bonds in this city like ye widney believe.' He grinned. 'Specially if Orr's coaching the Gary-boay.'

Tom flicked over stapled sheets of paper with one hand, tugged at his moustache with the other.

The grin faded. 'Whit's botherin' ye then?'

'You've heard about the Easterhouse gay-bashings?' Soft grey eyes from the paper to his. 'Out where you took me, that night, as it happens.'

Jas blinked. 'Disney strike me as the safest area tae cruise in, but it's isolated, quiet...' He suddenly felt the desire to explain the appeal. And an equally strong urge to leave Tom to his preconceptions. '... aye, ah read aboot the most recent wan at least. Whit's yer point?' He tried to keep the defensiveness out of his voice, for the first time sympathising with young Nick Galbraith.

'The entire division's gone into overdrive – leave's been cancelled, Fraser's trying to secure an emergency overtime budget to get on top of these... incidents.'

Jas took a sip of his coffee. 'Makes a fuckin' change...' The liquid was cold – colder than the trail of most homophobes, as far as Strathclyde Police were usually concerned.

'That's my point. I get the impression this sudden zeal is mainly for my benefit – you know E Division badly needs to get their detection rate up.'

Jas frowned but nodded. 'Still, if it gets the bastards responsible, or even saves a coupla guys fae a kickin' ah widney complain if ah wis you.'

The nod returned. 'Wednesday night's victim's due to be released from hospital today – mainly bruises and a couple of broken ribs. But it's still more than the first victim. Don't know if Fraser's playing to the press or not, but phrases like 'an increase in violence' are getting bandied about. And there's also the implication that other victims are not coming forward.'

His frown deepened. Jas knew the appeal of anonymous sex all too well. No questions. No explanations. Too many wives, families, girlfriends, boyfriends or employers in the background. Even these days, the odd cut lip was nothing to the hurt exposure could cause.

They stood in silence for a while. He was getting good at this. Jas listened to the growing sounds of traffic on the nearby Kingston Bridge and waited for Tom to get round to whatever else was on his mind. After much moustache tugging and pipe-fiddling, it came:

'Nick and I had another argument.' A sigh.

He moved between the rising sun and the sober-faced man. 'Whit wis it aboot this time?'

Another sigh. 'This is somewhat... awkward.' A pause. A long pause. Finally: 'That jacket of his – the one that got pinched when the Proton was done over?'

He watched tobacco-stained fingers stroke the ends of the thick moustache. 'Nick kickin' aff aboot it still?'

Throat clearing. 'Apparently, your phone number was in the pocket.' Tom stared at the ground.

Jas blinked.

Eyes slowly raised. 'Presume he obtained it one of the times you phoned Albion Street...'

The pinkening skin across Tom Galbraith's cheeks mirrored the growing blush Jas could feel on his own face.

'... evidently, you made quite an impression.'

He tried a laugh he didn't feel. 'Ah didney think ah wis his type...' Or the type Tom would have chosen as the focus of his son's affections? '... an' onyway, ah'm spoken fur.' The joke fell flat.

Tom stared at him, face a confused, accusatory mask.

Jas squirmed. 'Man, it's a crush – teenagers huv 'em aw' the time.' Did he have to say he had no interest at all in seventeen-year-old Nicholas Galbraith? Did he have to admit that the father was much more his type than the son?

Tom rubbed his face. 'I know, I know...' Words from behind moving palms. '... it was just a bit of a...' Face reappearing. Relieved laugh.

He managed a smile. 'Next week it'll be a rock-singer wi' tattoos or some rugby player. Ye ken whit...' He was about to say 'what young queens are like', then remembered who he was talking to. '... it's like, at that age.' Male-female, female-female, male-male: it was all the same.

'To be honest, I don't – too long ago.' Tom was now pushing the Malcolm Orr report back into the folder.

Jas laughed. 'Aye, same wi' me.' He knew it wasn't true. Being with Tom Galbraith made his balls sweat and his guts clench, had nothing to do with reality and everything to do with the appeal of the unavailable. 'So ye want Fraser tailed over the weekend?' He pushed the topic on from things he could do nothing about to the one thing he could.

Nod. 'Until further notice, I think. Ring you next week. Should be mobile again – picking up a new car in...' Unnecessary glance at wrist. '... fifteen minutes. Speak to you later.'

The vagueness of the arrangement was a disappointment. Jas watched a sports-jacketed back jog down concrete steps. He moved to the edge of the roof, lighting a cigarette.

Tom Galbraith was hailing a taxi on the far side of Bothwell Street.

Jas continued to watch. By the time the cigarette had burnt down he'd barely drawn on it.

Back at the flat Stevie was still asleep. It was 9.30 am.

By ten Jas'd had breakfast and showered.

At quarter past the phone rang. He let the machine pick up, then lifted the receiver as a familiar voice failed to identify itself. The message was brief:

'Your flat is under surveillance.'

Jas listened to the disconnection tone, letting DI Ann McLeod's single sentence repeat itself in his head.

So much for paranoia.

So much for Portacabins.

Just before eleven am he walked to the window, sifting through options.

Three loud bangs at the door interrupted the process. Jas drew back the security chain and stared at four uniformed officers and one plain clothed:

'Steven McStay?'

Jas blinked.

The plain-clothed officer stared at him. 'Are you Steven McStay?'

'Who wants tae ken?' Sleepy voice from the bedroom.

'We need you to come down to Easterhouse Police station, Mr McStay...' The plain clothed officer breezed past Jas, dragging the uniforms in his wake.

'Whit?' Panic tinged the sleepiness.

'Jist a wee chat, Mr McStay. Won't keep ye long...'

'Whit's this aw' aboot?' Jas looked at the uniforms, talking to the suit. Déjà vu from years ago filled his head.

The suit turned. 'And you ur?'

Jas sighed.

Fifteen

Procedure.

Protocol.

Par for the course.

'McStay – Steven McStay. He wis brought in...' Jas looked at his watch and cursed Donald's unreliable Astra. '... half an oor ago.'

On the other side of Easterhouse Police station's reinforced glass partition, the duty officer barely raised his eyes. 'Take a seat, sir.'

'Whit's he bein' questioned in connection wi'?' Even after years, the language was there like a mother tongue. Jas gripped his side of the reception counter.

'Ah canny tell ye that at this point, sir. If ye wanna wait fur him, take a seat.'

Jas frowned. 'He... goat legal representation?'

A sigh. Eyes finally raised. 'He's jist bein' questioned. If and when he's charged, he'll be informed o' his rights.'

He stared into a bored face. 'Will ye tell him ah'm here? James Anderson?'

Practised eyes met and returned his gaze. 'If ye wanna wait fur him, take a seat over there, Mr Anderson.' The head relowered itself, eyes returning to contemplate the *Record*'s racing pages.

His fingers tightened on the cold formica counter. Jas regarded the duty officer's balding pate then took the advice and walked towards a row of moulded, bolted-to-the-floor chairs.

To his right, the buzz of a controlled entry opening.

The sound punctuated the next hour.

People came.

People went.

A woman in a Puffa jacket enquired about her man, shouted at the duty officer then stormed out.

Jas sympathised with the reaction.

Another woman, this one crying, was escorted through the controlled entry door into the main body of the station by a plain-clothed female officer.

Jas looked away from the sobbing form.

Phones rang. Some were ignored, some answered.

Jas leant back in his seat.

Questioning could take anything from one to sixteen hours. With permission from the Fiscal, an extension could take it to thirty-two. Only with formal charging came the rights: to a phone call, legal representation, medical attention. Until then, Stevie was in limbo.

Time passed.

Jas stood up, walked around the small space. He read posters proclaiming Zero Tolerance and tried to find some of his own. He walked over to the reinforced glass. 'Whit's happenin' noo?'

Bored eyes raised. 'An' you are, sir?'

Jas went through it all again. And received the same response. He sat back down beside an old man who talked constantly to himself.

Jas knew how he felt.

An hour later, they were joined by two teenagers and a dog with a rope around its neck. The buzzing and the phones continued. When the outside door opened they all looked towards it for something to do.

Jas met and held the stare of a surprised pair of grey eyes, looked away and listened to the sound of Tom Galbraith's shoes on the scarred concrete floor:

'Afternoon, Len!'

'Inspector Galbraith...' More buzzing.

Part of him wanted to collar and interrogate his one friendly contact beyond that security door. A larger part knew Tom had to ignore him.

Two uniforms appeared and took the dog from the teenagers, who tagged after it. The sobbing woman re-emerged, talked softly to the mumbling old man. They both left.

Jas kept his eyes off his watch and his mind away from worst case scenarios. His thoughts filled with images of Stevie, scared and explosive, somewhere behind all the buzzing and reinforced glass.

'Mr Anderson?'

He leapt from his seat. 'Can ah see Stevie McStay?'

The eyes answered his question. 'Why don't ye go home? Ye can phone, see how things are.'

Jas stared at the face, noting a change in the voice. 'Naw, ah'll wait.'

'Could be a while, sir.'

He nodded. 'Ah'll wait anyway.' He sat down again.

Over the next two hours, he stopped registering the flotsam and jetsam which drifted in and out of the station. He ignored everything except the phone at the duty officer's elbow. He asked twice if he could see Steven McStay, three times if the desk sergeant could let Steven McStay know he was here. All five responses were negative.

For the first time he knew how it felt to be on the other side of the fence. Anonymous. Depersonalised. Just one more faceless member of the public enquiring after another.

It was 4.30 when the phone rang.

Jas stared at the scarred stone floor, worn down by thousands of feet over the years. Then:

'Mr Anderson?'

He raised his head, ready to insist he didn't want to go home and would wait as long as it took.

The duty officer's eyes were almost human. 'Message fur ye. Mr McStay says the... kids'll be turnin' up at the flat at five an' somewan has tae be there tae get them.'

Jas eased himself onto cramping legs and walked to the counter. 'Ony idea how much longer he'll be?'

'Phone when ye get home.'

'Is there a case number?'

A sigh. 'He's jist in fur questionin', Mr Anderson. Nae case number yet.' The duty officer looked almost sympathetic.

Jas half-wondered what had happened to soften the professionalism. Then he remembered the kids and stopped wondering. 'Thanks...' He peered through toughened glass at the ID tag on the front of the man's starched white shirt. '... Sergeant Matheson.'

'It'll no' be much longer, ah'm sure...' The gesture appreciated. '... ye can come an' collect him when it's aw' over.'

Jas managed a smile. As he turned and walked out though the door he'd entered five hours earlier, he remembered depersonalisation worked both ways.

The Astra sat in the visitors' car park. He pulled the keys from a pocket.

Sounds from the adjacent parking area cut through thoughts of Sam and Hayley and what he was going to tell them.

Jas's head swivelled. He kept walking.

Standing amidst squad cars and police vans, three figures – two in uniform, one in sports jacket.

Jas followed Tom Gabraith's eyes to what was left of the new hire car.

The younger of two uniformed officers was kicking pointlessly at one of four deflated tyres. Across the right hand side of the Ford Granada, still-wet paint read:

'Fenian Bastard Go Home.'

'Local yobs, sir...' The voice of the older uniform. '... ye shoulda parked it somewhere safer.'

How much safer could you get than outside a police station? Jas turned his head away, stuck the key in the Astra's lock and thought about yobs who liked a challenge. As he drove away, the nature of the graffiti tugged at his brain.

But it wasn't his problem. Not at the moment.

'Where's ma dad?'

'He'll be back soon.' Jas replaced the receiver and tried a smile.

'Ye said that before.'

'Want juice?' He got up from one of the sofabeds and walked to the fridge.

'Where is he?' Hayley followed.

'Ah telt ye – he'll be back soon...' He opened the fridge, fumbled for a can of Coke.

'Aye, but where is he?'

Jas held out the can.

Hayley McStay ignored it. 'Is he with ma mum?'

For the first time since Maureen's return to Glasgow, Jas wished Stevie was. He closed the fridge and walked through to where Sam was playing happily on the PC. 'Onywan hungry?'

Beeps from the PC.

Jas stood behind the small blond figure and watched a worm consume another dot.

'Is ma dad back at his work?'

He had no idea what to say. 'Wanna go tae the video shop?' Jas looked at Hayley McStay's suspicious face:

'You takin' us?'

He wondered what had happened the last time. He wondered what Stevie's children had made of his last arrest. Jas tried another smile. 'Ah canny – ah gotta wait here till yer dad phones.'

'He said he'd phone?' Brightening.

He nodded. 'Aye, he said he'd phone when he's comin' home.' Jas watched the eleven-year-old fiddle with a strand of blonde hair. He ran a hand over his own straggling scalp and pulled his thoughts from two questioning sessions which could last the weekend. Stevie's he could do nothing about.

His daughter's?

Jas smiled. 'Ah'm gonny wash ma hair – wanna dry it fur me?'

Blank look.

He elaborated. 'Style it, ah mean.'

A critical gaze over his head. 'Ye're no' goat enough length tae style.'

'Can ye dae onythin' wi' it?' Jas bent his neck and feigned frustration.

A genuine sigh. 'Ah'm no' promisin' nothin, but ah'll do ma best.' A small hand through an inch and a half of dirty blond.

Jas smiled at the carpet, then raised his head. 'You go through an' get yer... combs and clips while ah shove it under the shower, okay?'

'Ye want conditioner?' Her father's absence had not been mentioned for at least ten minutes.

Jas nodded. 'Wanna wash it fur me tae?'

The eleven-year-old girl folded her arms. 'Ye should eyeways use conditioner.'

He looked suitably penitent, then let her guide him towards the shower.

At eight pm he sat on a chair while she dried his hair flat.

By nine she'd tried two side partings, a French crop and gelled spikes.

By ten she'd washed it again and Sam was joining in.

By half past they were both yawning and wandering towards the sofa-beds.

His hair had never been as clean. He turned off the light and pulled the phone through to the bedroom. Jas switched off the PC and sat on the bed. He stared at the phone for the next hour and a half.

When it finally rang every nerve in his body jangled.

*

'Aw' Jas-man, they…'

'Where ur ye?'

'Jas-man, they asked…'

'Where ur ye, Stevie?'

'At the polis station – the guy behind the desk let me use the…'

'They let ye go?'

'Aye, Jas-man, they…'

'Ah'll come an pick ye up. Don't move.'

'Jas-man, whit's happenin? Why did they…?'

'Jist… don't move – ah'll be there before ye know it.' He forced himself to hang up, leapt off the bed and grabbed the keys to the Astra.

As he moved into the hall, two tiny obstacles to his action re-entered his mind. Jas edged the living-room door open a little.

In the half light, two faces relaxed in sleep.

Three options. He could wake them, take them with him…

Stability.

… he could phone Carole…

Consistency.

… or he could phone Maureen McStay and let her pick them up.

Stability. Consistency.

Jas stared at the tiny sleeping forms. Regardless of what ammunition knowledge of her estranged husband's arrest could provide in the ongoing custody battle, Maureen McStay was still their mother.

He closed the living-room door quietly and walked back through to the bedroom.

The number rang fifteen times before he disconnected.

Part of him wondered where Maureen McStay was at midnight on a Friday while another part of him punched in Stevie's sister's number.

Carole's man answered on the second ring, passed him over to a laughing Carole. Who quickly sobered.

Jas waited at the window for her taxi, then ran down three flights of stairs to the Astra.

*

Easterhouse police station was a different place at night.

Two vans screeched from the car park. Opposite the custody entrance, a third was disgorging its shouting, sportswear-clad contents into the waiting arms of four silent, uniformed officers. The place was bathed in blue/white flashes, full of noise and exhaust fumes. Jas parked beyond the gates, scanning the chaos for Stevie.

Crouched against a wall in front of a Disabled parking space, he spotted him.

Jas skirted an argument between a pair of drunks and two young kids, made his way towards the crouching, smoking figure. 'C'mon – ah've got the car.' He stared at the top of a ponytailed head.

Stevie's eyes focused straight ahead, cigarette pinched between thumb and forefinger.

His hand reached out to the tangled hair, paused then dropped. 'C'mon – before they change their minds.' Something like a laugh began in his throat but died before reaching his lips. 'Stevie?'

The head slowly raised itself. 'Whit you doin' here?'

'You phoned me, 'member?' He sank onto his hunkers. 'We're goin' home noo, Stevie...' Talking to another child. '... c'mon, the...' A door opened behind.

'Mo?' Amber eyes glinted past his towards the Public entrance.

Jas stared.

Stevie was on his feet. 'Hey, Mo... sorry fur draggin' ye oot in the middle o' the night, hen.' And moving.

Jas heaved himself upright.

Flanked by two uniforms, a slender blonde figure moved towards a waiting squad car.

Maureen McStay's absence from home at midnight on a Friday explained itself. The reason?

'Thanks fur tellin' them, Mo-hen...' Stevie bobbed around in front of the trio, which kept walking. '... thanks fur the alibi. If it wisney fur you ah'd still be in there.'

Maureen McStay said something in a low voice to one of the uniforms.

He nodded to his companion. They both moved a little away as the slight blonde woman turned to Stevie:

'Ah told them nothin'. Wherever you were that night, it wisney with me.' Word low and icy.

He watched Stevie's expression freeze.

Formal words. 'Ah have no recollection of bein' with you the night that... guy wis attacked.' Maureen McStay's face was a mask.

Silence. Then:

'But ah wis! Ye ken ah wis! Ah met ye fae work – we went fur a meal, 'member? Then back tae your place an'...'

'Go home, sir.' One of the uniforms was advancing on Stevie.

Jas did likewise. He grabbed a thick bare arm.

It wrenched itself free. 'Tell 'em, Mo – tell 'em ah wis wi' you!' Stevie's shouts were increasing. 'Please, hen – ye ken it's the truth. Ah...'

Jas grabbed Stevie again, both arms this time. 'Easy, easy...' Over the top of a tossing tangled head, he nodded to one of the uniforms, who steered Maureen McStay towards the waiting car.

Stevie's head followed them. 'Mo!'

'Calm doon...' In the half-dark, his lips brushed Stevie's ear. '... the polis didney keep ye the full time they could, an' ye wurney charged, so this is jist routine.' He continued to talk, feeling the tension from rigid muscle quiver against his hands. 'Come on... come on... take it easy...' He turned the man towards him, watching over Stevie's shoulder as the squad car left the car park.

Beyond both, Tom Galbraith's vandalised car was now surrounded by red/white SOCO tape.

Jas gripped Stevie's wrist and steered him over to the Astra.

The twenty-minute journey took ten.

The roads were quiet.

His passenger was quieter still.

Back at the flat, Sam and Hayley threw themselves on Stevie's legs. Carole McStay's knowing eyes pinned him. 'Ah'll take them home wi' me the night – you pair better sort yerselves oot.'

Jas nodded, phoned her a taxi. Stevie stood zombie-like.

When they left, he undressed the silent man, guided him towards the bed. As Stevie's head hit the pillow, their eyes met:

'They asked aboot Dalgleish, Jas-man: they asked aboot...'

'Shh...' A cold mist settled on his skin. '... go tae sleep...' He pushed tangles of brown hair back from the ashen face, moving onto the bed beside Stevie. '... we'll talk aboot it tomorrow.'

Amber eyes closed. Stevie turned onto his side, arms around Jas's waist.

He sat there, stroking the tangly head until the breathing slowed to a more even pace. When he was sure Stevie was asleep, Jas eased away and walked to the window.

It was just before two am. He stared out into a dark back-court, searching for the outline of a Portacabin.

Ann's single-sentence phone call.

Tom Galbraith's just a precaution.

The cold mist solidified into a frost of panic. He was still staring into darkness when the phone rang in the other room. His shin banged off one of the sofabeds as he moved quickly towards it. 'Anderson Investigations?'

'I'm on the mobile.'

Just a precaution now worked both ways. He was out of touch with surveillance techniques, but if the Portacabin contained long-range listening devices...

'You there, Jas?'

'Aye, sorry.'

'Thought you'd still be up. Just though you should know everyone with a record of any kind of... homophobic violence is being hauled in for questioning...'

The surprise in Tom's voice mirrored the nagging in his own mind. But at least he now knew why Stevie had been hauled in.

'... he's just another name on a list. Routine – nothing to worry about, I'm sure.'

The emergence of Ian Dalgleish's name in the process of just another routine interview was everything to worry about.

'The police are now convinced the attacks are the work of the same person or persons – certain details have been kept from the press, for fear of copy-catting, but there's a definite pattern. And two other blokes have come forward, who didn't report attacks at the time...'

Jas listened to Tom talk round questions to which the CIB officer really wanted answers.

Why wasn't I told Stevie had a record?

Why wasn't I told Stevie has served time?

What is a gay man doing living with a convicted gay-basher?

'... but they have to go through the motions, elimination et cetera...'

'Aye, ah know.' What did he know? His flat was under surveillance? He was being paid to keep Eric Fraser under surveillance? Eric Fraser, who was heading the Gartloch Bashings investigation?

Ian Dalgleish, the Portacabin and Ann's brief words danced together in his mind. Of all three, the first was the biggest problem.

The unsolved murder/vehicular manslaughter of Prison Officer Ian Dalgleish was just another statistic...

'Anyway, just wanted to check – you're still on for tomorrow?'

... a statistic on a detection chart of a division out to impress a visiting CIB officer? 'Aye, still on.' Dalgleish was a sleeping dog, suddenly awoken, whose bark he couldn't silence. And whose name he could not mention. 'Night, Tom.'

Surprise. 'Er... ni –'

He disconnected and continued to hold the receiver. He was just about to pull the phone-jack from the socket when it rang again. The early hours had turned out to be his busiest time. Jas raised the receiver. 'Aye?'

'Get yourself a mobile.'

The same, unidentified voice which had told him of the surveillance now confirmed what he'd suspected. Jas made a mental note of further favours owed to DI Ann McLeod and pulled the phone from its socket.

Ten minutes later he set the alarm for seven and crawled in beside a tossing-and-turning shape. Jas curled around Stevie's back and waited for sleep to claim him.

Sixteen

At 8.30 on Saturday morning he bought a Talk and Go cell-phone and twenty quids' worth of top-up cards from a supermarket in Dumbarton Road.

He was outside the Broomhill Drive address by nine am.

By ten he'd managed to switch the phone on and make sense of the codes. By half past he'd gone through his choice of ring-options, left his new number with Tom's answering service and played around with his own. Remembering Stevie, he almost phoned the Cumbernauld Road flat. Then remembered the Portacabin and the reason he'd had to buy the damn mobile in the first place.

At 11.05 Eric Fraser and his wife left the Broomhill Drive address and drove to B&Q. The garden had to be awash with strawberry netting already. Jas followed the Isuzu back to Broomhill. Then on to an address in Milngavie. Both Frasers left the car. Jas photographed their embrace by a couple of similar age. The woman had Lila's jaw.

At 1.15 pm Eric Fraser emerged alone and drove onto the motor-way.

Jas kept the Astra three cars behind, watching exits for city centre, Townhead then Dennistoun flick past. The turnoffs for Provan, Easterhouse and Ballieston also came and went. Twenty minutes later they hit the outskirts of Larkhall.

Union Jacks flapped from the upper-storey windows of rundown maisonettes. Red, white and blue bunting waved between lampposts along the main street.

Mid-July. Marching-season was well underway.

Jas looked from where a flute band was unloading itself from two coaches in the car park of a modern-looking church. His eyes re-trained on the Isuzu's rear number plate.

Fraser drove through Larkhall, turning right towards a dilapidated-looking sports ground.

Jas followed.

At one end, adjacent to a half-full seating area, a familiar blue mini-van. On the grass in front, a shortish man stood before twelve crossed-legged teenagers. Amongst their number, a platinum head caught light from mid afternoon sun.

At the other end of the playing field, a mirror image, minus star-player Gary.

Malcolm Orr's team were playing away.

Eric Fraser pulled in beside the Bridgeton Boys' Club van.

Jas slowed but kept moving. He edged the Astra round to the far side of the football pitch, parking as far away from the van and Fraser's Isuzu as possible. As he turned off the ignition and stared over his shoulder through the rear window, the camera caught his eye.

DC Malcolm Orr knew him as a part-time father. He had no idea what Jas did for a living. Local teams were always starved of publicity...

Grabbing the expensive Nikon from the back seat, Jas slung it around his neck and got out of the car.

... and he was a freelance photographer – of sorts. Locking the Astra and walking round to the other side of the football pitch, Jas hoped maybe actual lying would not be necessary...

'Oi! Mr Anderson?' Malkie Orr's gravel tones soared across the pitch,

... then cancelled the hope. Jas pinned a smile to his face and turned.

Orr jogged over, rubbing his hands together. 'Sam no' wi' ye the day?'

'No' the day...' His eyes roved over the stands behind the solidly built trainer, locating Eric Fraser at the far side. The head of E Division was in close conversation with a greasy-haired man in a baseball cap, who pointed enthusiastically towards Bridgeton Boys' Club's end of the field. '... guid turn-oot, by the way.' He returned his attention to Orr.

Questioning eyes to the Nikon. 'You a journalist?' And a presumption which saved him the trouble of lying.

'Wis thinkin' o' yer star striker, there...' Jas raised the camera and stepped back. Aiming the lens to where the platinum-headed boy was grinning and waving to the stands, he released the shutter and caught Eric Fraser and the greasy-haired man dead on. '... local papers eat up this junior league stuff.' He panned round, snapped Orr himself.

A laugh. 'Never hud oor very own photographer afore. Stick around afterwards an' ah'll get the team tae pose fur ye.' Orr slapped his shoulder.

A whistle blew.

'In fact, Mr Anderson – stick around here an' ah'll talk ye through the game. Ma boays ur gonny blow the Larkhall Blues aff the field...' Hands cupped around mouth, face aimed at the pitch. '... c'mon, Jamie – that's it! Git that ball aff him!'

The force of the yell made him jump then smile.

'Young Jamie's the... Gary! That's it, Gary-son! Git it up there! Git it – yes!'

A cheer from the stands echoed Orr's own bellow.

Jas turned to the field, just in time to see the platinum haired boy seized by three team-mates. Malkie Orr's enthusiasm was infectious. Jas raised the camera's lens towards the seated area and a now standing and applauding Eric Fraser.

Like the maxim said, it was a game of two halves.

And under the captaincy of platinum-haired Gary, Bridgeton Boys' Club dominated both. Against a backdrop of DC Malcolm Orr's breathless commentary, Jas kept his eye to the lens, sweeping occasionally to the stands where Eric Fraser and the greasy-haired man in the baseball cap had been joined by a third, heavier figure.

All three watched the game.

He watched all three watch Gary. Even a football-phobe could see the kid had talent. And something else.

Maybe it was the hair.

Maybe it was the combination of athletic grace and dogged determination.

Maybe it was charisma.

Something kept every eye on the young striker, even when he didn't have the ball. Which was rarely.

By the end of the ninety minutes, the score was eleven-nil and Jas was out of film. 'Yer boy played well.'

'Eyeways plays like a dream...' Orr was gathering up sports bags and water bottles. '... trains every day, nae tantrums or excuses...' He pushed a canvas hold-all at Jas. 'That boay's got a future – c'mon, ye can talk tae him yersel'.' Orr strode onto the pitch.

Jas fell in behind, eyes flicking between the approaching team and the suddenly empty seat in the stands.

Only when a platinum-haired vision broke ranks and rushed towards the long-haired man and his two companions did he locate Eric Fraser.

'Say hello tae Mr Anderson, Gary – he's gonny git yer picture in the papers...'

Jas looked briefly at the pink face beneath the blond hair. His heart hammered.

'Mr Anderson, this is Bobby Devine...'

He nodded at the portly figure in a shell suit.

'... Gerald – Gerry Corrigan: Gary's dad...'

His eyes flicked between the pink face and the sallow. There was a resemblance. Facial only.

Gerry Corrigan was talking to his son.

Jas could smell the drink on the man's breath. Standing in front of Orr, the trainer's proud hands on his shoulders, Gary continued to look at Jas.

'... and this is Mr Eric Fraser.'

They stood in the middle of the strip of muddied grass. Four men and a boy. Jas touched the strap of the Nikon briefly and stuck out his hand.

Fraser smiled. 'Mr Anderson an' I already know each other...' The arms remained coolly by his sides.

Jas's heart hammered again.

'... by reputation only, though.' Fraser glanced at Gary. 'Away ye go an' get changed, son. Well talk later.'

The platinum head swivelled round to Orr, who was staring at Corrigan Senior. 'Aye, go on Gary.'

The boy left.

The four men remained.

Jas continued to stare at Eric Fraser. The oblique words circled in his head. In the background, Orr and Corrigan Senior's voices framed the loaded silence:

'Will ye put Gaz up fur trial noo, Malkie?' Lager-breath filled the air.

'Don't put pressure oan the boay. Another season should...'

'Ye said that last year, man! Eric can fix it – Eric kens the guys oan the selection committee. Eric...'

'Eric's no' his trainer, Gerry.' Anger in the voice pulled Jas's eyes from Fraser's vaguely amused gaze.

Malcolm Orr was glaring at Corrigan Senior with barely disguised irritation.

'Ah'm his faither, but. Ah've put a lot intae Gaz's future tae, ye know.'

'Ye really think turnin' up pished tae watch the boy play's a guid idea?'

'Ah'm no' pished – me an' Boabby just hud a wee drink oan the bus...'

If there was a football equivalent of a stage mother, Gerry Corrigan seemed to be casting himself in that role. Jas was scrutinising the star player's father when Fraser finally spoke:

'Ah didn't realise ye liked football, Mr Anderson.'

The statement returned his attention to the object of the last three weeks' work.

He'd been discreet. Had kept in the background. Okay, it was never a good idea to get quite this close to a surveillance subject but he'd been careful...

'McStay no' with ye?'

... one simple question told him he was wrong. The Orr/Corrigan exchange eased off. Both men turned their attention to Jas and Fraser. Who talked on:

'Ye did time thegether, eh? That him in trouble again?'

The urge to split hairs burbled on his lips. Jas bit it back.

'Ah didney ken you an' Mr Anderson knew each other, Eric.' Confusion in Orr's voice.

Jas glanced from Fraser's smug face to the previously genial one. Behind the trainer, Corrigan Senior was staggering off towards where his son was talking with a group of players.

'Small world, eh?' An attempt at understanding from Orr.

Fraser answered for him. 'That wis McStay's kid ye wur with, Saturday doon at the Green, eh?'

Too late to deny it. Uncertainty as to how much Fraser knew continued to blur his response.

'Ah thought...' More confusion from Orr. '... ah mean, ah goat the impression...'

'C'mon, Gaz-son... we'll git oor pictures taken fur the papers, eh?' A slurring roar in the background made them all turn.

Corrigan Senior had hold of Corrigan Junior's arm and was attempting to drag him away from team-mates.

'Will ye lea' the boay alone, Gerry!' Orr jogged off towards the fracas.

Then it was just him and Fraser.

The tailer.

And the tailed.

The hunter and the prey.

Jas removed the camera from around his neck, set the film to rewind and gave Fraser the opportunity to confirm one way or another if his cover was blown.

A sigh. Then a hand on his shoulder. 'Hope ye got some good shots of the team. Mibby see ye again, Anderson.'

Jas watched the broad-shouldered man turn and make his way towards where Malkie Orr was trying to talk loud sense to Corrigan Senior. Relief slowed his heart over the sound of raised voices.

Not his problem.

But there was a problem.

As he turned and walked back to the Astra, Jas was still trying to make sense of Eric Fraser's response.

It nagged at his brain through Saturday afternoon traffic along the motorway.

Employing outside assistance in an internal investigation was not without precedent. Tom was well within his rights...

Jas indicated at Blochairn, drove down towards Alexander Parade.

... the proximity of himself and Fraser, fifteen minutes earlier, still made him uncomfortable. And made continuing to follow the man too much of a risk.

Above his head, an illuminated, unnecessary 'Slow'. Jas eased down into first gear.

The Astra coughed.

Jas pushed his mind away from uncertainties and back onto surer ground. For the first time, he had film full of faces and names to go with them.

DC Malkie Orr Tom already knew about.

Bobby Devine was new.

Platinum Gary had solidified into Gary 'Gaz' Corrigan, son of drunken Gerry.

Looming over this quartet, the patriarch Eric Fraser.

Malkie's boss. Acquaintance of Devine. Friend of Gerry – they sat together during the match – and unofficial sponsor to his son?

Eric can fix it – Eric kens the guys oan the selection committee.

Corrigan Senior's phrase echoed in his head. Another example of Fraser using his influence to provide rather than deny?

The rear lights of the car in front turned red.

Jas shifted into neutral and wrenched on the hand brake. His mind returned to the adjacent drama and the obvious tension between Orr and Gerald Corrigan. He frowned, drumming fingers on the steering wheel. Something about the trainer's attitude tugged at his heart.

But he had other things to think about...

The car in front moved off. Jas shifted into first then second, taking the turn off onto the Parade then right at the traffic lights into Cumbernauld Road.

... and as he parked then locked the Astra in front of Number 247, he could already hear the sounds made by one of them.

'You're scum, pal! Spyin' oan people – takin' money tae poke yer nose intae other folk's lives! How can ye sleep at night?'

Shouts echoed in from the rear court and amplified themselves up four floors of stairwell.

Jas ran towards the open back door, pushing through the small crowd which had gathered around the Portacabin.

'How much is she payin' ye? Is it enough? Enough tae salve yer conscience?'

Pinned to the structure's door by a large, furious hand, a man in an acid-yellow hazard jacket flinched under another roared rhetorical from Stevie and tried to retreat back inside. 'Lea' me alone! Ah'm jist doin' ma job!'

Children giggled and stared.

Women folded their arms and shook their heads.

The few other men present stood silently, watching.

Jas grabbed two solid shoulders. 'C'mon...'

Stevie shrugged off the grip. 'Bastard, ya...!'

He didn't have the patience to reason – not now. Police training returned with a vengeance. Jas seized the arm which pinned the Portacabin guy to the door, applied pressure at the elbow.

Stevie yelped.

Taking advantage of the slightly loosened grip, the Portacabin guy ducked free.

Jas twisted the wrist up Stevie's back. He wrapped his free arm around a thick neck. And pulled.

They both staggered backwards.

'You should be locked up, pal.' Voice hoarse from the pressure, the Portacabin guy was rubbing his throat and backing into the Portacabin.

Jas shoved Stevie's wrist between angular shoulder-blades, forcing him around to face the tenement. Over his shoulder, he glowered at a closing Portacabin door. And met the weary eyes of someone used to such treatment.

'Lemme go! Ya fucker, lemme...!'

Then he was pushing a struggling Stevie through a parting sea of curious faces, into the building and up three flights of stairs.

Only when they were inside and the door was locked did he release him. 'That wisney very clever – he could press charges. There wur plenty o' witnesses...'

Stevie charged to the window.

Jas was behind him. '... an' it's nothin' tae dae wi' Maureen.'

'Ah'm gonny kill that bastard!' Stevie tried to open the window, the violence now reduced to verbals.

Beyond, a figure in an acid-yellow hazard jacket was now locking the Portacabin door.

Jas moved between the window and Stevie. 'Will ye listen?' He pushed his hands against the bulky man, palms flat on Stevie's chest. 'It's nothin' to do with Maureen. Or you.' He shouted the words into a pink, furious face. 'It's me they're after.'

Stevie blinked.

It was all making sense.

Fraser's oblique comments, at the football match. The fact Ann was aware of the surveillance. Stevie's impromptu visit to Easterhouse police station, last night...

Jas repeated the words.

... confirmed by the way the Portacabin guy had met and held his gaze for the briefest of seconds. He knew a cop when he saw one.

This was a police job.

Tension slowly left Stevie's face. Fists uncurled.

Jas let his palms remain on the solid chest. 'The case ah'm workin' on...'

Stevie's hands settled on his waist. 'Ah'm finally gonny hear about that?'

'The morra...' Once he had officially resigned from Tom Galbraith's employ. '... but ah've got a feelin' your wee visit tae E Division yesterday wis causa me, too.' Not to mention the raising of the unsolved murder of a certain prison officer, two years ago.

Discredit a CIB officer by discrediting a PI in his employ?

In his inside pocket, the mobile beeped.

Amber eyes to his chest.

Jas frowned. Time to test the answering service. He let the mobile beep on, nodded through to the other room. 'Ah'm no' sure if that wan's bugged or no', but it's somethin' tae bear in mind when ye're usin' it.' He stared at Stevie.

Rage fading into confusion. 'So it's... no' Maureen wantin' ammunition?'

He shook his head. And not his problem. Not directly.

But the way Ian Dalgleish was rising zombie-like, to threaten in death the way he had done in life, was.

Stevie released his waist. 'Christ, whit a mess.' Two broad palms rubbing face.

Jas wondered if he had any idea how much a mess. Then he stopped wondering and moved to the bed and sat down. 'Tell me whit the polls said tae ye, yesterday – everythin'.'

The face emerged from behind the hands. Stevie frowned, then sat on the floor at the edge of the bed. And began to talk.

An hour later, a tangly brown head leant against Jas's knees.

His hand rested on Stevie's head. 'Ye've goat an alibi fur the night he wis run doon, aye?'

A nod. 'Yer pal… whit's her name – Marie? – set that up, along wi' the car. The polis didney ask where ah wis that night, but – jist kept goin' oan an' oan aboot how you an' me had been part o' the riot, an' how we'd saved Dalgleish fae gettin' whit wis comin' tae him oan the roof.' Wry laugh.

Jas frowned, pushing his fingers beneath the ponytail. It was something and nothing.

Maybe.

A way of sounding out him through Stevie.

Maybe.

Stevie himself had suffered no more, no less at the hands of Ian Dalgleish than any other inmate in the Bar-L at the time of Hadrian Security's management of the place. And had no more, no less a motive than all of them.

Maybe.

But he was living with someone whose beating and rape Ian Dalgleish had orchestrated.

Someone who had a long-term friendship – if you could call it that – with the woman whose brother Ian Dalgleish had killed in cold blood.

Someone who was now in the employ of the CIB officer investigating E Division.

'They wur jist fishin', man – okay, they gied me a hellova fright but there's nothin' tae connect me an' Dalgleish.' Stevie turned, resting his face on Jas's thigh and looking up at him.

Threads from the past stopped him sharing the easy confidence. Threads which joined himself, Stevie and Marie and God knows who else. Threads which should have been cut long ago. Threads with loose ends, should anyone decide to apply a little pressure.

Stevie lowered his face, manoeuvring his body between Jas's thighs. 'Ah'm sorry ah went fur that polis in the Portacabin...' Half laugh. '... actually, ah'm no sorry. Ah shoulda laid the bastard oot fur messin' wi' you.' The tangly head rubbing against his stomach.

Out of the mouths of babes?

His hand moved down beneath the neck of Stevie's tee-shirt, rubbing the warm skin on the man's back.

He had to know.

He had to make sure all tracks had been covered.

And only one person could reassure him. Slipping one hand into the slightly damp pit beneath Stevie's arm, with the other he pulled the mobile from his pocket. And punched in a number he didn't need to look up.

'Tight as a virgin's cunt, Big Man...'

Marie's harsh voice crackled down the line to him.

'... the car wis lifted fae a car-park, Stevie wore gloves, nae witnesses, an' ah've goat half a dozen lassies'll swear he wis drunk an' causin' a ruckus doon at Mr Simpson's when it happened...'

It was plausible: on release from prison, a lot of guys headed straight for the pub or the brothel.

'... you ken the money came fae Michael Johnstone, but Stevie ainly ever dealt wi' me. Nae-wan can prove nothin', Big Guy.'

He wanted to share her confidence. A soft rumble from his chest told him Stevie had fallen asleep. Jas tilted his head and looked down at the relaxed, snoring figure.

'Whit suddenly brought aw' this back, onyway?'

Jas thought about sharing the story so far. But if he couldn't tell Stevie, he certainly wasn't in a position to share confidential information with Marie. 'Somethin' an' nothin'...'

Sceptical laugh. 'Be like that, then.' A pause. 'Ah hear ye wur really nice tae Maggie – but no' much use, Big Guy.'

The Joseph Monaghan case pushed its way back into Jas's mind. 'Ah did whit ah could, Marie...' Like the murder of Ian Dalgleish, the death of Margaret Monaghan's son would most likely end up a statistic on D Divison's detection records. '... whit ah did find's been reported tae the collator in charge, doon at London Road.'

'Maggie telt me, Big Guy. She's still no' heard onythin' fae them, though.'

Not his problem.

Not now.

A sudden glint caught him full in the face. Reflected in an open window on the far side of the back court, sun flooded his vision. Jas blinked. Time had passed. He glanced at his watch: nearly seven. 'Thanks fur the reassurance, oan that other matter, Marie.'

'Nae sweat, man. Gie ma best tae Big Stevie, eh? An' tell him the polis'll never prove nothin', if that's whit's worryin' him.'

It wasn't. 'Ah will.' He disconnected, moving his eyes from the glare. Jas knew what he had to do. It was just a matter of whether now, or later.

'Whit's happenin'?' A mumble from his chest.

Later. 'Nothin'...' Jas leant back on the bed, moving his hands beneath Stevie's sleep-heavy arms and hauling the man up beside him. One arm threw itself across his chest:

'Ah hud a weird dream...' A warm face snuggled in at his neck. '... dreamt Mo jist... disappeared an' everythin' went back tae normal.' Regret in the laugh which ended the sentence.

He felt the relaxed heaviness of the body next to him. 'Mibby she will.' He knew it was what Stevie wanted to hear.

Another snuffle against his neck. 'Ah'm kinda past carin' tae be honest. Whit's gonny happen'll happen, whether ah worry aboot it or no', eh Jas?'

The courtesy returned. But the words sounded truthful.

'As long as... things're okay between you an' me, that's aw' that really matters, eh?'

Truth or dream?

'Things are okay, eh?'

Jas buried his face in tangles of sweaty hair. Tomorrow he'd resign from the Fraser surveillance. His lips brushed Stevie's ear. 'Aye, baby, things ur fine.'

Seventeen

He slept deeply and soundlessly, one arm numb beneath Stevie and a half hard-on against the man's thigh.

Kids' voices from outside woke him just before eleven. Further away but nearing, the distant tramp of feet and the chirp of flutes along Cumbernauld Road.

Jas eased himself out of bed and walked to the window.

Three girls were skipping on the spot where the Portacabin had stood.

Jas wondered vaguely when it had been dismantled, then grabbed the mobile and picked up his message from yesterday. In the other room, he returned the call.

Tom answered on the third ring. Straight into an enquiry on the progress of the tailing.

Jas broke in. 'Ah need tae talk tae ye.' He thought about the Portacabin's moonlight flit.

Tom ran through his schedule, looking for openings.

Jas walked quietly into the door way. He glanced through to the main reason he had to resign from CIB's employ. Despite Marie's reassurances to the contrary, he could not afford any interest in Stevie's past.

'Okay – one o'clock at the usual place?'

The atmosphere between himself and Stevie still clung to his body, a second warm and welcome skin he didn't want to lose with distance. 'Whit aboot...' In the light of 'The Greek', Jas considered a cryptic arrangement for 'The Macedonian'. Then reconsidered. 'Ye ken Alexander Park?'

'Can find it.'

Jas smiled and gave directions. He enquired about the fate of the second hire-car and was told E Division had provided a replacement vehicle of their own. 'A hideous dark blue Fiesta.' The hint of a grumble.

Jas laughed, terminated the conversation and walked towards the shower.

It was just before noon.

'Back by three. Don't go anywhere.'

By quarter to one he was writing a note for the still-sleeping Stevie.

Dead on one, he sat on the first bench just inside Alexander Park, watching for a dark blue Fiesta. In a Farmfoods bag beneath one arm, notes, names and the as-yet undeveloped role of film from yesterday.

Ten minutes later, he walked out onto the Parade and stood in front of a row of No Parking traffic cones. Ten minutes after that he met Tom's frustrated eyes through the windscreen, pointed him round into Eastercraigs and followed on foot.

The Fiesta was manoeuvring itself into a space just in front of Number 7 by the time he arrived. Jas looked up to the second floor and wondered who lived there now.

The slam of a car door. Then: 'There some sort of event happening here? Police cars everywhere. Nowhere to park.'

Jas shook his head. 'Jist yer normal July Sunday in Glasgow, pal.' He nodded to the same gap in the railings which had been there for years. 'Let's keep walking.' He glanced over his shoulder, in case Portacabin Man had been replaced with On-foot Man.

The street behind was deserted.

They stood at the far end of the boating pond and watched women with kids feed swans.

Jas handed over the Farmfoods bag with a short recap of yesterday afternoon's events.

Tom took it, listened.

As Jas recounted the Portacabin-episode, Tom remained silent. His eyes roved constantly over the noisy activity. The pipe was produced. Sucked. Finally lit when Jas concluded his speech:

'Ah can recommend another coupla private investigators, if ye wanna continue Fraser's surveillance.'

Serious grey eyes focused over his shoulder. 'A game of cat and mouse. With both changing place.'

Jas followed the eyes and acknowledged the logic. 'They've been watchin' me fur at least two weeks noo, if that Portacabin's onything tae go by. Makes sense they'll be keepin' an eye oan you too, ah suppose.' The sound of flutes barged through kids' chatter.

In the adjacent swing park, a variety of families engaged in family-type stuff. Beyond, on the Parade, a more active cavalcade was approaching.

Jas frowned. 'Ah canny see 'em havin' the manpower the day, though.' He nodded to the scene.

Tom's head turned.

Traffic crawled along behind the procession. On either side, a line of uniformed police kept pace and provided a human barrier between those on the road and those on the pavement. Jas listened for the strains of 'No Surrender', then remembered Glasgow District Council's ban on overtly sectarian anthems and recognised an arrangement of 'Abide with Me'. It was mildly appropriate.

'This some sort of historical thing?' Amused curiosity.

His frown twisted to a scowl. 'Aye, ye could say that.' The bass drum thumped enthusiastically at the end of each verse. At the head of the line of marching men, women and children, a group of three in dark suits and fringed sashes carried banners proclaiming Lodge-affinity and an embroidered picture of a man on a horse. Bringing up the rear, a police van.

'Very... um, colourful – what are they celebrating?'

The defeat of the Irish by William of Orange's army, on July 12th over two hundred years ago?

An army augmented by several hundred Highlanders?

A Dutch king's victory at the Battle of the Boyne?

The victory of Protestant over Fenian?

The same fight re-enacted every time Rangers met Celtic on the football field?

Jas stared at the embroidered portrait of King Billy. 'Racism, sectarianism, bigotry, hate – take yer pick.' He began to walk towards the edge of the park. His own days in uniform flashed back into his mind.

Tom followed.

'This sorta thing's goin' on all ower Glasgow an' the West coast, the day – an' next weekend...' He frowned. '... every cop dreads it – worse than the Auld Firm matches.'

A hand on his shoulder. 'You've lost me, I'm afraid.'

He stopped at the railings, staring through at the stony faces of the long crocodile. His voice was low. 'Ye ken aboot Drumcree?' Every year, on the other side of the Irish Sea a stand-off between Protestant marchers and the local Catholic community made the headlines.

'Of course, but that's... Northern Ireland. There's a war on, over there – despite the Peace Process.'

Links between the West Coast of Scotland and Ulster had been forged centuries ago. Jas watched Union Jacks flutter in the fists of small children and considered the irony, in a country which had only recently achieved its own parliament and some small measure of autonomy.

'The Province is a divided community.' Tom's head swivelled. 'Scotland's not...'

Sceptical blue eyes met confused grey. 'There wis a joke aboot Glasgow, till recently: even the buses ur Orange.' He recalled the 'Go Home Fenian Bastard' scrawled on Tom's second hire car. 'Man, ye're a Papist yerself!'

Small smile. 'Somewhat lapsed.'

Jas looked back at the end of the human cavalcade, watching rows of children too young to fight the indoctrination. 'No' a divided community, is it? Wi' separate schools, fitba' teams – Rangers'll sign Muslims afore they'll sign Catholics – an' there's at least three firms o' buildin' contractors'll no' employ a pape.' Not to mention Strathclyde Police's position on such matters.

As if on cue, the van moved into view. Inside, at leasta dozen uniformed officers, prepared for trouble.

Jas turned to the man at his side.

Tom was holding the pipe, tapping the bowl thoughtfully. 'No idea things were so bad up here.'

Jas smiled wryly. 'This isney... bad – this is normal. It's so ingrained, maist people don't even think aboot it. A walk tae a church, some sorta service then intae the bus an' back tae the Lodge tae get drunk an' sing 'The Sash' aw' the way home.'

He could still remember the words of the song, taught to him in primary school by his best friend Jimmy Morrison. Had hurled abuse and stones at the kids from St Peter's down the road with Jimmy, in between games of cowboys and Indians which always ended with Jimmy tied to a tree.

Jimmy's father had a sash. A flute. Even a bowler hat. Two six-year-olds played dressing-up with the regalia, until Jimmy father caught them and gave Jimmy the hiding of his life.

Jas's mother had seen him spit outside a chapel, like Jimmy did. She'd given him the one and only slap of his life and forbidden the friendship. He found other boys to tie to trees.

Jimmy followed in his father's footsteps. Joined St Andrew's Lodge Flute Band at nine. Apprentice Boy by twelve. Up through the ranks swiftly, under paternal guidance. Last thing Jas had heard, Jimmy Morrison was married with three kids, a leading light in St Andrew's Orange Order.

If Jimmy's kids were boys, the process would be repeating itself.

'Jas?'

A hand on his arm brought him back to the present...

He pushed the past away and laughed. 'Sorry.'

... a present which would continue to set the tone for Glasgow's future, as long as the tradition of hate was kept alive.

They were now strolling back towards Eastercraigs and the parked Fiesta. 'Get your invoice in the post to me soon as you like – I'll make sure it's settled promptly.'

'The retainer'll cover maist of it an'...'

'Know this work hasn't been easy for you, Jas. Don't want any favours.'

He grinned. 'Yes, sir!

They climbed back through the gap in the railings. Just in front of the Fiesta, Tom glanced at his watch. 'Look, you fancy grabbing something to eat? Got an hour to kill, till I need to be at Easterhouse and it's not worth going home.'

Not the most gracious offer he'd ever received. For the first time since he'd begun the work, he realised Tom Galbraith was about to disappear back out of his life.

Part of him was glad...

Jas looked at the tall, square-shouldered figure with the easy manner and the difficult job.

... another part of him?

'On me – to say thanks for all your hard work?'

Jas laughed. 'Okay – you choose.'

'Indian?'

There was a good curry house down in Shettleston. Jas nodded, suggested The Bengal Tiger.

Tom smiled, nodded and held the passenger door open for him.

The service was slow. They barely noticed. The conversation veered away from Eric Fraser and his football-mad cronies to more general matters. The Tiger still let patrons smoke.

Jas inhaled the scent of pipe tobacco and ate pakora he hardly tasted. Tom had the samosas then the chicken dansak. Jas took the prawn korma.

By the time coffee arrived, the conversation had come full circle:

'Give it a week or so more – that's all I can do ...' The pipe re-lit. Its stem fingered thoughtfully. '... if I can't get something concrete soon, I'll be forced to submit a clean report.'

Jas smiled and lit a cigarette. 'Pity ye didney say that in ma flat, before Stevie chased aff Fraser's boays in the Portacabin.'

Thoughtful expression deepening. Grey eyes to his. 'Sorry if the job caused any personal hassle for you, Jas. Truly sorry.'

He shook his head. 'Goes wi' the territory.' He'd never had a case which hit so close to home. And never wanted another.

The bill arrived. Tom paid by Amex and left a good tip. A grinning Bengali with a broad Glasgow accent brought their coats.

Outside the restaurant, they stood in front of the Fiesta. The distant thump of another bass drum signalled another march in process. And the end of what had never been more than a business arrangement? Jas stuck out his hand. 'Watch yer back, Tam.'

'You too, Jas.' His fingers gripped, tightly squeezed.

He felt the one-sided frisson, withdrew his fist before his body ruined this. 'Ah'll get a mair formal final report in tae ye, in the next coupla days.'

'Drop you anywhere?' Key into driver's lock.

Jas stared at the nape of Tom Galbraith's neatly shaved neck. 'Ah'm in the other direction – the walk'll dae me good.'

The head turned. A last smile. 'Be in touch, with your payment.'

Jas walked off along Duke Street before he said something he'd regret.

The smell of burning twitched his nostrils as soon as he pushed open the door to flat 3/1.

Something in his brain followed suite. Jas glanced at his watch:

4.30 pm. He sighed, moving through to the kitchen. 'Sorry ah'm late. Ah...'

'It's ruined – fuckin' ruined!' Stevie stalked from the tiny cooking area, cigarette clamped between lips. Pushing past Jas, he wrenched open the living-room window.

Jas continued into the hazy kitchen, opened the oven and peered in at one of Stevie's home-made lasagnes. 'Naw, it's fine – bit dried up, but ah'm sure it's edible.' He closed the oven door, noticing the large bowl of tossed salad atop one work surface. He sighed again and moved past it to where Stevie was now leaning against the window frame, cigarette gripped between thumb and forefinger.

'Ye said three o'clock – it's been ready since...'

'Ah'm sorry, man – things wi' Tam took a bit longer than...'

'Ye've been wi' him?' Cigarette end tamped out between fingertips, flicked though the open window. 'Again?' Smouldering brown eyes to his.

Jas met and held them. 'Aye, but that's me aff the case.' He smiled. 'Listen, ah've eaten onyway, so why don't we...?'

Levering himself from the window frame, Stevie headed for the bedroom.

Jas moved in front of the sullen figure, hands on Stevie's shoulders. 'Whit's wrang?'

'Lea' me alone!' The large body swerved away then got back on route for the other room.

Jas lowered his hands. 'Ah said ah wis sorry – it jist took longer than ah thought.' He watched Stevie duck into the hall, grab a jacket and head for the door. 'Where ye goin'? Where ye...?'

A slam semi-answered his question. He stood there, listening to rapidly descending footsteps.

Part of him wanted to go after Stevie...

Jas sat down on a sofabed. More than the lasagne was ruined. He stared towards the hall, thinking about last night's closeness and how little it took to replace it with distance.

... another part wanted to replay his last hours with Tom Galbraith over and over again. Alone. With no distractions.

He denied himself either indulgence. Stevie would be back, after he'd blown off steam. Tom would fade into the past, where he belonged.

Jas rubbed his face, got up and walked through to the PC.

He typed up the last day's surveillance by memory. At the end of his report, he added his usual recommendations: based on two weeks' observation, he could find nothing in Superintendent Eric Fraser's behaviour to indicate anything out of the ordinary.

He called up 'print' then prepared an invoice, to be included with the report.

He placed everything in an envelope, wondering if Tom wanted it sent to the Albion Street flat or E Division headquarters. In the end, he left the address blank and switched off the PC.

He undressed down to jock, warming up with five minutes' jogging on the spot.

One hundred press-ups later, his body sheened with sweat. Lungs ached.

One hundred crunchies after that, the sun was lower in the sky and he was vowing to give up the fags again.

Jas repeated both sets until his arms were lead and the muscles in his thighs trembled. His mind still raced.

He considered a wank. Jas peeled off the jock and leant against the edge of the sofabed. His cock responded to the fondling. Vague images of Stevie naked and Tom Galbriath's sports jacket flitted in and out of his brain.

After five minutes he lost interest.

A cold shower took care of what remained of his hard-on. Jas washed his body vigorously, scrubbing desire for two men from his skin but unable to dislodge either from his mind.

Drying himself in the living room, he tried to remember if this was a Maureen or Carole weekend, for the kids. Then remembered it was a Stevie.

Would he be bringing Sam and Hayley back with him?

Jas looked at the unaddressed envelope three times as he tidied up both rooms then cleaned the shower.

Just after ten, he crawled into their bed and waited for the sound of keys in locks.

An hour later he was still waiting. Fifteen minutes after that, he was asleep.

The sound of the shower woke him...

Jas's eyes opened enough to see red illuminated figures in the dark room: 01.25.

... the lack of kids' stage-whispers kept him that way. He lay there, listening to the patter of water on plastic. When it stopped he rolled onto his side and pulled the covers back. And waited some more.

Eventually, a shape made its way through the darkness towards him. His arms reached for the man. 'Ah'm sorry. Ah'll make it up tae ye.'

The bed dipped. The shape grabbed the corner of the duvet and pulled the quilt around itself. Stevie turned to face the wall.

Actions had always spoken louder than words, with them. Jas kissed the back of a still-damp neck, nuzzling through the loosened ponytail.

Stevie tugged at the duvet again.

Jas slid an arm across the man, fitting his crotch against the curve of Stevie's arse.

More tugging. Augmented by an inching away.

He pressed the side of his face to the solid back and refused the hint.

Then the inch became a mile. Stevie pulled away, moving to the far side of the bed.

Jas stared at the dark outline of the man's skull. 'Let me hold ye.'

No response.

His stomach clenched. 'Please?' He'd never begged anything from anyone before. But he needed to at least make physical contact, even if the distance between them in other ways was widening by the minute.

Still no response.

The clenching in his stomach firmed to a cold, sick feeling. Jas watched the rise and fall of Stevie's left shoulder. Then he gave up and rolled onto his back.

His eyes had barely shut when the lids sprang open again.

A beeping from somewhere in the other room.

Jas instinctively thumped the alarm button above illuminated digits which read 03.04.

His second thought: smoke alarm. He leapt out of bed, recalling an uneaten lasagne and trying to remember if the oven was still on.

His leg banged off the edge of a sofabed. Jas cursed under his breath, breathing in smoke-free air. The beeping placed itself.

In moonlight he groped through the pockets of his jacket. Fumbing on the keypad, he pressed the cell-phone to his ear. 'Aye?'

'Sorry to wake you, Jas – didn't know who else to phone…'

He heard the strain in the voice. 'Whit's happened?'

'… Nick's been picked up. They're holding him at Maryhill police station. I couldn't get much sense out of him when he phoned but…'

'You're up there?'

'Yes – well, outside. They told me to wait. Jas, I don't know what to…'

'Stay where ye are. Ah'll be right up.' He disconnected, heart pounding, and moved through to find his clothes.

Eighteen

'Refuses to talk to me – according to the desk sergeant, he's refusing to say anything. Just keeps asking to be informed when his solicitor gets here.' The voice was low.

Déjà vu…

The waiting area inside Maryhill police station was crowded and noisy. Tom sat on a generic plastic seat. Nicotine-stained fingers tugged constantly at the neat moustache. 'One phone-call, telling me where he was and asking me to arrange a good lawyer.' Gruff laugh. No humour in the sound. 'Like he was in some American film.'

… another lost, confused man in another faceless police station. Jas took an adjacent seat, turning his back to just another Saturday night/Sunday morning melee and leaning closer to the slump-shouldered figure. He heard the hurt in the low voice.

'Stupid bugger – stubborn, stupid little bugger!' Anger eclipsing the hurt. 'All a game to him!' Tom stood up abruptly. 'Some stupid game to get back at me for that bloody jacket! Has he any idea of the position this puts me in? Has he…?'

'Sit doon, eh?' His hands on another distraught father's deltoids, firmly lowering Tom Galbraith back into the moulded plastic seat.

Another man's deltoids.

Jas removed the grip. His brain ground into action. 'He's bin charged?'

Tom's head hung between his shoulders. 'Must have been, if they let him phone.'

'Ony idea whit he wis picked up fur?'

A mere headshake, this time.

Nick Galbraith was seventeen: a case could be argued for the presence of an adult, in loco parentis, but it might be dodgy. There was another way. 'Stay here.' It was Jas's turn to stand.

Tom Galbraith looked up at him. Surprise in the grey eyes.

Jas managed a smile then walked to where the night sergeant was arguing with a drunk. 'Ye're holdin' Nicholas Galbraith?'

Above the white shirt/black tie, a long suffering face to his. 'You his solicitor?'

'Ah will be advising him.' Most chose someone with a law background, but under Scottish Law, an individual in custody could assign anyone he liked as legal counsel. 'James Anderson, sergeant. An' ah would like to see my client.'

Weary nod. 'Ah'll git somewan tae take ye doon, Mr Anderson.' Buzzing. 'Mibby you can talk some sense intae the boy.'

Jas pushed the security door, heard it slam shut behind. He could try.

In the bowels of Maryhill police station, a female custody officer unlocked a holding cell three from the end. From inside:

'I'm not talking to anyone until...'

'We know, we know – your brief's here, son.' The woman whose name tag identified her as Sergeant Shaw hauled open three inches of thick steel.

'Thank you...' Jas stepped inside, eyes fixed on the pale-faced youth within. '... ah'll give you a shout when ah'm finished.'

Another door slammed behind.

The pale face looked at him. 'Ja-zzzz...' A grin. '... my knight in shining armour come to rescue me!'

He looked at the slim boy in tight tee-shirt and baggy cargo pants.

The blond hair gelled up into short spiky points. A hint of liner framing the large eyes. On the side of the neck, the faint bruising of a love-bite.

Jas frowned. 'Ah've come tae find oot whit the hell you think ye're playin' at.'

'Ask them who's playing games.' The teasing tone vanished. 'They think they can get me for Indecent Exposure cos they caught me taking a leak, they can think again!' Eyes to the door. 'It's persecution, that's what it is. I was cutting across that park to try and find a bloody main road and...'

'From the beginnin', pal...' Jas held up a hand and sat down on the uncushioned bed. '... tell me the whole thing fae the beginnin'.'

Nick Galbraith pursed bee-stung lips and ran a hand over blond spiky hair. He sat down.'The club closed at two-ish...'

Jas blinked: there were no 'clubs' in Maryhill. At least none that would interest Nick.

'... I left alone, and lost my bearings...'

Jas looked at the love-bite and doubted Nick Galbraith ever lost anything he didn't mean to.

'... I was looking for a taxi, but there was nothing around – no traffic, nothing...'

Jas had passed three taxi ranks on his way up here. Maryhill Road was busier at two in the morning than two in the afternoon.

'... then I saw the park – the gates were open...'

Glasgow Parks Department secured and locked all their premises at ten pm on the dot.

'... so I thought I'd take a shortcut...'

For someone who claimed to have lost their bearings, Nick Galbraith showed an enviable knowledge of Maryhill geography.

'... I was just taking a piss beside a tree when three cops leapt out from somewhere...'

Locked gates worked both ways. Jas nodded. 'Go on...'

A sigh. 'They shone lights in my face – Christ, it was like something out of a nightmare. All shouting at once, asking me where I'd been, what I'd been doing...' Knowing grey eyes to Jas. '... who I'd been doing it with.'

His own eyes returned to the bruise on the boy's neck. 'An' when ye widney tell 'em, they arrested ye fur Indecent Exposure?'

Bee-stung lips pursed again. 'I wasn't hurting anyone. Hell, if I'd found another soul in that fucking park the first thing I would have asked is "where's the damn main road"!'

Beneath the bravado, the same hint of panic Jas had seen in Tom's face. He nodded slowly. Amidst the many gaping holes in Nick's account of his movements, the presence of police officers in a locked park at two in the morning bothered him most.

'So what do you advise – as my legal advisor, Ja-zzzzz?' The mocking tone was back. The long fingers of one hand casually traced the outline of the love-bite.

He noted the movement, remembering the phone number in the pocket of the stolen jacket and the implication of a crush. Jas met the wide grey stare.

Nick held it, all innocence. A giggle.

The eye-colour was the same. There the resemblance between father and son ended. Jas rubbed his face. Whatever the motive for all this, Nick Galbraith had instinctively got one thing right. 'Ye've telt 'em nothin'?'

A wink. 'Not one word...' Sobering. '... I know my rights.' Thin arms folded across tightly tee-shirted chest. Bee-stung lips set firm. 'I have no criminal record, it'll be my word against cops' and everyone knows how much that counts for, these days. The CPS'll laugh in their faces if they try to take this to court and...'

'Shut it an' listen!' He grabbed one of the skinny arms, hauling the boy to his feet. 'You're gonny dae everythin' ah say an' keep that shut except when ah tell ye tae, okay?' He nodded to the now-scowling mouth.

Grey eyes to the grip. 'Like the rough-stuff, do you Ja-zzzz?'

He tightened his fist.

'Ow!' A wriggle. 'Okay, okay...' Grin. '... but don't ask me to come quietly. I never come quietly.' The voice low, husky.

He released the boy, ignored the innuendo. 'Ah'm doin' this for yer faither, no' you. If it wis up tae me, ah'd let ye stay here an' stew.'

Nick was rubbing a skinny biceps, with the same expression as when he'd fingered the love-bite. A mock-sigh. 'Always the brides-maid, never the bride. The story of my life, Ja-zzzz.'

Jas turned, thumped his fist against three-inch steel. 'Okay, sergeant!' To Nick. 'Remember whit ah said.'

'Always.' A giggle.

Then the door was unlocking and he was talking to the custody officer in a low voice.

'You're a visitor to Glasgow, Nicholas, and you're young...'

Half an hour later, Jas'd talked her round to a verbal warning. The Indecent Exposure charge would be dropped. In Sergeant Shaw's office, Jas stood beside a frowning Tom and a for-once obedient Nick.

'... but I would advise you to stick to the city centre in future.' She slid the contents of his pockets across the desk towards him.

Jas watched Tom register four loose Trojans amongst an assortment of chewing-gum and loose change before his son swept the lot up and stuffed it back into his jacket.

'Indecent Exposure is a serious offence. Our parks are not public conveniences. They are designed for everyone's use and as such the police are duty bound to...'

'I'm surprised the Glasgow police have nothing better to do with their time than arrest visitors to their precious city!'

Jas groaned silently, waited for Sergeant Shaw to lay into the kid.

She ignored the remark. Her attention moved from son to father.

He watched the look speak volumes.

'Take him home, Mr Galbraith – and keep an eye on him.' Silent threat made verbal?

'We'll dae that, Sergeant Shaw...' Jas took over, herding both Galbraiths towards the door. '... and thanks for yer understanding.'

'All part of the job, Mr Anderson.' Her face was a mask. 'Good night.'

With the confidence all charges had been dropped, bee-stung lips began to move in a parting jibe.

Tom beat Jas to it, this time. He placed a broad hand between his shoulder blades and pushed his son from the office before Nick said something they'd all regret.

They stopped for petrol at an all-night garage.

Jas bought an early *Record*.

'Homo Bashing Number Five' screamed at him from the front page. In the silent car, he absorbed details on the journey back to Albion Buildings.

Late last night, the unconscious body of a man had been discovered by a shift-worker in the grounds of Gartloch Hospital. He was now recovering in The Royal, with head and chest injuries.

Both editorial and police speculated about an increase in the ferocity of attacks. Witnesses were again requested. There were fears of a murder before long if this 'madman' was not caught soon.

Jas sighed.

Tom gripped the steering-wheel, knuckles white, jaw rigid.

He stared from the side of the tense face to the sulking teenager in the back seat, then returned his attention to Ingram Street and the slowing of the car.

It was just after 4 am on Monday.

Eileen Galbraith met them in the hall, face streaked with tears. She threw her arms around a sober-faced Nick and led him off to the kitchen.

Jas followed Tom into the lounge.

Trembling hands unscrewed the top of a bottle of whiskey, turned to Jas, who shook his head.

He watched the man half fill a tumbler, down it in one:

'Thanks – don't know what you did or how you did it, but thanks.' Tumbler refilled, emptied just as quickly. 'Just give me a minute and I'll run you back to...'

'Nae need fur either...' He moved to the drinks cabinet. '... but a coffee widney go amiss.'

The whiskey bottle still gripped in his fist, Tom paused in the pouring of a third. 'Of course.' He replaced the top, then bottle back on the surface.

Jas watched the man leave the room. Coffee was the last thing he felt like, but at least the request had stopped Tom drinking more. He frowned, glancing around.

On a table in a corner, a laptop computer and a pile of folders.

His eyes followed a wire from the machine, looked for a phone socket. Saw none.

Minutes later, Tom was back, clutching two mugs.

Jas took one. 'Eileen okay?'

A nod. 'Talking to him in the kitchen. Told her to leave it, but...' A shrug. Mug to lips. '... what the hell was he doing up there?'

Good question. Jas sat down on the sofa. He mused over the cock-and-bull story Nick had told him, then his own interpretation of events. Then remembered the warning look in Sergeant Shaw's cool eyes. He looked at Tom.

Pacing now. 'Calls me, to say he's been picked up but refuses to see me? Then refuses to talk to me when I get there and offers no explanation afterwards?'

'The boay got a fright, man...' He tried to catch a narrowed grey eye. '... give him time...'

Tom veered back to the drinks cabinet.

'... onyway, it's aw' over, eh? He got aff wi' a warnin', he's home safe an' sound an'...'

'Why?' The words soft over the pouring of another whiskey.

Jas stood up.

'He knows what I do for a living. So why does he purposely set out to embarrass me at every opportunity?' Glass to lips.

Jas sighed. To be seventeen and not embarrass one's parents was rare. He watched Tom down a third whiskey and kept his mouth shut.

'Did you see what he was wearing? Did you see that...' Voice slowly raising. '... mark on his neck? Looks like some... cheap little tart!' The hand reached for the bottle again.

'Fashion, Tam...' Jas moved swiftly, grabbing the strong wrist. '... ah came hame wi' a mohican when ah wis fourteen.' He tried a laugh. 'Ma faither telt me he'd no' huv a freak in his hoose an' either shave it aff or get oot!'

The well-built man in the sports jacket spun round. 'You know what I'm talking about, don't you?'

The fact that this particular kid's father was a high-ranking police officer? The fact that his son was articulate and mouthy? Or the fact he was gay and made no bones about it? He maintained the grip. 'Aw' ah ken is ye're reactin' the way ony father reacts when his son gits himsel' in trouble wi' the polis.' He stared at an ashen, half-furious half-distraught face. 'Keep this in perspective, eh?' Despite his words, the presence of police officers in a Maryhill park at two in the morning and Sergeant Shaw's knowing look refused to leave his mind.

A flicker in the grey eyes. 'Losing him, Jas...' The military cropped head lowered itself onto his shoulder. '... I'm losing him and there's nothing I can do about it.'

His free arm draped itself instinctively around no-longer military shoulders. Jas rubbed the sports-jacketed back and inhaled the smell of pipe tobacco.

It was the drink.

It was the strain.

It was five-in-the-morning desperation...

The muscles in his stomach clenched.

... it was everything except the one thing he wanted it to be. Jas stood there, fighting the beginnings of a hard-on and holding a man with whom he had more in common than Tom knew.

Stevie's moods.

Stevie's rages.

Stevie's problems seeping through to taint everything around him.

'Dad, I – oh, sor-rey!'

They leapt apart like two virgins.

'Am I finally going to hear some explanation of your behaviour?' Tom stormed to where the slight figure stood in the doorway rubbing wet hair with a pink towel. The love-bite on Nicholas Galbraith's neck stood out like a trophy:

'Maybe you need to explain to mum that you send her to bed then snuggle with men in the living room!' Semi-amused grey eyes to Jas then back to his father.

A snort. 'Watch that mouth, Nicholas.'

'I'd rather watch yours…' Mock-thoughtful finger to jaw, head tilted theatrically. '… does that count as incest, I wonder?'

'You filthy little…' Tom's right arm flew forward.

'Take it easy.' Jas strode forward, catching and preventing the slap. He saw a glint of shock in Nicholas Galbraith's eyes before the boy stepped back and pulled the droll expression back into place:

'Now, now, daddy dearest. That would be assault. Think of your reputation.'

'What were you doing up there?' The question repeated, this time from between clenched teeth.

Jas released Tom's arm

A shrug. 'Like I told Ja-zzz, I got lost on my way back from a club.'

'What club? Who were you with? What were you doing?'

Exaggerated yawn. 'Ask Ja-zzz, if you're really interested. Now I'd love to stand and chat with you boys all night but I really need my beauty sleep.' A grin. 'Nightie-night, kiddies.' Throwing the towel back over his head, Nick turned and walked slowly from the room.

Tom took a step into a conditioner-scented wake. 'Get back here, you little…'

'Leave him.' Jas moved in front, hands raised. 'He's just tauntin' ye. Don't gie him any more ammo.' He could still feel the weight of Tom's head on his shoulder, feel the warmth from the man's body seeping through fabric onto his. 'If it's ony consolation, he telt me the club story too – an' ah think he did jist go intae that park fur a piss.'

Disbelief in the eyes. Then narrowed grey, slowly uncreasing.

Jas nodded beyond Tom's shoulder. 'Settin' up yer ain private Internet café here, eh?' They both needed distracting.

Wry laugh. 'Working from home, now – can use the mobile as an online connection, access to PNC directly.' A sigh.

'Still no' takin' ony chances wi' phone-taps?'

A slow headshake. Tom, stuck a hand into his pocket, pulled out the mobile and wandered over to the table. 'Was in the middle of all this when that little bugger phoned.' He connected the sprawling cable to the side of the cell-phone. 'Something you said this afternoon's been going round and round in my head.'

Despite his son's arrest and most recent outburst, mind back on work in seconds. For the first time, Tom's priorities came home to him. But at least he showed no further inclination to rage after Galbraith Junior and slap that pretty, cocky face. 'Whit wis it?'

'You said... patrolling Orange Walks and Old Firm matches are the most hated jobs on the Force. What did you mean, exactly?' Tom sat down at the table, pulled out an adjacent chair.

Jas took it. 'Ye ken that fur all their purported historical celebration, Orange Walks ur mainly aboot... religion?'

A nod.

'Auld Firm matches may be aboot two football teams oan the surface. Underneath, it's the same thing. Rangers ur the Orange – Protestant – team, Celtic ur the Fenians.'

A cloud over the interested face. '"Go Home Fenian Bastard" – that was scrawled on my car.'

Jas nodded. 'Whit Manchester an' London go through wi' the race issue, Glasgow an' the West Coast git wi' religion.' So many similarities.

A class issue. A wealth issue. An immigrant issue. Less visible than a colour-of-skin thing, but equally strong. If you knew the signs to read.

'Yes, okay, I get all that – so why's it a problem for cops?'

Jas sighed. 'Divided community, man – like ah said. You apply tae ony Force, religious denomination's always oan the form. Same here – same in the RUC...' The Royal Ulster Constabulary had been given several sets of guidelines, to ensure a reasonable percentage of Catholic officers were employed. The reality was somewhat less easy to control. '... how many black officers did the Met huv durin' the Brixton Riots? Or Greater Manchester, at Moss Side?'

Tom looked at him.

Jas talked on. 'Society's changin' ootside the Force... but inside, black officers still get a hard time, as dae Asian wans – an' Catholic. Mibby the politicians ur tryin' tae redress the balance, but canteen culture's still white, male, heterosexual – an' Protestant. Oh, they'll tell ye they'll work wi' women, chinkies, blacks, pakis, poofs an' Fenians. But it's still them against us, when it comes tae policin' the streets – an' if "them" happens tae be Catholic, it gits... complicated.' It was a gross oversimplification of a far more complex problem.

A thoughtful tug on the moustache. Then fingers to the laptop, eyes on the screen. 'You saying those refused application for transfers could be sectarian in origin? Anti-Catholic victimisation?'

Jas listened to a series of beeps from the mobile. 'Ah'm sayin' it's worth checkin'.' Why hadn't it occurred to him before?

They waited in silence. Jas stood up, leant on the back of Tom's chair and watched record after confidential record flood the screen. Then a sigh:

'Four Church of Scotlands, one Muslim – Jim Afzal, the collator down at E Division.'

A dead end – or was it? His fingers tightened on the back of the chair. 'The whole system's sectarian: huv a look fur preferential treatment of lodge members...'

Tom's head swivelled. 'Preferential treatment of what?'

Jas smiled. 'Masonic membership's practically compulsory around here.' His own colleagues, when he was in the Force, couldn't believe he had no interest in baring his knees and chanting once a week. 'E Division's version of The Old Boys' network.'

'Ah...' Understanding dawning. Head back to the screen. Fingers again tapping the keyboard. Then a sigh. 'Wouldn't know where to start – this'll have to be analysed on a case-by-case basis.'

Jas watched hundreds of names scroll up in front of him. If nothing else, it had been a useful reminder just how few Catholic police officers were in the employ of Strathclyde Police.

'Christ, look at the time...' Tom grabbed a disc from a pile, shoved it into a slot in the base of the laptop then hit a key and turned. '... let me just save this lot and I'll run you home.'

Jas smiled. 'Nae need – an' ye've hud three whiskeys, remember.' He could stay here all night.

A frown. 'There's got to be some perks to this job. One flash of my ID and any beat cop'll be prostrating himself on the ground for me.' Tom stood up, unplugged the mobile and withdrew car keys from his pocket.

Jas laughed. 'If ye're sure.'

'Least I can do, friend.' A hand patted his shoulder.

The touch revived his half hard-on. As he followed Tom Galbraith towards the door, the wall clock read five fifteen am.

At half past, the Fiesta's engine was idling in front of 247 Cumbernauld Road.

He reached for the handle.

'Thanks, Jas...'

He turned his head.

'... for everything.' Tom's face was a jutting shadow in the dark.

He longed to run his fingers down the outline of that strong jaw. Jas gripped the door handle. 'Forget it...' Like he had to forget the effect this man had on him, mind and body. '... ah've done ye an invoice, by the way – plus a formal report on Fraser's surveillance.' He changed the subject and looked away. 'Will ah post it?'

'Hand it in – I'll be at E Division tomorrow...' Soft laugh. '... later today, rather.'

Jas opened the door. 'That no' a bit risky?'

'Not now – you no longer work for me. And anyway, there was no secret about my using an outside agency. Only the nature of the work called for discretion.'

Outside agency.

Using.

His stomach clenched. Jas almost laughed at himself. 'Okay, ah'll drop 'em aff later oan. 'Night, Tam.' He studiously refused to look at the man as he left the car.

'Goodnight, Jas.'

He stood on the pavement, watching the Fiesta drive off up towards the Parade. As he turned, his eyes drifted upwards...

... just in time to see the curtain fall back into place at the bedroom window of flat 3/1.

Nineteen

At least he was ready for it when it came...

'Where the fuck huv you been? Ah wis worried sick! Ah woke up, nae note, nae you, nae nothin'!'

For once Jas had an answer. 'Ah thought ah'd be back before ye knew ah'd gone...' In the hall, he edged past the frantic figure in baggy underpants then crouched. He hauled open the fridge door, reached inside for water. '... Tam phoned an' ah'...'

'Him?' The angry voice dropped from a roar to something more ominous. 'Ah thought ye wurney workin' fur him ony mair?'

Jas removed the bottle of mineral water, unscrewed the top and drank deeply. 'Ah'm not...' The fridge door remained open, illuminating, from the knee down, pale hair-covered legs. He nudged it shut and stood up. '... if ye'd let me finish, ah wis gonny say his Nick goat himself lifted over in Maryhill an' ah...'

'Ye went away up there? An' ye dinny even work fur the guy noo?'

The sun was rising. Pink light flooded the side of a furious, confused face. Jas turned away from it, walked through to the room from which he had been watched emerging from Tom's car. 'Ah went as a friend, no' an employee.' He leant against the sill, took another drink from the mineral water bottle.

'Oh ah see...' Stevie remained in the doorway. '... friends is it, noo.'

Jas heard the implication. He laughed. 'Ah've known Tam fur years. We...'

'Oh aye – ye're such guid friends ye didney even ken who he wis when he phoned here three weeks ago.'

Three weeks.

Only three weeks.

Before that, they'd met – what, twice? Over the space of fifteen years.

He placed the bottle of water on the sill, searched his pockets for cigarettes.

'Whit is it wi' you an' him?'

He sparked the lighter, bathed in dawn glow. Good question – and one for which he had no answer. Jas moved the flame to beneath the end of the cigarette. 'The guy's got a lot oan his plate – ye met his Nick. Ye ken he...'

'Ah ken Tam Galbraith says jump an' you jump, man.'

A smile played around Jas's lips. He inhaled on the cigarette. He tried to explain something he didn't really understand himself. 'Tam wid dae the same fur me – that's whit friends ur...' The words died in his throat. Jas glanced at Stevie.

At a man who had worked down at the Hovis bakery for eighteen months and never mentioned as much as a co-worker's name, let alone a friend.

A man whose sister was the closest thing he had to a confidante.

A man whose life consisted of work, sleep, weekends with the kids and a relationship with another man which had yet to be defined...

His mind turned to his own existence.

... another man whose life he dominated, nonetheless...

The smile slipped. The glance sharpened into a stare.

... a man Jas realised he barely knew.

'Ah never ken where ye're goin' or who ye're with, these days.' Stevie's face was an unreadable shadow.

Less implication, more accusation – and with foundation? Jas found himself bristling. 'Ah could say the same fur you, pal. Where wur ye earlier, onyway?'

The shadow flinched.

'Ah waited up – ah said ah wis sorry...' The bristle solidified into more than irritation. He knew he was being defensive. '... ah wis ready tae make up wi' ye...' He knew he was being irrational. '... an' whit dae ah git?' He knew it and could do nothing about it. 'Nae explanations, more silences an' more pullin' away fae me!' Jas realised he was shouting. 'You ken where ah've been – so where did ye get tae? Where wur ye?'

'Oot.'

'Oh, very helpful – very informative! Oot... where?'

'Jist... oot!' Two words echoed in the room. Then the slam of the bedroom door.

Jas stared into the space where Stevie had been. He continued to stare until a burning against his index finger reminded him he'd lit a cigarette.

Part of him wanted to follow, take Stevie in his arms and communicate the way they communicated best. Another part of him knew sex wouldn't help – not now. Not with Stevie.

Jas opened the window, stubbed the cigarette out on the edge then tossed it onto the street below and walked towards one of the sofa-beds.

Early afternoon, he showered, shaved then grabbed the Fraser case-report and left the flat.

He had no idea if Stevie was still asleep or not. Didn't really care.

A twenty-minute taxi journey later:

'James Anderson – could ye tell Inspector Galbraith ah'm here?' Jas slapped the folder down on the reception desk of Easterhouse police station and smiled at another sergeant. It made a change not to lie or hide.

The smile returned, exponentially. 'Take a seat, Mr Anderson – ah'll jist buzz him, see if he's free.'

Same procedure as before. Jas nodded towards the door. 'Ah'll huv a smoke...'

'Aye, oan ye go.'

He moved past a duo of beaming uniforms who had entered behind him and wondered what had happened to put grins on every-one's faces.

Outside, huddled around a No Smoking litter bin, he found out.

'Aye, CID's lookin' affy pleased wi' themselves.'

'SOCO git somethin' fae last night's wan?'

'No' sure Harry, but ah heard DC Murray say there wis gonny be a press conference later oan...'

'They arrested somewan?'

'Dunno – ah asked Maggie doon in Custody an' she jist tapped the side o' her nose.'

A snort. 'We're eyeways the last tae be telt onythin', 'course. Guid enough tae spend aw' night poundin' around that fuckin' loch, but. You seen the midgies oot there? The size o' fuckin' seagulls!'

'Hey, remember the overtime, pal.'

A laugh. 'Aye, that's true – far as ah'm concerned, they can keep kickin' the shite oota poofs long as they like. Ma bank manager's happy fur the first time in his life.' More laughter. The conversation moved on to a discussion of overdrafts.

A little beyond the smoking group of beat cops, Jas leant against the side of the building.

A breakthrough in the gay-bashings. With a CIB officer on the premises. It would be wide smiles all round if E Division could bring in whoever was responsible while Tom was here.

Jas extinguished his cigarette with the sole of his boot. He was just about to light a second when the door opened behind him:

'Mr Anderson?' The Laughing Policeman stuck his head around the corner and beamed at him. 'Inspector Galbraith's no' in the day...' He held out the folder. '... want me tae lea' this oan his desk?'

His eyes narrowed. It was all above board, now: nothing damning in his report, one way or another. And he was now officially off the case.

'Eh?' The folder flicked.

The information within those cardboard covers was still confidential. 'Ah'll hang oan tae it, thanks onyway.' Jas took the report from the desk sergeant.

A happy shrug. 'Please yersel – the Inspector'll probably be at home, if he's no' here.' Then the head disappeared.

Jas tucked the folder beneath one arm and levered himself from the wall. As he walked out onto Westerhouse Road, the huddle around the litter bin had dispersed.

A squad car slowed to let him cross.

Two small boys leading a dog, which looked very like the one he'd shared a waiting room with on Friday, walked back through the gates...

He could always post his report. Or hand it in later.

... Jas strolled towards the shopping centre and Post Office.

A taxi passed.

He stuck out his hand. It stopped. He got in. 'Albion Buildings, pal – Ingram Street?'

'Right ye are, son.'

Jas sat in the back, watching Easterhouse streak by outside and wondering if Stevie had a point.

Eileen Galbraith was out for the day, visiting old friends in Coatbridge.

Loud bass-y thumps from behind a closed door indicated Nick was at least awake.

A sober-faced Tom, in shirtsleeves, led Jas into the lounge.

On the table, the laptop and the mobile. Plus a large brown envelope.

Tom picked it up, withdrew a sheaf of glossy paper and held it out. 'Found this on the doormat when I got back from running you home.'

Jas took the photos, flicked.

All were large, police-lab-format forensic shots. Four showed the faces and/or bodies of badly beaten men, injuries livid in full Technicolor. He recognised at least one from the front page of the *Record*.

The fifth featured a slim blond youth half-in, half-out of a taxi. Nick Galbraith sported the same distinctive green and white O'Neill jacket he'd been wearing the first night Jas had met him.

Nicotine-stained fingers held out a sixth exhibit.

Jas stared at a sheet of A4 paper. Typed dead centre and laser printed, one short sentence:

Do you know what your son does at night?

The hair on the back of his neck stood on end. 'You reported this?'

'What does my son do at night?' Tom slumped into a chair, head buried in hands. 'Think I want to sit here and have a shower of uniforms ask me questions to which I have no answers?' Face reappearing. Helplessness radiated from the man in waves. Tom looked older. Dark rings semi-circled tired grey eyes. A film of stubble covered the strong chin.

Jas frowned. 'Nick seen these?'

Weary headshake.

'Huv ye talked tae him, since last night?'

Wearier sigh. 'He's locked his door and I'm not up to a shouting match.'

Something in the face tugged at Jas's heart. The frown slipped into a scowl. Before his brain had time to engage, Jas was moving away from the table and towards the sound of thumping.

He added less rhythmic pounds to the electronic drums from the other side of the bedroom door. 'Nicholas? Nick?'

The thumps stopped abruptly. Sounds of unlocking. Then: 'Ja-zzz! What an unexpected surprise!' A bare-chested vision in Adidas trackies and bare feet stood in the doorway. The love-bite purpling against pale skin. 'Come in, come in!' Nick moved back into his bedroom, bee-stung lips stretching into a smile.

Jas followed. 'This isney a social call...' The scowl stayed in place. His eyes scanned the array of not unexpected chaos: midi hi-fi system, small tv, another laptop. A pair of Calvin Klein briefs draped themselves casually down over its screen. Jas watched the boy sweep an armful of assorted clothes from the unmade bed then sit down. '... you ony idea wit ye're puttin' yer dad through?'

Bare feet swinging. 'He'll just have to get used to it...' Bright smile. '... sit down, Ja-zzz.' The space at his side patted theatrically. 'I'm not about to hide my sexuality from anyone, and if Big Daddy through there doesn't like it, he can...'

'Save the speech, pal...' Jas remained on his feet. He looked down at the slim, oblivious teenager on the bed. '... your faither loves ye, ya stupid wee bastard. He'll eyeways love ye, even if ye dae go oota yer way tae make his life a misery every chance ye get.'

The bright smile fixed. Mock-jaded grey eyes rolled. One palm raised. 'Save the lecture – pal.'

The urge to slap the boy was stronger than ever. This approach was not working. Jas sighed, sank to a crouch and tried a new tack. 'Listen, Nicky: ye're dad's workin' wi' guys who make him look like... Peter Tatchell, in the acceptance stakes.' Something which had been circling in the back of his mind took form. 'It's starting tae look like there's a smear-campaign in process, 'cause of whit he's workin oan. They've awready tried to git at him through me an' Stevie...'

A flicker in the jaded grey.

'... an' if they can damage him through you, they'll no' hesitate. Internal Investigations officers huv gotta be whiter than white...'

Bee-stung lips parting into another jibe.

'... ah ken it's no' fair...' He talked through the boy. '... but that's the way it is.' Jas stared at Nick.

The feet had stopped swinging. The raised palm slowly lowered itself. Grey eyes looked away from his.

Jas caught a glimpse of the ordinary, confused teenager Nick Galbraith struggled to hide at other times. He sat down on the bed.

'It's none o' ma business an' ah've nae right tae ask, but whit wur ye really doin' up in Maryhill last night?' If the son had some boyfriend he visited up there, regardless of how unpalatable this was to the father, it was better Tom knew. 'It's important.'

A long pause. Then: 'A guy in a pub told me Dawsholm Park's good, Saturday nights. I was checking it out.'

Jas blinked. 'Whit dae ye mean... good?'

Eyes returning to his. 'Action-wise.' No hint of the jaded now. Just sparkling grey. 'No-one told me there's two parks up there – I went to the wrong one.' A frown of self-reproach.

Realisation dawned like a black sun.

No boyfriend.

No clandestine assignations.

No stolen kisses – he should have known no-one would ever have to steal anything from Nick Galbraith. Jas prayed against what his instincts were screaming at him that the kid was just another giggling watcher in the bushes.

Blasé. 'I do them all: Queens' Park, Kelvingrove, Gartloch, Strathclyde Park – although that one's a bit difficult, if you don't have transport.' Earnest expression. 'Cruising grounds are the real heart of any city's gay community, Jas...'

Gartloch.

'... real people – real men. Not clubs filled with...' Bee-stung lips twisting in distaste. '... old queens and stupid kids...'

Gartloch.

'... looking for...' A groan. '... long-term stable relationships. They're just imitating straights. As gay men, we make our own rela-tionships, don't we Jas? You know what I'm talking about.'

The kid hadn't received that love-bite from watching in bushes. All he knew was that Nick Galbraith was using an area for casual sex – an area where, at the moment, cruisers were under attack.

'Long-term stuff's great – but it's never enough, is it?'

Jas stared at the young, earnest face. All flirting dropped, the boy smiled: 'The excitement – hell, the danger. The feel of a man's hand on your cock – a man whose face you can't see and whose name you'll never know. Christ, there's nothing like it in the...'

'Thanks fur bein' so honest.' He didn't want to hear any more. Jas stood up, aware his face was reddening.

The first frown. 'You're not gonna tell him, are you?'

He sighed. 'Ah huv tae, Nicky – there's stuff goin' on here, an' he's gotta ken.'

Bee-stung lips pursed. The start of a scowl. Then the scowl swept away by mock-jaded eyes. 'I'm grounded anyway for the next week...' Head swivelling to the laptop. '... back to the chat-rooms for now, I suppose.' The blond head turned away. Nick Galbraith scrambled over the bed. The Calvins whipped from the screen. 'You and Stevie use the Internet, Jas?' Fumbling at the wall socket.

'Watch whit ye're doin', pal...' He ignored the question, wondering if Nick would obey the grounding-punishment. Jas backed towards the door.

'Yeah, yeah – I always use a condom.'

It wasn't what he meant. Jas wondered if Nick Galbraith could possibly be unaware of the attacks out at Gartloch. Then remembered the optimism of youth and saved himself a lecture. As he left the room, he could already hear the tap of fingers on keyboard.

And the panic in Tom Galbraith's voice when he told him the news.

He took it well. Only a slight faltering in the attempt to light his pipe.

'So somewan's hud Nick under surveillance too...' Jas pointed to the photograph and didn't give the man time to dwell on his son's nocturnal activities. '... an' ah think we can presume it's the same somewan responsible fur the Portacabin in ma back-court.' He stabbed a finger at the sheet of A4 paper and the short, typed phrase. 'It's veiled, but it's a threat aw' the same.' Like the flexing of muscle which had taken Stevie in for questioning because of his record was a threat.

Indicative of what that muscle could do, should it chose to exert itself fully?

'But why?' Tom gave up with the pipe, pulled a cigarette from Jas's packet. Jas lit it for him. 'Tae warn ye aff, man.'

'Warn me off what? We've found nothing on E Division.' A cough. Then a longer drag on the cigarette.

'Ye're scarin' someone, Tam – they think ye're gettin' tae close an' that...' He pointed to the four photographs, noticing another sheaf which had appeared during his absence. '... is tae gie ye a wee hint whit they'll dae if ye dinny back aff fast.'

Tom Galbraith's face creased. 'They'd attack my son, and blame it on the homo-basher?'

Jas flinched. The term was straight from the pages of the tabloids. He turned his attention to the other photographs, found himself staring at images of Malkie Orr's Great Platinum Hope, Corrigan Senior and Eric Fraser.

'Find that hard to believe, Jas.'

Anything was possible, if the stakes were high enough. Jas continued to flick, allowing his brain free rein. 'We're presumin' whatever E Division's tryin' tae cover-up is internal.' He stared from Eric Fraser's glossy face to a bruised and battered one. 'It disney huv tae be. Okay, you came up here tae investigate a complaint from an officer. But mibby the real dirty washin's fae another laundry basket.' He raised his gaze to Tom.

A tug on the moustache. Sceptical eyes met his. An eyebrow raised. 'What are you suggesting?'

He had no idea. But something told him to look where Tom had not looked before. What did the police fear most? Internal complaints could be hushed up, smoothed over. External were a different matter. 'You can hook up tae the PNC fae here?' Jas ran with the thought.

Quizzical nod.

Jas turned to the laptop. 'Call up every case E Division's worked oan, in the past... twelve months. Concentrate oan any complaints from the public aboot how they wur treated, how a case wis handled.'

No response.

He glanced over his shoulder. 'Worth a look, eh?'

A sigh. Then Tom was moving his chair closer to the table and the cell-phone was squawking with electronic noise.

At the end of the first hour, Jas made coffee.

After the second, Tom made sandwiches.

By the third, Eileen had arrived home and Nick was skulking around in the background. Jas's eyes hurt from staring at the laptop's screen.

Hundreds of minor offences ricocheted around his head.

The usual drugs deaths, alcohol and joyriding-related crime, possession, housebreaking, assaults common and aggravated.

Just another year in the Greater Easterhouse area.

'This is a waste of time...' Tom sat back in his chair and rubbed his face. '... that makes... two formal complaints in the past year...' He tapped the keyboard. '... one withdrawn, the other resolved by the disciplining of the officer concerned.'

Jas frowned. Given the state of police/community relations in Glasgow's East End, he was amazed anyone bothered complaining at all.

Slashing tyres was easier.

Stoning the police station made more impact – and got press coverage.

A policy of general non-co-operation with anything in a uniform or a squad car was the normal reaction of an area disillusioned with any attempt to enforce the law.

Jas stubbed his cigarette out in the ashtray, got up and wandered over to the bay windows. Opening one, he let petrol fumes from Ingram Street below fight the fug both in the room and his head.

At the back of his mind, the gay-bashings refused to lie down. He tried to remember who had found the first victim...

'Access the Gartloch stuff a minute.'

Weary fingers complying on keyboard. Five minutes later, the report was on screen. With names and dates.

... the unconscious body of Mr Andrew McNeil had been discovered by the proverbial dog-walker. Mr Robert Devine.

Saturday afternoon. Larkhall. A heavy man in a shell suit...

Bobby... Bobby Devine.

... sitting in Larkhall Junior's stands beside Superintendent Eric Fraser. A friend of DC Malkie Orr's.

A cold shiver ran down Jas's spine. He turned from the screen to the pile for photographs from Saturday's surveillance. As he fumbled for what he was looking for, he brought Tom up-to-date with his thought processes.

Colour drained from the already sombre face. 'Are you implying officers in the employ of Strathclyde Police are beating up gay men to distract the attention of CIB?'

His laugh was wry. 'Naw, they're no' stupid – too many guys willin' tae dae the dirty work for 'em.' Either free. Or for a price.

Muscle came in many forms. A beating was well down the list, cost-wise. But he had a feeling Eric Fraser would only use untraceable professionals.

'This is all mere speculation, you know...' Tom pulled the last cigarette from Jas's packet.

But speculation they could eliminate or firm up, with one phone call.

Who provided most 'services to the community', the length and breadth of Glasgow these days? Van-hire, to the uninitiated. Guns. Ammo. Faceless men with baseball bats and no conscience? Men with all too familiar faces with grudges, behind the wheels of stolen cars?

He pushed Stevie from his mind.

Tom lit the cigarette. '... and wild speculation, at that. You're suggesting a Superintendent in Strathclyde police would employ thugs to beat up innocent members of the public?'

Thugs in uniform did it every day. At least the motives of hired muscle were reassuringly financial. Jas frowned at the man's naiveté, withdrew his own mobile from the pocket of his jacket. 'Ah'm suggestin' we make some enquiries.'

The one person whose knowledge of who was providing what could always be counted on to be up to date shimmered in his mind. He punched in a phone number, covered the mouthpiece when it was answered. 'Ony mair coffee goin'?' He looked up at Tom: the man was still a cop.

Confusion. Then. 'Oh. Right.'

Jas watched the man get up from the laptop and leave the room. Only when he heard voices from the kitchen did he uncover the mouthpiece. 'It's me. Ur the Johnstone brothers still intae van-hire?'

Harsh laugh. 'Who you wantin' disciplined, Big Guy?'

He ignored the question, filling Marie in on the background.

A pause, then: 'Jimmy's bin moved tae Carstairs. Neil's still in Peterhead...'

One brother in Scotland's only unit for the criminally insane. Another serving twenty to life on the north-east coast.

'... did ye hear Liam's gone straight?'

Jas almost laughed. 'Whit happened?'

Snigger. 'Found himsel' a guid woman, apparently. Big white wed-ddin', last month. A wean oan the way tae. Ah gie it a year, tops.'

He grinned. 'You're too much o' a cynic, Marie.' Marriage had been the makings of worse than Liam Johnstone.

Full laugh. 'Realist, that's me.'

'So if ah'm lookin' fur a van, ah'm wastin' ma time wi' the Johnstones?'

'Ah didney say that.' Pause. 'Michael's goat a new branch in Princes Square noo. Franchisin', tae...'

Muscle or hairdressing? Jas presumed the latter. 'He still in the business?'

'Far as ah ken – an' if he's no', he can point ye in the direction o' who might be.' Voice quieter.

Michael Johnstone...

A frown slipped in to replace the smile Marie always managed to generate.

... Jas's age. His orientation. There the similarity ended. As the second eldest member of Glasgow's most notorious criminal family, Michael and Jas had crossed swords many times, during his years with Strathclyde Police.

'He'd talk to me?' The man responsible for the incarceration of both younger Johnstones? Michael had a memory like an elephant, and believed grudges should not only be held but nurtured.

'You mention Stevie's name an' ye'll be welcomed wi' open arms, Big Guy – you ken that.'

He knew all right, but wasn't about to trade on associations. Not if it was at all possible. 'Princes Square, ye said?' The idea of Michael Johnstone owning a salon in Glasgow's premier upmarket shopping precinct was both surreal and strangely believable.

'ShortCutz. Second flair...' Noise in the background. Then: 'Guid luck, Big Guy.' The connection severed.

Jas switched off the mobile. It was a long shot. He shoved the cellphone back in his pocket and looked at the laptop's screen.

But maybe a visit to ShortCutz could shave off some of the length.

'Anything?' Tom appeared at his elbow, bearing another cup of coffee.

Princes Square was ten minutes' walk from Albion Buildings.

'Mibby.' He shook his head at the coffee and got up from the table. Jas grabbed his jacket, moved into the hall.

Tom lifted the sports jacket from a row of hooks. 'I'll come and...'

'Ye'll stay here.' His territory. His contacts.

If Tom was to keep his nose clean, being seen with Michael Johnstone wouldn't help.

Solemn face. 'This is my son we're talking about. I have to...'

'You huv tae stay here. Ah'll be in touch.' Jas pushed past the disappointed man and left the flat.

Twenty

Princes Square closed at six pm.

Just before five-thirty, Jas took the escalator steps two at a time. He scanned the second floor for something flashy and Johnstone-like.

In the far right hand corner, sandwiched between the Lacoste shop and a branch of Waterstone's, a matt black frontage caught his eye. He had to look twice to see it at all, a third time to notice the discreet ShortCutz logo etched along the bottom of the window.

Very tasteful.

Very understated.

Very un-Johnstone. Maybe Liam wasn't the only member of the family to be smartening up his act.

Jas stepped from the escalator and strolled towards the black frost-ed doors.

The salon was small. But busy. An anorexic girl with hair off the colour-spectrum sat behind a narrow, Lucite desk.

'Michael around?' He smiled at her.

'You got an appointment?' Huge eyes flicking from his to the crown of his head.

'Ah jist wanna word, no' a haircut.'

A bony-shouldered shrug. The angular, immaculately made-up face tilted upwards, eyes focused beyond him. 'Micki? Someone to see you.'

Micki?

Jas followed the receptionist's eyes past half a dozen assorted sexes sporting varying degrees of wet hair, to a tall slender redhead with bare swimmers' arms and a small tattoo on the right biceps...

The grin slipped.

... a redhead who was a complete stranger. Then the man glanced in his direction.

Tanned. Fit-looking.

No scraggy ponytail.

Even the coke-addict's teeth had been replaced by a too-white, too-crowded mouthful. A tiny silver-coloured stud glinted in the lower lip.

Which winked at him as both lips tilted into a smile. 'Well, well well – Jas Anderson.' Knowing, narrowed gaze.

The voice was the same. The eyes never changed either.

Michael Johnstone's younger, leaner alter-ego patted the shoulders of a woman whose skull was a series of foil-wrapped spikes, then shouted to the receptionist. 'A coupla coffees, eh Whitney-hen?'

Seconds later, Jas found himself ushered expansively into a back office.

A lithe, silver-haired boy sprawled on one of two pale suede sofas, flicking through the pages of a *Vogue*. He didn't as much as glance in their direction.

Michael Johnstone ruffled a shock of platinum hair in passing, perched on the edge of another Lucite desk and folded tanned arms across his chest. 'Tae whit dae ah owe the pleasure?'

Jas searched for irony in the voice. Found none. He glanced at the lolling boy on the sofa. His mind was read:

'Don't worry 'boot Sandy – hear nae evil, speak nae evil.'

The youngster continued to flick through the magazine, oblivious to everything.

Something else hadn't changed: Michael still liked his meat fresh and vacant.

Jas returned his attention to the newly reinvented Micki Johnstone and began to talk.

*

He paused when anorexic Whitney knocked to deliver two expertly made cappuccinos atop a Lucite tray.

Sofa-Sandy's eyes looked up briefly from his *Vogue* to follow her no-arse out of the office.

Jas finished talking a few minutes later.

Michael Johnstone took a thoughtful sip from the large cup, licked froth from an upper lip. 'Queer-bashin' in Easterhoose?'

Jas cut to the chase. 'You involved?'

Small smile. 'Gotta draw the line somewhere, Jas Anderson...'

Part of him was pleasantly surprised.

'... ah never work wi' polis.' Laugh. 'Present company excluded, of course.'

Strathclyde police's fitting-up of younger brother Jimmy for a murder he did not commit – while in custody for one he did – was a stronger motive than any gay-solidarity.

'Ony idea who might no' be so choosy?'

'Nae-wan in their right mind.' Slow headshake. 'Too risky. Ye canny trust polis. Nae firm worth the name'd huv onythin' tae dae wi' providin' a van oan their behalf – never mind how much dosh they're offerin'.'

'Micki, I'm hungry.' West End whine from the sofa. 'Can we eat soon?'

The question ignored. 'Disney sound tae me like a professional job.' Provanmill eyes met his. 'When money's involved, these things git done properly.' Laugh. 'Nae loose ends fur nosy PIs tae pick up oan.'

'Micki...' A louder whine.

'How's Big Stevie doin' these days, by the way?' Michael Johnstone sat the empty cappuccino cup on the Lucite desk and fingered the outline of his tattoo: a love heart, cupping the initials MJ and AL.

'He's fine.' The implication was clear. Jas pushed Stevie's past connections with the family from his mind and wondered if Sandy was short for Alexander. There were worse things than having your name on a Johnstone brother's arm...

'Tell him ah said hi, eh?'

'Micki...' Louder whine. '... you said we were going to...'

'No' when ah'm talkin', eh?' The sharp crack of flesh on flesh.

... but not many. The sound of a hand across the beautiful face made his guts clench. Sandy's squeal echoed in his ears.

'Guid guy, your Stevie...' Michael smiled, once more the picture of affability. '... he kens when tae keep his mooth shut. Hey – mibby we could make up a foursome, some evenin' .' He perched on the edge of the leather sofa, one finger stroking a cheek which was already bearing his hand-print. Voice indulgent. 'Ye'd like that, wouldn't ye Sandy?'

Tearful. 'Yes, Micki.'

Iron fists in velvet gloves came to mind. And wee straight boys who would quickly work out Michael Johnstone was no soft touch.

'Whit aboot it, Jas Anderson? Dinner? Sandy's real proud o' the kitchen in the place ah've jist bought oot in Kirkhall. Dyin' tae show it aff, so he is.' Another ruffle of the silver hair.

The boy pushed against the hand, wayward puppy to long-suffering owner.

Another message, more oblique than Sandy's slap. The second invitation in as many weeks. One he'd rather chew his own arms off than accept. 'Kinda busy right noo...' And for the foreseeable future, as far as any closer connection with Michael Johnstone was concerned.

'Nae problem...' An expansive wave of the tattooed arm. '... geez a ring, when yer caseload eases aff a bit.' The other hand lay possessively on the top of Sandy's silver head. Thoughtful frown. 'Whit did ye say the name o' that polis wis, the wan ye're investigatin'?'

'Fraser – Eric Fraser. Chief Superindentant oot at E Division.'

The frown increased. 'Yon Proddie bastard?'

He'd forgotten the Johnstones were Chapel. For the smallest second, a vision of Michael Johnstone cementing the paper-thin bond between them by inflicting his own type of justice on the man flashed through Jas's head.

Then the frown was vanishing. Michael aka Micki Johnstone slid smoothly onto the body of the sofa. He hauled Sandy onto his lap.

The boy flung thin arms around his neck, face buried in the finely muscled chest.

'Widney take oot ma knob tae piss oan him if he wis oan fire.' Michael's bottom lip dragged across the top of the lowered head, silver on silver. 'But if ah hear onythin' aboot onythin', ah'll gie ye a ring, Jas Anderson.'

Of all the offers of help ever extended, this was the strangest.

'Gimme yer mobile number.'

But this was the Johnstone family: over the years, he'd learned to expect the unexpected.

Specifically, this was the man who'd provided the money and the car with which Steven McStay, on his first day of freedom from Barlinnie Prison, had killed ex–prison officer Ian Dalgleish.

Fingers snapping. A laugh. 'Ye huv goat a mobile, ah take it?'

Jas flinched. And lied. 'Naw, sorry – an' ma business phone's tapped at the moment.' This was close – closer than he wanted to get. '... tell ye whit, ah'll ring you, eh?'

A flicker in the Provanmill eyes – eyes accustomed to deceit. Michael Johnstone stroked Sandy's skinny back. 'Aye, you do that, Jas Anderson.' A knowing smile.

He began to back towards the door. 'Thanks fur yer time.'

The smile stayed in place. ''Member an' say hi tae Stevie fur me – an' guid luck wi' yer poof-bashers.'

He nodded, glanced one last time at the boy curled in the arms of one of Glasgow's most dangerous men. 'Seeya, Michael.'

'Aye, Jas.'

They were no further forward.

Not really.

Jas pressed the buzzer outside Albion Buildings. The oblique threat to Tom, regarding his son's nocturnal activities and the fate of other cruisers out at Gartloch was as cloudy as ever. And therein lay its power.

The power of the implied.

'Hello?'

Not Tom. 'It's Jas Anderson, Nick – is yer…'

Buzzing.

He pushed the door, made his way towards the stairs. Half way up the second flight, Nicky was waiting for him, in Adidas trackies and zip-top:

'Um… can I have a word?' Grey eyes glancing up, then down.

This wasn't really the time for a heart-to-heart. Silver-haired Sandy refused to leave his mind. Jas was surrounded by young men who had got into situations way over the tops of their bleached heads. Micki Johnstone's present paramour he could do nothing about. Jas paused, then lowered himself onto a step.

Nick scrambled down, took a place by his side. 'Um…'

Jas waited, looking at the pink face.

Sigh. 'Those… guys?'

Jas frowned. 'Whit guys?'

'The guys out at the loch? In the paper?'

Jas cocked his head to the boy.

Footsteps from above. Nick leapt to his feet. Jas did likewise. A woman with a small dog smiled at them and made her way down.

Nick slumped back against the stairwell wall. 'I've been thinking about what you… said…' Eyes upwards. '… about… his work, and stuff and…' Deep breath.

Jas stared at the serious, now-reddening face.

'… um… I think I sucked one of them off. Maybe two – maybe them all.' Words tumbling from bee-stung lips

'Ye whit?' His voice was louder than he'd intended.

'Shhhh!' Anxious glance two floors up. 'This is none of his business

– none of anyone's business. But if… what happened to those guys has anything to do with what he's working on, I thought I should tell you.'

Jas frowned and wondered how Tom would take the news. But it was the least of his problems. Something was starting to make sense. 'This wis recent?'

Headshake. 'Over the last month or so.'

Jas stared at the side of the boy's neck and thought of Michael Johnstone's tattoo. Other less blatant but equally damning links were available. If you knew where to look. DNA. Blood and saliva samples. Tiny ties which could become ropes around necks. He stood up, mind reeling with possibilities.

Nick did likewise. 'Don't tell him – he'll go daft and I don't need more hassle right…'

He began to walk up the stairs.

'Jas?'

He kept walking.

'Jas!'

He pushed open the door to the flat and ignored the shouts. An implicit threat to rough-up a CIB officer's gay son had suddenly become a little more complicated.

Tom stared.

Jas glanced from the array of injured faces and bodies to the photograph of a happy-looking seventeen-year-old getting into a taxi. He repeated his theory. 'Your Nick's no' jist usin' the same pickup ground as these guys. He's hud relations wi' at least two o' them. That puts him right in the middle o' this. ' He picked up the sheet of A4 paper. 'This isney a threat tae beat him up – it's wan tae implicate him.' Jas looked at the pale face and watched Tom Galbraith age ten years:

'A fit-up?' The voice was faint, all the strength drained from it.

Jas nodded, recalling the gossip he'd overheard around the litter bin out at E Division headquarters. 'And there's talk o' some sorta breakthrough in the case, so they're serious.' Fitting-up usually involved the planting of some vital piece of evidence. Was the odd trace of Nick Galbraith's saliva on the cock of a gay-bashing victim enough for an arrest?

Tom Galbraith sat down heavily, face buried in hands.

Soft footsteps behind.

Jas turned.

Nick was standing inches away, wide grey eyes focused on at his father's slumped form. Eileen Galbraith shadowed her son.

Jas looked at the two scared faces.

Nick moved close to his father, one hand inching towards a hunched shoulder. He opened his mouth.

Jas shook his head, nodded to Eileen who gently took her son's shoulders and steered him back towards the kitchen. He waited until they were no longer in sight then moved to behind Tom's chair. His own hands came to rest on blue-shirted shoulders. And started to move.

A low sound, somewhere between a moan and a sigh from the still-buried face.

Jas continued to rub. Muscle bunched beneath his palms. He ran his hands forward, wanting to ease the tension. Wanting to help wanting to...

'I can't...' The words were muffled.

Jas rubbed on.

He could.

He wanted to.

It took every shred of strength to release the shoulders when Tom's head slowly rose.

'... I can't stop.' The face turned, looking up at him. 'Not now – not when someone at E Division is desperate enough to try and implicate my son in a crime.' A scowl. 'What does that say about me, Jas? Does it make me a monster?' Tom stood up abruptly and began to rifle through the heaps of notes and photographs which littered the table. 'Some sort of inhuman, unfeeling beast?'

Maybe...

He watched power return to the man's form. Saw order resume control over the emotional chaos of minutes before. Felt cold determination replace hot, messy passion.

... which was why he was DI Galbraith. And with CIB. It took a high degree of detachment to do any police job. Internal Investigations more than most...

'Whit ye lookin' fur?' Jas pushed the laptop to one side, clearing space for more sorting.

... and, if he was honest, it was what attracted him to Tom.

A sigh. 'This is big – bigger than even my suspicious mind let me believe. Fraser's involved in something he's willing to risk his job to hide. And I'm going to find out what.'

They began with the earliest surveillance names and photographs, ran everything through the PNC.

Twice.

Nothing. Ordinary men doing ordinary jobs.

Two hours later, light was dying. Tom switched on the table lamp and reached for Saturday afternoon's haul.

'Orr we've awready checked-oot...' Jas read from his own notes. Robert Devine had emerged as D Division's civilian collator. 'The Corrigan kid's still at school – nae juvenile record. Ah...'

'Who's the joker in the baseball cap?' Tom thrust a photograph at him.

Jas peered at a long-distance shot of Eric Fraser and Corrigan Senior, tête-à-tête in the stands at Larkhall. 'The kid's father – Gerry. Gerald Corrigan. As far as ah understand, he's suckin-up tae Fraser causa his connections wi' some selection committee an...'

'Corrigan, G...' Fingers tapping keyboard...

Jas stared at the angular face beneath the baseball cap, taking in the way the long, lank hair hung down from beneath the head covering.

'... 5-6-1962?'

'He's goat a fifteen year old son – so aye. Sounds like him.' Jas continued to scrutinise the photograph.

Caught motionless by the camera's lens, something which had escaped him in the flesh now seemed vaguely familiar.

A low whistle. 'Mr Gerald Corrigan, come on down.'

His eyes flicked to the laptop.

On the small screen, offences dating back to 1984 scrolled up. Mainly public order-related…

Jas read down the list.

… four disturbances of the peace. Three drunken disorderly: two at Old Firm football matches, the third in Duke Street, two years ago, on July 12th. Two actual bodily harm – both brought by a Mrs Annie Corrigan. Both later dropped.

A sigh. 'Sweet character, this Corrigan…'

July 12th.

'… but it's all small stuff…'

July 12th.

… more tapping. 'Ah – he's also a member of the same Lodge as Fraser and Devine… and Orr…'

July 12th. The date of the Battle of the Boyne. Jas frowned. 'Aw' Orange boays – ah shoulda guessed.' The information on the screen was blurring. He rubbed his eyes, looked away. 'Onythin' mair recent oan Corrigan?'

'Hold on…'

Jas refocused on the screen. Seconds later, a name leapt out at him from the array for flickering sentences. Alarm bells rang.

'… here we go. Ah, just last year. Seems our friend Corrigan was briefly a suspect in the murder of a… Joseph Monaghan…'

Loudly.

'… a witness to the attack picked him out from the photo-books. A line-up was arranged. The witness failed to identify a second time.' Sigh. 'And Corrigan had an alibi for the time of the attack.' Tom continued to talk. 'Couple of other minor offences…'

Jas no longer heard him.

The words of a middle aged financial advisor in a well-kept West End flat came back to him in a rush. And a baseball cap – a cap the dead boy's mother swore he didn't own. The same cap Guy Walker had been unable to wrench from a dying kid's hand. A cap bearing a three-letter name.

Joe?

He grabbed the photograph of Fraser and Corrigan from Saturday, peered at it.

Or Ger?

Atop the greasy head, three blurry letters were just visible. His stomach turned over. Both Gerald Corrigan's arrests for disturbing the peace were at Celtic-Rangers matches. The guy was a lodge member. The sectarian issue refused to go away.

'… Jas?'

He looked at Tom, then lit a cigarette. And began to talk.

Ten minutes later he'd filled the CIB officer in on the generalities of the Joseph Monaghan case.

D Division, not Easterhouse.

Bobby Devine was collator with D Division. Malkie Orr had recently transferred from the same branch. The latter trained Corrigan Junior. The former was a friend. Uniting all three?

Superintendent Eric Fraser.

Fellow cop.

Fellow lodge-member.

Jas frowned. 'Whit wis Corrigan's alibi? Who provided it?'

Tom scrolled back up the screen. A pause. Ten eyes back to his. 'Malcolm Orr.' Disappointed tug of the moustache. 'Can't get much more solid than that.'

Not normally. Normally, an alibi from one of Strathclyde's finest was above reproach. Beyond suspicion.

Now?

Jas looked at Tom. The unspoken doubt picked up:

'His son's trainer and football coach...'

'... a guy whose transfer intae CID suddenly went through, jist efter that...' Jas ran with it.

'... and who owes it all to Eric Fraser.'

Touchdown.

Would Eric Fraser go as far as to suppress evidence to get a friend off a murder charge?

Jas pushed his chair away and stood up. 'The case is still open, officially ...' He stubbed out his barely smoked cigarette in the overflowing ashtray. Margaret Monaghan's sad, stoical face shimmered in his mind. '... they hud an eyewitness – an eyewitness who gave a guid description of at least wanna wee Joseph's attackers.'

And a baseball cap. With three letters on the front.

Jas glanced from the photograph of Gerald Corrigan to Tom Galbraith.

'And we've no proof, Jas.'

Two cases came together, knitting themselves into one gigantic cover-up...

He walked to the window.

... a cover-up he himself may have unwittingly nudged into insecurity, with one simple phone call. 'Ah left a message fur Bobby Devine. Last month. Ah rang D Divisions, gave ma name, telt them aboot the baseball cap.'

The sound of a lighter sparking near his ear. Jas turned, watched Tom hold the flame to the bowl of the pipe:

'We need proof...'

He frowned. Alibis... cover-ups... details suppressed and evidence removed from the crime-scene.

'... and if Corrigan's got an alibi – provided by a police-officer – that's going to be hard to break. '

Jas inhaled the smell of smouldering tobacco. He watched slender wisps of fragrant smoke drift from the bowl of the pipe and twine themselves into a thicker knot.

Regardless of its girth, every rope consisted of slender strands. And every break in every rope began with the fraying of a single one of those strands.

Jas closed his eyes. Eric Fraser, Bobby Devine, Malkie Orr and Gerald Corrigan swam in his brain.

Who was the weakest skein in the rope?

A memory of barely concealed antagonism at Saturday afternoon's football match returned.

Who was both in the deepest and most approachable?

A sigh near his ear. Then: 'Look, let me phone my superiors, tell them what we've unearthed and...'

'Ye got Malkie Orr's address?' He raised his eyes from the slowly dispersing smoke to the face beyond.

Tom raised an eyebrow. 'Don't think that's a good idea.'

Maybe if he hadn't met Margaret Monaghan. If he'd not seen her face when she talked about her dead son, or the shrine she'd built to his memory. Maybe if Jas had never heard of seventeen-year-old Joseph, how he'd sobbed as he bled to death in the back of a financial advisor's new car on the way to the Royal after three thugs had shattered his breastbone, he could agree with Tom and let official channels handle this.

'Just a word – ah git nothin', you can phone yer... superiors.' Margaret Monaghan's son was not a mere detail in another case.

Joseph deserved better than that.

He continued to stare. 'You gonny gimme that address or dae ah huv tae tackle that thing masel'?' Jas nodded to the laptop.

Lips pursed themselves around the pipe stem. Then Tom sat down at the table and the keyboard tapping began again.

Twenty-one

The taxi pulled up in front of a small semi in Bridgeton.

One of the new houses. Neat, well-kept front garden. Roses. Nearly gnomes.

Jas paid the driver and walked up a paved, weed-free path to a royal blue door. He'd liked Malkie Orr. Right from the start. He remembered the man's easy way with both himself and young Sam, two Saturdays ago. It took a special kind of guy to give up afternoons and weekends coaching a bunch of kids...

Jas pressed his index finger to a small, recently polished bell.

... the same kind of guy who would lie, on the instructions of a senior officer, to save the skin of his star-striker's father?

Ringing somewhere beyond the royal blue door.

Jas waited, pressed again.

How much had Malcolm Orr wanted that move from uniform to plainclothes? How much did he...?

The door opened. Breathless. 'Sorry, ah wis...' The round, ruddy face creased, mid-apology. Recognition flickered in small brown eyes. And something else. 'Mr Anderson, isn't it?'

'Can ah huv a word?' Jas tried to read the something else.

Antagonism?

Annoyance?

Panic?

The guy was under no obligation to talk to him. He could slam the door in Jas's face and be well within his rights. And then he could put two and two together, phone Fraser and inform him the envelope sent to Tom Galbraith's flat had done no good.

From somewhere inside the house, the sounds of cheering and a sports-commentator's enthusiastic voice-over. Jas repeated the request, eyes moving from the man's face to the leather football held under one arm.

He waited for the refusal. Braced himself for it. Jas was just about to take a step back towards the street when the something in the small brown eyes identified itself.

Resignation: he – or someone like him – was expected. Without a word, Malkie Orr moved back.

'Thanks – ah appreciate it.' Jas walked in, closed the door and fol-lowed the man through to the living room.

Another blond.

Sprawled on another sofa. Floral-covered, this time. And the blond was in shorts and Rangers' Away strip. One hand held the tv remote. The other a can of juice.

'Another twenty minutes on yer dribblin' skills – oan ye go.' Voice studiously casual, Orr tossed the football to Gary Corrigan, who laughed and caught it:

'Nae sweat, Malkie.' Remote placed on top of the tv. Tv switched off. A vaguely curious glance to Jas.

He stared around the small, army-neat room...

The sound of patio doors opening, then closing.

... army-neat, but cluttered. Every available surface held its share of framed photographs.

All featured boys. Grass. And football strips.

Some recent, some yellow with age. In between, hair style and length bore testament to football's influence beyond the field. Kevin Keegan perms nestled beside Stanley Mathews-esque short back and sides. Ponytails. Spirals. Dreadlocks. Amongst the most up-to-date, Gary Corrigan's Beckham-style bleached crop shone out at him.

'Whit can ah dae fur ye, Mr Anderson?'The tone was flat, cool.

Jas sat down on the recently vacated sofa.

Malcolm Orr took a matching chair. The face mirrored the voice. Hands lowered onto armrests, fingers curling into the dense rose pattern. Eyes past Jas to the photo display. Tensed. Waiting. Prepared?

Jas leant forward on the sofa. 'You wur with Gerald Corrigan, oan the afternoon of Saturday October fifth, last year?'

Curled fingers dug into the rose pattern. Small brown eyes to his.

Jas held them, repeated the question…

'Oh – aye. Yes. Gerry an' me spent aw' that afternoon in Coia's café, up in Duke Street.'

… and watched tension pour from the tightly held body, like someone had opened a floodgate. 'Guid memory you've got there. No' many people can recall where they wur nearly a year ago that fast.'

Orr leant back in the armchair. A sigh. 'No' everyday ah huv tae alibi wanna ma players' fathers, Mr Anderson – an' before ye ask, another six folk at least can confirm Gerry an' me wur there.' Orr rubbed his face.

Jas could feel the relief, even at this distance.

'He wis drunk – again. An' rowdy. Ah doubt there wis a soul in Coia's didney notice the big stupid bastard.'

The exact time of Joseph Monaghan's death throbbed in his mind. 'Ye wur wi' Corrigan aw' afternoon?'

A nod. 'Ah wanted a word. Telt him tae drop by the hoose.' Frown. 'Gerry showed up at the community centre – where ah take the under-elevens, Saturdays? Wan in the efternoon an' he's awready drunk as a skunk. Couldney let him go hame like that, could ah? We went fur breakfast, up tae Coia's café. Shovellin' food intae Gerry usually works. This time it didney, so ah fed him black coffee aw' efternoon. Auld Jimmy Coia phoned us a taxi 'boot five.'

He searched behind the words for some hint of theatricality. A suggestion of rehearsal. And found none. 'Whit did ye want tae talk tae Corrigan aboot?' He looked at the man. 'Fae whit ah've seen, the two o' you urney exactly best buddies.'

Orr stood up. Wry laugh. 'Aye, ah could see him far enough, at times. Gerry's a waste of space. But he's the waste o' space that's bringin' up that boy oot there.' Eyes to the garden.

Jas followed the gaze. Beyond the glass patio doors, a platinum-haired figure was playing keepy-up.

'It's aw' aboot role-models, Mr Anderson. ' Eyes still focused on Corrigan Junior. 'Yon Saturday, ah tried tae talk tae Gerry – no' fur the first time – aboot mibby settin' a better example fur young Gaz.' Eyes from the garden to Jas. 'Ah dae whit ah can, but ah'm jist his trainer. A boay looks up tae his faither, that's ainly natural.' Genuine concern in the voice.

Jas nodded.

'Annie finally found the guts tae leave her man, two years ago. Since then, it's been jist him an' Gary, up there in Ruchazie – the boay wanted tae stay wi' his faither.'

Jas recalled Malkie Orr's automatic – if inaccurate – reading of the relationship between himself and Sam, that first day they'd met down at Glasgow Green.

'Values, Mr Anderson. Boays gotta huv values – they gotta ken right fae wrong. Gaz's settled doon a lot, in the last ten months or so. But back then, he wis wan helluva loose cannon.'

Jas found himself drawn into the earnest words. He glanced at the rows of photographs, pausing at a faded black-and-white shot of a round-faced youngster with small, sparkling eyes.

The glance noted. Self-conscious laugh. 'Nineteen seventy wan. Ah pulled a tendon, the week efter that wis taken. Didney tell the coach – played a full game plus ten minutes' extra time, ah wis that keen.'

Jas looked to where Malkie Orr was rubbing his right thigh:

'Stupid bastard, so ah wis. Oh, ah'm no' sayin' ah coulda bin another John Greig. But the scouts wur interested.'

Living his life through the potential careers of other sixteen-year-olds? There was no hint of fame-by-proxy in the voice. Jas smiled. 'So The 'Ger's loss wis Strathclyde polis' gain?'

'It's a job. Ah'm no' wanna they career-cops, Mr Anderson. Never huv been. It pays the bills an' it's reasonably secure – as much as ony job is these days.'

He was wasting his time here. For all his dodgy connections, DC Malcolm Orr's words rang true. Whoever Guy Walker had seen running away from the scene of Joseph Monaghan's murder, it wasn't Gerald Corrigan.

'An' ah ken it's no' everywan's cuppa tea, but.' Curiosity. 'You wur in the Force, eh Mr Anderson?'

Jas nodded again, eyes back on the rows of photos. 'Long time ago.'

'Aye, ye can eyeways recognise ex-polis.'

Three down from a single shot of platinum-haired Gary holding a ball and beaming, another team photo.

Same blue Bridgeton Boys' Club strip. His eyes scanned rows of faces, looking for the boy.

Three red heads he recognised from Saturday's match in Larkhall. A few sandy blonds. Mostly anonymous dark brown. Jas abstractedly searched for a hair colour with more to do with fashion than genes, wondering why the team's star striker had missed this photo-session...

'Can ah dae onythin' else fur ye, Mr Anderson?'

... and paused.

In the front row, a ball between his feet.

Same eyes.

About eighteen months younger, but the same face.

No platinum crop. For the briefest of seconds, Jas saw Corrigan Senior sitting posed amongst ten grinning fourteen-year-olds.

Long brown hair. Baseball cap.

With the bleach job, there was little resemblance. Without it, they could be brothers.

Jas reached out towards the mantelpiece. Guy Walker's words circled in his head:

I could have sworn it was him. But the build was all wrong.

He lifted the photograph. In the background, Malkie Orr was saying something. It failed to register. Jas's eyes zeroed in on the cap which perched on top of Gary Corrigan's head.

And the three embroidered letters on the front.

Not JOE

Not GER.

GAZ.

His fingers smudged the photograph's glass covering. Malcolm Orr's voice edged into his ears:

'Whit chance dis the boay stand, Mr Anderson? Ye've seen his faither – seen whit Gary comes fae. Football's his way oota aw' that. Fuck Rangers – ah want the scouts fae doon South tae see Gary play. Git him ootta Glasgow, afore it's tae late...'

Too late had been and gone.

'... he's a guid kid, is Gary. Underneath it aw'. But ye grow up wi' hate, it seeps through yer skin afore ye know it. There's a phrase – the sociologists use it. Internalisin' values.'

Sectarian values. He couldn't take his eyes off the cap. The cap the medics couldn't wrench from between Joseph Monaghan's bloody fingers. The cap which had gone unlisted from the crime-scene details.

The pound of leather against stone made him turn. Jas followed Orr's gaze through the patio doors.

Beyond, Gary Corrigan was now kicking the football against a wall. Totally absorbed.

Jas glanced at DC Malcolm Orr. 'You still goat it?'

Slow headshake. 'Bobby took care of that.' Eyes never leaving the boy with the ball.

Bobby Devine. The collator at D Division.

Jas frowned.

Malkie Orr's eyes remained trained on the solitary platinum-haired boy. 'Ah wis oan the seven-to-three shift, that Saturday. The first shout we got wis up at The Royal...' Eyes narrowing. '... pick up the... deceased's effects.' Sigh. 'Ah recognised Gary's baseball cap straight away. At first, ah thought he'd bin hurt...' The round face falling. '... then ah saw the Celtic scarf an' ah knew it couldney be him.' Muscles around the man's mouth slumped. 'Ah phoned the hoose, oan ma break. Gerry wis oot fur the count, in his bed. The boay admitted whit he'd done, right away...' Glance to Jas. '... gotta give him that, Mr Anderson.'

He couldn't believe he'd missed it.

'Fourteen, he wis...' Eyes back on Gary Corrigan. '... jist a wee boay...'

A wee boy who'd kicked another wee boy to death in broad daylight.

'That shift wis a nightmare. Ah knew ah hud tae tell somewan – dae somethin'...' Sigh. '... two in the mornin' ah phoned Eric. We're in the same Lodge. He phoned Bobby doon at the collator's office...' Throat clearing. '... stuff gits misplaced aw' the time, Mr Anderson. You ken that.'

Jas stared at the side of Malkie Orr's face.

'Whit guid wid ruin' another boy's life dae? Widney bring the Monaghan kid back, wid it?'

It would give his mother closure. Let her sleep at night.

'We thought we wur clear – ootta the woods.' A sigh. 'Then you phone up D Division, askin' aboot the fuckin' baseball cap an' we jist... panicked.' Frown. 'We hud tae ken how much you knew, Mr Anderson. So Eric authorised some surveillance, on the quiet.'

The Portacabin.

The fuckin' Portacabin!

Erected not by one of Maureen's McStay's spies. Or because Jas was working for a CIB officer. But because he had called D Division, passing on information on another crime.

The murder of seventeen-year-old Joseph Monaghan.

'Ye coulda knocked us doon wi' feathers when it came tae light you wur workin' fur DI Galbraith. Think we panicked before?' A hand over the balding head. 'The last thing we wanted wis CIB stumblin' in oan aw' this...'

'So ye dug around some more – an' found ah'm livin' wi' a gay-basher?'

Nod. 'That wis too guid tae be true, far as Eric wis concerned. Haul in McStay, gie you somethin' else tae worry aboot...'

And flex some muscle.

'... same wi' Galbraith's boay. We thought if we... muddied the water enough, you an' him wid gie up an' look elsewhere.'

Jas didn't tell Malkie Orr neither he nor Tom would have made any connection between E Division and the death of Joseph Monaghan, had it not been for Fraser's muddy water.

'Ah shoulda known it wisney right. None o' it wis right...'

Jas searched for some satisfaction in finally knowing the truth.

'... ye canny pile wrong oan wrong an' expect right tae somehow come oota it aw'.'

... and found none. Jas looked beyond Orr to the garden.

The kicking had stopped. Gary Corrigan was now standing watching them, platinum hair glinting in slowly setting sunlight.

'Wan mistake, Mr Anderson – that's aw' it wis. An' he's bin a changed boay since – ye've seen him.'

One mistake which unalterably changed the lives of both Joseph Monaghan, his mother and everyone who had known the seventeen-year-old. Jas pulled the mobile from the pocket of his jacket.

'Can ah stay wi' him, Mr Anderson?' Small brown eyes to his. 'In loco parentis, kinda thing – when they take him away?'

'That's oota ma hauns...' He punched in a number.

'Can ah at least... tell Gary whit's gonna be happenin'?'

He nodded to the garden. 'Gimme a coupla minutes, okay?'

Gratitude flooding the round, sad face. Orr moved swiftly, drawing the patio doors ajar and slipping through the space towards a confused-looking Corrigan Junior.

Jas watched him go, wondering if Orr was aware of the consequences of what he'd done. Then Tom Galbraith's voice was in his ear.

'Football? Three police officers have put their careers on the line because of some kid who plays football?'

He heard the disbelief. 'Get real, pal.' Jas frowned. 'Whit's that quote – football's no' a matter of life and death: it's mair important than that.' Demonstrably more important than the worthless life and pointless death of a young Celtic supporter. He glanced at the floral sofa.

At some point during his conversation with Tom, Orr and Gary had come in from the garden.

Both now wore jackets.

Gary was crying quietly. Orr had his arm around the boy's shoulder.

Jas searched again for some sense of satisfaction in all this. Tom's voice jangled down the line:

'Think Orr'll spill the beans, for immunity? Name names, in a formal statement?'

Jas stared at Orr's round, distraught face. He somehow knew his own and the careers of the two other police officers involved in the cover-up of Gary Corrigan's crime were the least of Malkie Orr's concerns. 'Nae problem.'

'Excellent, Jas. Good work, man! Keep them there till I organise transport.'

He watched Orr fumble for a handkerchief in the pockets of his Adidas jacket, pass it to the sobbing boy.

Margaret Monaghan's shrine to her dead son shimmered in Jas's mind, overlaying itself over the figures on the floral sofa.

So much misery.

So much pain.

'Be there as soon as I can.' The line went dead.

Jas continued to hold the mobile. He stared at another potential statistic on Strathclyde police's detection rate, who was now wiping his eyes with the handkerchief and leaning against DC Malcolm Orr.

A crime was a crime.

Murder was murder – and there would be no doubt in any jury's mind of the deadly intentions with which Gary Corrigan had attacked Joseph Monaghan.

Wrong was wrong. And right was right.

No room for grey areas or mitigating circumstances...

Jas closed the mobile and shoved it back into his pocket. Gerald Corrigan's drunken face refused to leave his mind.

... so why did he feel there were more victims in this room than perpetrators?

Twenty-two

The door bell rang fifteen minutes later.

DC Orr wordlessly guided a white-faced Gary Corrigan into the back of the car.

'Call me paranoid, but ah'm no' riskin' this at either Easterhouse or London Road...' As the Fiesta pulled away from in front of the neat, well-kept garden, Jas sat beside Tom, punched in DI Ann McLeod's mobile number.

She was surprised to hear from him.

Her surprise decreased when he told her why his flat had been under surveillance for the past month and asked if he could bring a suspect in the Joseph Monaghan case directly to Pitt Street. Ann agreed to say nothing to her colleagues until both Orr's and Gary Corrigan's statements were on tape.

Half an hour later, Jas sat across a table from Tom in Divisional Headquarters' canteen, drinking machine tea. A sense of anticlimax hovered overhead. An old case was now about to be well and truly reactivated: his request to phone Margaret Monaghan and tell her the good news had been politely but firmly denied. And although DC Malcolm Orr's statement would thoroughly incriminate both Eric Fraser and God knew who else, the process culminating in their arrests would be cop-time slow.

'Where does the gay-bashing fit into all this?' Tom fiddled with an unlit pipe.

Jas drained his polystyrene cup and repeated Orr's assertion. 'Jist somethin' else fur Fraser tae use, git your attention away fae stuff he didney want ya pokin' around in.' He fingered the empty cup, turning it over in his hands. Eric Fraser et al would be kept in the dark until Tom had the evidence to bring charges against them.

'So it was all a bluff.' A frown.

Something twisted in his stomach. Jas's fingers tightened on fragile polystyrene. The security blackout surrounding the arrest and charging of Gary Corrigan was double-edged: as far as Fraser was concerned, nothing had changed. Tom was still investigating E Division. The pressure had not eased up, regarding attempts to dissuade the CIB officer to abandon the investigation.

Jas's thumb sank into the cup's polystyrene surface. And tore a large hole. The plan to stitch-up Nick Galbraith could be going ahead and, if what Jas had heard down at Easterhouse station that afternoon, going ahead swiftly.

But based on what – how did they intend to link the boy with the gay-bashing? The usually incontrovertible DNA evidence would be laughed out of court, given the numerous body fluids exchanged out at the loch.

Jas picked at torn polystyrene. Something else.

Something they'd overlooked.

Something which had Nick Galbraith's name written all over it. Jas looked at Tom. 'There onywan ye trust at aw', at E Division?'

'Jim Afzal – the collator? He's... okay.' One eyebrow raised. 'Why?'

No point in starting a panic if his worries were groundless. Jas nodded to Tom's mobile. 'Gie him a ring. Find oot whit this breakthrough is, in the Gartloch attacks' case.'

A frown. 'That's external business – I have no jurisdiction and...'

'Jist dae it, eh?' He had to know. He had to make sure. Maybe the threat to incriminate young Nick Galbraith was mere bluster...

Tom sighed, lifted his cell-phone.

... but the suppression of evidence in a murder inquiry was a high stake. And Jas had the impression Eric Fraser played to win.

'Okay...'

The polystyrene cup was now in so many pieces.

Nod. '... I see...'

Jas pushed them around the table top and tried to read Tom's expression.

'Thanks anyway, Jim.' The cell-phone snapped shut. 'Looks like your breakthrough was for the press's benefit and general division morale purposes. As far as suspects go, they've got zilch and even less, evidence-wise from SOCO. Dozens of used condoms, but that's worse than useless.'

Which meant anything intended to implicate Nick Galbraith in the offences had still to be planted. Jas gathered tiny fragments of polystyrene into a pile and wracked his brain.

Tom sucked thoughtfully on the unlit pipe.

They sat in silence for another while. In the background, the late shift wandered in. Jas listened to the sound of the machine delivering more machine-tea and divided his polystyrene fragments into two separate heaps.

'The irony of it – and it wasn't even CIB business.' A sigh, then: 'Fraser certainly tried his best to put me off the scent...' Wry laugh. '... doubt Avis'll ever rent me a car again, what with the number I've gone through. Still...'

Tom's voice faded.

Something clicked in Jas's head. 'That first time yer cor wis done over – whit wis taken?'

Curious look. 'Told you at the time: my briefcase, your first report, nothing particularly incriminating or that couldn't be replaced...' Pause.

The click echoed. Jas watched its reverberations on Tom's face.

'... the jacket. Nick's bloody jacket.'

With Jas's phone number in the pocket. He stood up. 'An' he's wearin' it in the photo that arrived along wi' the note and the injuries

283

stuff.' The draught from the movement sent the polystyrene fragments whirling to the floor.

'Sit down…' A hand on his arm. Voice low. '… it's over. Anything Fraser and his cronies try now will be…'

'They don't ken it's over, dae they?' He shook his arm free. 'They still think you're gettin' way too close an' they'll dae onythin' tae cast doubt oan your professional standin'.'

Including planting evidence damning enough to at least cause a scandal and force Tom's resignation from the case – perhaps even negating any of the work he had already done. He stared at the CIB officer.

'Jim's a good collator…' The voice still hushed. '… anything from the gay-bashing crime-scenes has already been logged. He knows I'm watching him. No way he'd let anyone – even his commanding officer – slip in something to the logged evidence of a previous crime.'

Jas's stomach clenched.

Not on a previous crime.

A crime yet to be committed?

Who would know – who was part of it, albeit a part which had now seen the error of his ways?

Jas turned and made his way past other tables and chairs towards the door.

Fifteen minutes later, they both stood in DI Ann McLeod's office. Jas looked at the slumped form of soon-to-be-ex DC Orr:

'Aye, Eric got summa the boays tae dae DI Galbraith's cor. Ah dinny know aw' the details – didney want tae. But they goat somethin' they wur pleased wi'.' Eyes from Jas to Ann. 'How's Gary doin'? Ony chance ah can see him, ma'am?'

'What's this all about, Jas?' She ignored the question.

He quickly brought her up to speed.

She listened, face clouding. Tom sat silently.

'Lemme dae surveillance oot at Gartloch, the night at least – keep an eye oan things.' He perched on the edge of her desk. 'If Fraser's boays huv ony bright ideas aboot plantin' evidence at a fresh crime scene, ah can...'

'No!' Two voices spoke at once.

Tom open his mouth to protest further, then deferred to the officer in charge.

Ann scowled at Jas. 'This is police business.'

He scowled back. 'It's ma business tae – ma flat's bin under surveillance, an' ma phone number's in the pocket of Nick Galbraith's fuckin' jacket.' He'd been fitted up in the past: it would not happen again.

'We'll handle it.' Ann's eyes were cool.

'Then get somewan oot there undercover. Somewan ye trust. Somewan that's no' E Division.'

The scowl hardening. 'Don't tell me how to do my job.' She picked up the phone, tapped in an extension number.

'Ah'm no' – ah'm offerin' assistance.' Jas tried to keep his tone even. His own stake in this was only part of it. He remembered the distaste with which the group of smoking uniforms had discussed the patrolling of the cruising ground. 'Ah'm no' scared o' gettin' ma hands dirty.' Jas locked eyes with Ann, waited for her to take him up on the offer.

Receiver to ear. 'Andy? It's DI McLeod. I need an unmarked car. This evening.' Palm covering the mouthpiece. The eye lock returned. 'Leave this to me.'

Jas ran a hand over his head. The road around Gartloch circled a good five hundred yards from the main area of activity. Anyone in a car would be hard pushed to notice anything in daylight, let alone at night. 'Listen ah can...'

'You've done enough, Jas.' Tom's hand on his shoulder. Words over Ann's hushed telephone conversation. 'More than enough.' The hand squeezed.

Jas flinched. For the first time since all this had started, he felt distance between himself and his old friend.

Tom Galbraith had more in common with DI McLeod – even Malkie Orr – than himself. The bond of the blue. The security of the serge. The prop of professionalism.

Despite everything he'd been through with Tom, Jas knew the man shared that deep sense of detachment which separated police from civilians.

Never mind that his son was gay. Never mind that gay men were under attack out at Gartloch. Voice in his ear:

'Give you a ring tomorrow, bring you up to date, okay?' The hand removed itself.

He let it go…

A wry smile twitched his lips. Naiveté was a hard trait to lose.

… the way he knew he had to let it all go. None of his concern. He was a civilian – the paid help.

Tom was right. Ann was right.

He looked to where two officers – strangers until under an hour ago – were now deep in conversation. His eyes flicked to Malkie Orr, who was staring desolately at the floor between his feet.

Then Jas was slipping unnoticed from the room and jogging down stairs out into the night.

He could hear the tv before his key entered the lock.

Jas closed the front door quietly, walked through the ex–living room into the kitchen. He filled the kettle, switched it on then sat down on a sofabed. In darkness, he began to undress.

Civilian.

Civilian.

But still bound by police procedure and, as such, secrecy? Part of him wanted to go through to the other room and tell Stevie everything. He was under no obligation not to…

Jas pulled off boots, then tee-shirt.

… tiredness tugged at a speedy brain. Another part was just glad of the silence…

The sound of a door opening.

... which was short-lived. 'Where you bin?'

Jas continued to pull off socks, listened to the breathing beneath the question.

'Eh?'

'No' noo, eh?'

'Aye, noo!'

'Stevie, it's bin a long day.' Irritation creased his forehead. 'Ah don't want ony mair arguments.'

A click. Then illumination as Stevie switched on a lamp. 'Ah'm no' arguin' – is it too much tae ask where ye've been aw' day an' half the night?'

Spoiling for a fight. Jas could hear it in the breathing. 'Go tae bed, eh?' He pulled off another sock, hands moving to jeans' waistband.

'Ye've bin wi' him.'

In the kitchen, the kettle switched itself off. Jas moved towards it.

'Is he guid?' Stevie followed. 'Is he... better than me?' A growl.

He almost laughed. It was a joke. Jas Anderson, with a crush on another married man.

'Go oan... say it.'

Jas shook his head, lifted a mug from the rack and grabbed the coffee jar. Whatever ridiculous, irrational fantasies he'd nursed of himself and Tom had vanished the moment they'd both stepped into Pitt Street police headquarters.

Something about seeing the man in his natural milieu.

Away from his family.

Amongst those with whom he was closest.

Any desperate notions he'd ever entertained of himself and Tom Galbraith had turned to dust, the drying dregs of a wet dream. Jas spooned granules into the mug and lifted another from the rack. 'Want wan?' He turned .

A lightning movement knocked both mugs from his hands. 'Will ya fuckin' answer me?'

Jas flinched. Smashing around his bare feet. He stared at the furious outline a yard away. 'Will you git a fuckin' grip?' He seized a bulging forearm, pulled Stevie towards him. 'Ah've bin wi' Tam, aye – an' his son an' his wife an' assorted cops an' wee boys.' He spat the words into Stevie's face. 'Ah wis workin' – okay? Workin' tae earn the money so's we can git a bloody mortgage fur a proper hoose an' you can huv yer bloody kids stay weekends wi' us withoot every damn social worker in the area hangin' around to make sure we're no' fucking in front o' the wee darlins!' He tightened his hold, then spun Stevie away and pushed past him into the ex–living room.

He knew he was shouting. He didn't care.

Something crunched beneath his bare feet. He hardly felt it. Jas fumbled in the darkness, rifling through the pockets of his jacket for cigarettes.

'Ah thought ye liked Sam an' Hayley.' The voice was soft.

Jas found the packet. Empty. He crumpled it in his fist then threw it at the wall. 'Ah dae! Ye ken ah dae!'

This had nothing to do with Stevie's kids.

Or Tom Galbraith.

And he knew it. 'Ah jist...' Jas fumbled for the words. '... oh, Christ, ah don't ken.'

A loaded silence draped the space between them. Then: 'Ye're no'... interested in me onymore.'

Jas turned.

Stevie's face was lowered. 'It's okay – ah've seen this comin' fur a while.'

His stomach flipped over.

'The kids ur the thin end o' the wedge...'

At the thick end of which stood what was really pushing them apart. Jas wanted to reach out, wrap his arms around the unhappy man who stood less than a yard away.

'... ah... hurt people, Jas. Ah hurt people like... you.'

He frowned. 'Ye did yer time, Stevie. That's aw' in the past.' A ghost hovered between them, unmentioned and unacknowledged.

'Ah'm useless wi' yer... friends – ah don't feel... right wi' you ootside this flat.'

A memory of another dinner-invitation pushed itself into his mind. Would Stevie feel any more at ease, in the company of Michael Johnstone, the man who had paid him to kill an ex–prison officer? 'That's goat nothin' tae dae wi' it. Ah've never felt the need o' a social life in the past, an' ah dare say ah can survive withoot wan in the future.'

Even the fact that Stevie had killed in cold blood he could live with. The reason for that act? Jas stared at rigid shoulders.

'Ah'm problems ye don't need...'

He sighed. That much was true. Jas remembered the Portacabin and knew he brought his own share of difficulties to any relationship.

'... but ah love ye, man.'

Irritation hardened his mouth into a frown.

Words.

Just words.

Meaningless, easy to say words. He knew what was supposed to happen now. He'd repeat the phrase back to Stevie. They'd embrace. Hugging would twist into sex and they'd be all right again.

Till the next time.

Jas sat down on the sofabed. 'Why did ye dae it?'

The head shot up. 'Why did ah dae... whit?'

The frown slid into a scowl. 'Why did ye kill Ian Dalgleish?' Jas knew the answer, knew it was at the root of everything.

No response.

'Ye'd done yer time. The slate wis wiped clean...' Cleanish, at least. '... you coulda had a fresh start – a real wan. But oh no, you hud tae...'

'Ah did it fur you. Ye ken that, Jas-man.' Stevie sank to a crouch in front of him. 'That bastard... hurt ye. Dalgleish let they guys...'

'Ye think that helped? You honestly think huvin' that oan ma conscience really helped?' They were getting closer to it, now.

Stevie stared up at him. In the reflected beam of a back court street-light, amber glints shone. 'He didney deserve tae live – after whit he did tae you, he didney deserve tae...'

'You ony idea how that feels?' Jas rubbed his face, forcing himself to say what he should have said fourteen months ago. 'Knowin' you're capable o' that?' He removed his hands, scowled down at the crouching man. 'That you'd ... dae that, in the name o' whit you ca' love?' Not to mention the extreme discomfort which came from this new connection to the Johnstone brothers.

... ye canny pile wrong oan wrong an' expect right tae somehow come oota it aw'.

Malkie Orr's words came back in a rush. 'You're as bad as they are, man – worse.'

Stevie's face was a mass of confusion. 'Whit did ah dae? Whit did ah dae that wis so wrang? Dalgleish killed Paul McGhee – Marie's wee brother. He wis responsible fur... Christ kens whit, on top o' whit he did tae you. The bastard hud it comin' – the courts widney dae their job so ah did it fur them.'

So many add-on justifications. So many reasons to look past the real damage Stevie had done that night. Jas sighed. What passed for love, as far as Stevie was concerned, had a power and ferocity which scared him.

Partly because it was unpredictable. Mainly because Jas knew he could never live up to it. Or equal it.

And that scared him more than memories of a prison gymnasium and an attack long over and done with. 'Ach, forget it!' Jas ran a hand through blond hair. Four hours' sleep and two days' work caught up with him in a rush.

'You sayin' ye'd rather ah hudney killed him?'

He laughed. 'Well, no' tae put too fine a point on it, aye! Dress it up aw' ye like, ye're still a murderer, plain an' simple. Ye're gonny have tae live wi' that the rest o' yer life!' As was he.

'But ah did it fur you, Jas-man! Ah love ye – ah hud tae! Ah couldney... live wi' the thought that bastard wis gonny be walkin' around free efter whit he'd done tae...' Stevie stopped abruptly.

Jas watched something sink into that thick, beautiful head...

Stevie turned away. 'Ye never say ye love me, man.'

... the wrong something. Jas stared at the profile bathed in orange sodium from beyond the window. 'Jist cos ah dinny... run aff at the mooth, disney mean ah don't.' He didn't have the words – never had.

'Then say it.' The head flicked round.

Jas looked away.

'Say it...'

A hand on his shoulder.

'Fuckin' say it!'

Two hands. Shaking him. Instinct cut through exhaustion. His right fist balled then shot up, catching Stevie on the side of the face. The punch regretted as soon as it was thrown. Jas staggered backwards, pushing the man away with the other hand before he did more damage.

'Ah, ya...!' Stevie lurched sideways, grabbing a lamp for balance. It fell, smashed.

'Oh Christ, ah'm sorry – ah...' Jas stumbled forward, knuckles stinging.

Then noise. In the sudden darkness. And movement.

'Stevie!' By the time he regained his balance, the front door was slamming. Jas moved swiftly towards it. Only when his bare feet hit lino did he realise he was still half undressed.

Back in the lounge, he located shoes and jacket: tee-shirt and socks were irretrievable blurs in a room full of shadows.

Then he was racing from the room, grabbing keys and pounding down three flights of stone steps.

It was just before midnight.

On Cumbernauld Road, he scanned left, then right.

Then left again.

At the intersection with the Parade, a bulky figure with a ponytail hurriedly crossed the street.

Jas broke into a sprint, following Stevie up and round past the traffic lights...

Engine sounds.

... which turned green just as he reached them. A stream of cars, buses and taxis coursed past him.

Jas dodged between them, got as far as the pedestrian island. He cupped hands around mouth. 'Stevie!' The shout drowned by a slowing bus. He stared across Cumbernauld Road, watching the bulky figure stick out his hand.

The bus slowed further.

Stevie got on.

The bus pulled away just as traffic stopped and a green man winked at him from the pedestrian crossing.

Heart pounding, Jas raced into the bus's wake. He was just in time to catch the number.

A 51. Barlanark via Cranhill. Stevie was going to his sister's. To a sympathetic ear.

Jas scowled. Numerous other times he'd let him go.

Not this time.

Not now.

Frustration spangled in his veins, joining the adrenaline. Turning away from the departing bus, he gazed into oncoming traffic. And stuck out a hand of his own.

The first taxi drove on past.

The second indicated, drew into the kerb.

Jas hauled open the door and leaped in. He tried to remember Carole MacStay's address. Something in Starpoint Street... or Corran Street. His eyes never left the rear lights in front.

'Where to, pal?'

Jas frowned. 'Follow that bus – the 51?'

A laugh. 'Man, ah've waited a lifetime tae hear somewan say that!'

The driver screeched away from the kerb, overtook two cars. 'This is like the movies, eh?' Eyes in the mirror.

Jas scowled.

'Ah... well, mibby no'.' For the rest of the journey, the driver kept his mouth shut.

Edinburgh Road came and went.

The bus wound left up into Cranhill. The taxi driver slowed when it slowed. Paused when it paused.

Jas scanned every bus stop every time passengers disembarked.

Cranhill came and went. As did Blairtummock Road. Finally, just outside the shopping centre on Westerhouse Road, a bulky figure with a ponytail emerged from between pneumatic doors.

Jas pulled a fiver from his pocket, thrust it at the driver and got out. The meter read £2.50.

'Cheers, pal!'

Jas slammed the door, looking to where Stevie was now jogging down towards the old sports centre. Then veering abruptly left, off the street and into the waste ground...

His heart thumped.

... and towards the fields leading to the loch.

Twenty-three

The sky was clear and full of stars...

Jas plunged after Stevie, still dazzled by the streetlights. Dew from knee-high grass soaked his jeans. Feet squelched and stumbled into boggy ground.

... unlike his mind.

Ah hurt people, Jas. Ah hurt people like... you.

His eyes never left the outline of the figure twenty-five yards ahead...

Gartloch. Attacks on cruisers. When had it started? After he'd begun working on the Fraser job? After Stevie had become convinced he and Tom were somehow involved. No – before that: earlier victims had come forward.

... a bush reared up out of the darkness and raked his face. Jas inhaled sharply, pushed it away...

About the same time Maureen McStay had returned to Glasgow, bringing with her demands for access, the first skirmishes of a custody battle: problems Stevie didn't need?

... the dark outline in front was pulling ahead. Jas walked faster, avoiding the branches of a second hawthorn bush. His heart pounded in his ears...

Sexuality was an ongoing war within Stevie. Always had been, always would be. Jas's sexuality. His own sexuality. A sexuality he managed to handle if he didn't have to face it.

But if he did?

... underfoot, grass became worn earth. Stevie was leading him onto a path.

Stevie had been here before.

His eyes were starting to acclimatise to the blackness. Jas quickened his pace and tried to narrow the distance between himself and the man in front.

The undergrowth was becoming thicker. And he could smell the damp wet notes of the loch. He ducked under the thick bough of a ancient tree, hand slipping on its mossy trunk. He couldn't duck the thoughts...

The storming out. The early morning returns. A sudden taste for nocturnal showers. The attack on the Portacabin guy. Explosions of temper followed by tears and regrets.

... had, for once, E Division hauled in the right suspect for questioning?

Jas trudged on. No...

The attacks were increasing in violence.

... no...

Stevie's moods had grown more erratic over the past three weeks. And with it his confusion?

... no...

Steven McStay was a convicted gay-basher. And a murderer.

Jas shook his head to clear it and stumbled on. Somewhere to his right, a duck squawked. The mocking laughter echoed around him. He tried to get his bearings. Despite the quacking, the damp wet smells were receding. Jas followed the pathway, felt it curve around the loch side.

Ahead, the dark outline turned sideways and slipped through the gap in the same rusting cast-iron railings he and Tom had slipped through from the other direction.

Jas felt the scratch of bramble bushes as he did likewise, emerging into a grassier, drier area...

He swivelled his head.

… an area devoid of life.

He frowned, scanning left then right.

Nothing. No-one.

Ahead, he could just make out the incline leading up towards the grounds of the derelict Gartloch Hospital. Left?

Jas blinked.

To the west, movement. And shape.

Jas strode towards it.

He was ten yards away when he saw that the figure approaching him was smaller. Slighter.

And was rubbing the front of baggy cargo pants.

He swerved as they passed, ignoring the invitation on the stranger's face…

So much for the warnings in the press.

… the slight man smiled, shrugged good-naturedly and disappeared into a clump of trees.

Jas walked on, ears now working better than eyes. He followed each rustle, investigated each rip of lowered zipper and half-choked-back gasp of release. Elbowing his way through a cluster of shadowy outlines, he watched one man kiss another, then push him to his knees before an open fly. He searched the shaded faces of every figure he passed, peering closer than was necessary for the purposes of anonymous sex.

His interest was noted.

Jas shrugged a hand from his shoulder. Another from his arse.

No-one spoke. No-one said anything at all.

This wasn't about words. This was about making contact in the oldest way. The feel of another's cock. Another's hand on yours. The rasp of a stranger's stubble against your thighs. And the sour tang of a man's spunk in your mouth.

Amongst the rustles and the heavy thud of bodies on grass, the occasional alarm-beep of a wristwatch called its owner back to reality.

A cell-phone trilled softly, eliciting a curse then a laugh from thigh-high grass.

Jas continued his search. He was half-hard without realising it, sucked into the atmosphere and the smell of male bodies.

All ages. All physical types. All backgrounds and income groups.

Cruising: the great leveller. The only requirements a cock, a mouth and a need.

After a fruitless fifteen minutes, Jas veered away from the main area of activity.

At the top of the incline, taller trees. Pines. And the corresponding lack of undergrowth beneath. He scrambled up the hill towards them.

On his arrival, three blurred outlines merged back into the darkness.

Jas leant against a tree and rubbed his face. The moon slipped from behind cloud. Needles and haystacks shimmered in his mind. This was useless. Pointless. He'd never find…

A sharp crack sent shudders up his spine.

… his head snapped round at the sound of the breaking twig.

Two.

Two men.

The face of the guy on the ground was hidden.

Standing rigid against the trunk of a pine tree, fists balled at his sides, the expression on the other's was all too visible. And familiar.

His stomach flipped over. Jas stared.

Stevie focused neither on him nor the head of the man who gnawed at his groin. Dull amber eyes were tiny, narrowed slits, staring straight ahead out over the Easterhouse marshes. Full lips parted in a hard line, more pain than passion.

Jas's cock flexed against the zip of his jeans. He looked away, eyes zeroing in on the man on his knees.

The guy had one fist wrapped around the lower half of Stevie's half hard-on. The other fumbled somewhere in the crotch of his own clothing.

Jas watched the blow job, watched the skill with which this stranger licked around the head of a cock he knew so well. Then the face dipped, the tongue moving to flick over Stevie's balls.

The guy was making guttural noises, the hand in his own crotch moving faster.

His eyes returned to Stevie's pale, creased face. Nothing. Not a sound. Just an increase in the scowl and a tightening in fists which hung from tensed shoulders.

Jas wanted to intervene. Couldn't. He wanted to look away. The face he'd stroked and kissed so often held his eyes in a vice...

Fear, affection, jealousy and arousal swamped his brain.

... with effects three feet lower. His cock strained against the fly of his jeans. His stomach twisted into knots. Sweat poured from his pits, cooling on night-chilled skin.

Another twig snap behind.

It barely registered.

The soft crunch of boots on pine-needles. The brush of breath near his neck. The warmth of a palm on his shoulder.

Jas moved right, away from the hand and closer to Stevie and the guy.

The owner of the boots lingered, watching with him. Then a soft, departing crunch.

He could smell them now. Above the dry tang of the trees and the earthy odour of dew-soaked ground, a saltier scent drifted into his nostrils.

The guy on his knees shifted. The hand which had been busy in his own crotch now pushed Stevie's tee-shirt up from his stomach. A mouth Jas couldn't see roved over lightly haired skin he didn't have to.

And the fists tightened.

Wet, nuzzling sounds. Beneath that, the moans deepened towards climax.

He wanted to close his ears. He wanted to walk away. Babysitter and voyeur, Jas stood there and let the damp head of his own cock throb against his stomach.

Still no sound from Stevie. Nothing at all.

Then the mouth was back, the hand returning to crotch. A low, guttural sigh at the double contact. The blow-job recommenced.

He blinked to clear the sting from his eyes. And continued to watch.

The shaking began in his stomach, a low tremble radiating outwards. Jas fought it, then gave up and went with the shivers. Every hair on his body stood erect. His mouth was dry, lips cracking as he watched what filled another's mouth.

So much contact: one-sided contact.

Stevie continued to gaze out over marshlands. His face was shadowed. A sliver of moonlight cut through the trees and glinted on whitened knuckle.

Just when it seemed the sucking would go on for ever, the guy on his knees broke off the blow-job, raising his head to Stevie's face...

'You okay, pal?' A whisper in the dark.

... and breaking the silence. As he did so, Jas caught a glimpse of five flaccid inches between four confused fingers.

Then tensed arms were moving for the first time in over twenty minutes. Stevie grabbed the guy's shoulders. The noise which came from his mouth was half-sob, half-snarl.

The guy gasped.

Powerful arms hauled him from his knees.

Jas watched Stevie draw the man closer. The sound mostly snarl now.

Ah hurt people, Jas. Ah hurt people like... you.

Like slow-motion. Action replay – from four years ago? Or Saturday night?

Jas's eyes focused on the anguished, pain-filled face. He saw the loathing there...

Lashes sparkled wetly.

… self-loathing. Which nonetheless lashed out to hurt everything around itself.

Jas moved from the shadows. He seized a rigid arm, smashing his elbow into Stevie's kidneys and pushed the other man away:

'Whit the hell…?' The guy staggered, then regained his balance. 'Whit's goin' on here, ya…'

'Beat it, pal!' Jas gripped Stevie by both shoulders.

Confusion from the third party. 'Ye might huv asked, at least…' Confusion into irritation. '… we wur…'

Stevie's knees buckled. Jas held on, draping one arm around his shoulder.

Irritation into understanding. A stranger's eyes flicked between Jas and Stevie. 'If you two ur playin' some sorta… wee game, mibby tell folk next time, eh?' A grumpy laugh. And the sound of retreating feet.

He half-pulled half-dragged Stevie from the clearing deeper into the body of the wood:

'Ah, Jas-man…'

He ignored the voice.

'… haud oan, willya – ow'! Ya…!'

He ignored the way the trees ripped at their arms.

'Listen… man, listen…'

He ignored Stevie's attempts to wrestle free and tightened his grip.

'Haud oan, will ya!'

The impact of a fallen tree with his shins called a halt to their progress. Jas yelped, released Stevie who spun round to face him:

'Man, ah didney mean fur ye tae find out – no' like this, ah mean…'

Jas rubbed tingling bone and focused on his stinging shins. After twenty minutes of staring at it, he couldn't look at the distraught face now.

'… ah'm sorry… man, ah'm so sorry…'

His head inched up.

'Ah dunno how it aw' started...' Stevie was sitting on the fallen tree, face buried in hands.

He didn't want to hear it.

'... been doin' it fur... coupla months, noo...'

He'd been Father Confessor too long already.

'... somethin' inside me jist... snaps. Ah canny help masel' – when ah feel like this, ah jist wanna...' The hands removed themselves.

Dull mahogany eyes met his.

'... how did ye ken where tae find me? Did Nick tell ye?'

The unexpected name hit him like a rabbit punch. 'Ah followed ye oot here – an' whit's Nick Galbraith goat tae dae wi' aw' this?'

A sigh. 'Couldney believe it when he walked intae that room, grin-nin' at me...'

Dinner with the Galbraiths. The jibes. The footsie under the table.

'... bumped intae him a coupla times, oot here – before an' since...' A frown. 'It wis Nick that twigged me tae you an' his... faither.' Amber lights glinted in the dull mahogany. 'Telt me you an' Tam wur seein' a lot o' each other. Ah'm no' daft – ah ken he thought he wis jist... stirrin' between you an' me, but ah knew different.' Pause. 'But whether there's onythin' between you an' Tam or no', you dinny love me ony mair, Jas – if ye ever did. Ah ken these things jist... happen...'

He moved forward, opened his mouth.

'... nae-wan's fault, really...' Stevie talked through any protests. '... but ah had tae ken it aw' – you widney tell me nothin', so ah...' Scowl. '... gave Nick the phone number, asked him tae keep me informed.' Wry laugh. 'Talk aboot wantin' tae make it worse fur yersel'?' A wet glint in the mahogany.

Not his phone number in the pocket of Nick Galbraith's stolen jacket.

Stevie's.

'There's so much goin' oan, Jas-man...' The glint sparkled. Stevie wiped his nose on his sleeve. '... Mo, the kids... me an' you... Dalgleish – Christ, that fucker's causin' mair misery deid than he did when he wis walkin' aroun'!' An attempt at a laugh. It turned into another sniff. Jacket sleeve smeared across eyes this time. 'Ah'm trouble, Jas – eyeways huv bin, eyeways will be. Ah'll move oot the morra, okay? Doss doon on Carole's floor till ah git maself sorted oot...' Jacket sleeve from eyes. The amber glints now a shadow of their former selves. '... an' ah'll go tae the polis, tell 'em everythin' – if that's whit ye think ah should...'

'No...' So far, no-one had been killed. Jas closed the distance between himself and Stevie, sat down on the fallen tree. Before he knew what he was doing, his arms were around now-heaving shoulders.

They'd get help.

Counselling.

Advice.

As other, less rigid arms flung themselves around his neck, a set of four SOCO photographs depicting four sets of vicious injuries shimmered in his head.

Jas pushed them away and pulled Stevie closer. 'It's okay...' He nuzzled a cold ear. '... everythin's gonny be okay.'

How much was his fault? How big was his part in the circumstances which drove Stevie to attack and maim innocent men? Maybe if he'd been there more often. Been more understanding.

Managed to shift the three words which huddled in the back of his throat onto his lips?

'Ah'm sorry... ah'm sorry...' Stevie's hands roved up and down his back.

Jas shifted position, straddling the fallen tree to get a better grip. The movement dragged rough bark against the surface of his balls.

His hard-on flexed.

Then one hand was on Stevie's neck, tilting the tear-steaked face from his chest and groping for the mouth. The other pushed down into the man's groin, searching for the cock a stranger had failed to harden...

Stevie moaned, gripping the sides of Jas's face and returning the kiss.

... and finding eight inches of stiffening flesh. His fist tightened around it.

Stevie groaned, deepening the kiss and pushing Jas back.

He went with the motion, pulling Stevie onto him as the man thrust a knee between Jas's own thighs.

He didn't know who broke the kiss.

He didn't know who started to undress first...

Jas tore at the fly of his jeans, watching Stevie wrestle arms free of jacket then tee-shirt.

... and he didn't care. His shaft pulsed against his own palm. His other hand reached out to stroke the scars on Stevie's chest.

Then their mouths met again and his hands were on goose-fleshed arse cheeks, schoolboy fingers stuttering towards the opening to the man's body.

No lube.

No condom.

The thought shared.

Stevie jerked away. The sound of phlegm hawked from throat. Then the shadow of movement in the dark.

Jas watched Stevie grease himself up, spat on his own palm. His cock flexed with need as he smeared saliva over the sensitive head.

At the back of his lust-addled brain, part of him knew this was madness. Another part told him Gartloch was at present safer than it had been for months.

A foot away, a convicted gay-basher was now kneeling in front of the fallen tree. Ponytailed head turned sideways, cheek pressed against rough bark. Two large hands wrenched other cheeks apart, holding them there.

Jas's prick flexed in his fist. Before his brain could rationalise further, he was crouching behind Stevie's pale outline. He rubbed the head of his cock against the crinkled arsehole, the fingers of his other hand pushing up under the ponytail.

The drag of already drying spit. Tensed thighs trembled against his. His balls clenched. Jas leant forward, mouth open on Stevie's spine. And pushed between those parted arse cheeks.

A harsh, low moan. From two sources.

The muscle resisted.

He continued to push, lips widening in a half-scowl of pleasure.

Then other lips opened in parallel. The warmth of Stevie's body surrounded the sensitive glans.

His teeth came together, sinking into the skin on Stevie's back. His prick sank further into the hot vice.

A grunt of satisfaction. The hands left the arse cheeks. One arm braced against the fallen tree trunk, the other grabbing his own cock, Stevie turned his head.

As he continued to move ever upwards, their eyes met.

Something in his stomach torqued, relaxed and torqued again. Jas lunged forward, slamming the last two inches of himself into Stevie. He tried to kiss the man.

His balls impacted with shivering arsecheeks. His lips met air...

The clenching clenched again.

... then Stevie was pushing back onto his cock, grinding down onto him with both arms braced against the tree trunk.

Jas fumbled for jutting hipbones and held on.

At some point during the fuck, the vice tightened around his aching shaft and he knew Stevie had come.

Calves cramping, the smell of sex and wet earth in his nostrils, Jas thrust faster...

Wanting to hurt. Wanting to punish. Wanting revenge on behalf of the four men Stevie had beaten senseless over the past month.

... needing it to be over so he could hold and stroke and kiss this man whose arse he pummelled like a punchbag.

When he did come, it was on him in seconds.

Stevie reared up off the fallen tree. Hands pawed at Jas's arse cheeks, pulling him further inside. His cock shuddered and pumped into the hot body.

They were both on their knees. His right arm circled Stevie's waist. The left was a sweaty stranglehold around a bristling neck. Hair from a wet ponytail stuck to his face. His balls contracted again, surrounding his prick with another slitful of warm spunk.

Someone was shouting. With the receding force of the orgasm, he recognised his own voice.

Stevie's palms reached up and back, clasping either side of his face.

His cock remained inside the warm body until the shouting was soothed by low, hoarse whispers and one of Stevie's hands was tight in one of his.

After a while, he felt himself slip out.

Flaccid and tacky, his prick nestled between Stevie's legs and buffeted the loose ball sac. Jas nuzzled a pattering vein on the side of a stubbly neck and let his breathing return to normal.

With it came reality. And reality's problems.

Jas eased away and hauled up his jeans.

Stevie continued to hold his hand. 'Whit happens noo?' Said without turning.

'Go home...' The reply was automatic. '... stay there till ah come an' get ye, okay?'

'Okay, Jas.' No arguments. No questions. One last hand squeeze, then Stevie was fumbling on the damp ground, cursing softly before locating jeans and tee-shirt.

He found cigarettes in the pocket of the denim jacket, lit one and sat on the tree trunk. Jas watched Stevie dress, pulled another from the packet and held it out...

'Cheers...'

... then lit it. In the yellow flame, the pale face looked younger. Golden lights glinted in shining, amber eyes.

They smoked in silence, thighs touching on the fallen tree trunk.

Somewhere between shoving his cock into Stevie and easing it out, something had happened.

He had no idea what. He had no idea where they could go now...

Movement at his side.

... Jas watched Stevie extinguish the end of his cigarette between thumb and forefinger, toss it into the darkness:

'Don't be long, eh?'

'Ah'll see ya later.' He did know that somewhere around the Gartloch cruising ground, there was the chance someone was waiting to plant evidence.

Catch whoever it was with Nick Galbraith's distinctive jacket and a whole lot of loose ends could be tied up...

Stevie stood up.

... distracting the eye from others which would forever hang dangling?

Throat clearing. 'Um... whit way dae ah go – never bin up this part before.'

Jas almost laughed. He waved vaguely through the trees. 'Get back doon ontae the main path then cut across the marsh – it's dry as a bone, this time of year.'

A nod. A shuffling of feet. More throat clearing. 'Jas-man, ah...'

'Will ye git oota here?' He thrust the irritation into his voice and threw the smouldering cigarette into the undergrowth.

No response.

Jas stood up. His eyes followed Stevie until the outline became blurred by trees. Then he turned and walked back up the hill towards the main action.

Twenty-four

Same bushes.

Same rustles.

Same action...

Jas side-stepped two shapes on the ground, necking like teenagers. The moon glinted off the back of one near-bald head.

... different participants.

Safer participants, now the gay-basher was on his way home.

He scrambled through dense undergrowth, down onto the main road which skirted around the old hospital and the loch.

Two parked cars.

He strolled towards the first, remembering DI Ann McLeod's promise. Steamed-up windows and telltale rocking prompted him onto the second.

A dark-coloured Jag. Way above any division's budget, undercover or otherwise.

Jas sauntered past, caught the eye of the car's sole occupant.

The man gestured, smiled.

Jas glanced at the hard flesh protruding from the open fly of what looked like Armani tailoring, shook his head and turned back into the undergrowth.

In over an hour's total wandering, he'd encountered the odd, solitary figure, more intent on watching than engaging in the sex on offer.

He read the body language. Smelled the shyness. Or the lack of courage. Or empathised with the voyeur's thrill. Some sixth sense helped him eliminate all non-participants as potential evidence-planters...

'Got a light, pal?'

Jas held out his cigarette to a figure in a biker's jacket. The guy took it.

... another, less esoteric instinct told him he was wasting his time here.

Literally.

Maybe not wasting.

Buying.

Buying time.

Putting as many seconds and minutes between going home and what he knew he had to do there.

'Cheers...' The cigarette held out.

Stevie.

Jas took it, wandered off towards the wooded area.

Stevie.

Loose ends never went away.

Stevie.

The way Ian Dalgleish continued to haunt their lives was proof of that.

Stevie.

... ye canny pile wrong oan wrong an' expect right tae somehow come oota it aw'.

Jas frowned. He had more in common with Superintendent Eric Fraser and DC Orr than a previously shared uniform. The more you tried to hide something, the more it pushed its way up from the depths.

Stevie.

Denial had a habit of finding expression for itself elsewhere.

Stevie.

Jas ducked past pine trees, twigs firing underfoot like gunshots.

Emerging from the forest, he found himself on higher ground. He paused.

It hadn't been hard to sweep ex–prison officer Dalgleish's murder aside as something that needed doing. The faces and bodies of four innocent cruisers were less easily dislodged.

His eyes moved over the skyline, from the twinkling lights of the Easterhouse estate to the darkness of the marshland. Striking against the flatness of the latter, a bulky outline was making its way back towards a still-distant Westerhouse Road.

Jas blinked. Stevie had obviously got lost. But at least now he was walking in the right direction.

So quiet. So peaceful. So...

... a loud trilling from somewhere close shattered the silence.

Irritation jangled through his bones. Jas frowned around at nearby trees then realised the sound originated in his own jacket. He pulled the mobile from his pocket. 'Aye?' Only one person had the cell-phone number.

'Um... Jas?'

One person with a seventeen-year-old son. He frowned. 'Whit is it?'

'Um... I wanted to tell you this earlier, but you...'

'Nick, this isney a very good time.' Another heart-to-heart was the last thing he needed.

'Let me say this. Um... I know it's none of my business, but with what's been going on out there, Jas, I think you should know... your Stevie cruises.'

Old news.

He almost laughed. Before he could get words out, Nick's voice again:

'We – me and him – we... sort of had sex. It didn't amount to much, though: I wanted him to fuck me, but he couldn't get it up. Maybe I shouldn't be telling you this, but I...'

He was no longer listening.

Wheels within wheels circled in his head. Surveillance wheels.

While he'd been tailing Eric Fraser, the chief of E Division had been keeping track of Galbraith Junior's sexual proclivities – down to the identity of each partner.

'Jas? Jas? You there?'

At least two of Nick's tricks had been attacked. Gay-basher or not, Stevie was also a previous – if abortive – partner of Nick Galbraith's and, as such, a highly convenient next victim, if evidence was to be planted to discredit his father.

'Jas!' A blast in his ear.

He stared at distant marshland.

The bulky outline was still visible, a silhouette against the glowing city skyline...

His heart hammered. Jas disconnected then reconnected, a rigid finger punching the same button three times.

... new on the scene was the group of three-four men approaching the bulky outline from the east...

'Which service to you require?' A new voice in his ear.

... approaching at speed. 'Polis – police...' Then he was running. The phone jolted against the side of his head. Jas pushed through undergrowth, back into the wood and out the other side.

A different new voice. The signal whined, broke up and whined again.

'Hello? Hello... ah, fuck!' Cursing at a bank of thick bush, he ploughed through it onto what felt like a tarmac path.

'Police – how can I help you?' The voice was clearer now.

'Easterhouse...' Jas tore past the burnt-out nurses' home. '... the marshes...' The incline gave him greater speed. '... there's an assault in progress.' The words jerky as he reached the bottom of the hill and jumped the wall onto the path.

'What is the nature of the assault, sir?' The voice studiously calm.

'Does it fuckin' matter?' Momentarily disoriented, he scanned left then right. 'Ah need polis and' ah need 'em noo, so...'

'Can I have your name?'

'Jist git someone oot here!' His sense of direction returned. 'Gartloch – west, oot by the marsh.' He vaulted the broken fence, plunging thigh deep into bulrushes and giant hogweed. One foot sank into bog. Jas stumbled. The mobile slipped from his fist. Palms met scrub-grass, tightened and pushed upright again.

Then he was sprinting between dead trees and old bed-frames. His chest was tight. He dodged potholes and wet areas, feet leaping between raised clumps of dry ground and rusting shopping trolleys.

Heart pounded in his ears.

Eyes never left the group of what he could now see was five men, who were gaining on Stevie's outline. His shoes filled with water. Jas ran faster.

The tapering outline of four baseball bats in four fists was now visible...

'Stevie!' The shout came out a hoarse whisper, died in the darkness.

... the fifth held something less solid but equally deadly.

'Stevie!' If he didn't hear the shout, he had to be aware of footsteps behind...

Lungs burning, Jas found his second wind and put on a spurt.

... then remembered where they were and his last instructions to Stevie. For once, the guy was doing as he'd been told: going home and studiously ignoring any attention from anyone who might approach him.

'Stevie!' Jas yelled again.

He was less than twenty-five yards away when the first raised bat caught the bulky outline on the back of the neck. Jas howled.

Stevie's legs buckled.

Fifteen as a second blow knocked him from knees onto face.

At ten yards, the pounding in his ears became a whir. Then a roar...

Legs leaden pistons, Jas raced up behind the circle of men, watching baseball bats impact on someone he could no longer see.

... and his eyes focused on the distinctive logo of the O'Neill jacket clutched in Gerry Corrigan's hand.

Jas bellowed. The roar in his ears increased. He grabbed the man nearest, pushing him aside. A raised elbow caught another in the throat. A crunching sound. A moan.

Pain shuddered down his own arm as attention shifted briefly from the foetal shape on the ground to the unwanted interruption.

He felt himself grabbed, held.

Feet flailed, paralleling the heavy boots which impacted again and again with the base of Stevie's spine...

Then the area seemed to lighten, as if the moon had exploded. Marsh grass swayed violently in a sudden wind.

... and the roar in his ears placed itself:

'This is the police. Remain where you are.' An amplified voice soared down from overhead.

The grip on his arms slackened abruptly. Caught in the beam from the police helicopter above, five men dropped bats and scattered in five directions.

'Please remain where you are.'

Jas fell to a crouch, palms tentatively making contact with the back of a warm tee-shirt. 'Stevie?'

Over the retreating battery of feet and the whir overhead, the distant blare of sirens.

'Stevie?' Jas lowered his face to the hidden one.

No blood. No sound. His right hand instinctively moved to the bristly throat. Beneath his fingers, the pulse was shallow but there.

Then the whirring was moving off and they were in darkness again.

Jas moaned. 'Aw', Stevie...' He gently manoeuvred the inert shape onto its side and into the recovery position. His fingers brushed the cool face and came away wet.

The strength left his legs.

Jas sat down hard on damp ground, easing the lolling head onto his lap. '... Stevie...' He struggled out of his jacket, draping it over the unmoving shape and stroking the cooling body through it. '... it's okay, baby... ye're gonny be okay.' The tightness left his chest, seizing his guts in an iron grip.

Then his eyes swept upwards. 'Git an ambulance...' He continued to stroke. '... git a fuckin' ambulance over here noo!'

Twenty-five

A month.

Four weeks.

Twenty-eight days...

He sat down on the chair, struggled out of his jacket and draped it over the hard plastic back. 'Sorry ah'm a bit late.'

... day twenty-nine. The recording of his statement, at Pitt Street in the presence of DI Ann McLeod had taken longer than he'd anticipated.

'Couldney find a taxi...' He leant back on hard plastic.

A week ago, formal charges of conspiring to pervert the course of justice had been brought against Malcolm Orr, Robert Devine and Eric Fraser.

'... an' when ah finally got wan traffic wis hellish. Mibby a cor's no' an bad idea after aw' – whit dae ye think?'

Their part in suppressing vital evidence – the baseball cap – after fourteen-year-old Gary 'Gaz' Corrigan had, with two others, set upon seventeen-year-old Joseph Monaghan and kicked him to death following a Celtic/Dundee United match was now on record.

'Ah'll git a *Times* later, eh? Mibby huv a look at the ads.'

Gary Corrigan had already made his preliminary appearance at the High Court, in front of The Right Honourable Mr Justice Clark.

'Donald over at Parade Motors huz a wee beauty.' He forced a laugh.

The kid was pleading guilty to manslaughter, with mitigating circumstances and had been remanded to Shotts Prison to await background reports from Social Services. Jas didn't care.

'He telt me whit kind it wis, but ye ken ah dinny huv a clue aboot cors. A wheel at each corner's enough fur me. '

He didn't care about Fraser and the rest of the goons.

'Metallic green – emerald, he calls it.'

He didn't care about a shortish, balding DC who'd been more than a father to Corrigan Junior than greasy-haired Gerry – not to mention the rest of Bridgeton Boys' Club. He didn't care that two careers were over. Gary's and Orr's.

'Wanna they… low-slung joabs. Eats the petrol, but looks great. We can go round thegether an' check it oot, eh?'

Jas reached across stiff white sheets and slipped his hand under Stevie's. Fingers closed around clammy digits, avoiding the needle-tipped tube which protruded from just beneath the third knuckle.

'Whit aboot it?' He stood up, lowering lips to brush the damp forehead just below half an inch of cropped hair. The skin tasted vaguely of antiseptic and felt like perished rubber. Jas's stomach twisted.

Along with four other men, Gerald Corrigan would stand trial for the attempted manslaughter of Steven McStay. There was, however, no evidence to link them with the other gay-bashings at Gartloch. All five had attested, in their statements, to merely taking advantage of ongoing offences. Corrigan Senior had been only too happy to point the finger at Eric Fraser, as instigator of the plan to implicate Nicholas Galbraith in the crime by leaving a jacket identified as his at the scene. And, courtesy of Mr Portacabin, the final nail in the Chief Superintendent's coffin, was to be the illegal surveillance of flat 3/1 247 Cumbernauld Road.

Jas could care less about any of it.

'Mibby next week, eh?' Jas raised his head and sat back down again. He continued to hold the hand, looking away from the other tubes leading from Stevie's nostrils to the drip above his head. 'Nice day, ootside...' From the overheated stuffiness of the Royal's Intensive Care Unit, he gazed past the cathedral's spire to the necropolis beyond. 'Sunny – no' too warm, but.'

He could care less about Margaret Monaghan's tearful, gratitude-filled tones on the phone. He'd returned the extra two-grand which had arrived in cash by registered post three days ago, only to receive it again that morning. This time he'd keep it. It was less effort than sending it back a second time.

Tom Galbraith's sombre-but-content face hovered just this side of disinterest. He'd done the job he'd been sent to do – E Division had been well and truly cleaned up: Eric Fraser was to be disciplined inter-nally before standing trial in a civilian court.

Another matter had been laid to rest. On the day before the fami-ly left for Manchester, Jas had sat on the sofa of the Albion Buildings flat and listened to seventeen-year-old Nick come out to his father.

His mouth moved automatically. 'Jist in time fur the schools goin' back, eh? The weather eyeways does that.'

Not that it was necessary. Not the words, at least. The gesture, how-ever, was long overdue. Jas had sat there, smiling and nodding and thinking about another admission.

Maybe it would have made a difference...

His eyes lingered on the cemetery's green peaks, then turned to the motionless man in the bed, by way of the life-support unit.

... or maybe not. Different time. Different circumstances. Different men...

The attacks at Gartloch had stopped as abruptly as they'd begun, three months ago. Although the perpetrator of the gay-bashings was still actively sought, E Division had no concrete leads. But it was just a matter of time before those with a history of such crimes were hauled back in for a more thorough questioning.

... and what difference did it make, in the long run?

Behind, the door opened softly. The squeak of trainer-soles on lino.

319

Out of habit, he withdrew his hand and leant back in the hard plastic chair. 'Hey, the troops ur here!' He beamed at two small, sombre faces.

Sam and Hayley McStay approached the bed, mouse-like. The first couple of times, he and Carole had joked about installing drips and heart-monitors up at her Cranhill house, in an attempt to replicate the behaviour where it would be more appreciated.

'How wis school?' Jas beckoned them closer. 'Whit's that ye've got there?' He nodded to the CD in the eleven-year-old's hand.

Hayley mumbled something, eyes everywhere but her father.

He didn't push it. Jas patted his side of the bed and turned his attention to her brother. 'Ye bin practin' yer defence skills, Sam?'

'Ah made the school team!' The eight-year-old grinned, bounded over and scrambled onto the bed.

'Well, don't tell me – tell yer dad…' On the other side of the perspex window between the room and the nurses' station, Jas caught the eye of the overweight Nursing Sister from Pollok who'd first come up with the idea. She winked, clenched a meaty fist and raised a thumb.

'They can hear you – studies huv bin done. Talk tae him, son – talk tae him an' keep talkin' tae him. Gie the boay somethin' tae come back fur.'

'Shoulda seen me, dad – not wan traffic cone knocked over!' Sam MacStay continued to detail every second of the school football trials and his selection for the team.

Jas watched Hayley, who was now reading the messages in cards – the same messages she read on every visit. It was harder for her, more difficult to acknowledge the silent, unconscious man in the blinding white bed as her father.

'First match is against St. Brendan's, next week, dad. We're gonny kick their arses!'

'Hear that, Stevie?' He tried to keep his voice bright. Part of him envied eleven-year-old Hayley's ability to detach. Jas knew Maureen McStay had prepared both kids for the inevitable.

The head and spinal injuries were severe. The doctors had done all they could. After the second operation to remove a blood clot from Stevie's brain, they'd all sat in the Relatives' Room and listened to the Fife-accented words of the auburn-haired neuro-surgical consultant.

He knew what she was going to say before she said it.

A machine had been breathing for Stevie, for the last month. Drips fed him. A catheter pissed for him. Snarls of wires and clips kept him tied to this world when everyone knew he was destined for another.

'Who wants tae come wi' me an' git some juice?' The voice of the overweight Sister cut through his thoughts.

Hayley was immediately walking towards the door.

'Can ah, dad?' Sam was now leaning over Stevie's inert form, fiddling with his ear.

Jas smiled. 'On ye go – ye can finish aff the story when ye git back.' He patted the small back, then watched the eight-year-old scramble over to his sister and the nurse.

She met his eye again. 'Bring ye back a cuppa tea, son?'

'Naw, ah'll git wan later.' He watched them leave the room then turned back to Stevie, fighting what Hayley felt. 'Did ye see whit came, fae the boays doon at Hovis, by the way?' He lifted a large 'Get Well Soon' card, full of signatures. Scrawls blurred in front of his eyes. 'They're keepin' yer job open fur ye, man...'

Every day. Every day for twenty-eight days.

'... an' yer boss says no' tae worry aboot onythin'...'

Morning visiting. Afternoon visiting.

'... take aw' the time ye need...'

When they shooed him from the IC unit at four-thirty he got a taxi home, washed and ate whatever was easiest. Then back in the evenings. He stayed all night when they let him, watching and listening to the beeps.

'... yer job'll be waitin' fur ye, when ye feel up tae it.' Jas smiled at the ashen face. '... but there's no rush, eh? You enjoy the rest.'

Stevie's skin was unreal. Too still. Too young. Sometime over the past fortnight he'd stopped looking like Stevie and started looking like someone else. Carole McStay had noticed it too:

'Gimme summa whit he's oan. Takin' years aff him, it is.'

The overweight Sister had laughed. Jas had stared at the new crop of lines around Carole's heavily made-up eyes and knew she felt it too.

Maybe it was why hospitals put hopeless cases on life support. Maybe it was easier if the relatives saw only the husk of their loved one lying there...

Jas frowned.

... when the machines were finally switched off. 'Onyway...' He laughed and took Stevie's hand again. '... ye might no' be goin' back tae Hovis at aw', if things work oot the way they should...'

He had no proof.

'... ah've bin thinkin' – you wur right...'

Maybe Stevie's garbled confession, that night five weeks ago, pointed towards his extra-relationship activities.

'... ah need help wi' ma record-keepin'. Nae-wan can handle that computer the way you can, man...' Jas squeezed inert fingers.

Maybe he'd been storming out into other men's arms, to suck the cocks of strangers when Jas wouldn't let him touch his.

'... so...' His free hand plunged into the inside pocket of the denim jacket. Jas withdrew a sheaf of small white cards, plucked one from within the elastic band holding them secure and held it up. '... whit dae ye think?' Gold-embossed lettering caught the sunlight flooding in through the window.

Maybe he had nothing to do with the injuries of six gay men.

'Anderson & McStay Investigations, eh?' Jas held the newly print-ed business card in front of closed eyelids. 'Ye'd be a full partner, man – mibby help wi' the legwork tae.'

So many maybes. But Stevie had no alibi for any of the times of the attacks.

'Ye like it?'

Beeps.

He lowered his arm. 'Ah'll lea' it here so's ye can look at it later.' Jas propped the business card against a box of latex gloves which sat on top of the bedside cabinet.

The possibility of a higher justice hovered in his mind. The gay-basher bashed.

'And...' He stressed the word theatrically, aware he was following the nurses' habit of talking to coma-patients like they were small children. '... ah've got mair guid news – well, ah think it's guid. An' you will tae, if ye jist... think aboot it for a minute afore ye jump doon ma throat.'

He'd sell his soul to hear just one dismissive word from that full, motionless mouth.

'We're movin'...' Jas linked his fingers with pasty damp digits. '... well, hopefully we ur. Ah've... put in an offer oan a flat.' It was something to do in the times he wasn't here.

He'd detailed their specifications to an estate agent by phone.

'Golfhill Drive – along near the auld cigarette factory?'

Three bedrooms. Not ground floor. Access to a garden. Kid-friendly.

'Great view – ye can see right ower tae Castlemilk.'

Wandering soullessly through empty, lifeless rooms, trying to visualise himself and Stevie there, the kids on alternate weekends. And failing.

'Think ye'll like it, pal – ah want ye to...' Something tight and hot rushed up from his guts and wrapped itself around his throat. '... Stevie, man, ah...'

The beeps faded.

All sound faded.

Jas took the still, clammy hand in both of his and moved onto the bed. 'Ah canny dae ony o' this withoot you.' Heat on his face, spreading down beneath the neck of his tee-shirt. 'Ah don't wanna dae ony of it withoot you.'

The truth-blush intensified. His face was on fire. Flip comments fought for expression.

Jas scowled, pushed them away and lay down beside the inert body. 'Don't leave me, man.'

Of all the tests he'd ever faced, this was the hardest.

Instinctively, his knees pulled up towards his chest. Jas pushed his head into the crook of a recently shaved neck. He lay there, curled around the unconscious man. 'Ah love ye, Stevie.' The words stripped it all away.

His eyes were wet. Jas kissed the new scar on the side of Stevie's skull. 'If ye hear nothin' else, baby, hear that.'

He lay there, nuzzling half-inch brown spikes of hair and mumbling three words he'd never said to another living soul. After a while, the beeps became audible. Reality seeped back in.

Self-consciousness prickled on the back of his neck. He laughed and eased away. 'Listen, ah'll be back in a minute, okay? Don't go onywhere.' Jas sat up, swung his legs from the bed and fumbled in his jacket for cigarettes.

As he turned towards the door, a pair of eyes met his.

Jas stiffened. He wondered how much she'd heard. And seen. He continued to walk towards the door and past Maureen McStay. 'It's okay – ah'm goin' fur a fag.'

'No, please...' She grabbed his arm. '... ah need to say this.'

The tone of her voice made him pause. He glanced back at Stevie, then moved to the far side of the room.

'Ah didn't know...' She followed, still talking. '... no, that's no true.'

He leant against an eggshell wall.

She talked to beyond his head. 'Ah always knew – fae the beginnin', ah knew there wis somethin'. Stevie an' me wurney... right. We goat married too young, then ah fell pregnant wi' Hayley an'... things that shoulda got talked aboot never did...'

He knew the feeling.

'... then before ah knew whit wis happenin', we wur doin'... family stuff.' Sad smiled. 'Ah'll never forget his face when he saw his wee girl fur the first time. Same wi' Sam. He's a great dad, never bin ony-thin' other than a great dad...' Sigh. '... ah think that wis mibby whit finally made me dae the leavin' when he didney huv the guts tae dae it first.' Maureen looked down at her hands. 'He didney need me – the kids didney need me...' One thumb rubbing steadily just beneath the other. 'You ken whit that feels like?'

He'd never needed anyone till five minutes ago. Or never admitted it.

'But walkin' away didney help. Jist made it worse, ken? Everythin' got twisted up inside, an' when ah got offered a transfer back to Glasgow ah thought okay, you made me miserable fur years, pal. Now it's your turn.' She looked up.

He saw weeks of guilt and years of regret on her pretty face.

'Some women jist urney... the maternal type, ken?'

He nodded.

'Ah love 'em cos they're mine. But if ah'm honest, ah'd huv tae admit at best ah'm a part-time mother. Ah care aboot Sam and Hayley – Christ, ah widney want onythin' tae happen tae 'em, but they're Stevie's kids. An' hurtin' him hurts them.' A glance to the bed.

He followed her eyes.

'Ah wis oot tae cause trouble for Stevie an'... you ony way ah could. Ah'm no' wantin' sole custody – hell, whit wid ah dae wi' them aw' day?' Pause. 'He talked aboot you aw' the time...'

The past tense made him flinch.

'... the kids still dae. An' ah can...' Her voice broke. '... see how much he... means tae you.'

Another flinch, at something private suddenly made public. He frowned at the side of her face.

'Fur aw' his faults, Stevie's eyeways hurt himself mair than he's hurt onywan else...'

He wondered vaguely if six innocent men on the receiving end of a kicking would agree. The vagueness of the wondering bothered him. But only vaguely.

'... which is why ah went tae the polis, after work the day.'

Jas's heart missed a beat.

Maureen's head turned slowly. 'Stevie wis with me, the night wanna they... queers wis beaten up. He wis beggin' me no' tae take his kids away fae him.' Strain bunched the skin around her large eyes. 'An' the mair he begged, the mair ah wanted tae hurt him so bad ah...'

He didn't hear the rest, over the sound of his now-galloping heart. Not Stevie. Not Stevie. Not Stevie.

Jas gripped her shoulders, turning her towards the bed. 'Tell him – tell him so he knows too an'...'

'Ah can't!' She pulled away, tears streaming down her face. The door slammed behind her when she left.

Heads shot up in the nurses' station in the next room. Jas met three sets of eyes, raised a hand in apology. The heads relowered themselves.

He walked slowly back towards the bed, sat down at the top and gripped Stevie's limp hand. He had no words. Jas leant back against the wall and watched a nurse put her arms around a sobbing Maureen McStay in the corridor beyond.

He waved to Sam and Hayley as they left, half an hour later.

Did words matter? He squeezed Stevie's fingers and suddenly felt very tired.

He woke up in darkness.

The beeps were faster. More erratic...

'Jas?' A hoarse croak.

... and a warm hand was squeezing his.